Lindsay, F.

D1338642

F/0178728

IDLE HANDS

By the same author

A Kind of Dying
Kissing Judas

After the Stranger Came
A Charm Against Drowning
Jill Rips
Brond

IDLE HANDS

Frederic Lindsay

Hodder & Stoughton

Copyright © 1999 By Frederic Lindsay

First published in Great Britain 1999
by Hodder and Stoughton
A division of Hodder Headline PLC

The right of Frederic Lindsay to be identified as the
Author of the Work has been asserted by him in accordance
with the Copyright, Designs and patents Act 1988.

10 9 8 7 6 5 4 3 2 1

All rights reserved. No part of this publication may
be reproduced, stored in a retrieval system, or transmitted
in any form or by any means without the prior written
permission of the publisher, nor be otherwise circulated
in any form of binding or cover other than that in which
it is published and without a similar condition being
imposed on the subsequent purchaser.

All characters in this publication are fictitious
and any resemblance to real persons, living or dead,
is purely coincidental.

British Library Cataloguing in Publication Data

ISBN 0 340 69537 4

Typeset by Hewer Text Ltd, Edinburgh
Printed and bound in Great Britain by Clays Ltd, St Ives plc

Hodder and Stoughton
A division of Hodder Headline PLC
338 Euston Road
London NW1 3BH

For Douglas

They call this Reflex-man a Co-walker,
every way like the man,
as a Twin-brother and Companion,
haunting him as his shadow.

Robert Kirk, *The Secret Commonwealth*

BEFORE IT BEGAN

T he night street tilting and the drops of water that gleamed under
the lights threatening to run down on me and fill my mouth. I lay
with the floor of the entry pressed against my face, fought it wouldn't
wouldn't wake up, night ooze leaking from mouth's corner down my
cheek to pool on cold stone. Footsteps along the pavement, little
hammers beating nearer.

Buses tall as houses and tenements like smoked red cliffs and a road to cross and that a
long time ago when I was (two years old, as I'd work out later, a long time later) and I
was on my way, escaping, to or from, from or to (assuming whenever I remembered it
that I must have been fleeing from my grandmother's house to the flat my mother and
father were getting ready to move into; and then one day wondering if the journey might
have been the other way, back from them to my grandmother's room and kitchen, the only
home I knew) and the street tilting to and fro and roaring metal dragons rushing down left
and right as I all the way to the other side made passage between them under the bright
ferocity of the sun.

The bright ferocious beam of the torch struck my eyes, jiggled (lying
there we must have startled Constable Plod; in those days thirty years ago
the streets were empty of beggars) and swung from me to Davie, spread
flat on his back, mouth open, peaceful as a baby with one arm across his
eyes.

'Don't you move!' Warning me as I got up, he leaned over to poke
Davie with the torch.

Davie spluttered and knocked it aside.

'Chuck it!' he said, without opening his eyes.

The torch prodded him again.

'Fuck off, Neil!'

He got lifted by the hair, one heave, his feet it seemed to me left the ground for a second, strong bastard Plod must have been.

'What's the game?' He put his face down close to Davie, elected him as spokesman, ignoring me, hands retracted in submission up into my sleeves.

'We're no' doing anything,' Davie said, clutching the top of his head with both hands, tufts of red hair sticking up between his fingers.

'Where you from then?'

'You near scalped me. That's out of order! It's no' right!'

'You're from Glasgow,' Plod discovered. 'You as well?'

I nodded more than once, admitting the accusation.

'You out a Home?'

'Course we are.'

'One in the West?'

'How you mean?'

'Which one? I'll no' ask you twice.'

'I stay at my house, and he stays at his.'

Plod hit him on the side of the head with the torch. Home with a capital H, he meant, as in Children's Home. Behind him, I watched the rain draw lines that shone in the glow of the street lamps. It had come on again while he was questioning Davie. Runaways, he thought we were.

When we came out of the doorway, he held Davie by the shoulder, but left me to walk ungripped on the other side. Even when I lagged behind a step or two, looking up at the Castle set up dark on the hill above the street, he didn't bother to glance back to check if I was following. He was right, I trailed along for a while then caught up. We'd been in Edinburgh for about eight hours, and neither of us had ever been there before or much of anywhere come to that. What else was I going to do?

'What's this? Babes in the fucking wood?' the man behind the counter in the police station wondered.

'We're ten,' Davie said. Not babies.

When he asked us our names, Davie said, 'I'm Donald, he's Peter.' I looked over my shoulder and saw Plod shake his head at the man. 'Second names?'

'Fraser,' Davie said, hardly hesitating at all. That was the name above one of the stores we'd gone into that afternoon to get out of the cold. 'Eh, both of us. We're brothers.'

'Bollocks,' Plod said.

'The Jenners Twins,' the man behind the counter said.

Brown hair on me, red hair on him, fat and thin. We didn't even look like brothers, which we weren't, of course. Jenners was the name of this terrific big store we'd wandered about in till a dame in a black dress asked us what we were doing. Davie had lifted a pot of jam and a tin of herring from the food bit upstairs so we took off in case she got us searched. We went into the park on the other side of the road, and sat looking up at the Castle. We didn't have a spoon or anything to eat the jam and we couldn't get the lid off the herring, so we rolled the jar under the bench and threw the tin after it.

'The Bollocks Twins,' Plod said.

'Sit down,' the man behind the counter told us. 'There! There! Are you stupid?' He pointed at the seats against the wall, and when we'd sat down warned us, 'Not a muscle!' Nobody wanted us to move. 'Have a wee think, get your head on straight and I'll talk to you when I'm ready.'

Plod went away. After a while, Davie muttered something and I whispered, 'What?' and the man said, 'Sssh!' and what felt like hours crept by. One time he wrote in a book, another time the phone rang. But then he went through the back, didn't say anything, just went away round a partition. I turned to Davie, but his head was rolled back against the wall and his eyes were shut. You'd think there'd be noise in a police station even in the middle of the night. There wasn't a sound. I sat looking from the empty space behind the counter to the door. I couldn't see the man but the thing was, of course, could he see me? He came back with a cup in his hand. 'None of that,' he said, pointing at Davie. 'Give him a dunt with your elbow.' He made an *ach!* of disgust. 'Not like a wee lassie! Harder, like you meant it!' Davie woke up gasping, and the man sipped at the cup and grinned at us.

Before he'd finished his tea, though, they brought this drunk in. His belly was bigger than the wee policeman holding his left arm, and he'd blood down his face. His head was hanging when he came in at first, but when his wallet dropped on the floor and one of the policemen picked it up he yelled and swung his arm, not like a punch more like swatting a fly. The man behind the counter came over it in one jump and there were three of them hitting him. The policeman who'd been knocked on his arse jumped up again, and that made four.

Davie pulled my sleeve and nodded at the door. They were too busy to notice us.

Outside, we ran until our legs gave up. We stood in a doorway gasping for breath, peeping out into the street to see if anybody was after us.

'See that fellow's ear?'

'Whose ear?'

'The drunk guy!'

'His ear?'

'Aye.'

'What about it?'

'You no' see?'

'Naw.'

'Hingan hauf aff,' Davie said. 'Saw it as soon as he came in.'

He stepped out and we set off again, walking instead of running. Walking fast.

'What happened to him? Think he was in an accident?'

'Accident!' He spread it out into three scornful syllables. 'That'll be right.'

We weren't hurrying any more, just wandering along, dragging our feet. It seemed a long long time since yesterday, when we'd seen these two guys getting into a car in Maryhill Road. Hibs supporters through for the game at Firhill, they'd a good drink in them. Davie spun a yarn; maybe they believed it, maybe they didn't give a fuck one way or the other, anyway we'd ended up in Edinburgh. Just as well it hadn't been Aberdeen the Jags were playing.

I wanted to sleep. Davie said he was starving. He was fed up and wanted to go home. He thought we should go back down to near the railway station and try and cadge enough money for our fare back to Glasgow.

'Or the bus station,' he said.

'What bus station?'

'We can ask somebody.'

'We'd never get enough.'

'Bet we would. Bus wouldnae be that dear.'

We started to quarrel. He couldn't understand it; I never argued with him. The funny thing is the whole thing had been his idea and now he wanted to give up and go home. I wanted to go on. I never wanted to go back, I never wanted to go back.

It hadn't been dark for a while, and now it was light. A man passed on a bike and then looking down through railings into a basement area I saw bundles of newspapers and a crate of milk stacked outside the door of a wee shop.

'That'll do me,' Davie said and I followed him down the steps.

We took a bottle each. I pushed a hole in the top with my finger and took a big gulp of the milk. It tasted cold and clean. It tasted good. I put my head back for another slug and saw a face looking down at me. Nothing special about it, just a man's face. Next minute, Davie saw him as he came to the top of the steps. He must have thought this was the guy come to open the shop for he made a breenge up the steps, shoved by him and away.

The man didn't make any attempt to stop him.

He came down the steps and took the bottle from me. Then he did a funny thing: he took a drink out of it himself. He laid the bottle on top of the pile of papers and it fell over and milk ran out. The sleeve of his jacket was torn under the arm. When you got a right look at him, he didn't look like a man who would own a shop.

'What's your name?' he asked me.

'Neil.'

'Aye, that right? I like it. Let's try that.'

'What?'

He put his hands on my shoulders and forced me down.

'Kneel,' he said.

LATER

In a strange city, not able to speak French, or Flemish come to that, Meldrum had equipped himself with a street map of Brussels and a plan of the Metro. He came up the steps out of the station map in hand, and was relieved to find himself in Avenue Gribaumont. It was pleasant walking along like a tourist in the sunshine, and the feeling lasted while he checked the numbers and was lost only when he arrived at the building Iain Bower had lived in. He crossed over to the other side of the street to get a better look. With white slatted shutters over the windows and narrow green awnings above them the effect was strange to him but pleasing. He recalled that Bower had been born in Eyemouth in the Scottish Borders. Last time Meldrum had been there, it had been as part of a group at the side of a fairway on the nine-hole golf course. Thin rain from a November sky had drizzled on the grey town on the other side of the harbour and into the grey sea at their back and down on them, the living, gathered round the place where a fifteen-year-old girl had been found dead. That had been twelve years ago, and though it was only sixty miles from where he lived in Edinburgh he hadn't ever felt like going back. Bower had come a long way.

He went into the outer lobby, and paused between two glass doors with a row of residents' post boxes on the wall to his left. He assumed the inner door would be locked, but it wasn't and he got into a tiny lift and rode it to the top floor. From there he walked down, reading names, none of which suggested an English speaker. That was a pity, since from what he'd been told Bower had lived here for a long time. If he'd been able to make himself understood, there were questions he'd have liked to ask. He'd thought about Bower a good deal since his murder and still had no picture of the kind of man he had been. His flat in this building had been on the second floor, but there was a choice of two doors and no way of knowing which would be the right one. Spanish name on the left, one that might have been German or Dutch on the right; either way, someone new, the furniture changed, everything of Bower's gone.

Coming to look at the building like this, he told himself, wasn't investigation, it was superstition.

Back in the street, he took a moment squinting into the sunshine to check that the Metro station was still where he had left it, then set off in the opposite direction. The European headquarters of CIMD was only two stops distant, and since the phone call changing his appointment he had time on his hands. Even so, being the meticulous type, normally he would have gone and located the headquarters, then found a café or gone for a walk having made sure he would be on time. He was irritated, though, by the delay; irritated even by the title of the man whose secretary had phoned him. Director of Human Resources, what did that mean? People as material, like office furniture, to be used up. Maybe that's why the death of Iain Bower wasn't important enough for an appointment to be kept.

At the end of the street, there was a market with stalls and stuff piled on the pavements and a crowd spilling on to the road. He looked at leather belts and piles of crockery and cotton shirts. He studied cakes in a bakery shop window and was tempted to buy chocolate from a stall, but didn't. There were worse ways of passing time, but he didn't feel at ease. Within quarter of an hour he was heading back towards the Metro until, realising what he was doing, he thought, Fuck human resources, and turned right instead down a thoroughfare lined with trees.

At first it was cheerful walking, warm in the sun. At intervals, people went by on the opposite pavement, a man with a briefcase, two girls holding hands, a woman in a coat with fur trimming at the collar despite the heat. All going the other way. For some reason, he had this side to himself. Perhaps it was the time of day; for the middle of a city, it seemed to be a very quiet street. The wall that edged the pavement was about ten feet high, a blank of grey stone blocks that reminded him of estate walls beside country roads at home. Studying it, he observed a sudden change in the quality of the light and, coming out from under the branches of a tree, looked up to see clouds had been gathering all this time without his noticing. Now they had sealed up the sun. Rain splashed a scatter of dusty circles on the pavement ahead. Heavy motionless air clung to him, until it began to seem this was a street that would go on for ever.

A hint of wind stirred and fell away; the rain came to nothing. There were more people now, the street was approaching a junction. Ahead, cars and buses went from left to right in a roaring stream, traffic must have been held up by the lights, and rounding the corner he came into a wide street (the word *boulevard* came into his head) with a prospect of department stores, pavements crowded with shoppers. He broke step, came to a halt. Rushing for an appointment was the last thing he felt like doing. He didn't want to think about how or why Bower was dead. He wanted to stroll among the crowds. He wanted to be on holiday. He wanted to sit with a coffee and watch the world go by. He wanted a different job. He didn't want to be who he was. In this moment of disorientation, he focussed on a woman coming towards him through the crowd. He glimpsed and lost her as a man cut across between them. Tall, very tall, six feet perhaps, slim, long black hair, delicate stepping like a cat, no, like a deer, her head was down, the hair swung across her face, he was shot through with a seizure of lust, she glanced up and someone else got in the way but not before he was sure she had seen him, that something had passed between them, he had time to think that he wasn't going to keep his appointment, something different was going to happen to his life. And then she was only three steps away and she was looking up at him and she was half smiling. And she was sixteen or maybe younger. Just as he realised that, a touch fell on his arm. Startled, he swung round to be faced by a man in a dark business suit, framed by a glass entrance behind him, beyond it a glimpse of a hall and reception desk. In the same instant Meldrum felt rather than saw the girl pass behind him. Perhaps the man had been waiting, there in the entrance, keeping watch; for he asked, 'Mr White?' and handed him a business card. Meldrum denied the identification and answered the man's apology, taking for granted they were talking in English, the man with an American accent. The exchange only took a moment and when it was over he didn't make any effort to look round after the girl. He stood as if lost in thought, though his mind was blank, parting the crowd like a rock in a stream. Turning the card in his fingers, he read the name NEIL HEUK; and, glancing up to where the name *Avenue Louise* was carved into the stone of the wall, set off again.

Time to keep his appointment.

Meldrum, not a much travelled man, was struck by the impression that the Director of Human Resources, in contrast, had probably been everywhere at least once, leaving aside the Valley of the Kings or the Taj Mahal or wherever else the package tours had fetched the crowd. Six feet, touch of grey at the temples, shirt, tie, suit, shoes, so elegant you'd swear even his underpants had to be hand-stitched by Italian virgins, Jean-Philippe Guichard, sleek as a seal, made Meldrum feel like an unmade bed.

All the same, he was lying.

'Iain was held in affection by all his colleagues.'

'Why would that be?' Meldrum asked.

'Why?' Guichard raised his eyebrows. That and his tone suggested not that the question puzzled him but that he thought it obtuse.

' "Held in affection",' Meldrum quoted. The phrase struck him as out of date and affected. To be fair, English wasn't the man's native language; but why be fair? 'That seems stronger than just liking him, getting on with him. Did you really mean that?'

'Since I said it.'

'My impression is people like some of the people they work with, don't like others. To be liked by everybody – no, more than that, for them all to be . . . fond of him? What made people feel like that about Iain Bower?'

'You put it more strongly than I would,' Guichard said. To Meldrum's ear, he might have been an Englishman, one who'd been to public school. Quite apart from his name, though, listen carefully enough and you would know English wasn't his native tongue, even if you couldn't have explained how. 'Do people really like or dislike those they work with? I doubt if most of us care enough to feel one way or the other.'

'You could be right. But, if you are, doesn't that make Bower more unusual?'

'I may have given a wrong impression when I spoke of *all* his colleagues. In fact, the number isn't as large as that might suggest. He was out in the field a great deal. I suppose, too, I had in mind those who had known him for a long time. And that's not so many as you might imagine.' He smiled. 'With a head office in Kansas, the European end is vulnerable to every downturn in the business cycle. People do get shaken out.'

'Is that what happened to Bower?'

'No, he chose to retire.'

'He was only fifty-one.'

'That's not impossibly early, not nowadays.'

'It seems early to retire.'

'He may have been intending to do some consultancy work. When you called me, I looked back through his records. He had been with the company for twenty-four years. I read the interview he had with my predecessor when he joined us. I found it quite poignant. What happened to him, to die like that. Terrible, unspeakable. Such an unnecessary thing to happen. At one time, I'm told, it had been his intention to retire to Spain. If only he had . . . It's natural, of course, to want to go back to your own country.'

Back to die. He didn't say the words, but in the faint disapproval he gave to the study of his hands folded on the desk there was some suggestion of them. Better for Iain Bower not to have turned his back on Europe for the cold end of an offshore island.

'How long do you keep records after someone leaves the company?' Meldrum asked.

Guichard, frowning in surprise, hesitated as if deciding what the firm's policy would be on a question like that, or maybe whether it was worth an answer.

'That would depend,' he said at last.

On what? Meldrum wondered, but didn't waste his time asking. Instead, he said, ' "Affection"? Can I ask you about this "holding in *affection*"?' and had the satisfaction of seeing Guichard frown again. 'I'm sorry to come back to this, but it might matter.'

'How could it *matter*?' Guichard's stress on the last word made it seem like a parody of the emphasis Meldrum had used.

'The more I know about him, how people thought about him, the better I'll be able to do my job. Like you said, what happened to him was terrible. I'm trying to find out why it happened.'

'He wasn't homosexual,' Guichard said, 'if that's what you're suggesting.'

It hadn't been, but it was a thought. If a man living alone, never married, was killed in his bed, it was always a thought.

'In the field,' Meldrum said, 'you talk about him being in the field. We've been told he was in Nigeria.'

'Why there particularly?' Guichard wondered. 'He did some work in Africa, but his main field of operations was Eastern Europe . . . And Russia, of course.'

'What exactly did he do?'

'You don't know?'

'According to his brother, he was an engineer.'

'That's how his brother described him?' Guichard sounded disbelieving.

'Wasn't he?'

'Among other things. His first degree in Glasgow. As I said, I've been looking through his file. He changed direction during his doctorate at Manchester University. And he was a good linguist. "Engineer" wouldn't begin to describe him.' He paused. 'What does his brother do?'

'Retired, I think.' If that mattered. 'He'd been a schoolmaster.' Something must have been said to leave that impression. The purpose of talking to Frank Bower had been to question him about his dead brother, not himself..

'Sibling rivalry,' Guichard said.

Meldrum, who took the point for what it was worth, gave Guichard a moment to appreciate his blank look; then asked, 'Why "of course"?'

'What?' asked Guichard, blank in his turn.

'Nigeria. Eastern Europe. And Russia, *of course*, you said. I wondered why.'

Guichard shot his cuff and looked at his watch.

Meldrum said, 'I'm not taking up too much of your time?' And before he could be answered, 'I always try hard, but it's human nature to try even harder when you hear how fond of him everybody was.'

'For what it's worth, if anything, I had in mind that his biggest contracts were negotiated in Russia. In fact, if it wasn't for Russia you wouldn't be talking to me. He'd have been working for another company years ago.'

Meldrum waited for him to go on, then asked, 'Why would that be?'

'Not because he wasn't good at his job! In the middle Eighties, a new chief executive called Flanigan came over from Kansas. An American born and bred, but he wasn't fond of the English. So in that particular shake-out, the British were the first to go.'

'But not Bower?'

'Not Bower. He'd started dealing for us in Russia when Brezhnev was President. The way things were done, they sat round a table and drank vodka until they ran out of toasts, then thought up some more. At the end of it, business was done on a handshake. If they trusted you, they didn't need a signature, and they kept their word. They didn't have foreign currency, a lot of it was barter trading, but it was still very profitable. Bower could hold his drink, and the Russians trusted him. And that was why Mr Flanigan kept Bower.'

'But he did get early retirement.'

Guichard shrugged. 'Things have changed since Gorbachev.' The calculated weariness of a man explaining the obvious. 'Since the collapse of the Communist regime, Russia's oil production is down from twelve million barrels a day to just under six. The biggest company in the country is Gazprom. It should be paying roughly a quarter of all tax revenues contributing to the federal budget. Difficulty is, only eight per cent of its domestic customers pay their gas bills. In today's Russia, there are investment opportunities, but short term the risks can be unacceptably high. And you don't do business on a handshake any more. Iain Bower's approach was out of date. And, what's even more important, so were his contacts. His last visit to Russia didn't go well.'

As if the thought had just struck him, Meldrum asked, 'Could Bower's work have made him enemies?'

'I can't imagine why.'

'What about that last time he was in Russia? Different contacts, you said. Could some of them have been gangsters?'

'Certainly not.'

'Hasn't Russian organised crime moved in on big business? With the country falling apart, I don't see how you can be sure who Bower was dealing with.'

'I'm sure.'

'Could you see your way to letting me have an idea of the companies Bower negotiated with? If it was possible to get a list of the people he met, that would help too.'

'There might be problems of commercial confidentiality, but I'll check. And the records may not be complete – after all, it's nine or ten months since Bower left the company. In a case like this, obviously CIMD is anxious to co-operate.'

'In the last year, say, before he retired. Not just in Russia, but Eastern Europe and Nigeria. Anywhere, in fact. We know Russian gangsters aren't confined to Russia any more.'

'I don't think you'll find an answer to your problem in melodrama.' It was said unsmilingly with a kind of fastidious distaste.

Meldrum responded by making a half circle with his hand. 'When Bower's head was smashed in,' he said, 'they found bloodstains four foot above the bed.'

Put the truth as starkly as that and there was no way of predicting the response. Often it was anger, or even inappropriate laughter, defensive or hostile. Fortunately, the effect on Guichard was to make him issue an unexpected invitation to come back at four. 'We're having a cocktail for someone who's leaving. Quite a small affair, he hasn't been with us terribly long. But there will be people there who worked with Iain, and there's no reason why you shouldn't talk to them about him – providing they're willing, of course.'

It was held in the staff dining area, high-ceilinged, with long windows looking out one way on to gardens, on the other to an arcade leading to the street. About fifty or sixty people were milling about, but it was a large space and Guichard was right, it didn't seem that many. Meldrum was introduced to two men who spoke warmly of Bower, expressed shock at the manner of his death, became nostalgic about the company as it had been when they'd joined it thirty years ago and finished up by talking more about themselves than the dead man. Par for the course.

Guichard rejoined them briefly: 'Time to go and start the proceed-ings.' Meldrum watched him make his way up steps to a microphone on a raised area at the back. He made a joke, people laughed, he called for the man leaving CIMD to join him, people applauded, he made a little speech and handed over a gift. It was a practised performance. Meldrum's attention, however, was held by the guest of honour, for it was the man who had spoken to him that afternoon in the Avenue Louise.

The recognition was immediate, and discounted at once, dismissed as too much of a coincidence. It had to be an accidental resemblance, reinforced by the fact that the afternoon man and the man making his acceptance speech both spoke English with an American accent.

The little ceremony over, Meldrum's two companions seemed to have lost interest in Bower. One of them was just back from holiday in England, and they were talking music and opera. Glyndebourne, had he been to Glyndebourne?

Meldrum glanced down at his questioner.

'No,' he said.

Above their heads, he was watching the man. At something that was said, Guichard nodded and turning his head caught Meldrum's gaze. Next moment the man was heading their way.

It was Meldrum's impression as loud pleasantries were exchanged that the two men he'd been talking to didn't particularly care for the newcomer.

'Neil Heuk,' he'd said, pronouncing it 'hook', holding out his hand for Meldrum to shake. 'Jean-Philippe's been telling me who you are.'

He was medium height, five eight perhaps. He had thinning brown hair and a moustache of a darker shade bushed out thickly on his upper lip with a somewhat unpleasant effect. His eyes, slightly protuberant, were of an odd bottle-green colour. Meldrum ticked these things off like items on a police blotter.

'I was telling Charles I'd been to Glyndebourne,' the back-from-holiday man was saying. His interest in Heuk perfunctory, clearly he was anxious to get back to his own concerns.

'Tell you something I saw once,' Heuk said, his voice more nasal. 'In a programme for *Peter Grimes*, they had a picture of E. M. Forster, Benjamin Britten and a fisherman out in a fishing boat with a boy. Forster is reaching out to touch the boy on the shoulder. And Britten's hand is reaching down to him as well. You've never seen such a long limp hand.

Like a jungle tendril. Christ! I thought, I hope the fisherman was straight.' He glanced from one to the other, smiling. 'A very sinister photograph.'

'Britten is Aldeburgh, not Glyndebourne,' the holiday man said. 'You've got it the wrong way round.'

'Arseways, you mean?' Heuk asked, and when the two moved off asked Meldrum, 'Sounds better than assways, don't you agree? At least to our ears, eh? Jean-Philippe tells me you're from Edinburgh. I'm from Glasgow myself.'

'Glasgow, Scotland?'

'Is there any other kind?'

'Your accent misled me,' Meldrum said. 'You must have spent a long time in America.'

'I've never been there.'

As Meldrum waited for that to be explained, Heuk kept watch from those oddly coloured eyes and smoothed his moustache with two fingertips. After a moment, he said, 'It's odd, isn't it? Two complete strangers. This morning we didn't even know one another existed. And we meet twice in the one day.'

'I wondered,' Meldrum said.

'In the Avenue Louise! Do you remember?'

'I told you I wasn't Mr White.'

'You saved my life.'

No, I fucking didn't, Meldrum thought. He hated that kind of extravagant meaningless talk.

'You mean you didn't want to meet Mr White after all,' he said drily.

'There was no Mr White,' Heuk said. Smiling tentatively, a stout girl had come up to hover nearby. He ignored her.

'Very interesting,' Meldrum said, on the edge of losing his temper. It had been a long day, and not a fruitful one.

'This thing of mine you saved,' Heuk said. His eyes flickered towards the girl. 'In some cultures they'd believe it belonged to you. From today I hold it only on loan from you.'

'I'll get out of your way. Give you a chance to speak to him.' Meldrum smiled at the girl. Over his shoulder, already moving away, he told Heuk, 'Nice to meet you.'

Nice to meet you. Both times.

Leaving, he thanked Guichard, who made the mistake of trying to tell him his job. 'I've been thinking about poor Bower. The likeliest thing surely is that he was attacked by a burglar. Why assume enemies at all?'

'Well, for one thing,' Meldrum said, 'at the funeral someone pissed in his grave.'

F/0178728

BOOK ONE

Home to Die

CHAPTER ONE

T he sheen of the sliced earth was blue-green where the weak sun struck down into the grave.

Why was it you could never remember the words? Not at his father's funeral. Not at Billy Ord's. Not from any of the ones he'd gone to; too many over the years. It didn't matter whether it was sitting in a church or in a crematorium chapel, squinting an eye open to watch the coffin sink under its cloth in a parody of committal to mother earth, or like now mother earth indeed opened and in wait under a grey sky. Priest or minister, you never remembered the words. Apart from *Dust to dust, ashes to ashes.*

Why *dust?* Dust maybe out there in Palestine. Here and now, clods of wet cold earth stacked under a green tarpaulin ready to be shovelled back into the hole. *Get your ashes hauled*: the black FBI man had taught him that one in New England when he'd gone out with Henderson in search of John Bellman's killer. Both the black guy and Henderson murdered by the killer, who'd got away, vanished into the great anonymity of the continent's hinterland. *Get your ashes hauled*: get a woman into bed. For too long his ashes, his personal ashes, had remained, as it happened, unhauled.

Flakes of snow wandering down out of the grey sky above Warriston Cemetery settled on the shoulders and melted on the hair of the mourners. Snow that wouldn't last or lie, but was unseasonal. Second week in April and cold enough to make the bones of your head ache. Meldrum turned up the collar of his coat. He had taken notice of the faces around the grave, two men at either side who had taken cords at the lowering of the coffin and remarked the others, eight of them in an outer half circle between the angle of the paths and a line of trees. Maybe not much more than a third of those who had attended the funeral service. Photographs as the congregation left the church would have been useful. If it had been about subversion or terrorism, Special Branch would have had a crew parked across the street from the kirk in a plain van, no problem. Simple murder, on the other hand, involved such considerations as civil liberties, good taste in a time of grief, indignation in the *Evening News*; in other words, no photographs, which was why he was out here in the snow, wishing he'd a handkerchief to blow his nose.

It was, anyway, an improbable notion that the killer would turn up for the funeral; a variant on revisiting the scene of the crime. Not that revisiting that scene would be easy in this case, since it wasn't a clearing in a wood or a corner of a city street, but the fourth floor in a new block of flats. Not easy to go up in the lift and stand outside the door, or hang around on that new lawn with its little struggling trees, without running a risk of being noticed. Next best thing, then, turn up at the funeral? Maybe, though except himself no one really entertained the possibility of the murderer obligingly turning up. Certainly not his sergeant, Bobbie Shields, who'd gone along to the church service sceptical but cheerful since he had an inherited taste for a good funeral. The pair of them had settled in early at the back of the church. A man in an anorak took a seat in the same pew at the other end from them. As Meldrum studied him, making no effort to hide his interest, what seemed to be the family mourners arrived in a group and filed into the pews at the front. Meldrum identified the stout, red-cheeked man leading the way as Frank Bower. He'd only spoken to him on the phone, but recognised him from a photograph of the two brothers on a table beside the bed in the murder flat. There was another older couple, two older men, three younger ones. Over the next quarter of an hour a handful of others scattered themselves in a way that seemed only to emphasise the church's near emptiness. At last the organ got them to their feet and as Meldrum mouthed the hymn, producing a noise not much above a hoarse whisper, he'd been disconcerted by the baritone at full volume beside him. No Mr Faint-heart about Bobbie Shields, hymn book in hand. *Onward* Christian soldiers, *marching* as to war. Tramp, tramp, tramp. Being in the Masons, maybe that had something to do with it. Or maybe not, since, religious or not, a funny handshake wasn't a bad career move in the police. Or at least did no harm, put it that way. Despite the difference in rank, Shields had been one of the late Chief Superintendent Billy Ord's court of drinking pals. Everybody liked Bobbie Shields.

Except possibly Meldrum, who didn't go in much for the hail-fellow-well-met stuff, and anyway had had a soft spot for Henderson, the sergeant whose place Shields had taken. True, a soft spot he'd identified too late, leaving it till after the man was dead.

Coming out of the church, he'd told Shields there wasn't any need to go to the cemetery. No argument from the sergeant, snow already in the air and the wind slicing through the black leather jacket he wore as a fixture. Shields was more than willing to go back and catch up on the paperwork. As for Meldrum, he'd followed on with the rest of the Christian infantry to the cemetery. To do what? Check among the mourners for a killer who'd used ten inches of African carved ebony to batter in a skull? Sell that to colleagues as the why of his being here; not to be admitted to them was a belief that other things being equal almost everybody – and not least a poor devil like this Iain Bower, unlucky enough to be beaten to death by the base of a phallic symbol – deserved a respectable turn out at the cemetery.

Call it an agnostic act of piety.

Someone among the mourners on the opposite side of the grave was watching him. Average height, glimpse of a long thin face when he eased back the blue hood on what looked like a cheap imitation of a Berghaus anorak. It was the man who had sat along from Shields and himself in the pew at the back of the church during the service. Taking the chance of a second look, Meldrum half thought he knew the face, then was sure he didn't, but had his gaze returned just long enough to be certain he hadn't been mistaken about being watched. Distracted, he was slow to register the stir and then sudden stillness on either side of him. The minister's voice had fallen silent. Reluctant to look away from the watcher, he hesitated, so that he must have been the last to see the man who'd appeared at the minister's side and was pissing into the grave.

Shock was probably the explanation most of the mourners would offer later: 'I was too shocked to try and stop him. And then it was over. It was over so quickly. The driver of the hearse said he watched the man get out of the taxi. Bit of a cheek, the driver thought, pulling up in front of a hearse like that. But, of course, he thought it was some relative or friend in a panic about arriving late.' And the man had set off walking up by the path, going round the long way. Any of the mourners catching his progress from the corner of an eye would have assumed he was on his way to visit a grave, perhaps one of those lined up along the wall with the estate of bungalows on the other side. 'And then – I didn't see him at this point, you understand – but apparently he *swerved* on to the grass, came up beside the minister, and next moment! When he finished – mean, he didn't take long, he didn't go on and on, you know what I mean – he turned and walked, straight route this time, no messing about, down to where the taxi was waiting. Run? No, he didn't run, but he moved fast. No one was chasing him. Except this one chap, policeman as it turned out, but he hadn't a chance of catching him. I don't know why the rest of us didn't react. Difficult to explain, but who'd imagine anything like that? Tell you the truth, we were in shock.'

That the man was big, very big, might have had something to do with it as well.

In pursuit, Meldrum, himself inches over six feet, reckoned they might be of a size in height. The man was broader, though, gorrilla-shouldered. And then seeing him loom above the taxi, Meldrum added another four inches at least, six six or even eight. Whatever the driver thought was going on, he ignored Meldrum's yell and gesturing arm. The taxi was already rolling forward as the passenger scrambled in.

When Meldrum turned, panting, the group around the grave was breaking up. Mourners streamed towards him, heading down the slope towards their cars. Rather than use up breath he didn't have, he ran his own car up ahead of the hearse, and drew it across to block the exit road.

At least now he had a reason to gather names.

CHAPTER TWO

Side by side, in shirtsleeves, the two men were in a garden with enough flowers and greenery showing behind them for it to be summer. The sun was shining and Frank, the taller of the two, was offering a wide cheesy grin to whoever was taking the picture while Iain Bower stared unsmiling straight at the camera. The contrast gave an odd effect as if Iain was scowling under the burden of his older brother's arm slung across his shoulders. On the other hand, maybe the sun was in his eyes or the button had been pressed at just the wrong instant.

'See that kitchen in there, some kitchen, wife would give her eye teeth for that kitchen. And him on his ownio,' Bobbie Shields said from the doorway. 'Better off than better folk. Makes you wonder.'

Getting no response to this folk wisdom, he disappeared again.

Meldrum sighed and put the photograph back on the table between the telephone and the box of sleeping tablets. There was an alarm clock, too, and a glass with a last mouthful of water floating a scum of dust. Iain Bower must have had some sentimental feeling for the picture. Among the first things he would see when he wakened: two men in a garden, one summer thirty years or so ago. Since he'd been killed in bed it could have been among the last he ever saw. Maybe he'd kept it there because it showed the brothers when they were young or maybe because it had been taken by one of their parents and the garden behind them belonged to the family home. In a murder case, you could demand answers and get them from everyone but the victim.

'He's here,' Bobbie Shields said.

'I heard. You buzz him up?'

'He should be in the lift now.'

Meldrum went along the hall into the living room. He listened to the door being opened and an exchange of voices. When Frank Bower appeared, he was in a hurry, nerving himself to get things over with quickly. He was a bulky man with a large soft face, and his handshake was a little too moist for Meldrum's taste.

'I appreciate your being willing to come here,' Meldrum said.

He watched Bower cross to the window. 'I like this view.'

Behind him, Shields muttered, 'Some place, right enough.'

'Would it be all right?' Bower indicated the patio doors, miming the act of sliding them open.

'I gather the place is going to belong to you,' Meldrum said.

'I suppose I was thinking of evidence. Fingerprints. That kind of thing.'

'That's been taken care of.'

'So it's all right?' And he nodded again at the doors.

'The weather that night was exceptionally cold. I don't imagine whoever killed your brother went out on to the balcony.'

Following Bower out, Meldrum found it was still cold enough for the metal of the railing to strike chill against his hands. The balcony was narrow but long enough to hold a small table and two chairs, a nice place to have drinks or to take lunch if a warm summer day happened along in the absence of the city's persistent gusting winds. The grey tracks of the artificial ski slope angled down the flanks of the Pentlands in the near distance. To the left there was the round summit of the Braid Hill; in front a show of old beech and oak in a patch of land framed between the high tenements.

'I've only been here once before,' Bower said. 'To think it belongs to me. It's an odd feeling. Under the circumstances.'

Under the circumstances. One way of putting it.

'Did you know your brother had left it to you?'

'Not the kind of thing you do talk about, is it? There was money as well. I was surprised how much. I didn't realise he'd done so well.'

Plenty of murders had been committed for an inheritance. Bower, however, seemed to have taken the question straightforwardly at face value.

'Did you get on well with your brother?'

'Before he retired, he'd worked in Brussels for about twenty-five years. That's a long time.'

'So you wouldn't have seen much of one another?'

'I'd always thought he'd retire somewhere to the sun. He has – had friends in Spain. I was pleased when he decided to come to Edinburgh.'

'Yes . . . Seven months, isn't it, since he came back?'

'Not long.' Bower shook his head and took a sighing breath. 'All the plans he had, he didn't get long.'

'Seven months. I thought you'd have been here more often.'

'Eh?'

'You said you'd only been here once before.'

Bower shivered. 'Can we go inside? It's colder than it looks.'

Meldrum followed him in and pulled the patio doors shut. Even with the central heating off, the room was warmed from the sun.

'Iain came over to look around for a place last spring. They were completing the block next door, and getting started on this one. He put down a deposit on the flat just from a look at the plans. The promise was it would be ready for occupation by September. Typical builders, of course, it was January before he got in. He'd four months in rented accommodation, his furniture in store in Liverpool.' He looked round at the couch and chairs, the bookcases and pictures. 'As soon as you lot are finished, I'll sell this place.'

'Do you have the address? Where he stayed, the temporary accommodation, I mean?'

'Somewhere in Leith. Short-stay rentals, foreign students, all kinds of people. Told me he was glad to get out of it. I have the address somewhere – I'll check on it when I get home. Tell me where and I'll send it to you.'

'Phone call would be fine,' Meldrum said, passing across a card with his details. 'I'm not there, leave the message and I'll get it.'

'Why do you want it anyway?' Bower turned his head sharply and frowned as Shields appeared through from the bedroom. For a moment, it looked as if he was about to protest, but if so he thought better of it. 'Like I say, he was only there while he was waiting for this place to be ready.' He watched as Shields came and stood behind one of the chairs. It was as if no one felt able to suggest sitting down. 'Do you think he might have met someone while he was staying there? I suppose, what I mean is, someone who killed him?'

'Did he mention anyone to you?'

'I was never near the place. Kilbracken is a long way from Edinburgh.'

'Were you there when you were contacted about your brother's death?'

'Where else would I be? It's home. I was there when Iain was killed.'

Bringing that up without prompting might suggest that, after all, he didn't expect his innocence to be taken for granted. As for Kilbracken, it wasn't as far as all that from Edinburgh. Meldrum had an image of road signs pointing off to it, one after the other, miles apart, after the way of country roads. He'd never had occasion to follow any of them; Kilbracken he supposed would be not so much a village as one of those handfuls of houses dropped among a prospect of fields for no obvious reason.

'We can't be exact about when your brother was killed, sometime during the Thursday evening, early hours of the Friday morning, either side of midnight.'

Unbidden, memories came back to Meldrum of what he'd read about the notorious Peter Manuel murders back in the Fifties. To check on an alibi, police cars had timed fast runs between a house near Loch Lomond and the murder scene in a bungalow at High Burnside outside Glasgow.

Bower took out a large linen handkerchief, carefully unfolded it and blew his nose. When he'd finished, he said, 'I was at a party for a few friends. Last-minute arrangement. Usually that evening midweek I'd have been at a Probus meeting. On a normal Thursday, I'd be home about eleven, read for an hour, then off to bed. You know about Probus?' Professional and business people; retired; getting together to pass the time. Meldrum nodded. 'The party, as it happened, went on quite late.'

'You live on your own?'

'Certainly not.' It was as if the question offended him. 'With my wife.'

Why had he assumed Bower wasn't married? Maybe because there had been no sign of him being accompanied at the funeral. The existence of a wife – now that would be a really stupid thing to lie about – made notions of an intricate timetable to dispose of his brother that much more unlikely.

'When you said about being in this flat once before, when was that?'

'Back in January. Just after Iain finally got into the place. He invited May and myself for an overnight stay. If you want to know when was the last time I saw him — that would be it. We've spoken on the phone, of course.'

'So when would be the—'

'Last time we talked? Month or so ago, something like that.'

'Did he ring you?'

'Can't remember. Does it matter?'

'Just that if you didn't speak often, there might have been a particular reason for the call. If he'd rung you, it might have been because he wanted to ask you about something. If anything was worrying him.'

'Nothing like that.' Bower dismissed the idea. 'Whichever one of us made it, it was just a getting-in-touch kind of call. It didn't last very long. In fact, it petered out more than anything.'

'You didn't have much to say to one another?'

'We didn't have much in common any more. I'm sure he felt the same way.'

'He's got a photograph of you beside his bed,' Shields said.

They both looked at him. He didn't say a great deal, Shields. He wasn't what you'd call a contributor; unlike poor Henderson, always trying to work things out, get there ahead of you. With Detective Sergeant Henderson you'd almost been able to hear the wheels going round, all the time up until he'd got himself killed in America. He'd been ambitious. In contrast, Shields's ambitions appeared to lie on the other side of collecting his pension. Until then, working his ticket, he favoured the quiet life, doing no more than he was asked, trying to keep down the paperwork. Truth was, as a second pair of eyes and ears he was pretty bloody useless. Getting lumbered with him wasn't a good sign. Once, Meldrum would have kicked up hell. Now, he let it go; maybe himself less ambitious than he'd been in the not so distant past; maybe too proud to complain. Perhaps too arrogant. They gave him dead weight, he could carry it.

On impulse, perhaps only because Bower had made no answer to Shields, he asked him, 'You like to see?' and led the way into the bedroom.

Once there, though, and seeing the taut look on Bower's face, the way his eyes avoided the bed, a feeling of shame constrained Meldrum. The man's brother had died in this room, been beaten to death on that bed.

'Here you are,' Shields said, lifting the photograph from the bedside table and holding it out; urging, as Bower hesitated about taking it, 'Don't worry. The lab boys have been over everything in here.'

Bower glanced at it, looked at the table. 'That's where it was?'

'Just there. You'd think it would have got knocked over,' Shields said. In the killing process, he meant.

Bower swallowed; the high colour on his cheeks seemed more vivid as he went pale.

It was possible Bower wouldn't recognise the spots on the headboard for what they were, or the splashed arc on the wall above it. Meldrum hoped so. The cover and sheets which had soaked up most of the spillage had been removed. Fortunately, there was no blood on the photograph.

'Can I keep this?' Bower asked.

Meldrum took the photograph from him and set it back on the table, careful to put it more or less exactly where it had been.

'Not just yet,' he said. 'We still have things to do, I'm sorry.'

'Things to do?'

'But as soon as possible, of course, we'll finish up.'

'And you'll let me know?'

'Of course.'

'As soon as possible . . .'

Shields would say later on, 'He's in a hurry to get his money for the place,' but Meldrum felt that kind of cynicism came too easily, missed the point as often as not.

'Do you remember where it was taken?' he wondered, indicating the photograph of the two brothers.

'A long time ago,' Bower said. Red-cheeked, he was still recognisably the man in the photograph, very light pale blue eyes fixed on the camera, teeth bared in a grin. There was an intensity about the man in the photograph, though, and that, if it was still there, was veiled in flesh as much as the neck or jowls. 'Some family occasion, I imagine.'

At the cemetery, like everyone else Bower had claimed the man who had pissed into the grave was a stranger to him. Now, back in the living room, Meldrum tried again.

'He'd be hard to forget, someone that size.'

'I agree,' Bower said, 'which is why I don't see any point in going over it.'

'When I spoke to you after the funeral, you were shocked at what had happened.'

'Everyone was.'

'There's always a chance of remembering something after the shock wears off. I've seen that happen.'

'Has that happened? Does someone know who he is?'

Meldrum shook his head.

'And you've spoken to everyone?'

'Briefly. We'll talk to them again.' Reminded by that, he asked, 'There was someone else I'd like to ask you about. When you were at the graveside, he'd have been among the mourners over to your left. Medium height, long thin face, blue anorak?'

'Means nothing to me. What was his name?'

'Davis, he said.' He paused for a response, just in case.

Bower shrugged his ignorance, turning down the corners of his mouth. 'What about him?'

'Just that he gave me an address as well. Real address, fake name. No one called Davis lived there.'

'Maybe he likes hanging around funerals,' Bower said. 'I've heard of people like that. It's not a normal thing to do, maybe he was ashamed to give his real name.'

'If I find him, I'll ask him.' Meldrum took a breath, let it out slowly. Grieving relatives weren't supposed to irritate you: that wasn't in the manual. 'Anyway, he claimed not to recognise the man who committed the offence at the graveside.' Nice official language, times it came in useful. 'Neither did anyone else. Don't you find that strange? If someone had a reason to hate your brother, don't you think somebody there would have recognised him?'

'I doubt if anyone hated Iain,' Bower said.

Even if they pissed in his grave?

'What reason could there be for an offence like that?'

'Maybe he mistook the funeral. People always liked Iain. I honestly believe it had to be meant for somebody else. Or maybe he was mad. In that case, it could have been anyone's funeral he disturbed. I'd check the mental hospitals, if I was you.'

'Iain hadn't ever spoken about having trouble? Getting threats? Being worried about somebody's behaviour?'

'I never heard a word of anything like that from him.'

'Is there any chance he could have spoken about some unpleasantness to someone else?' And as Bower seemed about to dismiss the idea,

Meldrum went on, 'There isn't an old friend perhaps or someone else in the family he might have confided in?'

'My parents are dead. I have a couple of uncles. A cousin and her children. We're a small family. Even smaller now. Iain wasn't close to any of them.'

'Would you say he was close to you?'

'If you call living in separate countries close!'

Meldrum looked at the photograph, Iain's withdrawn expression in contrast to the intensity of Frank's smiling concentration. Did it suggest a tension between the brothers? That unsmiling eighteen-(twenty?)-year-old, it wouldn't be hard to imagine developing into a reticent man, one who shielded his private life against intrusion. Assuming he had secrets, of course, or any worth keeping. No way of telling. A photograph caught a particular moment, that was all. Even then you could misread, totally misunderstand, what it showed. For sure, you couldn't learn from a photograph how a life had gone in the years since it was taken.

'So, as far as you're concerned then, Iain had no enemies?'

Bower made a gesture of impatience. 'What enemies could he have in this country?'

In this country.

That was the way with questions. You asked the same ones over and over in different words in the hope sooner or later of an answer that would yield something different.

CHAPTER THREE

'He was a big bastard,' the taxi driver said. His name was Archie Kerr, middle forties, not much larger than a jockey, with deeply furrowed cheeks that suggested he might have a stomach ulcer nagging at him. He was a reluctant witness, turned up by routine checking on the taxi firms. 'You're telling me I should start arguing with him?'

'You're telling me you didn't see me chasing him?' Meldrum asked.

'I was reading my paper. Look, we get to the cemetery. I mean, I could see the folk at the grave, the minister and the rest of you, and he gets out, tells me to wait. So I take it for granted he's one of the mourners, what else would I think? He'd a black tie on too, well, a dark one anyway. So I get my paper, have another go at the crossword and wait for him to come back.'

'He didn't take long and he came back in a hurry. You didn't realise anything was wrong?'

'Honest, boss, when I heard what he done, I was amazed. That's an awful thing to do. I've never heard of anything like that.'

'I wasn't that far behind him and I was shouting. You didn't hear me shouting?'

The little man shrugged. 'Like I say, he was a big bastard. See, when he got in, I could feel the cab going down at that side. The only shouting I heard was him shouting and when a guy like that shouts, get moving, you get moving.'

The question was, moving to where? The man who'd pissed in Iain Bower's grave had given the Bruntsfield Hotel as his destination, but stopped the cab and got out before arriving there. Reception staff were sure no one of that description was or had been a guest in the hotel. It struck Meldrum, however, that if the man was a stranger to the city he must have seen the hotel, and that made it likely he was staying somewhere nearby. In Viewforth, the street full of boarding houses that ran down from the side of the hotel, a door-to-door turned up a Mrs Campbell, who recognised the description at once.

When Meldrum and Shields went to talk to her late that afternoon, however, they'd already been told their quarry had flown.

'My heart turned over when the young constable told me that man was wanted. He'd only walked out the door an hour before.' Mrs Campbell put her hand over her mouth. The distress, if theatrical, seemed genuine. 'To tell you the truth, even before I knew he was in some kind of trouble he made me feel uncomfortable. He was a pleasant enough spoken man, mind you, actually he was very civil. As a matter of fact, he spoke too quietly, twice I'd to ask him to repeat himself. And the second time, he had a stammer when he answered me. I felt embarrassed for him. But even so I wasn't comfortable. It was the size of him! Not just his height, but his shoulders, he'd hands on him like a navvy's shovel. I thought, even if he doesn't mean any harm, I just hope he knows his own strength!'

With the pause, Meldrum took the opportunity to ask if they could see the guest book. And there he was: *Richard Nicolson*; the signature very plain, cramped between the upper and lower lines, touching neither. It was even possible that it was genuine. That might depend on whether what he'd done at the graveside had been an impulse of the moment or planned. And, of course, on what else he had done or planned to do.

But if he had killed Iain Bower, then he'd taken an enormous risk at the cemetery in such a public expression of contempt for the murdered man. It didn't seem likely that he could be the killer – unless, of course, you came back to the theory of impulse, irresistible, unplanned, overwhelming. After all the kind of impulse that could end, given the wrong time and place, with the battering in of a man's skull.

'Did he leave in a hurry?'

'I don't think he expected to leave when he did. He'd paid a week in advance. But I wasn't sorry when he got the phone call.'

'You didn't say anything about a phone call to the constable, did you?'

'It was just after one o'clock, I was watching the news. A man's voice, asking if he could speak to Mr Nicolson. I went up and knocked his door. He'd been lying on top of the bed with his clothes on, it was all rumpled. He was on the phone a while, ten minutes, quarter of an hour. I came in here and shut the door to give him his privacy. But it was after that, he came down with his bag in his hand and told me he was leaving.'

'This man who phoned. Could you describe his voice? Any kind of accent?'

'No . . . Not from the West or English or American, nothing like that.' She thought about it. 'All he said was, could he speak to Mr Nicolson. Sounded just like anybody you'd pass in the street. It could have been you.'

That was it. They'd missed Nicolson by the length of an afternoon, not much, but enough. It was back to headquarters and routine, which would go no faster than undermanning allowed. Situation normal, they'd need a bit of luck.

'We've already got descriptions of him to the bus stations, Waverley, the airport. Now,' he told them, 'we cover every hotel and boarding house in the city. If the guy who phoned the boarding house is putting him up somewhere, that makes things harder. One comfort, though, this Nicolson is massive. If anybody's seen him they'll know who you're talking about. There shouldn't be any way a guy like that's going to be able to hide.'

The way things were to turn out, it wouldn't be that easy.

CHAPTER FOUR

'I hope you don't smell anything in the lift,' the receptionist said.

Failure, did she mean? Loneliness? Maybe just transience, the smell of unsettledness. Already in the months since Iain Bower had left, more than half of the flats had new occupants. Enquiries had been made, coming back in the evenings, the building mostly empty during the day, until statements had been obtained from the rest.

To his neighbours, Bower seemed to have been the invisible man; but that was probably true for almost everyone in a place where no one stayed for long. A lot of police time for not much return, with what might be the exception of a young couple on the fourth floor. That interview had been flagged up for Meldrum, and now he and Shields had come to check it out.

There was a smell in the lift, very faint.

As he watched the floor indicator change, Meldrum had a sudden image of his daughter Betty's flat the previous evening. With a new baby, she wasn't working or studying. Earth mother stuff. Plump and happy. Ready to get fat, if she didn't stop eating chocolates. How could you love someone and be so irritated by them? On the other hand, her husband Sandy had looked too lean. The baby had come along unplanned and Sandy, just finishing art school, had swapped the chance to travel round Italy on a scholarship for a teacher training course. Fingers drumming on his knee, fresh from a day spent teaching art to kids who didn't want to learn about anything, he'd looked fine-drawn as piano wire. Sandy and Betty, kids themselves, how could he trust them to care for his only grandchild? The young didn't know how; and the old didn't have the energy for all that stuff, broken nights, milk and nappies.

'Piss,' Shields said.

'What?'

'Somebody's pissed in here.' The indicator went to 4, the doors opened and they stepped out. 'More than once.'

They went the wrong way along the corridor, checked and came back, past the lift and round a corner to where two doors faced one another. The door on the left opened to Meldrum's double tap on the bellpush.

Black as the earl of hell's waistcoat was how Shields spoke of them later, an inadequate description of the tall, graceful girl, the stocky husband, the solemn-faced little boy.

'Not well,' the husband said. He spoke with a careful emphasis as if taking precaution against being misunderstood. 'That's not a claim I would make.'

'But you had spoken to him.'

'I'm sure we didn't tell your people we knew him well.'

'If you spoke to him more than once,' Shields said, 'you hold the record.'

'I don't understand.'

Meldrum was conscious of how much he and Shields overcrowded the room. They had been given the couch, the husband sat on the only easy chair, the woman on a kitchen chair by the small table with the child on her knee. Behind them the back wall made a kitchen space, sink, fridge, work surfaces. Out of the window as he'd come into the room, he'd seen the waters of the Forth darkening as a cloud passed across the sun. By his elbow a shut door must give on to a bedroom; one lying open in the tiny hall had offered a glimpse of a bath with a shower screen. A clean place – the receptionist at the desk had spoken of a once-a-week maid service – and adequate enough. An impression impermanent as a hotel room, though, which made it depressing.

'Except staff,' Meldrum said, 'no one else in the building seems to have talked to Mr Bower.' Most of them claimed not even to recognise him when shown his photograph. Nodding 'Good day' in the lift was about as much as any of them would admit.

'Apart from you two,' Shields said.

That was simply the case, a fact the DS offered without emphasis, but the man frowned and the mother refolded her arms more tightly around the child. The Balewas were legally in the country while he studied for a postgraduate qualification in electrical engineering. They shouldn't have anything to fear from the police. But Meldrum knew nothing of Nigeria. Perhaps it had one of those governments which bred that kind of reaction; read the papers, there seemed to be no lack of them. Against that, according to the notes, Balewa was here on a government grant, which argued for him being in favour with the regime, whatever it was.

'Perhaps,' Meldrum offered soothingly, 'flats like these, it isn't easy to get to know people.'

'Oh, yes!' the woman cried. Silver dangling earrings chimed with the energy of her agreement. 'It is very hard. My husband is out during the day. I am a qualified nurse so I work at night. Poor Sanya, it is lonely for him.' Wide-eyed, the boy kept watch from the shelter of her arms. 'I will be glad when we go home.'

'Not true!' the husband said. 'We weren't the only ones who spoke to him.'

Catching up after a moment, Meldrum asked, 'Who else?'

The woman, however, went back to what her husband had said earlier. 'We didn't know him well, not really.'

The husband pursued the theme. 'Mr Bower stopped me one day. I was coming into the building, he was coming out. Were we from Nigeria? Yes, he'd thought so. He had been in Lagos several times in dealings for his company, and once to a conference in Abuja on petrochemicals. He was very pleasant, and I enjoyed talking with him about my own country.'

'Would you say you struck up a friendship?'

Balewa pushed out his lips in disapproval. 'That would overstate things entirely. You might say we were acquainted from that time.'

'Were you ever in his flat?'

'Yes.'

'Often?'

'Not often.' He glanced at his wife.

'We had afternoon tea with him one Sunday,' she said. 'These flats come furnished. So his flat was like this, though he had some pictures of his own and some books. It was if we were sitting in this very room.'

'They know,' Balewa said. 'They've seen Mr Bower's flat for themselves.'

As a matter of fact, they hadn't. Months since Bower had left his flat on the floor below, a new tenant in occupation, what would have been the point?

Meldrum didn't bother to contradict him.

Instead he asked, 'You mentioned you weren't the only ones who'd spoken to Mr Bower? Who else did you have in mind?'

'The clergyman,' Balewa said.

'Clergyman?' Living here?'

'No, no, no. Mr Bower went to church.'

'Which one?'

The man scratched his cheek.

The wife watched him thinking, then said firmly, 'You don't know,' and added as Meldrum glanced at her, 'Neither do I.'

'I don't suppose it matters,' the man said.

Inclined to agree, Meldrum was about to leave it at that when Shields cleared his throat as a signal for attention. 'Was he religious?' he asked.

The sergeant's mind was of no interest to Meldrum, but the way it worked occasionally took him by surprise.

' 'I never asked him,' Balewa said. 'But the clergyman came here to visit with him.'

'As a regular thing?' Meldrum wondered.

'Yes, yes. I think so.'

More throat clearing from Shields. 'If this clergyman came round the place as much as that, I'm surprised you don't know his name.'

'I was never there when he visited Mr Bower, of course I wasn't, why would I be present? Mr Bower mentioned on one occasion that this clergyman came to see him.'

'When we went for afternoon tea,' the wife said.

Balewa nodded impatiently, as if that had been too obvious to mention. 'It was my impression Mr Bower held him in high regard.'

'What gave you that idea?'

'He said, My minister's coming tonight. Something to look forward to.'

'Popping in,' the woman explained. 'He said, My minister's popping in. Something to look forward to.'

'Reverend Turnbull, was it?' Meldrum asked. Turnbull was the name of the minister who'd officiated at Bower's funeral.

'I don't know. Mr Bower didn't say.'

If Bower liked this minister, talked freely with him, it wasn't impossible he might have shared a confidence or two. Given the seeming isolation surrounding the murdered man, any scrap might help. It went to show even Shields could turn up something useful.

Perhaps the sergeant had come to the same conclusion. Showing a rare touch of the excitement of the chase, 'What was the minister's name?' he was asking again; and, meeting with the same denial, persisted, 'Funny it was never mentioned, like.'

Time, Meldrum felt, to call a halt to this limping version of hot pursuit.

'We'd be grateful if you'd think about it,' he said, getting to his feet. He gave Balewa his card. 'If anything occurs to you, the number on that will get me.'

They were on the landing when the wife's voice came from inside. 'Is this number the same as the other one we got?'

She had followed them into the hall, the child tagging along close behind. At some point, the husband must have passed the card to her for she was waving it in front of her.

'No,' Meldrum said, more or less over his shoulder. He was anxious to get away. 'The other one would just be the general contact number.'

'He didn't give us a number at all.'

'I'm sorry about that. You should have been given a number. But, in any case, the one I gave—'

'I *was* given a number. Wait! I'll show you.'

As she went back into the room, Balewa made a nothing-to-do-with-me face and shrugged. To Meldrum's irritation, she came back clutching one of the leaflets the teams had circulated.

'I don't see the problem,' he said. 'The number at the bottom there. That's what I meant by the general number. The one I gave you is—'

'Is yours, I understand! What I'm wondering is why your colleague didn't give us a number.'

For answer, Meldrum jerked a forefinger in the direction of the leaflet.

'Not him!' she said dismissively. 'The second one who came.'

Shields was grinning as if at an entertainment laid on for his benefit, but now she had caught Meldrum's attention.

'As far as our records go, you've only been spoken to once.'

'No,' Balewa said. He spoke emphatically, coming to his wife's defence. 'There was another. I was surprised. I gave him the leaflet and said to him, just what I said to you, We've already been questioned, what's going on?'

'This was a policeman?'

'Oh, yes, he insisted. He sat on the couch where you were and went over the whole thing with us.'

'Like you,' the wife said, 'he wasn't in uniform. Just ordinary clothes. One of those rain jackets, with the hood, you know?'

'What colour, do you remember?'

'Oh, yes. It had been raining, but he wouldn't take it off. The cushion was wet when he got up to leave. It was a blue jacket.'

'He asked you about Mr Bower?'

'Yes.'

'And he claimed to be a policeman?'

'Yes.'

'You should have asked him for proof of identity,' Shields said.

'We didn't ask you,' the wife said. 'He asked questions just the same manner as you. Why would we doubt him?'

'Can you describe him?'

'He was taller than me,' Balewa said. 'Not by too much. Five foot ten? He had grey among his hair. With white people, I'm not good at judging age.'

'He looked hungry,' the woman said. She sucked in her cheeks. 'He looked like he needed a wife to feed him.'

Meldrum tried to recall the false name the thin-faced man in the blue anorak had given him at Bower's funeral. Long shot or not, something told him this might be the same man. Davis. He'd called himself Davis. And given a false address.

'Can you remember the name he gave?'

The two of them looked at one another.

'Chief Inspector. Like you.'

Shields snorted, sounding more appreciative than indignant. 'Chief Inspector what?'

'Meldrum,' Balewa said. 'Chief Inspector Meldrum.'

'When you introduced yourself in the same way, it did seem strange,' the wife said. 'But then I decided, it must be a common name.'

CHAPTER FIVE

I t was a pity not to be able to get nearer the water, but it was good walking in the sunshine, a little breeze in his face and beyond the lines of parked cars and the white length of the latest version of a Scottish Office small waves chopping and changing in restless dazzles of light. Coming out of the rental flats, seeing the sunshine, he couldn't face getting back into the car, told Shields to take it, he'd make his own way back. In response he'd been given a glance of impure speculation quickly veiled. In Shields's book, going off by yourself meant something to hide, private business, a deal, a woman. From the Chief Constable down, police were in the suspicion business; and with lawyers billing every six minutes, computer screens monitoring their operators, men looking over their shoulders as they worked all the hours God sent, the rest of the world had moved towards them. Going off by yourself had to be wrong, when there were forms to be filled in back at the office. The flaw in all that was, when did you get time to think? His theory was that he thought more clearly in the open air; his father's people had been farmers.

On the other hand, steering a plough up and down stony fields staring at a horse's arse didn't seem much of a recipe for thinking. Though Rabbie Burns had managed it pretty well. More than could be said for himself at the moment, Meldrum reflected. As for his father's family, apart from a bible with some names and birth dates fading on the inside cover, none of them had left a letter behind far less a poem. Maybe what they'd passed on to him was just a walking gene.

Radio Leith sat beside the old docks like an aircraft hangar. Or a barn. An enormous barn. Could have got an EC grant if there had been corn stored inside, instead of compact discs. More by association of ideas than impulse, he cut across the grass and went into the station.

'Jim Pleat about?' he asked the girl at reception.

'He won't be long,' she looked at the clock, 'about ten minutes.'

It was more like twenty. He read the award citations in the glass cases, leafed through a magazine about sound effects and was making up his mind to leave and find something useful to do when the receptionist came over.

'He's free now.' She led the way round from the hall to the studio on the left. 'Would you like a coffee?'

'Please.'

Through the glass, he saw Pleat, headphones in hand, rolling his head from side to side.

'Tension. Gets it out of the neck and shoulders,' he explained as Meldrum went in. He rolled his head back and squinted along his nose. 'You should try it.'

'I'd get seasick.'

Pleat stretched his mouth wide and stuck out his tongue an improbable distance. When he'd put it back in, he said, 'They call that the Silent Scream. Exercises the face.'

'Glad you told me. I was just about to take offence.'

'I read about it in a magazine. You can do it in the morning while you're shaving. Cary Grant said it kept him looking young.'

Meldrum studied him in silence. What was left of Pleat's hair formed a faded ginger fringe round the edge of his skull. He had bags under the bags under his eyes.

'All right,' he said. 'So it takes a while to work.'

'I didn't say a word,' Meldrum said.

'You don't have to. I can read what you're thinking on your face.'

'I'll have to work on that.'

'Right enough, not a good idea for a policeman.' He grinned. 'Or a criminal.'

'Not much of an idea for anybody.'

'You're a gloomy bugger,' Pleat said.

It was a view of himself which continued to surprise Meldrum, though hints directed his way over the years suggested it might be a majority opinion. His ex-wife Carole, a primary headteacher, had made the same point, though not in those exact words. She'd told him, 'My work makes me find the best in people, you find the worst.' He'd been surprised by her too, since looking out from the inside felt like keeping cheerful in face of the evidence for pessimism. Remarkably cheerful. Given the weight of evidence.

When the receptionist brought in the two mugs of coffee, Meldrum found his had sugar in it. That had been a misunderstanding of hers the first time he'd been to the station, and one she'd obviously got fixed in her head. It was possible, of course, she gave everyone sugar.

'I've got quarter of an hour,' Pleat said.

'They keep you busy.'

'All right, half an hour, but I have to go pee as well.'

They sipped in a comfortable silence. He'd first met Pleat about six years earlier. That had been in connection with a murder too, and one not so far away from where Ian Bower had rented his temporary apartment. He'd used Pleat's programme to make an appeal for information and, for some reason, they'd got on well. Feeling comfortable with people wasn't a usual experience for Meldrum. Certainly, it must have more to do with Pleat than him. Maybe it was just something Pleat did. Like putting sugar in coffee.

'What brings you this way?'

'I was at the Doune Apartments.'

'What were you doing there?'

'You know them?'

'Aye, rented flats. Big turnover.'

'That's the one.'

'So?'

'What?'

'Christ!' Pleat sighed. 'It's like getting blood out a stone. What took you there?'

'Somebody's been pissing in the lift.'

'Be that way.'

Meldrum relented. 'All right, a murder. But nothing in it for you. I mean, it wasn't today – or in the flats even.'

'Don't tell me. Up Morningside way – eh, Bower, chap called Bower. He wasn't long retired, worked in Paris.'

'Brussels. Pretty good, all the same.'

'I'm a fan of yours. Anyway, Edinburgh isn't exactly the murder capital of the world. Random violence and domestics is our usual. Something different catches the eye. I take it this Bower *is* different?'

'I think so. I'm not sure how much yet.'

'The papers said it wasn't burglary. Was he a homo?'

'Nobody's said so.'

'Like it said on the Gay Pride banner in Yorkshire, "Nowt so queer as folk." It's not always easy to tell.'

'Apart from his brother, the people I've spoken to – like this Nigerian couple in the flats – hadn't even met him till the last few months.'

Or, even worse, had never met him at all, like the woman in the flat once occupied by Iain Bower. They'd talked to her for no better reason than Meldrum taking a scunner at the fusion of smells in the lift. On the way down after interviewing the Balewas, he'd caught on the trapped air the sweet tang of disinfectant and behind it a faint smell, unsuppressed, acrid, unmistakable this time. He'd pressed the button and got out so quickly that Shields, taken by surprise, had to elbow back the closing doors before he could follow. Odd the things that could make your gorge rise. Maybe it was because he'd missed breakfast. Fortunately, the floor was the one Iain Bower had stayed on, so he'd marched ahead until he recognised the number on a door and rang the bell. Not a moment of weakness, DS Shields, but a lesson in leaving no stone unturned. The woman occupant, after puzzling over why, reluctantly agreed to let them in. She knew nothing of Iain Bower, and answered questions brusquely, all the while keeping an eye on an elderly woman bustling around, dusting cloth in hand. Getting the place cleaned once a week was part of the tenants' rental contract, but all that determined spraying and polishing witnessed how thoroughly any trace of Bower must have been eradicated. The charade couldn't have been stretched much past ten minutes. As she closed the door rather too firmly behind them, Shields volunteered, 'That was a waste of time.'

Nice when people felt they could be honest with you.

'Nigerian,' Pleat mused. 'I've always had a thing for black women. Not that I ever do anything about it.'

'Chance your arm. Her man looked as if he could do with a good laugh.'

'Anyway, so what did they tell you? Anything useful?'

'According to them, they didn't know Bower well. They'd been once to have afternoon tea with him in his flat. Mr Balewa says they got

acquainted when Bower told him he'd been to Nigeria on business a few
times.'

'Had he been?' And when Meldrum raised his eyebrows, 'In Nigeria
like he claimed?'

'Well, Balewa says they talked about home, and he enjoyed it. So
Bower convinced him.'

'All the same, you should check with his employers. Ex-employers. In
Brussels.'

'I blame the television,' Meldrum said.

'What?'

'Everybody wants to play detective.'

'Be like that.' Pleat got up. 'Finished your coffee?'

Meldrum was out on the pavement when a sudden discomfort made
him turn and go back inside.

Crouched over a basin soaping his hands, Pleat glanced round as
Meldrum crossed to the nearest urinal.

'Never miss a chance to pee,' he said, sharing the joke with himself in
the mirror. 'Duke of Windsor claimed that was the only good advice his
father ever gave him.'

Meldrum sighed as the stream began to flow, he'd waited a little too
long.

'You know any ministers round here?' he asked, staring at the white
tiles in front of his nose.

'Donald Dewar and his merry men?'

'Not political, religious.'

'This to do with Bower?'

'Maybe.'

But when he turned round, Pleat was grinning and nodding. '*Maybe*,' he
repeated mockingly. 'I can think of one. Mind, his isn't the nearest
church to the Doune Apartments, but he'll be the one you want.'

'Oh?'

'When I read about Bower's funeral, the minister rang a bell. No,
that's priests, isn't it? Ringing bells.' He gave a last scrub at his hands and
lobbed the wad of towels into the bin. 'Noticed the name because I
interviewed him not long since. He'd written a book. Reverend Dr
Turnbull. Bingo, eh?'

'You don't get your detective badge for reading it in the papers,'
Meldrum said. 'Know anything about him? Interesting, I mean.'

'I interview folk here all the time. Most of them, couldn't tell one from the other after a week. I remember Turnbull, though. Something about him . . .'

Meldrum waited, then asked, 'Something?'

Pleat chewed at his lip. Finally, blowing out his breath like someone giving up on a maths problem, he said, 'He didn't go in for knock knock jokes, that's for sure.'

As a description that struck Meldrum as imprecise, but neither mockery nor probing as he walked Pleat back to his studio produced anything more useful. He'd given up and walked away, when Pleat called after him.

'Jim? That book of Turnbull's, it was about the Covenanters.'

'What about it?'

'*The Blood of the Martyrs*, he called it. It just came back to me. Don't ask me why.'

Taking pleasure in the sun, Meldrum paced himself and for a time wondered about Pleat's reaction to the minister. He had been so intent on studying those gathered for Bower's funeral that he'd hardly paid attention to the Reverend Dr Turnbull. He was left now with fragments: at the side of the grave like a black pencil stroke, gown pulled close about him, but younger than that suggested, certainly not old, the voice light, rapid. What else? Light, rapid. Fierce? He dismissed that as probably owing more to imagination than memory. Turnbull had written a book about the Covenanters: men who defied a King to worship Christ in hidden places in the hills, and for their faith been hunted down and killed. Old heroic images of belief and sacrifice. The blood of the martyrs is the seed of the Church.

He found himself staring through the window of Volvona and Crolla at drums of Gorgonzola and hanging lines of taut skin bursting with sausagemeats. Clouds had blown up and the air had cooled. He began to walk more quickly, his thoughts turning from Pleat and the minister to the visit Shields and he had paid to the Doune Apartments. As they'd come out of the flat once rented by Iain Bower, 'That was a waste of time,' Shields had said, the words no sooner out of his mouth than the door behind them opened again and the cleaning woman slipped out.

She'd put her fingers to her lips, the dusting cloth hanging from her hand. 'No need for her in there to hear. None of her business. Did you know about the babysitting?'

'Sorry,' Meldrum had said. 'If there's some kind of problem, tell the local police. We're investigating a murder.'

But he'd misunderstood her.

'That's who I'm talking about. Mr Bower. Did that pair upstairs tell you he used to babysit their wee boy? Well, he did! Big brown eyes, a lovely wee boy.'

'How do you know he babysat?' Meldrum asked.

'The black woman—'

'Mrs Balewa.'

'Aye, right. She came down to thank him for it when I was there. I gave her a look – not that she was paying me any attention. These young mothers – you're all useless, I thought.'

'Did Mr Bower look after the boy often?'

'I expect so.' She hesitated. 'That was the only time I heard of, right enough.'

A young couple alone in a foreign country, with no relatives to turn to, it was understandable. Perhaps there had been some function to attend; maybe they'd just wanted one night when they went out together instead of separately.

'Well,' Meldrum said, 'thanks for telling us.'

Shields was already moving away. Meldrum nodded to the woman and followed him. Her fierce whisper reached after him.

'To me it just wasn't right. What would a man want to babysit for?'

CHAPTER SIX

'I t bothers me,' Meldrum said to Cowan, who was a sympathetic listener as well as being good on bloodstains.

'*Doppelgängers*,' Knife Stanley said. 'They have that effect on people.'

Despite the Dr in front of his name, Henry Stanley was close to the last person Meldrum had been expecting to meet when he walked into the forensic laboratory. Stanley wasn't a medical practitioner and his doctorate wasn't in chemistry or physics, sciences dealing in the kind of weighed and measurable fact juries liked. He was an academic; a psychologist who had turned to anthropology and then taken a sideways step into the sociology department of one of the city's newer universities. At some point along the way, he'd become interested in the techniques pioneered in the United States to associate probable characteristics with types of offence. Not a modest man, he'd quickly discovered in himself a gift for this kind of work and volunteered his services over a series of assaults on schoolgirls. The suspect profile he had produced detailing age, occupation, family background, even district of residence, didn't lead in any direct way to the end of the case. That happened because a beat policeman had the dumb luck to be in the right place at the right time. All the same, once identified there turned out to be an uncanny fit between the attacker and Stanley's predictions, which he'd taken the precaution of sharing with a campaigning tabloid. As a result after the capture he'd obtained a measure of credibility and enjoyed a lot of publicity. Not even sceptics like Meldrum could be certain the attacker's increasing recklessness in the grip of his compulsion wasn't due in part to seeing himself so accurately described. Maybe half a dozen times since,

Stanley had been invited to help with a crime when the papers were criticising lack of progress. As the late Chief Superintendent Billy Ord had put it, 'Throw the fucking jackals a bone.'

'Double*what*?' Bobbie Shields asked.

Like any invitation to Stanley to explain, this was a mistake. Among themselves detectives called him Knife as much for his habit of wandering up the byways of any discussion as in reference to his surname. Cutting to the heart of the matter wasn't his way, and Shields' badly concealed sneer of disbelief brought out the worst in him. Even in physical type, the two were at odds: the sergeant a big sagging figure with a swag of beer belly, Henry Stanley an apple-cheeked little man, not much over five feet, dressed like a bank manager with a weakness for gaudy neckties.

'Not just a double,' he was saying. 'Not simply the old chestnut of everyone having a double. Kirk in his *Secret Commonwealth of Fairies* writes about the Co-Walker, the Reflex-Creature, the Companion who haunts a man like his shadow and after he is dead may be visible to some of the mourners at his funeral. That is what the Germans called the Doppel-gänger.' The look he turned on Meldrum was immodestly satisfied. 'Someone introducing himself as Detective Inspector James Meldrum, using your name, claiming your identity, stirs up a race memory of hauntings. Not surprised you're disturbed.'

'I think this one's solid flesh and blood,' Meldrum said drily.

'An act of faith,' Stanley said, nodding at the leaflet from the Balewas' flat Meldrum had laid on the bench beside Cowan. 'If that's your only piece of physical evidence.'

'Wouldn't hold out much hope, but I'll see what we can think of,' Cowan said.

'It was just on the offchance. Since we were seeing you anyway.'

'What about the SEM?' Stanley asked.

Cowan smiled and raised his eyebrows. A pleasant and courteous man, it was the only sign he allowed himself of the expert's disdain for the amateur.

Nettled, Stanley went on, 'It's not as if it's overused. From what I understand, it was only bought because Glasgow had one.'

Cowan slipped the leaflet into a drawer and told Meldrum, 'Ready when you are.' He explained to Stanley, 'We're going up to take another look at the flat Bower was killed in.'

'You amaze me,' Knife said. 'I thought you people were too busy to visit a scene of crime more than once.'

'Not even that often,' Cowan said, putting on his jacket. 'Most cases we have to rely on what's brought to us. That's why we run courses for policemen.'

Following along the corridor with Shields, Meldrum glanced through the sealed glass partition of the controlled environment room. On a half moon of desks, the Scanning Electron Microscope sat between two monitor screens.

'So why a second visit to the murder scene?' There was an edge to the question as if Knife Stanley might have glimpsed the fleeting grin Cowan gave Meldrum over his shoulder.

'Last chance before the keys go back to the owner,' Cowan said as they came out into the car park between the laboratory and the local police station.

'I take it there were some things you weren't happy about, then?'

As Cowan hesitated for an answer, Meldrum nodded to Shields and the two of them crossed to the car.

'Will I start up?' Shields asked. Without waiting for an answer, he switched on the engine. 'Can't wait all day for him.'

Almost at once, Cowan was opening the door and slipping into the rear seat.

'Practically suggested he should come with us,' he said with mild amusement. 'Henry's amazing.'

'One word for it,' Meldrum said, waving to Stanley, key in hand by his red Porsche, frowning as he watched them go.

Passing King's Buildings, he saw groups of students coming out of one gate then the next, among them a girl, Scandinavian blonde, very tall, a bag showing a racket hung over one bare brown shoulder. Ducks rose off the pond at the gate of Braid Hills Park. Cherry trees spun by pink and white in the opposite gardens. It was a day made for better things than thoughts of human violence. Edinburgh looked good in sunlight.

'*Is* something bothering you?' Shields asked.

Meldrum's head whipped round, startling Shields who was directing his question to Cowan in the seat behind.

'How do you mean?' Cowan seemed taken by surprise. Perhaps he too had been watching the city go by.

'You told Dr Stanley you weren't happy about something.'

'No,' Cowan said. 'He said that to me.'

'All the same,' Shields said.

They waited for him to go on but, leaving it at that, he went back to his driving.

'It's not anything I could put my finger on,' Cowan said to Meldrum. 'I just have this feeling there's something I missed. Usually, when that happens, whatever it was comes back to me. You know the way it goes, you put a problem out of your mind, think about something else altogether and the answer just pops into your head. You solve what was bothering you. Just by not trying too hard. Not this time. I had the feeling even while I went round Bower's flat, there was something I – we – something I was missing.'

Instead of answering, Meldrum turned his attention again to the passing street, a fat hedge, a line of metal railings painted blue. Though he could have given the dimensions of the rooms and drawn a plan of their relation to one another, only parts of the flat Bower had died in were clear in his memory, as if picked out by lights from a surrounding uncertainty. A print in the hall of the *Grande Place* in Brussels with red and green awnings down and a flag with a jaunty pawing bull; remembered for its name not its artwork, a reminder that Bower had come from Belgium. A wine bottle on the kitchen table: only one glass out of it, worth noting as suggesting Bower had eaten on his own that night; but why remember the way the bottle had been resealed (a tiny cork slid into a silver sleeve)? And in the bedroom, the red pattern of violence thrown against the headboard and wall, each stain with its tail indicating the direction and angle of a blow; he could envisage that and how on the murder weapon fragments of skull bone adhered to the bloodied end of the African carving. Forensics seized on such details; but that the background behind the smiling brothers in the bedside photograph was a summer garden or that the sleek bulbed carving used in the killing resembled a penis, did those things matter?

As they got out of the car, Cowan glanced up at the balcony four storeys above. 'Is that door open?'

Shields, locking the car, was last to give an opinion. 'No. Just the way the shadow is.'

A trick of the light, which for no reason made them uneasy so that not a word was spoken as they rode up in the lift. In fact they found the doors to the balcony were locked, and in the same way when Meldrum used his key to get them into the flat the outer door seemed secure. It was only later examination which suggested the lock might have been skilfully picked or maybe a key which needed forcing had been used.

'Fuck sake!' Shields said.

Looking round, there was no doubt about a break-in. Chairs lay on their side. The lamp had been knocked off the bureau desk. It lay in the corner by the patio doors among the scattered contents of drawers pulled out and emptied. With wardrobes getting the same treatment, the bedroom was in even more of a mess. Later, the search team decided a watch was gone, together with cufflinks, rings, some ornaments: the kind of stuff which suggested, if anything, an amateur in theft. Despite checklists, neither Meldrum nor anyone else could be one hundred per cent sure of what had been taken.

All the same, Cowan remarked almost at once that the picture of Frank and Iain Bower was missing from the bedside table.

Before Meldrum's day was over it was almost midnight. Even after eleven months, he came into his flat like a stranger. It had taken years after the divorce before he'd got round to selling the house Carole and he had bought not long after they were married. Unusually from all he heard, there had been no bitterness in their parting nor anyone else involved, not another woman, not another man, just that she had wearied of the little share of him left over from his job.

He put on a bar of the electric fire in the living room and went along the corridor to the kitchen to make coffee. The kitchen was small, like the rest of the flat: a bedroom, a little second room used as a dump for papers and files with a stack of cardboard boxes still unpacked from the flitting lined under the window, a toilet with a shower closet. He liked the view from the front-room window, coffee in hand looking down on the traffic on Leith Walk. Buses, cars, people. Even this late, there was always something to watch. He'd bought the flat on a mortgage, since he'd given most of the money he'd got for the house to Carole, and they'd agreed she'd find ways to pass it on to Betty and Sandy. Betty might take money from her mother she wouldn't take from him. Pride: her pride, Sandy's bloody pride. Betty was his only child; she was precious to him; and now she had given him a grandson, too small to be a person to him, precious as an idea, precious for the accident that the baby's eyes were the identical shade of blue that looked back at him from the mirror. Damn their pride.

He dozed in a chair and woke up stiff. It was just after one. Hardly muffled by the double glazing, an ambulance ululated from the street below. In the kitchen, he opened a can of corned beef and folded a slice of bread round a chunk of it to make a sandwich. He took a mouth-stuffing bite that made for dry chewing all the way back to the window. Opposite on the other side of the Walk, the tall spired church stood up under the floodlights like a stage flat. The mouthful he swallowed had no taste. He laid the sandwich on the arm of the chair and went to bed.

In the dark he remembered after a while that he hadn't checked if there had been any calls. He reached for the phone by the bed and heard the broken note. He hit the numbers on the pad by feel, not bothering to put the light on. One call, the disembodied voice said, and he told her, yes he'd hear it, yes.

'I've been thinking,' Henry Stanley said. 'Are you there? It's half past six, I thought you might be there. I started thinking. I wouldn't want to be alarmist, but maybe you should take this fake Inspector Meldrum more seriously. Someone fantasising, the Munchausen syndrome or whatever. It's easy to think of someone like that as pathetic or ridiculous.' There was a pause, something that might have been a sigh. 'But to live in a fantasy isn't a trivial thing. People like that can be dangerous.'

BOOK TWO

The Nice Man

CHAPTER SEVEN

The morning after he came back from Brussels, 'You still need to get that window fixed,' Meldrum told his ex-wife Carole.

He'd made the same point before. She'd part of the ground floor in a detached stone house that had been divided into flats. Sciennes wasn't a bad district, but in Edinburgh like any other city there wasn't any district so good you could leave a window round the back of the house with a broken lock. Divorce hadn't stopped him feeling responsible for her safety.

'You should get what's-his-name to fix it. No milk!'

'Since when?' Carole looked round, jug still poised.

'I've stopped taking milk in coffee.'

'I see,' she said, and patted his stomach. He reached round her and lifted the cup from the work surface.

'Or can he not use a screwdriver?'

'Who?'

'What's-his-name?'

'Would that be Phil What's-his-name?' she wondered, and stared him out until he grinned reluctantly.

'That's the one.'

'Don't tell me you don't remember. I know how good your memory is.'

'That window isn't secure. You could put a lock on it yourself. Or get Phil to do it, it's not difficult.'

'He's an Assistant Director of Education, not a joiner.'

'Have you stopped seeing him?'

'No,' she said, and led the way out of the kitchen into a narrow passage lined with shelves and with a door at each end.

The way the house had been divided the window of her front room looked into the garden at the side. It was raining. A wet summer, it rained most days. Rain was rain. It didn't look any better seeping through the despondent branches of a Kilmarnock willow. He turned from the view to see her laughing. He was sure she was going to make a joke about the rain, as if she knew him so well she'd read his mind.

Instead, she said, 'Phil did better than put a lock on. He turned up one Sunday with a pot of paint. Now I can't get *either* of the back windows open.'

'You were lucky. Imagine what he'd have done if he'd been the Director of Education.'

'No more jokes!' She held out to him the box of chocolates he'd got at Brussels airport. 'Leave the white ones, and tell me why you went to Belgium.'

To his surprise, she had read about the murder of Iain Bower. She'd always avoided accounts of crime in the newspapers. Perhaps it didn't matter so much now she was no longer married to a detective. He wondered if it was possible she might belatedly have become, like Jim Pleat, a fan; but, discretion being the better part of valour, didn't ask her.

She was a good listener, which he'd never appreciated during their marriage. Then he'd never talked about the job to her. When she'd asked, he'd told her he didn't want to bring the mess people made of their lives home with him. That had satisfied her for a time; and then there had been a time when she told him it came home with him anyway in his silences.

'And you still have no idea who he was?' she asked of the man who had pissed into Bower's grave. 'Such a horrible thing to do.'

He was amused by the emphasis she put on it.

'Not so *horrible* as getting murdered.'

'It seems like sacrilege.'

'Even if it was a Protestant service? I didn't think that would count.'

'That's not fair. You know I don't think that way.'

'I was joking.'

'You always had an odd sense of humour.'

'Nice to be told that,' he said. 'Nobody else thinks I've any kind at all.'

'Poor you.'

They sat together in a silence which he felt was comfortable, and then wondered why it was going on so long.

At last she said quietly, 'Some people must be genuine loners. Whatever you believe, I don't think you're one of them. You should find somebody.'

'Like who?'

'Somebody you can live with.'

'Isn't that immoral?' He held up a warning hand. 'Joking!'

'Half joking,' she said.

'What do you suggest? Should I ask Harriet Cook if she'd come back?'

Hearing the irritation in his voice, he realised that he'd felt as if he was being attacked. That was stupid, or a harsher word; and mentioning Harriet stupider. She'd been his only serious relationship since the divorce. Serious enough that he'd gone to live with her. In her twenties, she was twenty years younger than him: a gap he'd despised seeing it in other relationships. But with them, it was different. A lawyer, she'd worked with him to get the young Irishman Hugh Keaney out of prison for a crime he hadn't committed. They'd staked careers and lives in that good cause, and despite themselves fallen in love. Their affair had been intense and brief and flavoured with danger. And if they'd failed, it had been a gallant failure.

'No, I'm not suggesting you ask her back.'

'Sorry?'

'Saying you wanted her to come back—' She broke off. With a sigh, she asked, 'You don't seriously mean that?'

'Joking,' he said, quoting himself.

Half joking.

'John Brennan's wife came to see me a few days ago. He's told her he wants a divorce.'

He stared at her in astonishment, a dozen things chasing through his mind. He picked the least of them: 'Why would she tell you?'

'Parents do,' she said. 'Their daughter's in Primary Three now, a quiet little mouse like her mother.'

'I don't believe it. What about his Papal Knighthood? Brennan's too cold a fish. Why would he now? What age is he now? Nearer sixty than fifty? And she's only—' He cut off the flood. 'Why does he want a divorce?'

'Harriet Cook. Even if he is nearly sixty, and she's only whatever it is. He's been sleeping at her flat more than in his own house.'

'It doesn't make sense.'

'Maybe he's fallen in love.'

'He's waited a long time to do it.'

She looked at him thoughtfully. 'You sound bitter.'

'I'm not bitter.' But, frowning, he couldn't resist going on, 'She's not the first, she's the last in a string of them, everybody knows about Brennan's harem. Young women straight out of law school. Star-struck by the great John Brennan.' Brennan's affair with Harriet had been like that, the latest ambitious girl fresh from university, and in time he'd ended it and found her a place with another firm. She'd been humiliated and angry and started drinking too much. Then she'd met Meldrum, and it seemed to him that they'd been happy for a while. 'And when it's over he finds them a job – he's decent that way. But it's a job with someone else. Tidily out of the way. Because a fox doesn't mess round his den, and Brennan's a fox with a reputation and best friends with the Archbishop. And that's the end of them. He doesn't sleep with them again.'

He ended as abruptly as if he'd walked into a wall. Carole looked at him. She didn't have to say it. Fact was Brennan *had* slept with Harriet again, and that had been one reason for Meldrum breaking up with her.

'I'm disappointed in Brennan,' he said. 'I thought he was smarter than that.'

He's offered me a job, she'd whispered to Meldrum one night, lying beside him in the dark. *Not for the wrong reasons, I wouldn't if it was the wrong reasons, you know that. He wants me because I'm a good lawyer. And I want to take it, because there isn't any better place to learn. Jim? You understand, don't you?*

To work with the best criminal lawyer, most successful criminal lawyer, most flamboyant criminal lawyer in the country. Who could refuse ambition its chance to get up close and see how the magic was done, in the hope some of it might rub off?

'Of course, I can see what's in it for her. It's a good career move,' he said. 'Not to mention the money.'

Richest criminal lawyer in the country; that too.

'I don't think that's it,' Carole said.

'Don't tell me, let me guess. She's in love. Nice and simple.'

'She might be. But if she is I doubt if it's simple. From what you've told me there was always part of her hated the weakness of giving in to him. Maybe that's why she does it. Part of the reason anyway.'

'What?'

'To despise herself.'

After all these years, she could still surprise him.

CHAPTER EIGHT

'I 'm tired of being told Iain Bower was a nice man,' Meldrum said, rolling his chair back from the computer monitor. 'What good is that?'

'Who says?'

'Everybody says. His brother. The Balewas. People he worked with in Brussels.'

'What was the weather like?'

'Where?'

'In Brussels. It was pissing down here.' Detective Sergeant Shields spoke with the bitterness of a man left behind.

'No idea. I was too busy to look.'

Shields slid the file drawer shut. 'It was pissing here. Sicken your breakfast, make you boak, give you the dry heaves. Know what I mean?'

Shields scratching the belly that sagged over his belt was an unlovely sight. Meldrum studied it in silence. Reviewing the consequences, ranging from dismissal from the force to an extended period of sick leave, he was wondering almost seriously if, with a double grip on that belt, he could throw the fat man out of the window. Sumo style, it could be done. On the other hand, the belt cut so deep into the gut it would be a hard squeeze to get a grip. Anyway, the windows were double glazed.

'Nothing wrong with being nice,' Shields said. 'If only bastarding scum got killed, nobody'd give a fuck. We'd be out of a job.'

'What's wrong,' Meldrum explained, elaborately patient, 'is that nice people don't give you any reason to kill them.'

'Nobody's as nice as that.'

'It's what we call motive,' Meldrum said, and caught a look from Shields that indicated 'nice' wasn't the four-letter word he had in mind. 'In this job.'

'All right then. The brother gets the flat, *and* he said Bower left a lot more money than he'd expected. So what about money? That's a motive, am I right? I didn't start in this job yesterday.'

'Oh, money'll do it every time,' Meldrum said. For some reason, he felt more cheerful. 'Let's go and find out.'

'Today, you mean?' Shields looked sceptical. 'What's the name of the place he lives? Kilbracken? Is it far?'

Meldrum laughed.

Catching the lights at green, it took them about ten minutes to get to the Point Hotel.

'This was fixed up before you left for Brussels?'

Shields had asked the question already.

'I left you a memo,' Meldrum said. 'Remember memos? You should try reading them sometime.'

'I must have missed it.' Shields stared intently ahead, like a man wondering if there might be the makings of a hobby in watching lift doors slide open.

'Right,' Meldrum said, stepping out and leading the way along the corridor.

Frank Bower had phoned the previous week to arrange the meeting. 'The Simons have to be in Edinburgh, they're flying down to see their lawyer in London. Because I understand it can't simply be a matter of taking my word, I'd be happy for you to speak to them. I can be there when you talk to them or not, just as you wish. Or you can talk to them, and see me afterwards. I can understand you might not want to take statements from them with me there. All I'm saying is, if you did want to talk to me again, there wouldn't be any difficulty in me arranging to be in town at the same time. It seems a good opportunity, since they are going to be in Edinburgh anyway. They could come to the station, if that was needed. They tell me they wouldn't mind doing that, but the hotel might be easier for them. If the hotel was all right with you? They're not the kind of people who've ever seen the inside of a police station.' Before or just after Meldrum agreed, he'd said, 'I want you to use your time finding the person who killed Iain, not waste it checking up on me. So, if I can make it more convenient, I will, because that saves your time.'

Don and Rachel Simon were a surprise, though Meldrum would have been hard-pressed to put into words what he'd imagined they might be like. They're lovely people, Frank Bower had said. He's a writer, and she's originally from New York. So what had he expected? Woody Allen and a nymphet?

Don Simon was six feet or a shade more, a portly man with red cheeks and very clean white hair, who stood up to shake hands. 'It's quiet here. You ever notice Residents' Lounges are always quiet? We're having tea, if you want to join us. The cakes are just self-indulgence — to be avoided except when travelling. Like kippers for breakfast.'

The four of them settled round a low table with a tall teapot, milk and sugar set, and a cake stand, already heavily raided.

'Or coffee? If you prefer,' the wife said. She was lean, with delicate cheekbones, washed-out blonde hair worn long, and an air of fragility, which the down-turned corners of the mouth suggested might be deceptive. Her accent matched her husband's. Meldrum interpreted it as that of the comfortably off, privately schooled southern English; but had no ear for any finer social ranking, like the infinitely flexible signals by which bats find their place on a cave wall. For sure, though, there wasn't a trace of New York.

It seemed their opinions matched, too, though she confined herself to nods of encouragement and agreement.

'There were six robberies within eighteen months. I mean, all of them people we knew, one or two of them damned good friends. The worst was the last one. Old couple get home early, find the bastards in the house and are attacked. I mean, we're talking broken bones, not hard to do with a couple in their seventies. And not for any reason, not for fear of being caught, not to get at the hidden safe, none of that nonsense, the bastards had already got what they'd come for — had the paintings off the walls stacked to go. No, those two were beaten, use the right word, *tortured*,' here a nod from the wife emphasised the exactness of the choice, 'for the pleasure of inflicting pain. It was a turning point for us. A turning point.' More nodding. 'We'd sit at breakfast with the papers, and it seemed as if the world was going mad. Violence, robberies, cruelty. The stuff that made the headlines. You didn't have to search for any of that. It jumped off the page at you. Then Frank told us about Kilbracken, and we didn't hesitate for a moment. I suppose you could say we were ripe for it.'

They were there to provide Frank Bower's alibi. 'Frank was with us from half seven – half seven for eight, you know? – that Thursday evening until, oh, three the next morning . . . Frank and May, that's his wife, were the last to leave. Odd night for a party? I don't think so. It was a special day – we had just moved in. So Frank and May were there and some friends of his, we can give you their names. It was a celebration. Our arrival in Kilbracken, we were starting a new life. Anyway, none of us had to be up the next morning, put it that way.'

They had even written it all down in advance, and offered to sign it there and then.

'I don't think so,' Meldrum said. 'Let the sergeant write up a statement from his notes of what you've told us. He'll take what you've written there too, of course, and check it against that; very helpful. You're not leaving today? Fine. If you wouldn't mind coming into the station tomorrow, you can read the statements over and sign them then. Unless there's anything you want to add or change. It shouldn't take up too much of your time.'

If that irritated them, they made a good job of hiding it.

'Time's the whole point, isn't it?' Don Simon said. 'So you can get on with finding who killed Frank's brother. Can I ask how things are going?'

'It's early days yet,' Meldrum offered, which had the advantage of being indisputable (and true, in contrast to the usual bromide about enquiries progressing).

'By my understanding, most murders that are solved are solved quickly. Doesn't it get harder as time passes?'

Should have stuck to the bromides: hoping arrest soon glad of help fruitful lines enquiries progressing the sun has got his hat on I'm singing and dancing in the rain.

'Not always,' Meldrum said.

'It's just that it would be good to have something to tell Frank. You can imagine how he's feeling about this.'

But then, the way it often happened, the interview over, the Simons relaxed. She said how much they were looking forward to getting back to Kilbracken. A haven of peace, he called it, which turned him back to the robberies around their previous home in Sussex and the beating of the elderly couple. The final straw. Not the final final straw, his wife said.

'God, no,' Don Simon said. 'The last book I wrote got this hellish review in the *Telegraph*. It was full of malice and feminist dirt. The kind of thing made me feel as if some offended shopgirl was pelting me with sanitary towels.'

'Used sanitary towels,' his wife said.

'Oh, *used*, absolutely! But that wasn't what troubled me. The review was unintelligent and missed all the points it might have made, so normally I would have shrugged it off. I can cope with stupidity. What got to me was that I didn't know the woman who'd written it, I didn't recognise her name, I was sure I'd never met her, and yet the malice in it was *personal*. Can you see why that would trouble me?'

No, not easily. Meldrum could understand the point of getting troubled about murder, old couples taking a beating, even burglaries.

'I can see it might get up your nose,' he said.

'It *troubled* me, because it made me realise how much hatred there is out there. Hatred like an unshaped darkness, hatred without a motive, ready to release itself like lightning out of a cloud. Stalkers and crazies. How can you protect yourself against hatred like that? Did you ever go into a cupboard and find a piece of fruit in a bowl? And it looks all right, so you pick it up, and your fingers sink in through the skin. Waiting there in the dark, it's dissolved in its own corruption. Suddenly, I understood. England was like that now.'

'Kilbracken saved us,' Rachel Simon said. 'As for that woman, I hope she feels better for writing it out of her system. That kind of animus held inside can give you an ulcer.'

'Or a cancer,' her husband said.

Going down in the elevator and leaving the hotel, Meldrum was busy with his own thoughts. In the car, though, Shields, who liked to talk, broke the silence.

'One of my father's brothers was like that,' he said.

'Like what?'

'Thought Britain was finished. He took my aunt and the kids, just two of them then, to New Zealand. All that crap about a new life.' He paused as if to give Meldrum time to think about it, get ready for the twist. 'They were back within eight weeks. He claimed it was for the wife's sake, but my father always told him it was because he fucking hated it himself. I warned you, nothing but sheep, he told him.'

Meldrum hit the brake harder than he'd intended, jerking the car to a halt. I need to watch this idiot doesn't get to me, he thought, watching the crowd stream across the pedestrian crossing.

'Apart from the wee bit of family history,' he asked, easing the car into gear as the lights changed, 'did anything else occur to you about the Simons?' A glance to the side showed Shields directing a look of suspicion at him. 'Just as a matter of interest.'

'What way? They've put the brother out of the frame. That's obvious.'

'Looks like it.'

'So, what's to say about it? No reason to think they won't turn up in the morning to sign the statements, is there? Is that what you mean?'

'They'll turn up.'

'So?'

Meldrum began to regret starting this. It was a feeling Shields often gave him.

'I was thinking about that story about the woman who reviewed Simon's book.'

'I didn't see what he was on about.'

'It didn't strike you that for people who've travelled a long way for peace and quiet, those two have a lot of violence in them?'

'Nuh!' A grunt Meldrum interpreted as 'no'. But then, feeling perhaps that response might be too abrupt, Shields eased the seat-belt from his belly and offered second thoughts. 'Every wee town in the Borders is stuffed full of folk from London or wherever. Vote Liberal Democrat! Let's have a flag day for Africa! Fuck me, only reason they're up here is to get away from the darkies.'

It wasn't easy to find an answer to that; and by the time Meldrum had thought round the possibilities, they were pulling into the car park and he couldn't be bothered trying.

CHAPTER NINE

F ish suppers weren't what they used to be. Tired with walking, Meldrum stood on the pavement opposite Radio Leith and wondered about going in. Sitting down for a bit would be good. Probably, though, Jimmy Pleat wouldn't be there, or be free to talk even if he was. The interior glowed, throwing its light out into the darkness, but he couldn't see inside. He peeled more of the paper back, hooked out a couple of chips and pushed them into his mouth. Almost cold, they chewed to a slimy paste. He tore a lump off the fish, sparse flakes of haddock in a shell of soggy batter, and crammed it in after them. His watch showed ten to eleven.

He'd put on the Channel Four news about four hours ago, seen the image of a starving child with saucer eyes and ribs you could count, put it off and gone out. One drink had been the idea in the bar opposite his close. He'd been checking the faces round him out of habit, when between one sip and the next they'd blurred and refocussed. He'd found himself looking at them as Cowan would have looked at them.

That afternoon the forensic scientist had told him the evidence in a rape case wouldn't be strong enough to persuade the Procurator-Fiscal to go for a trial. 'She waited too long,' he'd said, which meant the ex-husband walked until the next time. The inevitable next time, unless he killed her first. 'I don't envy you,' Cowan had said, 'having to deal with such scum. I only have to deal with the traces they leave. I don't have to look at them or listen to them. And not just the bad ones. Take the druggies. We're down on ecstasy use, but we're up on heroin. We've been low on that compared to Glasgow or Aberdeen, because we'd the HIV plague here. But now — ancient history, the young ones don't know it happened. They're injecting again! There's no folk memory. Idiots! I keep my faith in the goodness of God, but thankfully I don't have to meet these people face to face.'

Of course, Cowan was a churchgoer, no wonder the bugger got depressed. And a teetotaller. But he'd put Meldrum off the faces in that pub, so he went to the next one. From there it had been like setting a stone rolling from the top of a hill. He'd drunk his way from the flat down the length of Leith Walk, and now it was time to go back except that he'd come out in the first place because the walls were closing in.

It was a dry night after a wet day. He began to walk again, heading the same way, telling himself just a little further, to clear his head, he'd turn back soon, soon but not yet. It was another of Edinburgh's one-sided streets, a rat's nest of tenements on his left, and on the other side of the road a restless crawling of water stretching away into the darkness of the estuary.

Some time later he was frowning at a building, wondering what about it had caught his attention. He studied the double glass doors with a glimpse of lobby beyond; looking up, fewer than a quarter of the windows of flats on the facade were lit, the occupants of the rest gone to bed or out on the town clubbing or pubbing PCP gin MDA acid rum dex vodka barbs hash coke speed smack crack shit E. For ecstasy, pop a pill; nice if it were that easy. Cowan had it right, he decided, world's full of fucking idiots. Like if you were going to get religion, which, as it happened, he wasn't, pick one that's been around at least a couple of thousand years — no Mormons Scientologists Jehovah's Witnesses — straight Christianity bottled by the Church of Scotland or Rome, stands to fucking reason. Stick to beer, stick to whisky. It made sense. He recognised the building as the Doune Apartments. Maybe those darkened windows were bedrooms. In that case, not out but in bed, everybody getting ready for another day. Up on the top floor there'd be a window for the Balewas, solemn husband, good-looking girl, nice little kid holding on to her. All three of them far from home. Sleep well, kid. No bad dreams. He raised a hand, farewell, benediction; and noticed the fish supper still wadded cold and greasy in his fist.

The next time he looked at his watch it was twenty minutes to midnight. On impulse he'd shot his cuff and checked as he came under the street light. Almost an hour. How had that happened? Time gone

stopped him in his tracks. Past time to go home. He swung round. Like a
pulled-out telescope, the perspective of the street narrowed away from
him. It had taken him for ever to come the length of it. High chainlink
fences between blank-faced warehouses shut off the opposite unpave-
mented side of the road. Receding, pools the colour of rape grass
dwindled in line from lamp to lamp. Just past the mid point of the
nearest, two men waded towards him through the acid light. Startled by
his sudden turn, they broke step then came on again. They moved fast
with the loose-hipped movement of young men, and the distance halved
before he heard the soft slap of their feet. They divided to pass on either
side of him and as they did he went through the gap. He took four steps
and spun round ready to battle. And they were walking on, going down
the street. Not a sound, except that fifty yards on they looked round, and
there was the sound of laughter, but quiet, almost muffled, not wanting
to draw attention to itself.

Instead of turning for home, he walked after them. Not hurrying, but
for no sensible reason. Maybe for the same reason that had made them
turn round and laugh. To show they weren't afraid. Maybe for that
reason.

There was a church on the corner. As he came to it, the two men were
out of sight. His pace slowed despite himself. The facade of the church
ended at a metal gate giving on to a path almost blocked by a dense
overhang of bushes. Out of this darkness, voices sounded, abrupt,
impassioned, mingled and echoing, one of them a woman's. He went
to the distress in that voice, hand stretched out to confirm the church
wall, branches snatching at his shoulder, not even considering whether he
had a choice.

A man and a woman, they were in a doorway that swung back as they
struggled, framing them against the light of a corridor. Meldrum gripped
the man by the shoulder and threw him off. As he hit the wall, he rolled
and Meldrum saw his face and then the unmistakable white band of a
clergyman's collar under it. Next moment the woman had sunk her nails
into the flesh of his wrist. Her hair was black, dyed and thin, so that the
skin of the scalp showed white like a fish belly. Her mouth gaped open
and from it, as if a bubble of gas had risen to the surface of a swamp and
split, there came an overpowering sweet stench of cheap wine. He pulled
and her nails dragged through his skin, she'd taken a grip it would hurt
her to break.

'Right, right, hit me, you cunt!' she cried.

'It's all right, Maureen,' the man said. He might have been speaking to a child. 'He's a policeman.'

It took a moment for the magic word to penetrate, then she let go. She retreated a step or two, ready for flight. 'See him! Look at him, look at him, I'm telling ye!' She pointed at the minister, not with a finger but with the whole hand, trembling and rocking at full stretch. 'He's a fucking saint!'

In the sidelong light, Meldrum made out gleaming gobs of vomit and understood the struggle he'd witnessed had been the man clasping the woman in his arms as she heaved on his shoulder and chest.

'That's enough, Maureen,' the minister said.

Now she subsided, ready to go. She combed down strands of hair with her fingers into some semblance of tidiness. When she spoke, it was quietly.

'You cannae see it,' she told Meldrum. 'I'm the only one that sees it. But I know he's a saint.'

CHAPTER TEN

'I recognised you from Iain Bower's funeral,' the Reverend Patrick Turnbull said.

'I'm surprised you're here as late as this.'

Turnbull led the way, only as far as the second door. The corridor that had seemed so bright from the outside was lit by dim bulbs, its scuffed walls dull green. 'I'm here in the evenings very often.'

'Should you lock the outer door?' Meldrum asked, glancing back as he followed him.

'The Church Officer and the Session Clerk think so. We had a burglary a month ago. They weren't happy with me. But sometimes people come in through that door to talk to me, who wouldn't get a chance at any other time.'

The room was small but the carpet looked new, and by the wall to the side of the desk two bars of the electric fire glowed red while fake coals spun a cheerful illusion of leaping flames. Not as uncomfortable as you'd expect for a saint, Meldrum thought.

'People who wouldn't dare to come into church on a Sunday. Are you a churchgoer? People the congregation wouldn't want sharing a pew.'

'Like that woman.'

'Poor Mrs Maguire. When her priest's had enough of her, she comes to me.'

The room was warm and Meldrum suddenly was fighting sleep. Turnbull waved him to a chair, asked if he wanted coffee and left saying he wouldn't be a moment. Meldrum let his legs sprawl in front of him and yawned. It struck him perhaps Turnbull thought he was another knocker on the door come to talk about being down on his luck.

Turnbull came back carrying a tray and laying it on the desk remarked again, as though he'd read his mind, about recognising him from the funeral.

'You spoke to me after the incident,' he said.

'I remember,' Meldrum told him. Like the rest of those present, the minister had claimed the man who'd pissed into the grave was a stranger to him.

'Even before that, though, everyone knew who you were, of course. How do you like it?'

'No milk, please, or sugar.'

Turnbull passed a cup, took one himself and sat behind the desk. Mid forties, greying hair worn too long, almost to his shoulders. Meldrum had a conventional taste in how ministers should appear. He'd taken off the vomit-stained jacket and had the look of a man who didn't eat enough, but the shirtsleeves rolled up over surprisingly muscular forearms. On a second glance, nothing gaunt or hollow-cheeked either about the face; lantern jaw, wide, thin-lipped mouth, the skin pale but with the fresh undertone of a man who spent time in the open air. That initial impression of hunger came from the eyes, Meldrum decided, a little too small for the face, dark, unblinking, the fact that they fixed on you without wandering; and the unrelaxed body, that seemed to be tight-wound as a spring. What was it Jimmy Pleat had said? Not a man who went in for jokes. Pleat had interviewed him on radio; some book he'd written.

'Were you coming to see me?'

'Just walking.' Meldrum drank from the cup. The coffee was bitter, too much had been used; but since it was instant coffee, the bitterness was muffled, almost stale.

'Stupid of me, how could you know I would be here? And at this time of night.' He glanced at his watch. 'I hadn't realised it was so late.'

'I heard the uproar. Sounded as though she was being attacked.'

'Years of drinking have made her like a child. You know how a child is overwhelmed by feelings? When a child is sad, the distress would break your heart. Pay attention, real attention, to a child's fear, and the hair stands up on the back of your neck. But offer some distraction or let five minutes pass and their attention will be taken up with something new.

That's not hypocrisy. The child's not playing a trick. Sometimes in the
street or a shop, you hear a mother or a father – it always sounds more
threatening in a man – shouting at a child whose mood has changed,
Don't try to make a fool of me! And you want to go up and tell him,'
Meldrum watched the hands on the desk clench into fists, 'Stop, in the
name of Christ! The unfortunate child can't explain the emotion is
sincere and felt passionately, but belongs only in the moment. That's
how it is with Mrs Maguire. Except that she isn't a child. She's an adult
with a brain damaged by drink.'

'Is that how you see children?' Meldrum asked. A policeman's job
meant questioning people; detectives were trained in the arts of inter-
rogation, but over the years they added habits of their own. If they were
any good, they kept what worked, tried to lose what hindered. Even so,
elements that went with the grain of their own mind persisted,
idiosyncratic as fingerprints. With Meldrum, a willingness to pick up
on what caught his attention, however oblique or seemingly peripheral,
could have a disconcerting effect. Now, frowning, he asked, 'Distress.
Fear. What about joy?'

'Joy? That's not an emotion Mrs Maguire feels.' Turnbull's fists
unclenched. He spread his fingers on the desk. 'And so there's another
way she differs from a child. Yes, they live in a continuous present, and in
a sense so does she. But she's not so lucky as they are. Damaged or not,
she's an adult and adults can't get free of the past. Like the rest of us, she
lives with her demons. Only children can really live in the present. Or
religious mystics, of course.'

'Getting crucified, you mean? Or burnt at the stake? Concentrate the
mind, all right. But I don't see that's about religion, it's about being for
the high jump. A guy in front of a firing squad or in the electric chair,
he'd be living in the present as well, bet he would.'

'I said mystics, not martyrs.'

'. . . Right.' I've drunk too much, Meldrum thought. That was all
right. A man on his own. As long as you did it in your own time. The
difficulty was that this wasn't his own time, not when he was talking with
Turnbull, who had buried Iain Bower. Though how could he have
known as he went from pub to pub that later he would encounter the
minister?

Or had he known? Without intending, had he come this way because
he'd pass the Doune Apartments; and once he'd got to them instead of

turning back had he walked on because he'd known the church wasn't far away?

He felt the minister's gaze like a weight. Turnbull had corrected his mistake, mystics not martyrs, without the flicker of a smile.

Could you be a saint without a sense of humour? No problem. Question should be other way round. How could anybody who had a sense of humour ever get to be a saint? Imagine in the middle of licking out a beggar's sores thinking, What the hell am I doing this for? Bad time to get a fit of the giggles. Think after you'd finished laughing, the taste you'd have in your mouth.

'You wrote a book about them, didn't you?'

'About what?'

'Martyrs.'

Turnbull stared at him in astonishment. 'You've read it?'

'Jimmy Pleat told me about it.'

'Pleat? Should I know the name?'

'You had an interview on his programme. On Radio Leith.'

'I'd forgotten.' The name presumably, though nothing in his tone suggested he might remember Pleat himself any better.

No reason why saints should remember people; easier to love humanity in the mass, excuse the pun.

Meldrum told himself, forget saints. How had saints got in his head? Forget saints. All the same, shouldn't ministers be like teachers or politicians, professionally good at names and faces?

'That interview wasn't something I wanted to do,' Turnbull said. 'I was astonished when they asked me.'

'Radio Leith's not all sport and playing records. They do books.'

'My book is about religious conflict in the seventeenth century.'

Meldrum thought about that. 'Local connections?' It was the best he could come up with.

'The point of it isn't battles or escapes across the moors. I wrote it to ask whether a Church that forgets those who were killed and tortured in its name deserves to survive.'

'Jimmy Pleat's a good guy. Didn't you find that?'

'He asked me about the battles,' Turnbull said flatly.

'So why did you go?'

'Because it was another way of preaching. Because people should know about the Covenanters. If I didn't believe that, why write the book at all?

The publisher phoned to ask if I would do it. He's not rich, he drives around in an old car delivering bundles of books. He confronts and shames booksellers into taking copies. Sale or return, mostly return. So, you could say, because I was grateful to him. Or say, because of vanity – isn't that the easiest thing to believe?'

It was disconcerting not to have a smile accompany the question. Vanity, you me everybody, tell me about it. And they did, confession time in pubs and clubs, and spewing it from television screens, can I share this with you? No, fuck off. And to accompany all the soul-baring stuff came the little smile they couldn't keep from offering with it, the nudge and a wink know-what-I-mean? smile that meant hey! we're all Jock Tamson's bairns, everybody's human, brothers under the skin, we all have our weaknesses. That kind of shit.

Turnbull asked the question straight, seemingly of himself; no smile, just a twist of the lips as if he wouldn't like the answer.

Meldrum took a deep breath that was half a yawn, scrubbed a hand down across his face. 'Would it be too late to ask some questions?'

'You do know I've already spoken to a policeman? He came here in the evening. Last night – or was it the one before?'

'Did he give a name?'

Turnbull shook his head without a moment's hesitation. 'I've no idea. I mean, I'm sure he would.'

'I don't suppose you remember what he looked like?'

'Not really. Does it matter?'

'The man I'm thinking of would be average height. Long thin face. He'd probably be wearing one of those blue anoraks with a hood.' In other words, the man who had sat in the pew at the back of the church during Iain Bower's funeral service. Turnbull's blank look indicated the description meant nothing to him, which might not mean much since, it seemed, people didn't impinge on him unless they were in trouble. Meldrum wondered about asking him, Did this policeman tell you he was Inspector James Meldrum? He's my *doppelgänger*. It was tempting, but chances were Turnbull wouldn't bat an eyelid. Religion should guard you from superstition. Instead, he said, 'It doesn't matter. Would you mind, though, going over it again with me? Unless it's too late?'

'Not for me. But I'd be grateful if you could give me a run home afterwards.'

'Problem there,' Meldrum said. 'I came out for a walk. Short walk that turned into a long one.'

Since it had got to be after midnight, if they had to walk, the obvious thing was to make a start. Meldrum waited while Turnbull locked the side door from the church. There had been a shower of rain, and fat drops spattered on them from the neglected shrubs along the path's edge.

They turned left away from the shore, a small cold wind blowing into their faces. Not another pedestrian in sight, as if they were the only two kept out of a unanimous secret decision to have a glass of milk and make it an early night. A couple of cars passed at speed, heading in different directions for bedtime, and the street was empty again.

'Did Iain Bower ever mention the Balewas to you?'

'What was the name?'

'Balewa. A Nigerian couple. They're on the top floor at the Doune Apartments.'

'No, but why would he?'

'No reason, I suppose. He got friendly with them, while he was staying there.'

'I didn't know. I imagine he was lonely.'

'That was your impression of him?'

'Oh, yes. Having lived abroad for so many years, he didn't know anyone in Edinburgh.'

'Is that why you went to see him? Pretty often, according to the Balewas. They say he looked forward to your visits.'

'They seem to have got to know him quite well. I wonder how that happened.'

'The husband and Bower got talking in the lift one day. Bower had worked in Nigeria, that broke the ice.'

'Nigeria? I thought he'd come back from Belgium.'

'He worked in Brussels. But he told Balewa he'd been at a conference in Nigeria, business trips, that kind of stuff.'

'The Doune Apartments struck me as one of those places where people kept to themselves. Impersonal. A soulless place. I wouldn't have expected him to make friends there.'

'He had them to his apartment for afternoon tea. And he babysat for them.'

Abruptly Turnbull broke step, using both hands to turn up the collar of his jacket against the wind. As Meldrum glanced round, his gorge rose at the smell of sour vomit from the sleeve.

'We're almost at my place. It's just down there. Is that on your way?'

'I've a flat on Leith Walk,' Meldrum said.

'Other direction then. Unless you want to come back with me – I could give you a lift home. You can see the manse from here.'

It was a street of substantial houses, which took Meldrum by surprise. Nothing about Turnbull, the hair, the stained jacket, went with a house like those. A flat in a bad tenement would have been more like it. He remembered, though, a manse had to have a certain number of bedrooms. Church rules going back to when ministers in country places would have to put up visitors, and families would be large. Unsuitable in the middle of a city for a childless man. What had the congregation imagined they were getting when they'd picked him? Maybe he'd worn a suit. There must be a faction by now desperate to be rid of him.

A lift back to his flat? He thought about it. Against tiredness and the wind, sharper here on the open corner, he set the idea of being trapped in the confined space of a car with that clinging sick smell. He shook his head. 'I'll be fine, thanks for the offer.'

'In that case,' Turnbull moved as if to go.

'Did he tell you much about himself?'

'Bower? He only attended my church while he was staying at the Doune Apartments. Not long, a matter of months.'

'I'll tell you the truth. As of now, I need to know more about Bower, and there doesn't seem to be anybody to tell me. I know where he worked, I know where he died. If I'm going to find who killed him, that's not enough. Make it simple. Did you like him? What kind of man was he?' And as Turnbull hesitated, added in a kind of ferocious disgust, 'Let me guess. *Nice?*'

'Troubled.'

The single word coming, after a pause, as if weighed, stopped Meldrum in his tracks. Adrenalin spiked through him, driving out the tiredness. 'What about?'

'I can't help you.'

Can't or won't? It couldn't be seal of the confessional crap. That was the other lot.

'You can't say he was troubled, and leave it at that. Troubled, what does that mean? In trouble, is that what you mean, he was in trouble with somebody? Did he give you the impression he was afraid? Did he ever mention a name?'

'Troubled spiritually. I'm a minister. Do you think I can't recognise when a man is troubled in spirit without having to be told?'

'How do you do that?'

'Not everything has to be put into words.'

'I'm trying to find who killed him. If you know anything, you should tell me.'

'After he left the Doune Apartments, he didn't come to my church.'

He took another tack. 'In that case, how come you did the funeral service for him?'

'I saw his death in the paper. When I enquired, he hadn't found a church after his move. He had no minister.'

'When he's in the Doune Apartments, a transient place, he goes to church regularly. But when he moves to his permanent home, he doesn't bother. You don't find that odd?'

'Where he died, he seemed to me like a stranger in a strange land,' Turnbull said. 'At least I knew him.'

CHAPTER ELEVEN

'I was hoping I might be able to help you,' Neil Heuk said.

'Why would that be?' Meldrum asked.

As he spoke, he noticed the second drawer from the top in the filing cabinet was pulled out. Leaving it like that was careless. That was Detective Sergeant Shields all right, a man who didn't care, clumsy-fingered so that things had a tendency to break in his hands, because he didn't care or maybe because, all the time without knowing, that's what he wanted to do. True, in a room on the top floor of regional police headquarters, security shouldn't be a problem. He had a strong impulse, all the same, to get up and shut the drawer on its secrets.

'When I got to the desk downstairs,' Heuk said, 'I wondered if you would recognise my name. It hadn't occurred to me until that precise moment it was perfectly possible you might not. Isn't that strange? That's why I sent up my CIMD business card. False pretences, I suppose, since I've left the company. That's a crime, isn't it?'

'Don't worry about it.'

Heuk nodded seriously. With two fingers he patted his moustache, the thick curve of bristles flattening and springing up again. The slightly protuberant green eyes held fixed and intense on Meldrum, who was struck again by, found he hadn't in fact forgotten, their odd brilliance, muddied like a mountain pool stirred by a stick.

'I realised the two of us meeting in the Avenue Louise like that had to mean more to me than you. After all, I was the one whose life was saved. I was on my way up to my apartment, and from that point the choice would have been either the balcony or see if I could get up on to the roof and jump from there. I pressed the button for the lift and waited. It was only when I saw the concierge smirking at me from behind his desk that I noticed the sign "lift out of order". It was a large notice, too, placed quite prominently. I suppose I'd been too busy with my thoughts. I could have gone up by the stairs. I'm in good physical condition. Four floors, I could have run up the stairs.' Unexpectedly, he spread his hands then pressed his fingertips against his mouth as if to hold in his laughter. 'I couldn't be bothered. Give life a second chance, I thought. I went back out into the street. If the first person I see answers a question in French or English, I decided, I'll jump; if the answer's in Flemish, I won't. You were the first person I saw.'

'I answered you in English.'

'Your accent was unexpected. So I lost interest.' He looked round at the office furniture, the view from the narrow window of a strip of grey sky, at Meldrum in suit and tie behind his desk, and smiled. It wasn't a pleasant smile. 'I don't suppose you can understand.'

'Try me.'

'What do you mean?' The smile went.

'I've heard most of the reasons for suicide.'

'At first hand, you mean?'

'The ones who could still talk.'

'Mine was dull. They were holding a cocktail for me in the cafeteria at CIMD, because I was leaving the company. I felt I hadn't been there long enough for that, not more than three years. It was unnecessary. It embarrassed me. I couldn't face it. I suppose there must have been other reasons, but that was the one I had in mind at the time.'

'At the time you were getting ready to jump off a roof?'

Heuk stared back without a trace of a smile. If he'd meant to be funny, he was hiding it well. And what about that accent of his, Meldrum wondered. How come a Scotsman spoke like an American? He'd never been in the United States, hadn't he said that? Yes, at the CIMD leavetaking in Brussels. Maybe he's worked for a lot of American firms. Maybe it was a kind of protective coloration. Maybe it will disappear now he's working back here.

'Did you travel through from Glasgow just to tell me this?' Meldrum asked.

'Glasgow?'

'I thought you'd come back to work there?'

'Not in Glasgow. I don't know where you got that idea. Maybe I told you I was born there, that might be it. But I got out as soon as I could. I wouldn't want to go back there to live or to work.' His smile this time seemed simply pleased with himself. 'I've taken a day off to see you, but I didn't have far to travel.' He made a gesture of apology. 'I should have come sooner. But there was all the business of getting my furniture shipped across, settling in to the new job. It's not an excuse, I know, but I was surprised when you left the CIMD cocktail without speaking to me again. One minute you're talking to Jean-Philippe Guichard, next I look round and you're gone.'

'Why would I have spoken to you again?' To listen to more suicide talk? Did he imagine policemen took some kind of Hippocratic oath that meant they had to listen to crap like that? 'I was investigating the murder of Iain Bower.'

'Well, exactly,' Heuk said. 'Didn't Guichard tell you I was the nearest thing Iain had to a friend?'

Meldrum leaned back in his chair and thought about it. He took his time thinking about it, but if that made Heuk uncomfortable he didn't show it. He didn't seem to mind waiting at all.

'Guichard gave me the impression Iain Bower had plenty of friends.'

'The man's a fool. Apart from anything else, Iain spent most of his time away from head office.'

'How long did you say you'd been with the company?'

'Just under three years.'

'Not a long time. And yet you were the one who made friends with him.'

'I didn't see much of him the first year. But the last two years, things were going badly in Russia. He wasn't away so often. We were both Scots. I think – no, I'm sure – he took a liking to me.'

'How did you feel about him?'

'He was a nice man.'

Meldrum grunted. 'In what way?'

'What way?'

'Was he generous with money? Did he tell good jokes? People say somebody was nice, it's helpful to know what makes them think that.'

'He was a good listener. If he didn't tell jokes, he enjoyed them when someone else told them. I never heard of him lending anyone money, but then probably he didn't know anyone who needed it. With being abroad

so much, he had a fund of good stories. He liked a drink.' Heuk
shrugged. 'Nice, what can you say?'

'So why didn't he have more friends?'

Heuk blinked. 'Like I say, he was—'

'Away a lot. He joined CIMD when he was twenty-seven and stayed
with them for twenty-four years. For a nice man that's plenty of time to
make friends.'

'I take the point.' Thoughtfully, Heuk patted the moustache from one
end to the other. 'Maybe he did. Maybe over the years people he'd got
friendly with moved on, to other companies or went back to the UK or
the States or wherever they'd come from. It's an expatriate community.
As a matter of fact, he did mention a friend, maybe more than one, who'd
retired to Spain. For a while, I think, he'd planned on retiring there
himself. All the same . . .'

It was Meldrum's turn to be kept waiting. 'Yes?'

'All the same, you're right. He was good company, but you didn't get
close to him. Oh, about being in Russia or Africa, politics and business,
plenty of that, but nothing personal. I don't think he wanted to talk
about his past. But from what I've seen, people don't become real friends
until they've shared bits of their past, how they got on with their parents,
not real secrets maybe but things they don't usually talk about. If for
some reason you can't do that, you make acquaintances not real friends.
That's been my impression of how it works, don't you think so?'

'According to yourself, you were the nearest thing to a friend he had.
But it sounds like no kind of a friend at all. Have you anything worth
telling about him?' Slow down! Meldrum told himself. He took a deep
breath and went on quietly, 'I appreciate why you felt you should talk to
me. You did the right thing.' He eased his chair back and stood up. 'If
you think of anything else, we'd be glad to hear from you.'

Heuk also stood up and moved, willingly enough it seemed, to the
door. As it was being opened, however, he asked, 'Have you spoken yet
to Keith Chaney?'

'Who?' But already Meldrum was pushing the door a fraction forward
as if in the act of reclosing it.

'That's mostly why I came, but then I thought you were bound to have
heard about him from someone else. After all, he lives in Edinburgh. He
would have been at Iain's funeral.'

'No one of that name was there.'

'That surprises me. They'd known one another a long time. Since schooldays.'

Meldrum closed the door. 'Would you mind?' He waved Heuk back to the chair, and seated himself again behind the desk. 'Did Bower tell you about this friend of his?'

'Better than that, I met him. This would be about a year ago in Iain's flat. Just the three of us. With Chaney being such an old friend of Iain's, I was flattered to be invited. Like I said, it made me feel he'd taken a liking to me. We'd drinks, went out for dinner. Chaney was very taken with the Grande Place. It was his first time in Brussels, he said.'

'Can you describe him?'

'Early forties. Brown eyes. Going a bit thin on top.' Heuk smiled. 'He could hold his drink. We drank a hell of a lot.'

'How tall was he?'

Heuk waved a hand vaguely. 'About my height.'

Not then the giant of a man who had pissed into Bower's grave; and it wasn't likely he'd turn out to be the man in the anorak, the police impersonator.

Meldrum pulled over a pad and pen. 'Keith Chaney, that right, Keith?'

'Keith. And C-h-a-n-e-y. But hang on a minute.' He eased up one haunch, twisting round to get at his hip pocket. After a brief struggle, he tugged out a leather foldover wallet. 'I've got it written down.'

Meldrum took the slip of paper and unfolded it.

As he did so, Heuk explained, 'He gave me his address in case I was ever in Edinburgh. I'm not trying to teach you your business, but wouldn't it be a good idea to talk to him?'

CHAPTER TWELVE

'Let's try anyway,' he'd told Shields.

It was the same restlessness he'd been feeling for weeks. He wanted to get out of the office, away from the desk, the phone, the computer. It didn't even much matter where, or if it would help to find who'd killed Bower. Just to keep busy.

'Nobody answered the phone,' Shields said once they were in the car. Going over a thing again was his way of making a protest, one of his ways.

'So you told me.'

'I tried twice.'

'Right.'

Shields tugged the belt clear of his belly and belched. He'd thrown his jacket on the back seat and rings of sweat were spreading from under his arms. The sour smell of him hung in the confines of the car. Meldrum tapped the button and rolled the window down a couple of inches. The rain was light but persistent. The wipers paused between single sweeps. As they started up Lothian Road, he was aware of Shields staring gloomily out of the passenger window at the church and then the shops, the familiar shops, in the same succession. On the square in front of the Sheraton Hotel the trees and the fountain had been cleared away. It made a nice uncluttered open space at the start of what they were calling the business quarter with its Conference Centre and new office buildings big as a cathedral or a castle, over the drawbridge and into the atrium.

'Down there,' Shields said, jerking a thumb. Meldrum opened his mouth to protest the best way to Chaney's house was straight ahead, but the sergeant went on, 'That place Heuk told you he worked, it's one of the new buildings down there.'

And what the hell was an archivist? That's what Heuk had called himself. He'd done that at CIMD as well as some external relations, and now he was doing it for a company in Edinburgh, whose name Meldrum had recognised. When he'd lived with Harriet Cook, she'd joked about it. A multinational, it was the biggest client of a firm of corporate lawyers who'd recently formed a relationship with John Brennan. Now they've got John as well as their corporation lawyers, Harriet had said, they'll be able to kill their clients instead of just stealing from them. With Harriet, he'd liked the glimpses she gave him into a different world. Like other good things, that ended when she'd let Brennan bed her again.

'Down that way, towards Haymarket. My sister-in-law works there. Small world, eh?'

'Small world.'

Small city. Make seven connections and you could join anybody to anybody — or was that the world?

As the lights changed, he spotted the African mother, standing hipshot, hair braided, child at her knees. He realised it was her he'd been looking for, vaguely and without knowing. He couldn't remember exactly when she'd appeared or why, something to do with Nelson Mandela, but the statue had stood for years in a central position at the front of the square. Now diminished in a corner, it looked out of sight out of mind.

The address Heuk had given him placed the Chaney house out in bungalow land. Because identical rows wound about each other like tangles in a love knot, they drove in the wrong end of a street so narrow two cars couldn't park opposite each other, went past the house and had to reverse back.

Shields, out of the car first, scratched the bristles on his chin and shook his head at the house. 'Would you believe that's worth a couple of hundred grand?' He took an interest in what things cost.

'Uh-huh.' Meldrum didn't.

At the back of an unweeded garden the house crouched in the shadow of a pair of overgrown yew trees. It looked like a house you would pay not to live in. Behind him a woman's voice called a girl's name, and he glanced round to see the child running to her across the opposite garden. The child scurried inside, and the door closed on them like a drawing aside of skirts. Mother and child had retreated into what looked like a nice house, grass cut, fences painted; just like all the others, both sides of the street and all the streets round about. Nice houses for nice people, driving along that was the impression he'd had. Only this one in front of him was different. In the front room on the left heavy curtains were drawn. The storm door was shut. He thought, this house is abandoned.

The woman who finally unbolted and opened the storm door stepped back in fright.

'What do you want?'

She was about thirty and would have been pretty except for dark circles under the eyes and her mouth dragged down at the corners.

'It's all right,' Meldrum said. 'We're police officers.' As they showed identification, she inched cautiously forward. 'We were wanting to have a word with Mr Chaney.'

'Keith isn't here,' she said.

'When are you expecting him?' Meldrum asked.

She stared at him. Her expression had the stressed blankness he'd seen on the faces of the deaf trying to work out what the question had been. He was about to ask again, when she shook her head and turned, gesturing for them to come in.

'I get nervous,' she said. She led them down the hall. 'It's worse at night, with me being on my own.'

'But I'm here.' The pale emphasis against the idea of her aloneness belonged to a child. About ten years old, he was at the door of what was probably his bedroom, the one with the curtains drawn.

'Of course you are,' the mother said. She turned away from him through the door on the other side of the passage.

'What's happening?' the boy asked.

Meldrum stopped to answer him, as Shields followed the woman into the room.

'My name's Jim. What's yours?'

'Sam. Who are you?'

'Policemen,' he said, 'but it's not anything to worry about. Just something your mum can help us with.' Behind the boy there was a glow of pale light. 'Are you working on a computer, Sam? Playing games?' At the word 'games' a twitch of disdain came and went. 'You should put the lights on. Working in the dark's bad for your eyes.'

In the sitting room, Meldrum felt as if Shields and himself crowded the space. The furniture packed into it, dark wooden sideboard, over-stuffed couch and chairs, made it seem even smaller than it was. What might have been a year's collection of papers and magazines were piled and scattered around. The air was stale with the smoke that had yellowed the ceiling. The woman cleared litter from the couch, lifted a full ashtray off the arm and invited them to sit down. Instead of sitting herself, she began to drift round, still holding the ashtray, doing the kind of tidying that consists of moving things from one place to another.

'I don't like to discuss my business on the doorstep. Round here you never know who—' she began, and broke off to ask, 'Would you like a cup of tea?'

When they refused, she asked what about coffee and looked disappointed when they said no again. She told them her name was Val. Having got over her fright, apparently she was in no hurry to be rid of them. Visitors have to be pretty scarce, Meldrum thought, for policemen to seem like company.

'Keith's working away from home at present,' she said.

Before Meldrum could respond to that, 'What does he do?' Shields asked.

Maybe it was his tone that made her blink and pause again.

After a moment's thought, she said, 'He had a garage business.' And then, as if realising that wasn't an answer, added, 'He can do anything with cars.'

'Can you tell us where he is?' Meldrum asked.

'Why do you want to speak to him?'

'He's not in any kind of trouble. We think he may be able to help us with some enquiries. If you let us have his phone number, we could contact him.'

'What happened with the business wasn't his fault. Nobody could have tried harder.'

'It's not anything to do with his business,' Meldrum said reassuringly.

Now, though, she was more puzzled than convinced. 'If you tell me what it is. Maybe I can help you?'

— Just give us the fucking address. Shields didn't need to say the words aloud. The noise he made clearing his throat, like a man getting ready to hawk and spit, didn't give Meldrum any translation problems.

'I think we'd have to speak to him.'

'Is it about that man who was murdered?'

Despite a charge of excitement, Meldrum had to make a decision before admitting it. The principle of getting information not giving it away had been instilled a long time ago.

'You mean Iain Bower?' She nodded. 'That's why we're here, yes. We've been told your husband was a friend of his.'

'Oh, I don't think so.'

'An old friend,' Shields said.

'I never heard Keith mention him.'

'Sorry?' Meldrum said. 'You just asked about him.'

'Bower's not a common name, is it? When I saw it in the paper, I noticed it, because Keith's gone to work for a man called Frank Bower. I wondered if they could be related.'

'They were brothers,' Meldrum said.

'There you are then. I was right. But Keith never said anything to me about – Iain? – about anybody called Iain Bower. It was just with it being an unusual name, that's the only reason I noticed. And he never said to me about being friends or anything – just that he was going to work for somebody called Frank Bower.'

It took another quarter of an hour, but there wasn't any more to be got out of her. When he was sure of that, Meldrum got to his feet. As he did so, by some accidental angle through the overgrown shrubbery he saw a man going by outside. There was the impression – his head in the act of turning away – that he might have been looking at the window. It was no more than a glimpse, but it was enough for Meldrum to recognise him.

'Stand in front of the window. Back to it, make it look as if you're talking to Mrs Chaney. Don't look out.' Shields was startled, but didn't argue. The room got darker as the bulk of him blocked the light.

'What is it?' she asked.

'I need to use your back door,' he told her. 'Sit there. I'll explain later.'

Meldrum went down the passage fast, covering the distance from passage into kitchen in three long strides. At his sudden appearance, the boy had half jumped back into his bedroom. All this time, he must have been standing watch. The man of the house, poor kid. Brave kid.

The back door was locked and he wasted a minute getting the key from the hook beside it.

A high thick privet hedge made the left boundary for the garden. The other side was a fence about six feet high. He pulled himself up, got a foot on top and jumped over. No one in the neatly kept garden. His luck held, not a sound of complaint, as he ran the path along the back of the neighbour's house. At the corner, he took a quick look. A drive with a parked car, a view of a section of the street. it was his guess the man had been standing opposite watching the house, then decided to risk a look because of the overgrown garden; the gamble was that he hadn't just walked away.

One peep past the end of the gable wall told him the front was even nicer, the lawn smooth enough for nail scissors, the hedge beaten to its knees and cropped into submission. Fortunately, Chaney's next-door jungle gave cover for the three steps that let him see along the street.

And there the man was. Other side of the street. Average height, glimpse of a long thin face when he eased back the hood on what looked like a cheap imitation of a Berghaus anorak.

The drive was covered with small chips. A stupid surface, the kind that got wedged into the welts of shoes and trailed into the house. Moving slowly, treading softly, still Meldrum heard it crunch underfoot. From one step to the next, he picked up the pace so that he came out of the gate closing the gap just fast enough to suggest how stupid trying to run from him would be. When he saw the man had got the idea, he took the last couple of yards at a walk.

' 'Meldrum, isn't it?' Meldrum said. 'Don't tell me. Detective In-spector. Isn't that right? I've been wanting to meet you.'

CHAPTER THIRTEEN

H is name was David Slater and, as Meldrum told Knife Stanley that
night, 'There wasn't anything sinister about him at all. Poor
bastard.'

All the way back to St Leonards, they could hear him muttering to
himself in the back seat where the doors were set only to unlock from the
outside. Shields tapped Meldrum on the arm, rolled his eyes back and
pulled a face. As they came to Tollcross, the muttering stopped.
Meldrum angled the mirror, and saw Slater pointing across the road.

'That's where I live. That close there,' he said. 'Do you want to come
up for a cup of tea?'

Shields, who'd clearly made up his mind what they were dealing with,
laughed and said, 'You got any biscuits?'

'I could get some. See, there's a shop there.'

'Another fucking time. Not right now, pal.'

There was a silence, then the voice from the back seat asked, 'Will I be
going home today?'

'Today?' Shields sucked air in through his teeth. 'Put it this way, I
hope you've fed the budgie.'

'I don't have a budgie.'

'Leave it,' Meldrum said. 'Let him alone.'

In the interview room, Slater asked if he could put the recording
machine on.

'I'm familiar with the procedure,' he said.

'Have you ever been convicted of a crime?'

'Oh, no.' He looked shocked, but then clasped his hands to his mouth, nodding and thinking about it. 'Well, I was arrested once. But that was a mistake.'

'What was that for?'

'Sleeping rough.'

'Just for sleeping rough?' Shields asked sceptically.

'Like I said, it was a mistake. It was a time in my life when I'd lost my way.'

'Do you make a lot of mistakes, David?'

'I'm quite methodical. Well organised, I keep full notes. I imagine you'll want to see them. I've put it all down.'

'What "it" would that be?' But even as he asked, Meldrum knew. 'Would these be notes about the murder?'

'Of Iain Bower. I thought the best thing would be to concentrate on it. Working on my own, my resources are limited.'

'You've been telling people you were a police officer, David. You know that's an offence? You've got yourself into trouble.'

'I did it so they would talk freely.' He fell silent, and then muttered something.

'What? I didn't hear that. Tell me again, David.'

'I think of myself as a policeman. I applied, but wasn't accepted. I hoped it would be different, if I showed what I could do.'

'But why did you choose Iain Bower's murder to investigate?'

'I saw you were in charge of it. I admired you.'

Meldrum heard Shields give a little muted snuffle. Dangerous thing, a sense of humour.

'Is that why you told people you were me?'

'Yes.'

'Both name and rank, isn't that right?'

'Yes.'

'Does the Reverend Patrick Turnbull mean anything to you?'

'He conducted Iain Bower's funeral. I was there.'

'Yes, I know.'

Slater nodded seriously. 'I saw you too. In the church, looking around, just the way I was doing. Taking note of everybody. There was always a chance the murderer would be there. That sometimes happens. I could tell exactly what you were thinking.'

'And the cemetery. Didn't you go there too?'

'Yes.'

Meldrum let the silence run, but Slater didn't expand on that. Perhaps he was worried that he'd given a false name after the man pissed in the grave.

'Did you see Mr Turnbull after that? After the day of the funeral?'

'I went to his church and spoke to him there. You know, the church we were in for the funeral service? I thought it would be easier for him if I did the interview there. Of course, I have his home address as well. Just as part of the dossier, though. Like I said, I try to be methodical. I don't suspect him of any wrongdoing.'

'I'll take a note of that,' Shields said. Even though they were recording, he couldn't resist.

'I interviewed him about the murder. And the black couple, they've been interviewed.'

'The Balewas.'

'Yes. Husband, wife and child.'

'Why?'

Slater sat with hunched shoulders and head hung a little forward as if it was too heavy for his neck. The anorak lay open, showing on one breast an old dull stain like a rub against wet paint. The question seemed to perplex him. 'Background. In a murder case you have to go into the background. That's what you do.'

'But why them? There must be what – a couple of dozen flats in the Doune Apartments? Iain Bower lived on the second floor. Why go all the way up to the top to talk to the Balewas?'

'I spoke to other people too.' Showing agitation for the first time, he slid the anorak zipper a couple of inches up and down over and over again.

'Could you give me any of their names?'

'I knocked at doors. Some people were in, some weren't. I took down their names. I have them in a book at home.' The zipper rattled up and down. 'The Balewas were the last ones. Maybe that's why I remember them.'

It was possible. All the same: 'So you remember talking to the Balewas. And telling them you were a policeman.'

'Yes.'

'And the minister, Dr Turnbull?'

'Yes.'

'And Mr Chaney, you wanted to talk to him?'

'Yes.'

'Which Mr Chaney would that be?'

'Keith Chaney.'

'That name hasn't been in the papers. Yesterday I didn't know that name. So how come you know it?'

'I followed you and you went into that house and then this woman with a shopping bag went past and I asked her and she told me who lived there.' He leaned back in his chair, pressed a curved forefinger to his lips and nodded his head. Little almost imperceptible nods, Meldrum counted five of them. Thinking about what he's just said, Meldrum decided, going over the links in his chain of reasoning. He must think it checks out. He seems pleased with himself.

'Do you have a car, David?'

Slater put his hands over his eyes.

'David, how did you follow us without a car?'

Without taking his hands away, he said, 'You're giving me a headache.' He began to rock back and forward.

Until not so long ago that would have been the signal to hammer him with questions. Over the moaning noises, certain on tape to sound even more desolate, Meldrum gave time and date; said, 'I'm ending this interview,' and did.

Finishing after eight or later, too often recently he'd had no taste for food. That night he decided not eating was a bad idea, and detoured to the Chinese restaurant in Frederick Street. It was there that Henry Stanley, on his way back from the lavatory to the dining area, spotted him waiting for the carry-out he'd ordered. 'Join us!' Knife, whatever his faults, had a liking for company, the more the merrier. He'd been invited to celebrate with the team that had just cracked a series of burglaries in Barnton. Modestly: 'I was of some assistance.' Lecherously: 'Mary Preston's there. Far too pretty to be a detective constable.' Resisting temptation, from wine to woman, Meldrum paid for his carry-out.

They were poised to go their separate ways when Knife asked, 'How are you getting on with your *doppelgänger*?'

'What?'

'The shadow Meldrum. Are witnesses still telling you to go away, you've already turned up on their doorstep?'

'We've got him. There wasn't anything sinister about him at all. Poor bastard. I doubt if he'll even be charged. Though it might get him sectioned again.'

'I expect he'll turn up on another doorstep.'

'Not if he's got any sense.'

Knife laughed. 'Well, quite.'

He was turning away when Meldrum said, 'There is someone I'd like to talk to you about.'

His words surprised him. It wasn't something he'd intended to say.

'Who would that be?'

'Who?'

'It's all right. When we've more time. This isn't the place.'

'Whoa! Not so fast. You'll regret asking for help, I know you. This is an historic occasion. Do it now, or there's a risk you'll forever hold your peace.' And, in response to Meldrum's shake of the head, added, 'It isn't about Mr Heuk, is it?'

'Who's been talking to you?'

'My spies are everywhere.'

'Shields been marking your card?'

'Not necessarily. A pleasant sociable creature, all the same, your sergeant. Anyway, from all I hear this Mr Heuk's a strange one.'

Meldrum waited. The couple who'd ordered after him got their carry-out, paid for it and left. There was a mid-evening lull.

'The strangest thing about him,' Meldrum said, 'is he claims I saved his life.'

'How did you do that?'

Though he would have claimed he'd dismissed it from his mind, he found that he wanted to talk about it. He wanted to talk about it quite badly.

'According to him, he was getting set to throw himself out of a window. This was in Brussels — when I was there. But he changed his mind. Or at least, this is the story he's peddling, he decided to bet on it. He went out into the street and asked the first person he saw a question. That was me. Do you believe in coincidence? With him turning out to be a friend of Iain Bower, that seems too much of a coincidence. But I don't see how he could know I would be there. I didn't know I would be there. I was just wandering around.'

'What was his bet?'

'If he got an answer in English or French, he'd jump. If it came in Flemish, he wouldn't.'

'And do you think he would have?'

'Yes.'

He didn't hesitate. There was no doubt in his mind that Heuk would have jumped. It wasn't something you could give reasons for believing. It was something you knew, the way a dog caught a smell off a man's skin.

'Wait,' Knife said as it struck him. 'Didn't you answer him in English?'

'He didn't expect my accent. The Scots accent distracted him.'

'As little a thing as that.'

'I'm sure he wasn't looking for an excuse. I still believe he meant to jump.'

'If he's what I'm thinking he is, I don't doubt it.'

But perversely Meldrum felt a surge of impatience with himself for seeking help. For a policeman, showing weakness was a bad move.

'I'd give a good deal to meet your Mr Heuk. It's my feeling he'll be a study for someone like me, sooner rather than later. Think about it. A man who doesn't commit suicide only because of some trivial thought or interruption, an existential accident,' Knife Stanley said. 'The very slightness of the dissuading accident uncovers the looseness of his attachment to life. That suggests to me what I'd describe as a cold pallor of the soul. It marks the type – like Hitler, who had to destroy peoples and nations to feel at all.'

A familiar impatience with the little man's air of omniscience, count that in too.

All the same, he'd stayed to listen, which meant the carry-out was cold by the time he got back to the flat. Not that it mattered since he'd lost his appetite.

AS IT BEGAN

'Twelve,' I told her, though I had some months to go.

'Shouldn't you be at school?' she asked me.

I'd already told her my name was Norman. I'd started out to tell her Neil when she asked me, but then I thought my name was none of her business. it came out 'Nee-nee-norman', so that she gave me a queer look and asked me again. Norman, I told her, and that time it came out clear and no mistaking.

There were only eight tables, I'd counted them, and I had the one by the window. There was a man on his own and two women together and then an old man came in, and they were all eating, they'd got served, even the old man who came in after everybody else got a plate of mince and potatoes and peas that were bright green round the edge of his plate. Me, I was still waiting, though I'd told her ages ago I wanted a plate of soup. Just a plate of soup, thank you. I hoped she'd bring a bit of bread as well. That's when she asked all the questions, she was a nosy woman.

'The school's shut the day.'

'What school would that be then?'

'Shakespeare Street.'

I'd no breakfast, I'd been in such a hurry to get out of the house. I'd kicked the schoolbag under the bed, and banged the door behind me so my mother'd know that was me away and there was no chance of a cup of tea in her bed.

Years would pass before we were together again. If I'd known, would I have served her the tea?

When I came out the close, I walked from Arden Street to the Botanic
Gardens. I sat on a bench in the park. The sun was shining, but because it
was October it was cold all the same and then the rain came on. I went
into the big glass house and looked at the plants, but a man was keeking
round them at me and then he started following me so I came out. I went
down Byres Road and looked in the shop windows. I was starving. I
bought a packet of crisps, and that was me practically broke. I asked a
woman the time and it wasn't eleven o'clock yet. I couldn't believe it,
how slow time can go. I walked all the way back up to Maryhill Road.
My feet were sore. I walked down to Queen's Cross and at the gushet I
could go one way or the other, down Garscube Road or carry on down
Maryhill Road and it didn't make any difference and I couldn't be
bothered one way or the other. What I decided: If the number of the first
bus I see adds up even, I'll go down Garscube Road; if it adds up odd, I'll
carry on down Maryhill Road. That was the bet. It was a 63, so that was
that and I carried on down Maryhill Road and I might have walked all
the way to George's Cross, I might have walked all the way to Sauchiehall
Street, if I hadn't been hungry. Or if the rain hadn't got worse. Or if my
sandshoes hadn't squelched, right, left, squelch, squelch, till I was sick of
it. ABORTION BILL PASSES PARLIAMENT. I stood and looked at
the placard and then I saw the shop next door to the newsagent's had
curtains on a sagging wire and where they nearly met in the middle there
was a card with LUNCH written at the top and under it *scotch pie and beans,
bacon egg and chips, stovies*, there was *rhubarb crumble* too; and *home-made soup*. I
asked for the soup since it was all I could afford. 'Just the soup?' she
asked. And then the questions started.

She talked to the old man, and he nodded up at her, mashing his
potatoes into the mince gravy, shovelling it in his mouth, all the while
staring over at me. While that was going on a man in his shirtsleeves
came out of the kitchen and he'd a look at me as well. I should have left
then, but I could see the food and the warm air was greasy with the smell
of it.

When I'd about given up hope, she did bring the soup with a roll on a
plate and butter on it. I'd never tasted anything better than that soup.
Half of it was gone before I thought of trying to make it last, and the rest
went just about as fast.

Thinking back, I'd a chance to leave then too, but didn't.

I was dabbing up the crumbs off the plate, when the woman leaned

over and said quietly, 'Take your bowl into the kitchen and see if he'll fill
it up for you.'

What soup it must have been. Nothing ever tasted as good again.

The man in shirtsleeves was taking potato slices out of a bag as I came
in. As he slid some out of his fist into the chip fryer, the fat leapt and
sizzled.

'I'm going to eat now,' he said. 'Sit at the table there and take a bit of
bread. You can have a share of these when they're ready.'

'Can I have some soup? It's rare soup.'

He laughed. 'Flattery'll get you everywhere.'

He put about a half ladle of soup into my bowl, which wasn't being
mean since the pot was nearly empty. It was cold too and not so nice as it
had been before. I finished it in no time, and got up to put the bowl
where the rest of the dishes were piled up for washing. A big policeman
was standing at the door. The woman in the apron was just behind him.
She must have gone out into the street to fetch him, and done it the
minute she'd got me into the kitchen.

The man in shirtsleeves was on the other side of the cooker from me.
He was leaning with his hands on the board, and his head turned to look
at the policeman. It wasn't one thing, it was everything: the way it was at
home, the dirty bastard in Edinburgh when Davie and me ran away, her
in the apron making a fool of me, him giving me cold soup, walking in
the rain that was the worst squelch squelch squelch. I took the spoon out
of the bowl and dipped it in the boiling fat, then I poured it over the
back of his hand.

The policeman in the car that took me away from court wasn't young.
He'd double chins and a bit of white in his hair. I thought, I wouldn't
mind having him for a father, which was a stupid thing, a really stupid
thing. The truth is since I'd watched the skin on that hand bubble and
split under the fat I hadn't belonged to myself not for a minute, it was as
if all I had left to be me in was a corner of my mind hidden away like a
cupboard at the back of a hall crowded with folk dancing and shouting.
That stupid thing about the copper for a father fell out of the cupboard.
It must have been because of how low I was feeling.

When he saw me looking at him, the policeman curled his lip in
disgust and contempt and told me, 'Too late now to say you're sorry.
The good times are over for you, boy.'

The idea seemed to satisfy him.

Crime and punishment, I suppose.

'You're for the nailer,' the policeman told me. 'That'll sort you out.'

When he said that to me I saw an image, like a Sunday school picture, of a naked man laid on a cross on the ground and a soldier in breastplate and helmet kneeling beside him.

And see it still, though now, aware of the century's bad dreams as well as my own, my centurion is like as not to have given place to a kapo with nails in his mouth and a wooden hammer in his hand.

BOOK THREE

The House on the Island

CHAPTER FOURTEEN

Meldrum's curiosity about Neil Heuk made him decide to get in touch again with CIMD, which should have been simple but wasn't. The first time he rang it was a national holiday or a saint's day or a strike of telephone workers or the firm's annual picnic. Anyway, Brussels was off planet that afternoon.

The morning after talking to Knife Stanley at the Chinese restaurant he tried again.

'Good morning, CIMD International. How can I help you?'

Very bright, businesslike, ready to help, very American in fact, though the accent sounded French.

'I'd like to speak to Jean-Philippe Guichard, please.' Silence. Though he felt she should know, he told her: 'He's your Personnel Director.' More silence. 'Sorry, Human Resources.'

'Could you hold on a moment?'

Not bright at all any more, which sometimes happened when people found it was a policeman on the line. But, of course, that was something she didn't know. She hadn't asked for his name. Maybe because she'd been in too much of a hurry to pass him on after he'd asked for Guichard? He couldn't see any reason for that.

There was music interspersed with a recorded assurance that he hadn't been forgotten. As he listened, he went through the returns on the search for the man who'd signed himself in at the Viewforth boarding house as Richard Nicolson. There had been no sightings at the transport terminals, and given his exceptional size that made it more than likely that he'd either left in a car or was still in the city. A blank had been drawn at city hotels, and from every phone call to a listed boarding house.

'Hello?' A man's voice.

'I'm still here,' Meldrum said.

'I'm told you wanted to speak with M. Guichard?'

He sounded wary and, Meldrum noted, made no apology for keeping him waiting.

'That's right,' he said.

'I'm sorry, I don't know who I'm speaking to.'

'I have the same problem,' he said. The point made, sensibly he went on at once, 'Detective Inspector James Meldrum, Borders and Lothian Police. I'm phoning from Edinburgh in Scotland.'

'Can I ask, what is your business with M. Guichard?'

Very wary. What's going on, Meldrum wondered.

'Is there a reason I shouldn't talk to *him* about that?'

There was an audible sigh at the other end.

'You make it difficult for me to know how to help you.'

'You could start,' Meldrum said, 'by telling me who you are.'

And again there was a silence, as if even this was information not to be given away lightly. 'Georg van Ostayen. Acting Director, Human Resources.'

'I was in Brussels last month. I saw M. Guichard then, and he was good enough to help with my enquiries.'

'What kind of enquiries?'

'Into a murder here in Edinburgh.'

'Was it a child?' The question came sharply, as if the word 'murder' had shocked it out of him.

It was Meldrum's turn to pause. 'No, a man called Iain Bower. He was a retired employee of CIMD in Brussels. That's why I asked for M. Guichard's help.'

'Why do you want to speak to him now?'

Consciously patient, Meldrum said slowly, 'Things have come up I'd like to check with him.'

'He's not here.'

'In the building? In the country? With the company?' Not so patient.

'He's no longer with the company. The best thing, Mr . . . ?'

'Detective Inspector. Meldrum.'

'The best thing would be to make a list of questions. If you would put them in writing, I would make every effort to find the information for you.'

Fuck this for a game of soldiers, Meldrum thought, suddenly not patient at all.

'I can think of one now,' he said quietly. 'If you could answer it, that would save us both time. There's someone else who used to work for CIMD – a man called Neil Heuk. Did you know him?'

'Yes.'

'Would you describe him as a friend of Iain Bower?'

'I'm not sure what you mean.'

'It's a simple question surely. Were they friends?'

Another sigh. 'When I say I knew Mr Heuk, what I meant was working in the same building. By sight. I wouldn't say I knew him well.'

'How well would you say you knew Iain Bower?'

'When he was here, quite well. He was away a great deal. But he was a very cheerful man.'

It struck Meldrum that working out a list of questions, typing them up and faxing them to van Ostayen was going to be a good deal more bother than the answers were likely to be worth.

'Could you tell me how I'd get in touch with M. Guichard?'

'Why would you want to do that?'

'Because I'm conducting a murder investigation. I don't know how you feel about that in Belgium. In Scotland we take it seriously.'

No sooner were the words out of his mouth than he regretted them. For a policeman the groups you could be rude to were pretty clearly defined, and they didn't include officers of multinational companies.

After a pause, however, van Ostayen said, 'I'd like you to believe that isn't fair. A week ago today, Guichard was arrested. They say he was a member of a paedophile ring. Apparently, the charges include the abuse of children, perhaps their actual abduction. God knows what else. I can only tell you that many of us here care about that kind of vileness. We care very deeply.'

While Meldrum was considering his response to this, he heard the phone go down at the other end.

When Shields came back from the canteen, Meldrum looked up from the piece of paper in front of him. On it he'd written the names Guichard, Iain Bower, Neil Heuk in a triangle. Round them he'd written a circle of other names, including that of Keith Chaney. For quarter of an hour, he'd been drawing lines between them and question marks and studying the results.

'Get your jacket on,' he told Shields. 'We're off out.'

It was only as they pulled up outside the Doune Apartments that he realised he hadn't told Shields where they were going. Or why, come to that. Turning over the possibilities, he'd been so preoccupied he'd hardly been conscious of his companion. As he switched off the engine, he turned, better later than never, but got Shields's back view, jacket strained across beefy shoulders as he scrunched down to squint up the steps at the apartment entrance. Next moment, he'd opened the door and got out, leaving Meldrum to follow. By the time he went into the hall, the sergeant was already standing by the lift. As Meldrum approached, the door slid open and they stepped inside. 'Four,' Shields said, 'I suppose,' and when Meldrum nodded, pressed the button.

Weekday mid morning, Meldrum had been hoping to get mother and child on their own. He was disappointed; the door was opened by Balewa, who raised his eyebrows and stared in surprise.

'I know who you are,' he said, when Meldrum offered his name. 'I just didn't expect to see you again.'

'It would be easier to talk inside,' Meldrum said.

'We told you everything you wanted to know.'

'I'm just trying to respect your privacy. We find people usually don't want their neighbours to get the wrong idea.'

'Please,' Balewa said. He moved aside. 'The difficulty is I don't have a great deal of time.'

As they went through, the wife appeared yawning from the bedroom. Her hair was ruffled from sleep. A very short dressing gown exposed long black legs. She clutched it across her breasts, while the five-year-old clinging to her tugged it open at the bottom to show a strip of sticking plaster on the inside of her right thigh.

'I heard the doorbell ringing.'

'Go back to bed!' Balewa told her.

'I'm up now,' she said, yawning.

'We are not accustomed to have visitors,' he told the two detectives, sounding almost apologetic.

'What do they want?' the woman asked, unsmiling.

'I'll attend to this. There's no need for you to be up.' He explained, 'My wife didn't get home until quarter past eight this morning.'

She worked as a nurse, Meldrum remembered. He said, 'I'm sorry we woke you.'

'It's done now.'

In the little room used for sitting, cooking, eating, they arranged themselves much as before, side by side on the couch with Balewa facing them. This time, though, the woman hovered above her husband, leaning with both hands on the back of his chair. Catching the boy's eye as he peeped round the arm, Meldrum smiled at him. The boy shot back out of sight like a startled rabbit.

'He's shy,' Balewa said.

At this the wife made an odd clicking sound, tapping her tongue on her palate in what could have been irritation or something stronger, like contempt.

'Still, Iain Bower must have got on well with him,' Meldrum said.

'The poor man who was killed?' Balewa asked. 'What do you mean?'

'Otherwise he wouldn't have been able to babysit for you.'

'Who said he did?' the wife demanded.

'Are you telling me that he didn't?'

The husband twisted round and looked up at her. 'Of course he did.' He turned again to Meldrum. 'It's not easy for us in a strange country. We appreciated the opportunity, it was wonderful to be able to get out for an evening. Otherwise our lives consist of classes for me during the day – I should be leaving for one now! – and then we're parted most nights. I long for it to be over. I long to be home again. I miss Iain Bower because he let us out together for a handful of evenings. What's wrong with that? It may be selfish of me to say so, when the poor man's dead, but it's the truth.'

Meldrum saw the child peeping out at him again. His brown eyes were wide with the excitement of his own daring.

He said, 'Your son – Sanya, isn't it? – Sanya may be shy, but he's a charming little boy. You must be very fond of him.'

Balewa nodded agreement and showed a lot of large white teeth in a grin of pleasure. Behind him his wife frowned.

'You didn't worry at all about leaving him with Iain Bower?'

'Worry?' Balewa's smile vanished. He looked puzzled. 'Mr Bower was a very responsible man.'

'Most men wouldn't be too keen on babysitting a child.'

'It was kind of him. There wasn't a woman to volunteer. He knew our situation.'

'Did he volunteer?'

'What?'

'Did you ask him if he would look after Sanya to let you out for an evening, or did he suggest it?'

But now Balewa was disturbed. 'What is this about? I don't know who suggested it.' He twisted round, glanced up at his wife. 'It came up naturally, didn't it, that first time? We were talking about my course at Heriot-Watt. I mentioned the end of term dance. You said how much you loved to dance, and –' he swung round again '– and he said he'd be glad to look after Sanya and give us a night on our own. Why does that matter?'

'Him offering like that didn't surprise you?'

Balewa stared at him. Instead of answering, he reached a long arm round the chair and pulled the boy in front of him.

'You liked it when Mr Bower came in to look after you. He read you a story, then you got a glass of milk and went to bed. Isn't that right?'

His big hands rested on the boy's shoulders, fingertips touching in the middle of his back. Meldrum couldn't see the boy's face, but the child didn't move or speak.

'Sanya?' The father's voice sounded thinner, somehow lighter. 'It was all right, wasn't it?'

'Mr Balewa—' Meldrum began.

'You stay out of this!' He put a hand under the boy's chin and tilted his head back. He did it very gently, and his voice was soft when he said to him, 'We have no secrets from one another in this family. Haven't I taught you to tell me the truth? Tell me the truth.'

The boy began to sob. Balewa made no resistance when his wife took the child from him. She crouched down beside the boy, and wrapped her arms round him.

'We can get a woman police officer to talk to Sanya,' Meldrum said to her. 'With you there, of course.'

'What for?' Balewa asked.

Meldrum never took his eyes from hers. 'It would help us. I'm not pretending it wouldn't help us. It's important we find out as much as we can about Bower. But it would help the boy, too. We can get you people trained in talking to children.'

'Are you telling me that something has happened to my son?'

As he spoke, Balewa was suddenly on his feet, picked up in one motion as if by a force outside himself.

'Don't speak to them!' his wife said.

Balewa squeezed his temples between clenched fists. 'Is it true? Is it what I'm thinking?' He glared down at the child. 'Wouldn't he have told us? Oh, that man should be alive. I would kill him!'

To Meldrum's surprise, he heard Shields at his side give the faintest of snorts. Was it possible the fat sergeant thought that was funny? *If he was alive, I'd kill him.* Like an Irish joke, one of those funny unfuckingfunny jokes.

'Sit down, Mr Balewa,' he told him. 'Please. This isn't the way to go about things. It doesn't help. Sit down and we'll talk quietly.'

'No!' The wife was on her feet. She took a half step forward as if to gather husband and child behind her. 'You don't think I know what you're doing? You think we are stupid people? We are not poor people, we are not stupid people. A man has been murdered. You need to find who killed him. But that is a hard task. Easier to accuse my husband. The black man did it. You are racist policemen.'

The ferocity of the attack startled them all, including the child whose sobbing took on an edge of hysteria.

'Time for everyone to calm down,' Meldrum said, getting to his feet. 'We may have to talk to you again. But let's leave it just now.'

He led the way out into the hall. Balewa was about to shut the door when his wife came after them and said, 'My husband knew nothing about it.'

'But she knew,' Meldrum said, talking it out in the car on the way back. 'I wonder when she found out. Maybe the boy let something slip. Maybe he was having bad dreams. One thing's sure. Either Balewa is a hell of an actor, or he genuinely didn't know. Mind you, I've said that before and got it wrong. But if he did, it would be all the motive any man would need.' He tapped the brake and then accelerated to get past a bus taking on passengers. 'Or woman either. She's impressive, a stronger character than he is. But not physically. I wonder if a woman could have had the strength to smash in Bower's skull.' He eased the car to a halt on the red, and watched the last pedestrians straggle across. 'What do you think?'

'I should have been briefed,' Shields said. They were the first words he'd spoken, Meldrum realised, since they'd got into the lift to go up to the Balewas'. 'If I'd known where we were going and why, I'd have been more help.' Might have been, Meldrum thought, *might*. Chances twenty-eighty? 'If my opinion's worth anything, that is.' Mind reader.

All the same. In fairness. Even if the guy was a dead weight.

'You're right. Sorry about that.'

Shields didn't say a word. Waiting for a gracious response would be a long wait.

'Tomorrow,' Meldrum said, 'we're off to see Frank Bower. Why? To ask him if he has any idea why his brother took early retirement. And when we're at Kilbracken anyway we'll take the chance to talk to Keith Chaney.'

Okay?

CHAPTER FIFTEEN

'What does this guy Keith Chaney do for Bower?'
'No idea. His wife didn't tell us. You were there.'

It was almost noon on another wet morning in a summer of wet mornings. Bad weather made Meldrum restless. He was glad to be on the road.

'I remember his wife all right.'

'You were there when she didn't tell us.'

For answer, Shields slumped lower in his seat and stared ahead at sheep munching hill grass under a grey sky. Clear as a bell, he'd decided to give up on the effort to take an intelligent interest; body language signalling: ah, fuck it. What was that saying about suffering fools gladly, Meldrum thought. With Shields, he hadn't, not suffered him gladly at all; though he should have tried just now, effort always being worth encouragement and even praise. Something he'd been taught in the Boys Brigade, along with the dead march, how to form fours and the trick of smoking a brass belt buckle over a candle before polishing it. All part of learning how to be a leader of men. Ah, as Shields might have put it himself, fuck it. Total up the number of fools he'd worked with over the years, no wonder the gladness supply had run out.

Shields let out a long breath, spluttering it in bursts between his lips. From the corner of his eye, Meldrum watched him twiddling his thumbs, away from his belly ten times, towards his belly ten times, fat thumb stuttering on the towards, away seemed to come more naturally to him.

'Fancy the radio on? Bit of music?'

'Fine by me,' Meldrum said.

'Pass the time, eh?'

Meldrum, if he thought about it, knew why he didn't try to get rid of Shields. Pure bloodymindedness. And, to be fair to himself, indifference. A harder question was why Shields didn't get away from him. Maybe, Meldrum pondered, he thinks it would look bad on his record. Or maybe he's worried I'd harbour a grudge if he applied for a transfer.

'What's the joke?' Shields asked.

'Just enjoying the music.'

'Aye, that's nice, isn't it?'

Was it? Truth was, Meldrum didn't have much of an ear for music. Country and Western, moody songs that told a story, he liked, and that was about it. Bobbie Shields, on the other hand, would browse along the dial, stop and listen to all kinds of music, sometimes for a surprisingly long time to music Meldrum would have imagined he'd have jumped away from at once. He played accordion in a band when he got the chance, and his big grumble about the job was it meant he didn't get all that many chances. 'Come the day,' he'd say about retirement. 'Roll on the fucking day!'

The result was long journeys could pass pretty well. Shields listened to the music, and Meldrum drove and had no need to share his thoughts.

They rolled into Melrose to something with strings on Classic FM, had lunch in the first pub they came to and rolled out to Liam and Noël, brackish water in the desert. Just after two, it was Runrig, doing one of Mr Anderson's Fine Tunes, and the mist had come down.

'Keep your eye open. The turning can't be that far away,' he told Shields, and as he spoke there it was signposted to the right: Kilbracken. So suddenly looming out of the white haar at them that he'd to stamp on the brake and jerk the wheel to take them across into the side road.

'How accidents happen,' Shields said.

'What?' Meldrum sprayed water on the screen, leaning forward to peer out as the wipers swept back and forward.

'Suppose a car'd been on the other side screaming along without being able to see what was coming. Smack. Straight into us.'

'Your side,' Meldrum said. 'Smack into your side.'

About forty minutes passed. He concentrated on following the lamps into a cave mouth hollowed out of fog. The road narrowed and curved back on itself, seemed to straighten out but only for a while; at last, for all he could tell, swung the car in a circle like a bone on a string. There wasn't any way into the cave.

A house came up on the left, then another.

'Looks like we're there.'

One on the right. And a noticeboard with a church vague behind it. Then nothing.

'Looks like we've missed it.'

'Brigadoon,' Shields said in disgust.

Meldrum slowed to not much more than walking pace. They needed a place to turn.

Edging over a rise, he spotted an opening on his left. He took the car past and started to reverse into it, then stopped. He couldn't see out of the back window.

'I'll guide you,' Shields said. 'Wind down the window, so you can hear me.'

He got out. There was a tap on the roof of the car. Meldrum started to inch back again.

'Hold it!' Shields's face filled the window space. 'It's the drive of a house. And there's somebody coming.'

Meldrum got out as a bulky man in an Arran sweater approached, a stick tucked under his arm.

'I heard the music,' he said.

'Sorry.' Meldrum reached back in through the window and turned off the ignition. Engine and radio fell silent.

'Are you lost?'

'I hope not. We're looking for Kilbracken.'

'Well, you're there. More or less. I'm the last in the village.'

Behind the man Meldrum could now make out the shape of a house, ground and upper floor, square-built and substantial. A thought struck him. 'This wouldn't be Kilbracken House?'

'What do you want there?'

Meldrum squared his shoulders by instinct at the abruptness of the question.

Before he could say anything, Shields said, 'That's police business.'

The man's response was a totally unexpected chuckle. 'Delighted to hear it,' he said. 'Are they expecting you?'

'Yes.'

'Can I ask who you spoke to? Was it Bower himself?'

'He wasn't available. I left a message for him.'

He chuckled again. 'And whoever it was didn't tell you the House is on an island?'

'I get the idea,' Meldrum said, not in the mood for a poor joke. It had been a woman who'd answered the phone. He'd taken it for granted Kilbracken House was in Kilbracken village, and she hadn't contradicted the idea. You can't miss it, she'd said.

'Would it be too much trouble to tell us how we can get to this island?'

He was prepared for the chuckle again; keeping his temper in check, because he wouldn't allow himself the luxury of losing it, despite being chilled by the raw mist and feeling a fool.

'Come into the house out of the cold,' the man said. 'I'll phone and tell them you've finished up here, which is good luck for you. I've a jetty for fishing at the back of the house. They'll send a boat and pick you up from there.'

Meldrum took the car another half-dozen feet back to clear the gate. By the time he walked down to the house, the two were inside, leaving the front door ajar behind them. Coatstand with umbrellas and sticks, polished wood floor, oval mirror, picture of a fishing boat, the hall came at him after the journey in dazzling segments. The sound of a voice led him along a passage. As he came into the kitchen, the man put down the phone. 'Somebody'll be over to collect you.' He glanced at his watch. 'I could run to tea or a coffee, if you want one.'

He bustled round, putting on the kettle, getting out cups. It was another brightly lit space, every surface cleared tidy as a ship's galley, a wood-burning stove on a plinth in the corner. He sat them at a table big enough for a farm kitchen, took one sip from his cup and said, 'Biscuits. Don't say, don't bother.'

'Don't—' Meldrum began, and stopped.

The man got up, laughing, 'Gives me an excuse to have one myself. Living alone, you need a bit of self-discipline. Name's Macdonald, by the way.'

'Meldrum.'

'Bobbie Shields. This is good coffee.'

At the cupboard, he glanced over his shoulder at Meldrum. 'DI?'

'Right.'

'Sergeant,' Shields said, tapping himself on the chest. 'Before you guess constable.'

'No, I'd have got it right,' Macdonald said, settling again at the table.

Meldrum put him in his early fifties, florid, heavily built. At a guess, he'd be a retired major, bowler-hatted out of the army. Major Macdonald, local worthy, local busybody, took an interest, might even be on the area Police Board. Not a type Meldrum cared for much. He prepared to stonewall questions about their business with Kilbracken House.

Shields, however, had been intrigued by the idea of having a jetty at the back of the house. He launched into his own set of questions about what size of loch it was out there, and what kind of fishing it offered. Macdonald answered patiently enough, though his glance kept wandering to Meldrum, who'd eased back in his chair, nodding, looking interested and saying nothing.

The clock chimed the half hour.

'Let's save whoever's come over for you a walk,' Macdonald said.

Outside struck cold again after the warmth of the kitchen. They went down a slope of grass, and where it steepened sharply so that muscles tightened on the backs of their calves came on the narrow landing place. Meldrum's foot slid a little on the watery scum that covered the surface of the planking. Beside him, Macdonald thrust his hands into his jacket pockets and leaned into the mist, cocking his head to listen. Clattering like a sewing machine under a blanket, from somewhere ahead the sound of an engine stitched its way towards them.

'Hello!' Macdonald called. There was no answer. He called again. 'That'll give him a mark to aim at,' he said quietly, and went on with no change of tone, 'Did I mention I was police myself? At the station in Annan for over twenty years. In charge for the last ten. I'd be there yet if my wife hadn't fallen ill.'

A boat slid out of the greyness bearing the shape of a man. The engine note quietened. There was a thump as it hit the landing, and Meldrum felt the boards judder under his feet.

'Take it slow,' the man said. 'Don't rock her.'

Meldrum stepped down after Shields into the boat.

'Their car's here, Mr Chaney,' Macdonald said. 'Don't pass my door when you get back, Inspector.' The boat swung free as he released his grip. 'I'll give you a dram for the road.'

The engine raised its note. The mist streamed past them.

'Can you find your way in this?' Shields sounded uneasy.

'It's better nearer the island,' the boatman said.

If it was going to improve, there was no sign of it yet. The three of them sat in a room with four grey walls.

'Mr Chaney, is it?' Meldrum asked.

'Yes.'

'Keith Chaney?'

'Yes.'

Meldrum left it at that.

'Why?' the boatman asked.

'Later,' Meldrum said. 'I'll let you concentrate on getting us through this.'

'I know where I'm going.'

'Fine . . . You know who we are?'

'Police.'

'Right.'

Now it did seem as if the mist was thinning, if only in patches with swirls still closing round them. Gradually a darkening on the grey curtain ahead solidified into a line of trees. They had arrived at the island.

Out of the boat first, Meldrum watched Chaney as he moored it.. Medium height. Early forties. Wiry body and fast movements, deft and full of nervous energy.

'You know why we're here?'

Chaney paused, his hands still for a moment. He tugged the line and stood up. 'To see Mr Bower.'

'That's funny,' Meldrum said.

'What is?'

'I'd have thought you'd call him Frank.'

Shields swung his arms to keep warm.

'I work for him.' Chaney said, not hiding his contempt for a stupid question. At once, though, he seemed alarmed to hear himself, his glance jumping from one man to the other. Placatingly, he added, 'He's the boss.'

Nervous, Meldrum thought. Does he think we're going to start knocking him about? All right, he's on his own, we're both bigger than him. But we're police, not thugs. So, no hero. What kind of police has he met?

'Still . . . With you being such a friend of his brother.'

'What brother?'

'The one who was killed. Wasn't that the only brother?'

'As far as I know.'

'You weren't at Iain's funeral.'

Shields began stamping up and down, the planks booming under his feet.

'We should get up to the house,' Chaney said. 'The boss doesn't like to be kept waiting.'

'Fine. Lead the way.'

The path up the bank turned almost at once into a track firmed with stones and gravel and wide enough to take a car.

'How many houses are on the island?' Meldrum asked.

'Just the one.'

Meldrum had imagined Frank Bower in a village with neighbours and the Simons as new arrivals living nearby. If the Simons had needed to come out to an island for that welcoming party of theirs, then on the night Iain was killed brother Frank had been doubly sealed off from the world.

'How far is it?' Shields demanded.

'Other side of the wall.'

They'd gone by a hedge and then by three intermingled trees crouched together as if for comfort. Now they were going along beside a wall, eight feet or so of dressed stone with a coping on top; an expensive luxury, as if an island wasn't privacy and protection enough.

When they came to the entrance, the fog was too thick to see far inside, but the gates, high, thick-barred, with wrought-iron detail at the top like a coat of arms, were in keeping with the idea of expensive seclusion. Chaney unlocked a small side gate, and as he relocked it behind them Meldrum was reminded of prisons. Meticulous turnkeys unlocking doors in Saughton, Barlinnie, Peterhead, and leading the way along grey corridors. On either side there was the sound of drops shedding from branches. They came to a flight of stone steps, uneven underfoot as they climbed. At the top, from a pattern of lit windows, hung blurred and glowing in the mist, Meldrum caught a sense of the scale of the house. As they came nearer, given glimpses of a crow-step gable, a corbelled stair turret, he recognised what it had to be. There were houses like it all over Scotland, and not least in the Borders. Nineteenth-century magnates in shipping or steel or tea plantations

memorialising their success in stone, robber barons infatuated with a
vision of castles.

Was Frank Bower rich? Maybe that was why he'd talked so casually of
inheriting from his brother. Living here, it didn't look as if money would
be a motive for murder.

A couple of times Chaney had cleared his throat as if intending to
speak. Now he said, 'I don't understand where you got hold of the idea I
knew Mr Bower's brother.'

'We talked to your wife.'

'But she didn't know.'

Meldrum laughed. After a beat, Shields joined in. The old ones were
the best ones, when they worked.

Realising what he'd admitted, Chaney tried to backtrack. 'What I
mean is—'

'Don't worry about it.'

'I wouldn't want you to misunderstand.'

'Don't worry about it,' Meldrum said again. 'Not now. There'll be
time. We'll talk once we're inside.'

A lamp at the entry guided them. They came into a porch the size of a
bungalow bedroom, and from there into the hall. There were stone flags
on the floor and a staircase going up in a double sweep out of sight.
There was a chandelier, splendid overhead but unlit. A couple of table
lamps emphasised the shadows.

'Not much but it's home,' Shields said. A cliché for every occasion,
often the same one. 'Nobody told us this guy Bower was loaded.'

A chuckling laugh sounded at this. It came from Frank Bower, not
that he'd heard Shields's comment, for the laugh seemed to be directed at
someone out of sight on the landing above him. He came running down
the last flight of stairs. He was in jeans and a light wool sweater, moving
down very lightly for so bulky a man, and looking years younger than he
had in the flat in Edinburgh. Difference of being on home ground,
Meldrum thought; master of all he surveyed.

'Terrible day,' he said, voice booming into space as he crossed the hall
towards them. 'Sorry about the lights. We have our own generator, but
we have to be a bit sensible about electricity.'

'I didn't realise you were on an island,' Meldrum said.

'Didn't you? Must have taken it for granted you did. Sorry about that.
We can use the library.' He nodded at a door on the left and started

towards it. 'Would you like a tray of sandwiches?' And went on without
waiting for a reply, 'Long journey, of course you would, eh? Wouldn't
mind myself. Do the honours, Keith, there's a good chap.'

As Chaney moved off without a word towards the rear of the hall,
Bower opened the door and waved them inside.

The library was a long narrow room with two high windows facing
them as they entered.

'Get a seat close by the fire. You might find it a bit chilly in here, I'm
afraid. We're used to it, of course. I look on it as a price well worth
paying to live in a place like this.'

In a hearth diminished under an ornately massive mantelpiece, a low
fire struggled dimly against the bad afternoon light. As Meldrum took
one of the chairs near the fire, the leather striking cold against his legs,
a quick look round identified a couple of single bookcases on either
side of the door and a chiffonier between the windows, showing four
shelves of books behind its glass doors, as a meagre justification of the
room's title.

'I'm surprised you found us at all,' Bower said, taking up a position
which blocked whatever of the fire's heat struggled to escape into the
room.

'We were lucky enough to find Mr Macdonald's house. Otherwise
we'd have been out of the village altogether.'

'Macdonald . . . yes. We don't have a lot of contact with the village.
We're pretty well self-sufficient. Islanders!' He laughed and nodded as if
the word pleased him.

'We were grateful to him. We might not have got here otherwise.'

'Travelling on a day like this,' Bower said, 'you must have felt it was
important.'

'No fog when we started,' Shields said. 'Raining in Edinburgh, but
nothing like *that*.' He gestured with a thumb.

Turning to the windows, Meldrum saw white pelts purr across the
glass.

Bower asked, 'Have you got any *news* for me?' And when Meldrum,
whom the word had taken slightly by surprise, didn't answer at once, he
went on with a touch of impatience, 'Are you any nearer catching my
brother's killer?'

'We're making progress.'

'I never know what that means when I hear a policeman say it.'

'Just what it says, sir. I want to find your brother's killer. I can't promise I will. No one could. We're doing our best.'

'I accept that. Of course I do.' He sat down. Resting his chin on his hand, he stared into the fire. With a sigh, he said, 'Iain was six years younger than me. As you get older, that age difference doesn't mean so much. But it never disappears. To an extent time stood still, you might say, perhaps because he was away so much. In one way, I realise now, looking back, to me he was always my little brother.'

'You must have been surprised, then, when he retired.'

Bower lifted his head and frowned. 'Why would I have been?'

'He was only fifty-one.'

'He could afford it.'

Meldrum couldn't help glancing around. 'Was money an issue with him?'

Bower said, 'He was good at what he did. He was successful. He saved his money. He wasn't born rich, if that's what you mean.'

'Would you say he enjoyed his work?'

'Of course. Most people do, if they do it well.'

'Yet he took the first chance to retire. I mean as soon as he'd saved enough.'

'I don't know if it was the first chance or the second chance or what chance it was. He'd a fair bit of money. Enough that, I imagine, he could have retired even earlier, if he'd wanted to. Presumably he didn't want to. Maybe he stopped enjoying it, when things started getting difficult in Russia.'

'Russia,' Meldrum said. 'Ah, yes. The Director of Human Resources at CIMD, Jean-Philippe Guichard, explained to me about Russia. Is that the reason your brother gave you?'

'Whether he did or not, what does it matter?' Bower asked. 'I don't see what you're getting at.'

Before Meldrum could respond, there was a knock at the door and Chaney appeared with a trolley. He pushed it over to the group by the fire, poured coffee and offered sandwiches.

He'd been told to leave the trolley and was turning to leave, when Meldrum said, 'I'm going to need to talk to you, Mr Chaney.' In recognition of what seemed to be Chaney's role as servant, he turned to Bower, 'I mean afterwards, of course. After we're finished. Then if there's a room available, my colleague and I could talk to Mr Chaney there. We'll make it as quick as possible, then he could take us back.'

'Chaney? What do you want with him? Let's have some light on the subject!' Stretching, Bower switched on the standard lamp beside his chair. As he sat back, Meldrum saw a line of sweat glisten on his upper lip. 'What do they want with you, Keith?'

'I've no idea.'

'Oh, I think you do,' Meldrum said. He appealed to Shields, 'We've already had a word with Mr Chaney, haven't we?'

It gave him a certain grim amusement that he got only a nod in return. The size of Kilbracken House seemed to have impressed Shields into handling its owner cautiously.

'If you've anything to ask him, do it now,' Bower said. 'No need to wait.'

'I haven't talked to them,' Chaney said. 'They've been talking to me.'

'You could hardly say it was much of a talk,' Meldrum said, as if he was genuinely thinking about it, 'either way. Just a word or two when you were fetching us over to the island.' He spoke so quietly and reasonably, it seemed offhand. It was in the same tone he went on, 'We were asking how well he knew your brother, Mr Bower.'

Bower looked from him to Chaney. The silence stretched. It was Chaney who broke it.

'And I told you, I don't know what you were on about.'

'That's why I'm asking again. Just to get things clear. You're telling me you never met Iain Bower?'

'Of course he did.' Frank Bower's voice rumbled across anything Chaney might have been tempted to offer. 'Don't be a fool, Keith. You brought my brother across to Kilbracken at least once.'

'In the boat, of course. Just the way he did with us today. I suppose you could say,' Meldrum added, smiling, 'he'd met us, but didn't really know us.'

Bower smiled and nodded. 'One way of putting it.'

'So you wouldn't describe your brother and Mr Chaney as friends?'

Bower's smile stayed, but somehow emptied of meaning, then at last it faded and, as the corners of his mouth drooped, so the whole face relaxed into its double chins and took on a look of petulance.

'Friends!' Chaney said, 'I asked them where they got that idea from.'

Frank Bower leaned back and tugged a handkerchief from the slanting front pocket of his jeans. He folded it and wiped his temples and cheeks, refolded it and patted his upper lip dry. During the whole process, he kept his eyes on Meldrum. Finished, he wadded up the handkerchief and pushed it back into his pocket.

'That seems a reasonable question,' he said. 'Who did tell you that?'

'Another friend of your brother's.'

'Is there any reason I shouldn't know? Are you going to tell me it's confidential? Good God, we're talking about my brother!'

'I'm sorry. You're quite right,' Meldrum said. 'It was Neil Heuk.'

If he was hoping for some kind of large reaction, he would have been disappointed. Bower sucked in his lower lip and stared. In Meldrum's experience, some faces were expressive, others weren't. Overall, people hid as much as they gave away. As well, you had to take faces in turn, so that by the time he glanced at Chaney, the first instant of reaction was gone. He could check later on Shields's impressions, for all they'd be worth. It was at times like this he missed Henderson, the detective sergeant Shields had replaced. A smart man. Ambitious. And dead, of course.

'Maybe you've heard your brother speak of Neil Heuk?'

'I know the name. He works for the company my brother was with in Brussels.'

'Well, he did work for them. He left CIMD. He's working in Edinburgh now.'

'I didn't know that,' Bower said; and added, 'But then there's no reason why I should.'

'Neil Heuk!' Chaney said suddenly. 'When you said Brussels, well, I was in Brussels, I met him there. This was a few years ago, well, a couple of years, I don't remember exactly.'

'How did you meet him?' Meldrum asked. 'Do you remember that?'

'I was with Iain.'

'Iain?'

'Iain Bower. I was on holiday in Brussels, and I went to see Iain.'

'Because he was a friend? In that case, I don't understand why you said he wasn't.'

'No problem in that,' Bower rumbled. 'Keith was a friend of my brother, and now he's working for me. Nothing to be embarrassed about, Keith.'

Chaney nodded and looked relieved. 'I'd a bit of business trouble. Mr Bower here was good enough to give me a job.'

'Right,' Meldrum said.

'I didn't see Iain often. Didn't get the chance. Not with him being abroad.'

'But you were friends. So how did you keep in touch? A lot of phone calls?'

'Not a lot.'

'What? New Year? That kind of thing?'

'Yes. And birthdays. He'd give me a ring on my birthday.'

'What about postcards? With all that travelling, I expect he'd send you a card sometimes? From Africa or Russia?'

'I've had a few of those,' Chaney said, brightening up.

'Letters too, eh?'

'Sure.' He paused. 'Not that I'm much of a letter writer.'

'But Iain was?'

'He'd write sometimes.'

'Did you keep his letters?'

'No. I mean, why would I do that?'

'Sometimes people do.'

'Not me.'

'What did he write about?'

'Just stuff. You know.'

'Did he write about his job?'

'Just about being places. Like you said before. Africa and that.'

'Did he tell you why he was retiring?'

'I got a letter saying he was stopping work and coming home.'

'But did he tell you why?'

Chaney shrugged. 'If you've got the money, who needs a reason?'

'What about his friends? Did he write about them?'

'How do you mean?'

'What he did in his spare time. People he knew.'

'I can't think of anybody.'

'Neil Heuk. We know he was a friend. Didn't Iain ever mention him?'

'No.'

'Not even after you'd actually met Heuk, when the three of you went out for a meal and a drink in Brussels?'

'Iain didn't write that often. Next letter I had from him was that one about planning to retire and come back home.'

'What about people at CIMD, where he worked? Jean-Philippe Guichard – did he ever write about him?'

'Never heard of him.'

'Did you see Neil when he was in Edinburgh, after he retired?'

'We had a drink, couple of times. Then Mr Bower offered me a job, and I came down here.'

'Did you visit him in his flat?'

Chaney shook his head. 'He was waiting to get into it. He was pissed off about it not being ready.'

'So this would be while he was still living in the Doune Apartments?'

'Is that what they were called? We met in town. Café Royal. The Dome.'

'Did he say anything about the Doune Apartments?'

'Bit of a dump. I said to him, you could be somewhere better, then, you've got the money. And he said, he never thought the flat would have taken so long, and it was too much bother to move. That was it.'

'Did he mention the name Balewa?'

'Come again?'

'Balewa.'

'What is it? Somewhere in Africa?'

'A husband and wife,' Meldrum said. 'And a little boy.'

Chaney looked back at him blankly. After a moment, Bower said, 'Well, if that's all?'

Meldrum nodded. Chaney wasted no time in heading for the door, but just as he opened it, Meldrum called, 'One other thing!'

He got up and went over to Chaney. He stood close, stooped over him and spoke softly.

'What age are you, Mr Chaney?'

'Eh? Forty-two.'

'I thought you'd be about that. But Iain Bower was fifty-one.'

'So what?'

'Can you tell me where the two of you met?'

'I don't remember.'

'Well, you didn't meet at university. You haven't ever been to university, have you, Mr Chaney?'

'No.'

'No . . . Maybe you met at work. Iain Bower was a scientist, who moved into marketing. Setting up deals in Russia and Africa. What was your own line, Mr Chaney?'

'I'd a garage.'

'Car mechanic to trade?'

'Nothing wrong with that.'

'Absolutely not. So he's a scientist, and you're a car mechanic. And you can't remember where you met. Servicing his car?' Chaney stared back balefully. 'What about school?'

'What about it?'

'Neil Heuk said Iain Bower and you had been friends for a long time. Since they were at school, he said. But now it turns out you were nine years younger than Bower. What about that?'

'Heuk got it wrong,' Chaney said.

He opened the door like a challenge, but then lost his nerve and hesitated. Meldrum let him go.

Coming back to sit down again, he was met by Frank Bower's frown and the sight of Shields intent on the study of his hands where they rested on his knees.

'What was that about?'

'I wondered what age Mr Chaney was.' He paused, but Bower only stared, starting to shake his head. 'He can't remember where he first met your brother.'

'Probably in a pub somewhere. Iain drank too much.'

'Of course,' Meldrum said. 'That makes sense. He'll probably remember something like that, once he has a chance to think about it. If he remembers any other stuff, he should get in touch with us. About when he was in Brussels, or whatever. It's a pity he didn't keep the letters your brother wrote to him.'

'I don't see why.'

'Oh, surely,' Meldrum said mildly. 'I have to know everything I can about your brother, if I'm to find his killer. That goes for his life in Brussels, as well as since he came to live in Edinburgh.'

'Couldn't he have been killed by someone who didn't even know him?'

'Let's hope not. Those are the hardest ones. That's why I said it was a pity about the letters. For one thing, I'd like to've known how well your brother knew Jean-Philippe Guichard. Did he ever talk to you about him?'

'I don't even know who he is.' But before Meldrum could pick him up on that, he said, 'Wait! You said, didn't you? He might have been the one who wrote to me. Offering bloody sympathy, company's and his own, for what either of them were worth.'

'As I said, he was CIMD's Director of Human Resources.'

'So he did his job! He wrote to me. If I can find it, do you want to see his letter? I don't see the point, but I'll look.'

'He's under arrest.'

'What?'

'I've been in touch with the Belgian police. They've charged Guichard with being part of a paedophile ring. Same morning they took Guichard, they made arrests in Brussels and Liège. In Antwerp, they arrested a man as he was getting on a plane at Duerne Airport. He was leaving in a hurry. It occurred to the police that he might have been tipped off.'

'What has this to do with anything?'

'I asked them about your brother.'

Bower sucked his lower lip between his teeth. He'd gone very still. It seemed to Meldrum that was the wrong reaction. From the corner of his eye, he saw Shields had lost interest in his hands and was leaning forward.

With a little wet smack, Bower released his lip. 'About Iain? Extraordinary thing to do.'

'I asked them, if your brother had been in Brussels, if he hadn't left the country, would they have arrested him with the others.'

'And?'

Meldrum shrugged. 'They weren't co-operative.'

When he'd told them Iain Bower was dead, they didn't even pretend interest. They had too many scandals on their plate to concern themselves with a murder in a foreign country.

'What makes you think you can talk to me like this?' That was closer to the response Meldrum had expected, though still Bower asked his question quietly.

'I'm sorry,' Meldrum said. 'I don't want to cause you distress. But it was a legitimate enquiry. If your brother was an active paedophile, that can't not have a bearing on what might have happened to him.'

'But he wasn't. That's the end of it.'

'Not quite, I'm afraid. I believe I have a witness.'

'You *believe?*'

'A witness who'll say he may have been attracted to children.'

'Not possible,' Frank Bower said, but he was thinking. 'Balewa . . . Husband and wife. And a little boy, you said. Is that your witness?'

'I can't tell you that.'

'I have a *right* to know!'

Meldrum shook his head. 'I don't think so. Telling you might hinder the enquiry. I'm sure that isn't what you'd want.'

'I've had enough of this,' Bower said. He stood up. 'I'll get someone to take you back.'

They went out into the hall.

'Wait here,' Bower told them. 'Someone will come for you.'

It was a tone Meldrum didn't care for. Although he made a point of not discussing politics, he believed in authority and hierarchy. Goaded by his left-wing daughter Betty, he might even make a case for squires, lords, estate owners, the whole of that bunch. His head had no problem with any of that; the difficulty came with the reaction in his gut to the reality of being patronised.

As Bower was turning away, Meldrum asked, 'I take it then you wouldn't say your brother was involved in perversion?'

The response was explosive. Bower's neck swelled. His voice boomed into the shadowy corners. 'I would *say* you've abused your position. I would *say* I'll complain to the Chief Constable. I would *say* you should get to hell off the island.'

As he stormed off towards the rear of the house, Shields blew out a long breath. 'You wound his clock for him.'

'Looked like that, didn't it?'

'I thought he was a cool customer. But when he does lose the rag, he goes mental.'

'I wonder if he was as angry as he seemed . . .'

'Long as he remembers to send somebody. I'd hate to get stuck—' Shields broke off. 'We're being watched.'

Meldrum was conscious of him grinning, as he turned to look.

There was a standard lamp set at the left side of the stairway, and a boy was caught in its upcast light. Slightly made, he appeared to be about seven years of age. At a guess, he must have been coming down from the landing, and stopped at the sight of Bower leading them out into the hall. His whole body drooped from where one hand at head height clutched the bannister. He stared and kept still as if even yet he might not be noticed, though he must have known the two of them had seen him.

It seemed to Meldrum he had never seen a child so disconsolate.

There was a murmur of voices from the passage down which Bower had vanished. A door somewhere closed.

'It's all right,' Meldrum said.

He found himself at the foot of the stairs without quite knowing how he had got there. He held out his hand.

A man he recognised appeared on the landing above the child.

'There you are!' he cried, and the boy turned and trudged up to him. His tone was kindly and, as the boy passed on his way back upstairs, he gave him a pat on the shoulder. 'You'd best get back to your room, before they know you're out of it.'

Don Simon came smiling down to them.

'I heard we'd visitors,' he said. 'Does Frank know you're here?'

There was a pause, then it was Shields who said, 'We've spoken to Mr Bower. He's gone to get somebody to take us back in the boat.'

'No need. I'll do it. Give me a minute to tell them we're off.'

'The boy seemed upset,' Meldrum said.

Simon nodded vaguely. 'Be right back. Quick as I can.'

They stepped outside to wait, though Shields came no further than the steps where he stood shivering and rubbing his hands. Meldrum wandered out on to the lawn. He'd felt as if he might suffocate if he stayed inside. He'd had enough of Kilbracken House.

He crossed the lawn and went down the flight of stone steps to the lower garden where the path led back to the gate. Full of his thoughts, he watched his feet imprint the wet grass and go tramping down the uneven steps, worn in the centre and furred with damp moss that made for uncertain footing. At the bottom of the steps, it was very quiet and still, not the faintest breath of a wind to stir leaves. He saw the circular net of a spider strung down between the branch and trunk of a dead tree like a web of skin between a thumb and hand. Then he noticed a line from that web which swooped across to a bush, and the bush was covered in a shawl of webs. Then at last he saw the webs were everywhere, on every bush, on every branch, all around him. He listened to the silence and the mist shone and glittered where it clung in drops to outline each and every thread. It was wonderful and strange, and the strangest thing was that there was no sign of a victim. In search of something trapped, he stepped off the path for a closer look at the web spun on the dead tree.

As he looked through it, he saw Simon come to the top of the steps, and a moment afterwards Shields joining him.

CHAPTER SIXTEEN

H alf-way over the engine cut out, and the boat drifted until Simon unshipped oars and began to pull. He didn't seem at all put out, dealing with the emergency like a matter of routine. It had happened before, he said; Chaney had tried a couple of times to fix it. No wonder his garage went down the tubes, Shields said, and Simon chuckled.

In the stern, where changing places had put him, Meldrum listened to them talking, their voices loud in the stillness. He watched the oars go in and out of the mist, which had settled in coils on the surface.

'What about the boy?' he asked.

'Terry, you mean?'

'The boy on the stairs. He went back up when you called him.'

'He wasn't supposed to be out of his room. He's been wetting his bed, and Frank said the best thing for him was to spend a quiet time before supper.'

'Why would that be? So he could think about it?'

'Frank knows what he's doing. He used to work with children.'

'Where was that?'

'Some kind of children's home.'

Ahead of him, from the waist up Shields and Simon rode above the mist. The water hidden below it smacked and sucked as it met the oars.

'Is Terry your boy?' Somehow he'd got the impression, talking to them in the hotel in Edinburgh, that the Simons were childless.

'Rachel wouldn't mind. He's a nice boy. No, he belongs to the Parkers, Milly and George.'

'Where do you live? Is your house on the island?'

Simon laughed. 'With sixteen bedrooms, Kilbracken House is big enough to hold us all. We're a community.'

'How many of you are there?'

'Eight couples, a dozen children.'

'Mr Bower must like company,' Shields said.

'In that sense, we all do. It's a human need.'

'Still,' Shields persisted, 'it's a lot of people to have in your house.'

'The house isn't Frank's. It belongs to all of us. Frank's the moving spirit, though. It was his advertisement that drew the original group together. And then Rachel and I came along as latecomers. Joining the community was the best thing we ever did.'

He said 'community' with a mixture of relish and reverence. It had been the same when he used it before. The word seemed to have some private significance for him.

'Take the line, will you?'

As Shields scrambled out in response to the instruction, Meldrum started from his thoughts. They'd arrived.

'Will you get back all right?'

'I'm a tough bastard,' Simon said, which certainly appeared to be the case, at least physically. He wasn't even breathing heavily. Yet his reason for coming to the island, according to what he'd said in the hotel in Edinburgh, had been to get away from the violence and dangers of the modern world. No accounting for people and the way their minds worked.

Meldrum nodded, and stepped up on to the jetty.

'Is that it?' Shields asked. At Simon's nod, he dropped the line back into the boat.

As it started to swing out, Simon said, 'Can I ask the same question about your business here? Is that it?'

Meldrum didn't answer, watching the boat drift away.

From a distance, 'I don't suppose we'll see you here again,' Simon called. This time it sounded more like an assertion than a question.

Again getting no answer, he took up the oars.

It would be a long drive back to Edinburgh, and Shields made it plain that in his opinion they shouldn't waste any time in getting started. Meldrum overrode his objections, however, and when Macdonald opened the side door he beamed at the sight of them. The ex-policeman

led them into the kitchen, insisted on making a pot of coffee and had to
be dissuaded from topping up Meldrum's cup with a shot of whisky. He
poured a generous measure into his own, and Meldrum turned a blind
eye as he did the same for Shields, who brightened with the first sip.

'Who brought you back?'

'A man called Don Simon.'

'Simon?' He shook his head at the name. 'Don't know him. But
normally, of course, those people never come near my landing place. If
you'd got proper directions, they'd have collected you at the other end of
the village. They've built their own jetty there – well, fixed up one that
had been let go to rack and ruin. And fenced it off, eight-foot fence, gate
and padlock.'

'Would you say they kept themselves to themselves?'

Macdonald smiled. 'You make them sound like respectable widow
ladies in a suburb somewhere. No, I'd say, if someone like you asked me,
in confidence and off the record – I've no desire to be sued for slander –
I'd say they were some kind of cult.' He gave Meldrum a shrewd
challenging glance. 'What would you say?'

'I wouldn't worry about slander,' Meldrum said. 'There's no law
against cults.'

'As such, eh?'

'How long have they been in Kilbracken House?'

'Just over a year.'

'Is that all?'

'You sound surprised.'

'I am a bit,' Meldrum said. 'I had the impression they'd been there for
longer than that.'

'Not them – they turned up from nowhere. The House had been lying
empty for near on two years. It wasn't a ruin, nothing like that. The Kerr
boys died in Normandy during the war, within a week of one another.
Old Sir John was never the same man after his sons were killed. He died
October the twelfth, nineteen sixty-five. Lady Kerr kept the place up.
She'd a house in London, but she was on the island a fair bit. But when
she died, it went to a second cousin, a doctor in Sussex, so they say. He'd
no interest in the place, so it went on the market. This was three years
ago, and although there were a few had a look, it didn't get a buyer.
Maybe they were asking too much for it. I mean, it's not a shooting
estate, just a fine house on an island of great peace and beauty. The Kerrs

never minded you walking or picnicking there. My father took us over manys the time when we were bairns.'

He lost himself in thought for a moment, then poured a top-up from the bottle into his coffee. Without asking, he did the same with Shields, then, noticing he'd emptied his cup, added some coffee from the pot. 'Then this man Bower turns up. On his own, the first time. He must have liked what they showed him, because he was back with some others within the week. They bought quickly, and for the first month or two the place was busy with workmen and gardeners. They even had three local women in helping with the cleaning. But that changed. Now they do everything for themselves. And they soon let it be known visitors weren't welcome on the island. That didn't go down well. After all, some of us had been back and forward to the island all our lives. Walking on the island was a thing I'd looked forward to when I thought of being retired. There were a couple of unpleasant confrontations. And after that the locals gave them a wide berth. They're not popular.'

'You should have stood up for your rights,' Shields said, drinking the last of his coffee. By Meldrum's reckoning, his second cup must have been half whisky.

'What rights? You've no rights against a landlord in this country.' Macdonald had a watery eye. It occurred to Meldrum that he might have had a few coffees on his own that afternoon. 'But I keep a watch on them. I've been to and fro to Edinburgh, tracing the sale, trying to find out as much as I could. Register House first, checked the Sasines, found the disposition. If they'd made themselves a limited company, I could have tried Companies House and maybe found out more.'

'According to Simon,' Meldrum said, 'they're a community. They bought it together.'

'That could be. Although I'd dearly like to know how much of his own money Bower put into the pot. But what I wanted to find out was what you might call the articles of association. What each of them put in, what rights that gave them, what would happen if one of them wanted to leave. It's not so easy leaving a cult. Moonies. Scientologists, I've done a lot of reading on this cult business. It's a fascinating phenomenon.'

'But that's youngsters. Baldie haircuts and orange robes,' Shields said. 'Harry harry cash an' carry,' he chanted. 'That stuff. The Simons are grown-ups.'

'That tells me you know nothing about it, Sergeant.' Macdonald paused before the last word and laid a little stress on the rank. Before he could say anything else, a bell sounded from the direction of the front hall. He excused himself and went out.

'Cults! He's got a bee in his bonnet,' Shields said, 'but he makes a damn good coffee.'

But Meldrum was listening puzzled to an echoing salvo of raised voices. One of them soared shockingly into a yell of what sounded like fright. As Meldrum ran into the hall, Macdonald swung from the open door to face him.

'That was Detective Inspector Meldrum! Come in and meet yourself, I told him, you're in the kitchen.'

Meldrum went past him at a run.

He reached the gate in time to see red rearlights receding. The mist was still thick, but he saw enough of the shape to be sure it was a taxi. Turning back, he saw a figure trudging towards him, stick tucked under one arm.

'One of you's a liar!' Macdonald shouted as he came.

BOOK FOUR

Maximum Jeopardy

CHAPTER SEVENTEEN

O ne moment the pushchair was there and the next it wasn't.
Carole had never much cared for pushchairs. For Betty, when
she'd been a baby, Carole had bought a Churchill pram and Jim had
taken turns with her to roll it along. A big pram wouldn't fold up in the
boot of a car, of course, and so they'd pretty much been replaced by these
light collapsible chairs. Bother was, they were harder to push, you got
tired, where with the big pram you could roll it along for ever. Worst of
all, a baby in one of them never looked quite comfortable, either with its
head lolling or somehow squashed up, poor thing.

God, where was the pushchair?

Betty and she had arranged to meet in the upstairs eating area at twelve
o'clock. The idea had been to do some shopping together and then make
their separate ways back to town. Assuming that I can eat, Betty had said,
depends what the dentist does.

It was quarter to twelve. Almost ten to. Betty was good about time,
she didn't often turn up late. She might already be upstairs there waiting.

Oh, God, she'd lost Baby Sandy.

She didn't believe it. It wasn't possible. It couldn't be happening. She
was a third of the way down James Thin's Bookshop. She still had the
book in her hand that she'd taken off a shelf to glance at. Just a glance
and her eye had been caught by a paragraph and she'd read it attentively,
remarking on how they got it wrong, all these experts on education and
the early years. And the pushchair had been by her side, she could feel it
with her foot, the wheel, but when she looked up it was gone.

Baby Sandy was gone.

The Gyle shopping complex was always crowded. Through the shop entrance, she could see people going by in the mall. She started to go out, then turned and checked the whole shop all the way to the back and it was no use. At the counter by the shop entrance, there were two assistants, a pretty girl slipping a book into a bag and a young man who was looking up something on the computer, have you seen a baby in a pushchair? she asked, not waiting till they were finished dealing with their customers, just asking them, they stared, of course they'd seen pushchairs there were children and mothers everywhere, she could see they couldn't help her, she had no time to waste with them. She stood in the mall looking right and left. She went all the way to the entrance beside Safeway and then she turned and came back. She wanted to shout and call out but he was only a baby how could he answer her?

Where are you, Sandy?

She found herself outside James Thin's and actually went inside again and the girl at the counter looked at her and seemed as if she wanted to help but plainly didn't have any idea what it was about and there wasn't any time to waste. She remembered there were public telephones outside the lavatories, and she hurried past the fountain and the ice-cream parlour and went in and, thank God, there wasn't anyone at the phones and she dialled the number, from memory she'd used it so often in her life with Jim, and when the voice answered, she asked, Could I speak to Detective Inspector James Meldrum, please?

Oh, Jim, help me, I've lost baby Sandy.

But he wasn't there. Would you tell him his wife called and it's very important, she said, and she'd hung up before she remembered she wasn't his wife, not any more. She came out and went the other way and she didn't run she walked quickly and perhaps she was talking to herself for people were staring at her as they went by or glancing or pretending not to look, no one wanted to be embarrassed. She went right to the end and then through Marks and Spencer's and then outside and she was faced by a sea of cars in the car park and if it was some mad woman who had *stolen her grandchild stolen Jim's grandson stolen Betty's child how could she face Betty, face Betty and Sandy and say I lost your baby* and if it was a mad woman then she might be in one of those cars and Baby Sandy on the seat beside her *would the woman have a car seat would she know about strapping him in he's only a baby* and she would drive off and be gone. The air was cold and Carole fought her panic and knew she should go inside and find someone from security.

She was half-way down a line of cars and had no idea of how she had got there. In the other lane of parked vehicles, a man was walking towards the storefront. She didn't notice him so much as realise suddenly that he was watching her. And then from the way he was moving she realised he was pushing something ahead of him. She went between a car and a van and he was only a few yards away. The pushchair was in front of him and she could see the colour of the baby's hood and it was light blue and that was right and the chair looked right though didn't they all look the same? And she had to go up in front of it before she saw and, yes, it was Baby Sandy. *Hail Mary, Jesus Mary and Joseph –*

'Is this your child? The pram was sitting in the slot beside where I pulled in. Christ, woman, anything could have happened!'

And he was so angry that she apologised, not caring about anything but that Sandy was safe. She crouched down and held him with her arms so tight round him he began to complain.

By the time she looked up the man was quite far away, though oddly enough now he was walking away from the shops instead of towards them.

CHAPTER EIGHTEEN

'I didn't feel you were taking me seriously,' Neil Heuk said.
'About what?'

'Nobody likes to be laughed at.'

Meldrum didn't feel there was any answer to that. One part of his mind was still wondering why Carole had phoned him. Very important, the message slip had said. Timed at 12.06. It was almost half past one now. But he'd had no chance to call her, because Heuk had been in the station when he got back, waiting of his own volition though even honest men had a tendency to avoid police stations, waiting patiently, it seemed, for twenty minutes or so. He didn't know what to make of Heuk.

Being pursued by a witness in a murder case was a new experience for him.

'I don't suppose you've even bothered to go and see Keith Chaney,' Heuk said.

'We tried the address you gave us, and spoke to his wife. But he's not staying there.'

'He's left her?'

'She didn't say that.'

'Well, did she know where he is?'

'Have you heard of Kilbracken House?'

'He's working for Frank Bower, then,' Heuk said. 'Poor little bugger. I wish I could say I was surprised.'

'Would you like to explain that?'

Heuk smoothed his moustache. What's he smiling about? Meldrum wondered. Like the cat that swallowed the canary.

'Keith Chaney's been Frank Bower's slave since he was ten years old.'

'What the hell does that mean?'

But even as he spoke something inside Meldrum chilled and saddened, like a cloud shadow blotting out the sun across summer fields. It was a premonition of a thing he didn't want to hear, or live with, a place he didn't want to go. Unreasonably, he felt an instinctive anger and aversion against Heuk. Calm down, he told himself, don't shoot the messenger.

He knew, before anything else was said, Heuk was a messenger.

'It means the Naylor Home,' Heuk said. 'N-a-y-l-o-r. Not nailer as in carpentry.' He smiled and laid his hands palm up on the desk. 'Would you like to see my stigmata?' There wasn't anything to see. Just a pair of hands. He'd a piece of sticking plaster on one of his thumbs where he must have cut himself. 'I'm sorry. That's a private joke. Don't be impatient with me. Frank Bower was one of the staff at the Naylor Home, not one of the most senior – he was only twenty-six. But when I arrived there as an eleven-year-old, Frank ran the place. You've met him. You must know what I mean. That extraordinary force in him. You felt it?'

'Didn't feel a thing. He seemed ordinary enough to me.'

Heuk looked genuinely puzzled. 'Do you really mean that?'

Meldrum nodded. 'I'm a lot taller than he is. I'm not looking up at him from the angle of a ten-year-old.'

'It's not a physical thing,' Heuk said. He sounded offended, almost petulant. What angle do you see him from now? Meldrum wondered.

'Chaney would be about the same age as you?' he asked.

'A few months younger.'

'Then what does this have to do with Iain Bower? You told me Chaney and him were friends at school. That doesn't make sense. Iain Bower must have been what – nineteen or twenty? – at the time you're talking about.'

'Did I say friends? I didn't say friends, did I? They *knew* one another.' He had a smile like a wound. 'More or less in the biblical sense.'

'I don't know what you mean.'

'Oh, yes, you do. That's what the Naylor was about. That's what happened there. And Frank Bower was at the centre of it. Maybe if he hadn't been there, it wouldn't have been like that. Maybe before he was there, it wasn't like that. Who knows whether you need Satan to have Hell, or whether the damned could arrange their own misery? That first

summer I was there, Iain Bower appeared. He was on vacation before
going into his third year at university. I'd never heard the word
"vacation" before. It made a terrific impression on me. It came from
a different world, one I couldn't imagine ever getting into. Funny the
things you remember. Oh, and you're right, he was twenty that year. He'd
his birthday while he was with us. Frank gave him Chaney as a present.'

Christ! Meldrum said to himself. He didn't want to listen to any
more. He didn't want to hear this. He didn't know why it was hitting
him so hard. He was a professional, he'd seen a lot of things, he'd
listened to a lot of things.

He didn't want to hear this.

'Go on,' he said, quietly. 'I'm listening.'

'There isn't much more to tell. I was at the Naylor till I was nearly
fourteen. Two years, give or take a bit. I'll tell you a funny thing. For a
long time I believed I'd been in that place for most of my childhood. I
know that sounds stupid, but I didn't think about it, it was just
something I felt while trying *not* to think about it. Till one night –
that was a birthday too, I was thirty – I was getting drunk on my own
and for some reason I worked it out – two years, give or take a bit. And I
couldn't believe it. Sleep in the same bed half your life with someone,
they say, and at the end you'll still be sleeping with a stranger. But it's
worse than that. Inside here,' he laid fingertips against his forehead,
'you're sharing with a stranger. Not a stranger you'll ever get away from –
not in this life. Don't you feel that?'

'Have you told anyone else about what you claimed happened in the
Naylor Home?'

'Oh, that's practical,' Heuk said. He sounded pleased.

'Have you ever gone to the police?'

'I haven't, and I doubt if anyone else has. And if anyone did, it
wouldn't come to anything. When I went to work for CIMD in Brussels
and found Iain Bower there, it was a shock for both of us. He didn't want
to talk about Frank, but I persuaded him.' From his wallet, he took out a
folded paper and laid it on the desk in front of Meldrum. 'I showed him
this. Frank Bower, leaving the Naylor Home. Nice picture, eh? He's
thirty-nine then – it says so in the article. They print all the speeches
about what a gap he'll leave, how much he'll be missed. Typical local
paper, they list as many names as they can find room for – three
councillors, two ministers and the local bishop among the guests. Oh,

and Chief Superintendent Hill and the chap who owned the local knitwear firm. Flowers for the wife, and a state of the art camera for him bought with his presentation money. He was always keen on taking photographs.'

'Where was he going?'

'Pastures new. Read it for yourself, keep it, I've got a copy. Going into a business opportunity. In London! Streets paved with gold, or would be for Frank who had so much energy and talent. Lucky he hadn't struck out on his own earlier – "only his devotion to children could have kept him with us for so long".' Heuk laughed silently, mouth a little open like a panting dog. 'I hope nobody ever went to the police. Frank had good friends everywhere.'

'Who else have you kept in touch with from the Naylor Home?'

He looked startled. 'For Christ's sake, class reunions? Have you understood what I've been telling you?'

'Well, you met Iain Bower again.'

'By accident. I didn't go looking for him!'

'Do you recognise the name David Slater?'

'No.'

Stupid question, Meldrum thought. At thirty-five, Slater, the fake policeman, was too young to have been a schoolmate for Heuk. You had to be careful about that policeman's impulse to tidy up the loose ends. There were plenty of bad homes in the world: you didn't have to have been at the Naylor to be a little crazy.

'When I looked up Iain Bower's funeral in *The Scotsman*,' Heuk said, 'I was surprised to see Paddy Turnbull's name. You know, the minister.'

'Why?'

'He was at the Naylor. When I saw he'd become a minister, I thought, that's another solution.'

'Solution? For what?'

'All that guilt.'

'What did Turnbull have to be guilty about?'

He heard his voice, too sudden, too abrupt, too harsh.

'You should ask him. That summer Iain Bower worked at the Naylor, Paddy Turnbull was fifteen. One of the big boys.'

Meldrum controlled his irritation. Don't shoot the messenger.

'Let me ask you about somebody else,' Meldrum said quietly. 'There was an incident at the funeral.'

Heuk smiled. 'The man who peed into the grave. "Relieved himself",
my newspaper called it. Pissing or shitting, I wondered when I read it.
That's the bother with euphemisms. But I suppose there wouldn't have
been time. I mean, if he'd dropped his trousers for a shit, you might have
caught him.'

Being needled calmed Meldrum. For Heuk, it struck him as refresh-
ingly normal behaviour.

'Just peed. The man who did it was unmistakable. I'd guess he was
about six foot eight. And built in proportion. You know anyone like
that?'

'I have a limited acquaintance. It doesn't run to basketball players or
circus freaks. Someone like that must be hard to hide. I'm surprised you
haven't found him already.'

'We're looking. He must have hated Iain Bower to do a thing like that.
That amount of hate probably goes back a long way. What do you
think?'

'No idea.'

'What about as far back as schooldays?'

'I think people mature as they get older. They get things into
perspective. They get over them.'

'Even the worst things?'

'Most people, yes, I think so.'

'Have you ever heard of a Richard Nicolson?'

'No. Is that the name of the freak?'

'The name he used in a B and B. You don't know or remember anyone
to fit his description?'

'That's what I said.'

'Fine.'

Meldrum sat back and let Heuk watch him thinking about it all.

'You've given me a good hearing,' Heuk said. 'I'm grateful. I won't
take up any more of your time.'

'How well would you say Iain Bower knew Jean-Philippe Guichard?'

'Oh . . . What an odd question. They worked together.'

'You wouldn't say they were close?'

'No. They'd both worked for CIMD for a long time, of course.'

'They weren't friends?'

'Absolutely not.'

'You and Iain were friends. But neither of you were friends with Guichard. The three of you weren't friends.'

'I've said so. I can't think of any other way to say it. What's this about?'

'Are you still in touch with people in Brussels?'

'I've no reason to be.'

'You should. Ask about Guichard. Then we'll have another talk.'

Heuk shrugged. 'I'll look forward to it,' he said, and got up.

Meldrum walked him out of his office along the corridor. He saw Heuk's head turn to look through the glass into the room with pictures of Iain Bower and the murder bedroom on the back wall.

As they waited for the lift, Meldrum asked, 'Do you want to bring a charge against Frank Bower?'

'What?'

'There isn't any time limit. Some recent cases of child abuse have gone back as far.'

'I won't bring any charges,' Heuk said. 'In fact, if you question me about the Naylor in front of anyone else, I won't know what you're talking about. That's a promise.'

CHAPTER NINETEEN

'It's worth trying,' he'd said in the morning. 'Give them some fresh air.'

'Could we not do it over the phone?' Shields had asked.

But petrol stations weren't fitted with fax facilities. You couldn't show a picture to staff over the phone; and so two teams of detective constables had been sent out to cover the fastest route from Kilbracken to Edinburgh, checking the records everywhere Frank Bower might have bought petrol on the night of his brother's murder.

Then there had been case meetings that had gone on too long. Chief Constable Baird believed in accountability, which was useful in second-guessing newspapers and politicians, but had its drawbacks if you were trying to catch a killer.

There had been one thing and another, including what should have been a court appearance. That had been cancelled because a witness hadn't appeared, but only after another hour had gone to waste. Plenty of excuse for a liquid lunch; then he'd got back to find Heuk waiting. Once that odd interview was over, it was almost three o'clock by the time he got together with Shields for an update.

'Oh, and one other thing,' Shields said. 'The uniforms that went to Slater's flat, they banged his door a few times but didn't get an answer. That would be about ten o'clock. Tried again about twelve. Same thing. He could be in and not answering.'

'What response did you get from the hospital about him?'

'I got a Dr Gunn. He says, We've adjusted his medication. I say, Why'd you not keep hold of him? There's a shortage of beds, he said.'

Meldrum growled in disgust. 'So what am I supposed to do? Spend the rest of my life getting told, fuck off, Inspector Meldrum's already been, thank you very much?'

'There's more,' Shields said. Now it struck Meldrum he was looking pleased with himself. 'Dr Gunn tells me Slater's got a sister. Apparently, she does her best to help him. And guess what the sister's husband does?'

'Impersonations of Baird?'

Shields's smile brushed the joke aside. 'Taxi driver! Name of Archie Kerr.'

'Why do I recognise that name? Wait a minute. The guy that took Richard Nicolson away from Bower's funeral? After he pissed in the grave? With me chasing the taxi and yelling? That one?'

'That one.'

'Well, well. Small world. We've got an address for him, haven't we?'

'No answer from the house, but I phoned round the taxi firms. Third call did it.' Call me Sherlock.

'We should talk to this clown.'

'I'll get him fetched in.'

'Better idea. Find out if Kerr has keys for his brother-in-law's flat. If the sister's been keeping an eye on her brother, chances are he might have.' He checked his watch. 'If he has keys, meet us outside Slater's close at four. If he hasn't, get his arse in here. Either way, let us know.'

Punctuality wasn't a police virtue. It was almost twenty past by the time they got to Tollcross. As they pulled up behind the taxi, the driver got out.

Kerr, jockey-sized, bow-legged, wearing a tartan beret half a size too large for him, wasn't happy. Crowding Meldrum getting out of the car, he cried, 'See that! That's a double yellow line. I could get a ticket. I can't afford to get a ticket.'

'Do you have a key for the flat?'

'I've *got* the key, but I'm saying—'

'Come on then.'

As they went up the stairs, Meldrum said without looking round, 'You're a stupid man, mister. You've told us lies. Don't make things worse for yourself.'

The grumbling behind him stopped.

Second landing, Kerr had said. As Meldrum stepped on to it, he was met by an open door. At first he thought there was no one there, then a sliver of white face showed round the jamb. As he watched, the door swung almost shut. Through the remaining crack, a woman's voice whispered, 'Are you the police?'

'Yes.'

'Where's your uniform?'

From the other end of the landing, Kerr said, 'Come on then, here's Davie's place. Over here.'

Ignoring him, Meldrum asked the woman, 'What is it? Did you send for the police?'

'One of the neighbours, maybe she'll have phoned. She'll have heard the noise he was making. He's smashed the house up.'

'Your man? Where is he now?'

Kerr said, 'Can we get on with it, please?'

'Shut your face,' Meldrum told him.

The woman whispered, 'He's fell asleep in the chair. He might be quieter when he wakes up. Sometimes he's worse.' As she spoke, the whole of her face came gradually into view. One eye was bruised shut.

'Sort it out,' Meldrum told Shields.

'What about?' And Shields nodded at Kerr, scowling at the end of the landing.

'I'll go in with him, have a look. Slater won't give any trouble.'

'Probably hiding under the bed.' Grinning at his own wit, Shields turned to the woman. 'In you go, love. I'll have a wee word with Mike Tyson.'

Kerr had the key in his hand. Meldrum stopped him from using it, and pressed the bell. If Slater was in the flat, there was no point in frightening him. Listening, he couldn't hear it ringing inside. He kept his finger on the button, and with his other hand rattled the letter box and then knocked.

Heels rang on the stone landing behind them. Shields asked, 'Is he there?'

'Doesn't seem to be.'

'Can you come next door?'

'You having trouble?'

'With that piece of shit? He's just piss and wind. But there's something you should hear. About Slater.'

'There's no harm in Davie Slater,' Kerr said. 'Blood's thicker than water, ken? Peg believes everything he tells her.'

'Any chance he could be with your wife?'

'No! At least . . . not before I left this morning. But more than likely he'll run to his big sister. That's Davie, that's what he'd do. Christ, that's exactly where he'll be.' Kerr sighed. 'I've been a right bloody fool.'

'If that drunk bastard along there gets his door shut,' Shields said, 'you'll have to kick it open.'

'Right, right,' Meldrum said. 'I'll talk to him. You keep an eye on this one.'

'Take a look inside, will I?'

'No, wait for me. I'll only be a minute.'

It didn't matter how often he went into this kind of set-up, Meldrum's heart sank. A policeman, if he didn't start out indifferent, should develop a hard skin. Some people could pick up hot plates and never feel it. Or you could develop calluses that protected you. But to keep on picking up plates and getting burned, that didn't make any sense. Not unless you wanted to be a chef badly enough.

The lobby smelled of poverty and defeat. The front room with the man sitting on the floor against the wall (had Shields kicked the chair from under him as he slept?) and the woman standing in the farthest corner with hand on hand folded over her mouth smelled of fear. The wallpaper had marks like bruises from thrown pots and cups. Violence sparkled like rats' eyes in the shards of broken glass.

In one long whine, the man on the floor offered, 'He's a poof. I'm not daft, tell his kind a mile off, I hate them. And now he's got some cunt of a bum boy living with him. You are here about him, aren't you? Your mate says that's what you're here for.' He scowled up malevolently. 'Or was it that bitch in the corner sent for you?'

'We're here about Mr Slater. Nothing else,' Meldrum said. 'How do you know somebody's living with him?'

The man struggled up from the floor. Encouraged by Meldrum's quiet tone, he spoke more assertively, 'Because I've got eyes in my head. He's there all right.'

'He's not there now.'

Swaying, the man mustered a sneer. 'As well for you. Fucking *enormous* monster. Rip your head right off.'

Meldrum spun on his heel.

'Get it open!' he called as he came on to the landing.

He pushed Kerr aside and went in followed by Shields. Two doors, one to a bedroom, the other would be to the kitchen. The flat had that indefinable air of being empty. The door to the left was partly open and he shoved it wide and stepped into a cramped space taken up by a narrow bed heaped with a mound of dirty blankets. Out of the window he could see the top of a tree, growing in the open yard between the tenement blocks.

In the lobby, Kerr called, 'Davie?' His voice was tentative and without conviction.

As Meldrum turned to go out, his shoulder brushed a pinboard hung on the wall where it would face someone lying on the bed. He steadied it with a hand and saw that it was covered in newspaper clippings. He recognised the headlines, saw his own face; old crimes, investigated by him.

Kerr's voice came again, sharp and high. 'What's that smell?'

Hands pressed to his face, the little man had beaten a retreat to the outside landing.

As he went through the door that had been opened into the kitchen, Meldrum gagged on the smell, like nothing else in the world, unmistakable. There was a two-seater couch and an easy chair; a window giving a view of the same tree. The only odd feature of the room was a camp bed, set up under the window. Beside it a bundle of blankets lay tangled like the shape of a man. Meldrum was crossing to look when the sound of a dry spitting made him turn.

Shields was standing in the recessed area tucked into the back of the room to take a cooker and a sink. He had found David Slater. The shoulders of the corpse pressed against a cupboard kept it from sliding all the way to the ground. Sprawled naked like a doll thrown in a tantrum into a corner, there wasn't any doubt about Slater being dead. Even from across the room, Meldrum could see by the way the head rested flat on the shoulder that his neck had to be broken.

Routine took over from shock.

In the middle of it, he was pleased to see Cowan. It was always better when a forensic scientist could examine the crime scene at first hand. His presence, too, helped in getting physical evidence with the least possible loss or damage from the process of gathering it, not always easy with scene of crime officers working round one another in small rooms and cramped spaces. After the police surgeon finished, Slater's body was straightened out and under the kitchen bulb had a strange, poignant, last brief integrity before it was bagged to be sent to the knife and saw.

When at last Meldrum emerged from Slater's flat, the closed middle door on the landing reminded him of the wretched woman inside. He hesitated at the door, but there was no sound from the flat. She was still in his mind as he came out of the close, guarded by a young constable, to be confronted by a couple of journalists and a photographer. Not an impressive media presence, but infinitely more than would have gathered to mark the day the woman with the bruised face had spent.

An everyday wickedness, there was no glamour in her tragedy.

CHAPTER TWENTY

'Y ou should be more careful.' Meldrum said. He'd been watching and the curtain hadn't stirred.

Carole had opened the door without checking from the window which gave her a view of who was ringing the bell. Though they'd been divorced for years, he couldn't get out of the habit of trying to look after her.

'You're too careful,' she said. 'I wouldn't like to live in your world.'

It was almost midnight, and she was in her dressing gown. He followed her through into the kitchen. Seated at the table, he fished the piece of paper from a pocket and held it out.

'Very important, it says.'

It was the message she had left for him at lunchtime.

'I was in bed,' she said.

'Sorry.'

'It's all right. Want a coffee?'

'You couldn't run to a sandwich as well? I'm starving, haven't eaten apart from a pie and a pint at lunchtime.'

'Can't imagine why you don't have an ulcer.'

He watched as she started to slice bread. 'I was on my way home, got stopped at the lights. I thought about something I should do tomorrow, so I looked for a bit of paper to take a note and found your message. I'd forgotten all about it. Sorry.' He sighed. 'It's been a hell of a day.'

'My mistake. I should have asked them to tell you it was a matter of life or death.'

His heart jumped. 'Was it?'

'No, of course not.'

'So what was it?'

She took some cold ham and tomatoes out of the fridge and made sandwiches. Finished, she said, 'Eat these first. It was nothing to worry about.'

'Sure?' he asked with his mouth full.

'Honestly. You must have had a busy day?'

He told her about it, the bad day, all the way through finding Slater to getting Archie Kerr's story.

Kerr had told how on the day of Iain Bower's funeral he'd been waiting outside the cemetery for Slater.

– I took him places when he asked me, as a favour for the wife's sake, call me stupid! You watch your funeral and come back, I'll be here, I told him. So I was looking at the paper when the taxi door opens and this big guy – seriously *big* – gets in the back and tells me to take him into the cemetery. You know the rest of what happened. And David was mad that I'd just gone off and left him – so I told him about the guy and that I'd dropped him near the Bruntsfield, just the same as I told you. But, I swear to God, I didn't know that he'd hidden him at his place. I don't even know how he found him.

'Same way we did, I imagine,' Meldrum told Carole, when he'd got to this point in the story.

'Poor man,' Carole said. 'He can't have been all that bad at playing detective after all.'

– And, when he asked me, Kerr had said, I drove him around – to the Doune Apartments, to that minister's church, down to Kilbracken – but I didn't know what it was for. I took him because he was wrong in the head. I took him because I felt sorry for him. I took him because Peg worried about him all the time.

'He took him,' Meldrum told Carole, 'because he was getting double and triple fare.'

'Did he tell you that?'

'Eventually. And since Slater was on the social, we can only assume the money was coming from this Richard Nicolson.'

'Is that his real name?'

'That's how he signed the register in the boarding house in View-forth.'

'Should someone like that not be easy to find?'

'In theory. We'll do everything we did before. And this time he won't have Slater hiding him.'

'Poor Mr Slater. He must have wanted to be a policeman very badly.'

'You can see why he was sectioned.'

'That's not funny.'

'No,' he said slowly, 'it's not. I'll tell you something I wouldn't tell anyone else. After the doctor had finished, I turned round and saw Slater lying there on the floor. I should be used to that stuff, seen it often enough. Not a stitch to cover him, ready to be taken away. I felt so sorry for him I could have started crying. Can you imagine how that would have gone down?'

'There's no shame in getting counselling.'

'They'd say I was cracking up.'

'Your generation's too macho for its own good.'

'I can imagine what they'd say. Wouldn't give them the excuse.' As she shook her head at him, he added, 'Just because you're paranoid, doesn't mean they're not out to get you.'

'All the same. Maybe you can see one horror too many. The effect of these things must be cumulative.'

'Like a boxer getting punched to the head.'

He'd meant that as a joke, but she didn't laugh.

Before she could say anything else, he went on, 'As far as we can work it out, Slater was just trailing around after me when he went to Iain Bower's funeral service and then on to the cemetery.' He kept it determinedly matter of fact. 'Part of this fantasy he had about being a policeman. He'd read about Bower in the paper – according to Kerr he'd get hold of a murder and go on and on about it. It was his bad luck that he decided to play detectives with Richard Nicolson. As for Kerr, the taxi driver, he's in trouble – so all he can do is keep saying anything he did was for his wife's sake, because she was so concerned about her brother.'

'Why shouldn't that be true?'

Because Kerr wouldn't risk lying to the police just for his wife's sake, Meldrum wanted to tell her. He didn't, though, since he had a feeling that might be one of those things men and women tended to view from different angles. Who says an old dog couldn't learn new tricks?

Instead he said, 'It might be part of it. But if Nicolson had a lot of cash, Kerr might have been getting paid off.'

'I can see money would be a more likely explanation,' Carole said, with a look he'd seen before, the one that suggested she'd just read his mind. 'Let's hope his wife believes his version.'

He drank his coffee, and wondered about asking for another sandwich. It was almost one o'clock. 'My God,' he said, 'look at the time. You've got your work to go to in the morning.'

'My fault. I shouldn't have phoned you. The honest truth is, I panicked.'

'Panicked?' The word startled him. She wasn't someone who panicked.' 'What happened?'

'I warn you, I didn't tell Betty. I got through lunch somehow, but she knew something was wrong. I told her I had a headache. And when I got home I did wonder about reporting it, but it was too late, and anyway what possible good could it do? Some poor woman. That's all it could have been. I don't want to think about it.' She spoke calmly, but too quickly. Half-way through she began to weep. 'I'm sorry,' she said, brushing at her tears, 'this isn't like me. It's just that when it happened, I felt so responsible. I didn't know how I could tell Betty or Sandy or you.'

Now, as she began to shake with sobs, he got up and knelt by her chair, putting his arms round her.

'Tell me what?'

When she had finished, he hardly knew where to begin to comfort her. She had been unfortunate that her path had crossed with some childless soul, and fortunate that some accident or other had interrupted the theft. He paid hardly any attention to her account of the man who had come up between the lines of cars bringing their grandson back to them, and none to the oddity that having claimed to have just arrived he had walked away from the shops rather than towards them.

'Don't cry,' he said. 'I'm sorry I took all day before I came. I'm ashamed that I took so long to ask, when you'd said it was important. I don't know why you ever put up with me.'

She smiled at him through her tears and said, 'We got used to one another when we were young.'

He was down on one knee holding her round the shoulders, and suddenly her thigh made him conscious of an erection, the length of an erection, pressed against that warmth of flesh. He became absolutely still. Everything in him focussed on that place.

After an endless time, she said, 'I went with John Brennan's poor little mouse of a wife to see the lawyer.' He let out a breath he hadn't realised he was holding. She hadn't moved her leg away. Had she realised? How could she not have felt the shape of his prick? He eased back. Weren't things complicated enough between them, as it was? 'Get up. You'll give yourself a sore back kneeling there. I'm fine now.'

He sat up again on the chair at the kitchen table. He took a sip at his coffee. It had gone cold.

Carole said, 'There didn't seem to be anyone else she could ask, or perhaps she was too ashamed. It's not as if I'm a friend or anything. Of course, she'd come and talked to me about the divorce. But that was only to let me know so the class teacher could keep an eye on the child. Even in a Catholic school, that happens all the time. For a headteacher now, marriages breaking up goes with the job.'

'It's not part of the job to go to a lawyer with her.'

'Just as well I did. He was a disaster. Here she's married for years to the great John Brennan. And when he tells her she needs a lawyer, she's so bewildered she picks one out of the Yellow Pages. A little man stumbling on an orthopaedic shoe, full of his own importance, but in a mix of excitement and panic when he learned she was John Brennan's wife.'

'I wish you wouldn't get involved.'

'Why?'

It wasn't easy to put into words. Harriet Cook and he had been lovers, and now John Brennan wanted to divorce his wife and marry Harriet. If Carole helped the wife, would it look as if he was jealous and trying to prevent Harriet getting married to Brennan? If he said that to Carole, she'd laugh and ask who'd imagine anyway that she'd do whatever he told her. And then she might quietly ask, how jealous was he?

Some things were best not put into words.

'You're too generous with your time,' he said. 'Don't overdo it.'

'Don't worry. I went with her to see this creature, and then worried all night over what I should do. I needn't have worried. She went home to find a letter from Brennan waiting for her. He wanted to know if she'd picked an idiot deliberately to embarrass him – so he's found her a better lawyer.'

'That's John. He's all heart.'

'He's a monster.'

'I'll tell him you said that.'

'When will you see him?' Carole asked.

Tomorrow night, he could have said, but didn't. The invitation to
dinner had arrived out of the blue. The difficulty was that it was being
held at Harriet Cook's.

He shook his head vaguely, yawned and got to his feet. 'Time to go.'

'You can sleep here if you like.'

'Thanks, but I've stuff I'll need for the morning.'

He took it for granted she'd meant the bed in her spare room.

CHAPTER TWENTY-ONE

C owan held up the tumbler 'Beautiful set on this, for example. Since we took Slater's prints, we assume these ones come from his murderer.'

'Richard Nicolson,' Shields said.

'They're all over the flat. But, of course, since apparently he lived there for weeks, you'd expect that.' He laid the glass down. 'Do you know if you'd no fingerprints you couldn't hold a glass? It would just slip through your fingers. Rather like this Richard Nicolson, eh?'

'Usually,' Meldrum said, 'you use prints to get a name. We've got a name, we've got prints. Bother is we don't know if it's his real name—'

'And his prints aren't on record anywhere,' Cowan said. 'But we got hair from a brush in the bathroom, we assume is his. And saliva from a handkerchief in the basket. We'll send the DNA record to Birmingham. But, of course, they're only allowed to keep and collate the records of those who've been convicted. I've a nasty suspicion your Nicolson hasn't been found guilty of anything.'

Meldrum leaned his weight against the bench and stared gloomily out into the corridor that led to the two search labs, carefully separated to avoid any contamination of samples between victim and suspect. 'He'd time after Slater was killed to tidy up at his leisure.'

'They always miss something,' Cowan said cheerfully. 'Like the apple that rolled under the camp bed. It gave us a beautiful set of teethmarks. What a size of jaw! From that alone I could tell you this was a man of exceptional size.'

'Which I knew anyway,' Meldrum said. 'Damn it, I *saw* him. I chased him down the hill at Bower's funeral.'

'I wonder, just as a matter of professional interest,' Cowan said, 'if the grave soil was examined, would there be anything that might have held his piss? Lovely idea, eh? I mean, if we hadn't already got a DNA sample.'

'Oh, we've got the lot. Fingerprints. DNA record. Descriptions. I've bloody well seen him. Everything but a polaroid. And we still have no idea who he is or where he came from.'

'Where he's gone to, that would do it. Settle for that,' Shields said. 'Before he kills number three.'

'You're sure he killed Bower as well then?' Cowan asked Meldrum. 'Of course not.'

'No, I didn't think you could be sure. I went back over the stuff we got out of Bower's flat. There's no physical evidence against Nicolson. Although, obviously, he'd be your best bet.'

'Not even that,' Meldrum said. 'I'd bet the other way. I don't think Nicolson killed Bower.'

'Why not?' Shields blurted out. His face had gone red.

'Because he sent Slater to talk to the Balewas and Turnbull. And then persuaded him to go all the way down to Kilbracken. We don't know why or who he was supposed to talk to, and Kerr the brother-in-law claims not to know either. But Nicolson must have wanted something pretty badly, and it's my guess he must have been trying to find out who'd killed Bower.'

'Why would he want to do that?' Shields said, in the same tone he might have cried, *Bollocks!* 'If he hated Bower, why'd he care who killed him?'

'Maybe,' Meldrum said, 'he wanted to congratulate him.'

Cowan started to chuckle, glanced at Shields and changed his mind.

'If it wasn't Nicolson, I'll tell you who my money would be on.' Shields's face had reddened more than ever. 'The black guy.'

'Balewa?'

'Him, like I said, that's what I said, him. And I'll tell you why. Because he found out Bower was interfering with his wee boy. That's a motive. I'll tell you this, if anybody laid a finger on my boy, I'd swing for the bastard, so I would.'

Since the death penalty had been abolished, this struck Meldrum as something of an empty promise. But then that kind of rant always seemed empty to him, heart on the sleeve, chat-show stuff.

Seeing, however, Cowan's quizzical look as he glanced from one to the other, Meldrum swallowed his distaste and let it go.

CHAPTER TWENTY-TWO

Councillor Nolan was a busy man. He hadn't neglected to tell Meldrum so himself. 'But if it's all that important, I've got half an hour before the Education Minister is due.'

As things turned out, this was rather less grand than it sounded. Shields and Meldrum turned up at the primary school to find what was essentially a photo opportunity. They were taken along by a small girl to the assembly hall, where they found a cluster of people and a table of home baking. Meldrum explained to the Head Teacher, a stout woman striving for an air of placidity, who they were.

'Councillor Nolan? He's not here yet. I don't know what he means by half an hour.' She looked at her watch. 'The Minister's due in twenty minutes.'

As they waited, the Deputy Head told them the occasion was to launch a new curriculum initiative being pioneered in the school. 'We're fortunate it's a dry afternoon. That corner of the hall leaks in heavy rain. Is it right you're here to talk to Councillor Nolan? Well, that's him now, talking to the Head.'

Nolan, with a swag of belly and a couple of rolls of fat under the chin, gave the impression of a man who lived well. His wife, Meldrum had been told, was said to be the brains of the family. Rumour had it that she'd begun by selling to friends out of a catalogue, gone on to organising parties for the selling of sex aids, and worked her way to near the top of some pyramid designed to sell expensive-looking jewellery worth less than it cost. She made a good deal of money, they said; but then so did he, they said, one way and another. A well-doing couple.

'I'm just telling Mrs Martin,' he said as he acknowledged Meldrum's waiting presence, 'don't worry about me handling the kids. I probably fathered most of them.'

Seeing the Head flinch, Meldrum recalled Councillor Nolan was Chair of the Education Committee.

The Head offered her room for them to talk. 'You can see the car park from the window,' she said, 'so you'll be able to see the Minister when he arrives.' By the time he'd managed to detach him and get him into the room, Meldrum reckoned he had about ten minutes.

'You stand by the window,' the Councillor told Shields. 'Give me a shout when you see him. You won't be in any doubt. Chauffeur-driven Bentley, and same again for the minders.' He squeezed himself into the chair behind the desk. 'Take a seat,' he told Meldrum. 'What can I do you for?'

'I'd be grateful if you would help me with some questions about the Naylor Home.'

'You told me that on the phone. I told you it was closed. Years ago, fifteen, it must be.'

'Could you tell me why it was closed?'

'Do you know how much money's been cut from local authority budgets in the last twenty years? We're down to the bone.'

'There wasn't any other reason?'

'Didn't need one. When you're shutting down outdoor education and dishing out part-time contracts, they're all hard choices.' The confident, hectoring voice was unchanged, but Meldrum took note that now his hands clasped together on the desk.

'The records from the Home seem to have disappeared,' Meldrum said. 'At least that's what I'm being told.'

'What would you want them for?'

'I'm investigating a murder. A man called Iain Bower.'

'Never heard of him.'

'Well, you knew his brother.'

'How?'

'Frank Bower worked at the Naylor Home, and you were Chair of the Visitation Committee for it.'

'Who told you that?' The question was over-peremptory. Perhaps Nolan thought so too, for he commented more quietly, 'It's a long time ago.'

'I was shown a newspaper account of Frank Bower's retirement dinner. You made one of the speeches. You said a lot of nice things about him.'

'He was well thought of. Is that what you wanted to know? Is that what you're taking up my time for?'

'I was wondering if you could help me to find the records. Iain Bower – the man who was murdered – worked at the Home one summer. I need a list of the pupils who were there at that time.'

'Why?'

'At this stage that would be confidential, sir.'

'Lots of kids were in the Naylor because they were a danger to other people apart from themselves. Some went on to be serious criminals. You think one of them might have murdered Bower?'

At the window, Shields said, 'That looks like your man just getting out of his car.'

Nolan jumped to his feet. 'No point in coming to me about records. Local government's gone from districts to regions and back again – of course stuff's got lost. Not anything I can do.'

He was already at the door. To hell with it, Meldrum thought.

'In the course of our enquiries, sir, we've had an allegation made against Frank Bower. He's accused by a former inmate of the Naylor Home of serious sexual and physical abuse.'

Nolan stared at him, frozen-faced.

'I wonder if anything like that was ever brought to your attention – as Chair of the Visitation Committee.'

The door closed emphatically behind Councillor Nolan.

CHAPTER TWENTY-THREE

'I love,' John Brennan said, 'all these rumours of panthers in the English countryside.'

'Not just English,' Harriet said. 'I read someone claimed to have seen a big cat in the Pentlands.'

'I prefer to think of it prowling in Sussex or Kent, somewhere like that. In fact, not "it", *them* – and them *breeding*. Point is, that kind of countryside, rolling parkland, orchards, little villages, is a gentle land-scape and one free of risk. That's why Ted Hughes can write a poem about getting into a muck sweat because he was being menaced by a horse.'

'A horse can be menacing.' Samuels, a dapper little Englishman, who was some kind of professor at Edinburgh University, made his point with more than academic certainty.

'Nonsense,' Brennan said cheerfully. They were in the middle of a good dinner, and he enjoyed his wine.

'Nonsense, yourself,' cried Samuels. 'This is the man,' he addressed the table at large, 'who told me cricket was a game for wimps. Have you ever faced a fast bowler, I asked him.'

Brennan made a large dismissive gesture. 'I've faced Lord Byers scowling down from the Bench. But leave bowlers and Byers and such beasts out of it, for the moment. My point is that one panther, the remotest chance of a panther, would make it impossible to have that loving concentration on trivia which is the delight of the English countryside and comes entirely from feeling secure. From being, in fact, unmenaced.'

'I wonder,' Harriet said, 'if the lack of other predators doesn't let us concentrate on the most dangerous beast of all – man.'

'And the voice of the feminist shall be heard in the land,' Mathieson said.

He was a partner in the firm of corporate lawyers who had recently formed an association with Brennan. Of the dozen people round the table, Meldrum guessed most were there through a business conection. Samuels perhaps there as a friend of Brennan's. And himself? He had been at dinner at Brennan's house a couple of times, but that had been when Harriet Cook and he had been living together. Perhaps he'd been invited because it satisfied Brennan's competitive nature to invite an ex-lover of the woman he'd just decided to marry. Or maybe it was more complicated than that and he wanted to say, look, I'm not the bastard you and everyone else thought, see, I'm marrying the bloody girl.

Why Meldrum had accepted the wretched invitation was another question. Masochism? Or because he couldn't resist a chance to see Harriet again? It would be flattering to think he'd come because Neil Heuk was going to be one of the guests; but the truth was he hadn't known that until he arrived. Even for Heuk he could see a business reason, since Heuk apparently was, among other functions, acting as archivist to a treasure trove of documents inherited, in the course of their latest takeover, by the multinational Mathieson's firm represented.

Interestingly, although they were in Harriet's flat, he took it for granted – as everyone else seemed to be doing – that the dinner party was Brennan's. On the other hand, Harriet seemed to be more assertive with Brennan than he'd ever imagined she could be.

'Take, for example, the strange case of the giant panda,' Samuels was saying, making Meldrum wonder if he'd missed something. 'Like man, it is a carnivore, related to the tiger, but it lives almost entirely on bamboo. It's had to evolve a false thumb to hold the stalks and big incisors to strip the outer integument. Advantage: bamboo is plentiful and disliked by other animals. Disadvantage: it offers little nourishment to the short gut of a carnivore and so the panda has to eat constantly, lying on its back to save energy, eight hours eating, four for sleep, then up again at night for eight hours eating, four sleeping.'

'A dear friend of mine – I've known her since we were at school,' Mathieson's wife said, 'looks exactly as if she follows that regime.'

Undeflected by laughter, Samuels went on, 'It will eat a carcass if it finds a dead deer, but it couldn't spare the energy to chase one. It is only three hundred calories from starvation every day of its life.'

'I've got a friend like that too,' Mathieson's wife said.

'If there's a God, he's played a pretty bad joke on the panda,' Heuk said. 'I wonder what Paddy Turnbull would say to that,' he asked Meldrum. And to the others, 'We share a friend who's a Church of Scotland minister, and by way of being a saint.'

'Isn't that a contradiction in terms?' Mathieson's wife asked, unwise enough to try for three in a row.

Her husband frowned at her. 'My father,' he said, 'spoke of seeing George Macleod, who founded the Iona Community, holding up a drunk as the man vomited on him. There were elements of the saint in Macleod.'

If being vomited on is all it takes, Meldrum thought, I can vouch for Turnbull. The difficulty was he could stand witness on the same grounds for a number of nurses and doctors; not to mention police, at least the ones who'd refrained from violent retaliation.

'Neil, I hear, is not long back from Belgium,' Brennan said. Heuk nodded in acknowledgement. Meldrum was sure Brennan hardly knew Heuk; the connection, so far as there was one, seeming to be through Mathieson. Those sensitive antennae of Brennan were working, though, and Meldrum was conscious of the advocate's speculative gaze going from Heuk to himself. 'Did you come across many saints there?'

Heuk grinned and shrugged, but before he could say anything, Samuels had taken flight again.

'Are there any Belgian saints? Moderation, heavy furniture and *pommes frites* are surely antithetical to the requirements of sainthood. Take Magritte, for example.' Examples taken were, it seemed, a speciality of Samuels. 'Magritte was your absolutely typical Belgian bourgeois. He was married to the same woman all his life, a good parent, out to the café for a game of chess, everything domestic, unvarying, ordinary. Not a hint of the bohemian about him. If you'd been in a gallery showing Magrittes, the little fellow in the corner was the last one you'd have picked out as the artist. He was the very incarnation of the boring Belgian.'

'Except for his art,' Brennan said. 'And the point may be, not that he is so very different, but that every Belgian may have a winged bowler hat in his cupboard.'

'It's a dull man, who doesn't have something in his cupboard,' Mathieson's wife said.

'Now isn't that true!' Heuk cried. 'I can't tell you about a saint. But when I was in Brussels, I worked with a man called Guichard. One of those glossy high-born French types. Tall with a touch of grey at the temples. You'd have taken him for a diplomat, you know? To be honest, I was a bit in awe of him. And now – I was on the phone the other day catching up with the gossip – it turns out he's been arrested.'

'Looks like a diplomat? Let me guess,' Harriet asked. 'Industrial espionage?'

'Padding his expense account!' Mathieson offered, joining in Harriet's game with almost too eager an enthusiasm.

Two or three other increasingly improbable suggestions were made.

'Come on, Jim. You're the professional,' Brennan challenged Meldrum.

'Unfair,' Heuk said. 'No professionals allowed.'

A saturnine man called Connor offered, 'Stealing spoons from the company canteen.'

'Child abuse,' Heuk said. 'He was part of a ring of paedophiles. They're going to be charged, apparently, with the abduction and murder of children.'

A chill fell on their laughter. One of the women made an exclamation of disgust. Yet in another moment, Connor was talking about a recent case in London. Brennan followed with scandals in the Belgian police, Samuels cited FBI statistics on serial killers in the United States and Mathieson's wife a discussion on Oprah Winfrey. The conversation was livelier than ever.

One of those odd pauses, in which everyone falls silent as if listening, was ended by Harriet, who said of it, 'When that happened, my grandmother would tell us an angel had gone by.'

'I was thinking about *Pinocchio*,' Heuk said. 'In the Walt Disney film, I mean. I'm not one of those who despise America or popular culture. I suppose everyone has their own favourite. The bit I remember is when the fox persuades the puppet to come away with him. Come away and join all the other boys, he says. A life of joy, a life of ease, a life of doing what you please. I saw that when I was at school. We didn't see many things like that, and I've never forgotten it. It came back to me when we were talking about Guichard being arrested in Belgium.'

Looking round, Meldrum saw people who had been smiling stop.

'Am I being stupid?' Samuels asked. 'The connection escapes me.'

'When you wish upon a star,' Brennan said. 'Young Jodie Foster in a taxi, perhaps?'

'You're too clever for me,' Heuk said. 'I was just thinking how children love adventure. Whatever the price.'

Again Meldrum had the sense of Heuk, eager and sociable, at a smiling tangent to normality.

'Whatever the price?' he asked.

'Oh,' Heuk said, 'there's worse things than to be a donkey.'

The evening went on, but the words blurred for Meldrum, faded to gaping mouths, widening eyes; grinning faces like masks hung around the table. At first, he was most aware of Heuk and watchful Brennan. Soon, though, he was watching Harriet. Between one glass of wine and the next, she had drunk too much; he knew her so well, had held her from that line other evenings, and sometimes failed and watched her cross it. He caught Brennan's eye and looked down to hide his thoughts. Now she was laughing too much. She looked at him and laughed, perhaps because she could read his scowl. He saw Mathieson's glance rest on her, flicker away, return, and the thick red tip of the man's tongue lick, and lick again, across his lips. He told himself he despised Harriet, was sorry for her, angry with her. He wanted to feel the weight of her breasts in his hands and press his body against hers.

They rose from the table; a couple, going abroad in the morning, took their leave. The rest of them sat talking round the fire. Samuels announced he had to go, and Heuk, on impulse it seemed, jumped up as well. It got late and at last there were only the Mathiesons, Brennan and himself. And Harriet, who had slid down in her chair. Part of his mind told him he was behaving like a fool; part of him resolved to wait them out. And suddenly, the Mathiesons, come to the parting of the ways, were leaving; and Brennan was seeing them out. Meldrum knew it was time for him to go; this was a contest he couldn't win, and shouldn't be in. He scrubbed his hands down his face, and told himself he was being a fool and began to will himself out of his folly. Brennan came in from the hall, smiling, shrugging into his coat.

'Court in the morning,' he said. 'I'll say goodnight.'

Meldrum watched him leave. Listening, he heard the outer door close.

He got up and went out into the hall to make sure. When he came back, Harriet, who'd appeared to be sleeping, had her eyes open.

'Alone at last,' she said.

'Why would he do that?'

'Why should you care?'

'Maybe he's hoping I'll change your mind and you'll let him off getting married.'

'I notice,' she said, her speech unslurred, 'you displayed your usual hesitation when that fool of a woman asked what you did. Why do you dodge admitting you're a policeman?'

'Only because people can be a bore about murders.'

'If you're ashamed of what you do, tell them you're in traffic.'

'I've done that,' he said dourly.

She began to laugh. 'Remember the first time we went to bed? You took off your clothes and folded them all neatly and laid them on a chair. He hasn't done this often, I thought. That must have been his routine when he'd a wife to fuck.'

He pulled her off the chair, and they tore at one another's clothes until they were naked more or less. She sank her fingernails into his shoulders and he fucked her. He was too excited to make it last, and when he'd finished fell asleep as if he'd been bludgeoned. In the middle of the night, he woke up and she was asleep with her face between his legs. The central heating had gone off and when he touched her shoulder it was cold. Gently he eased her head to the floor, gathered her up and carried her through to the bedroom.

They were in bed and he'd cuddled her to him thinking she was asleep when she began to talk. Her voice was quiet, no more than a whisper in the dark.

'When I was five, we lived in a house with a shed at the bottom of the garden. It had a fire in one corner the men used for bending metal. One of them came up to the house to say there were mysterious noises in the chimney. My father took me by the hand and we went down to the shed together. The men said, those noises have been going on for a while. We think it might be Santa Claus, but he won't pay us any attention – so we wondered if maybe it needed a child to call him. Sure enough, just then I could hear it, this banging on the roof just by the chimney. Call him, they said. Go on, my father told me. And I did, I leaned forward and called, Santa? Santa! And then – I don't know how they did it, how it managed to avoid the fire, the fire was on, but down it came with a great *whoosh!* a parcel – and dropped right at my feet. Inside it was a pair of silver shoes, for me to wear on the Saturday which was Christmas Day. I wore those shoes until they fell apart, and nothing in my whole life was ever as magical as that moment.'

He lay trying to think of the right words to say, but by the time he'd come on them she was settled against him, each breath leaving her like a sigh, and so instead he told her he was sorry and then how he had lost the sense of who he was and how near he felt himself to the crack-up.

He wasn't prone to self-pity, but comforted himself with the thought she slept and did not hear him; though next morning this felt to him like a false consolation.

CHAPTER TWENTY-FOUR

On the first occasion the man had taken more exercise than he cared for, following the boy as he walked down into Bruntsfield, to Holy Corner where three churches stood. He'd stood in a queue behind him and followed him on to a bus, got off after him at the foot of Lothian Road and in Shandwick Place had queued again and taken a second bus. He'd sat near the door on the bottom deck so that he could keep an eye on him, but the boy had never raised his head from a book. Haymarket had gone past, and the Zoo on its hill to the right. They'd come to Corstorphine and the boy had stood up and come down the aisle, going by unheeding though so close he could feel him brush against his knees. Book tucked under his arm, the boy had wandered past a line of shops and started across the road at the roundabout, with never a backward glance. Strolling along behind him, the man wondered as he had done before at how little attention people paid to their surroundings. They went about with shut eyes and ears, as well be blind and deaf. They would be easy prey in a jungle. But this wasn't a jungle, of course. No panthers in Edinburgh.

He'd still been smiling at the thought, as he'd watched the boy cross the road at the roundabout and go into the PC World car park.

Held up by the traffic, he'd lost touch with the boy and had to go up and down the aisles in search of him. Among the computers, he'd been standing in front of an Apple Mac. The man had joined him, well aware of the boy's startled look, but carefully paying no heed to him, instead studying the Mac; oh, very intent, cradling his elbow, rubbing a thoughtful finger on his lip, lost to the world you might say. 'What do you think?' he'd said at last, almost as if to himself. For the first time, he let his glance meet that of the boy. 'Isn't a shape like a jelly bean good fun? And now they're all much the same, isn't a fun shape as good a reason as any for picking a computer?' That was too simple, and the boy hadn't been able to resist explaining why. Soon the boy, who more than most might have had good reason for being wary, was chatting away happily. A common interest was a wonderful thing.

It wasn't difficult. Like everything else, practice made perfect.

On the Saturday morning, the boy, not truanting this time, was there again and seeing the man broke into a smile as if catching sight of a friend. The man talked about needing a modem and they looked at several, discussing whether it was better to have one independent of the computer or not, until the man settled for a Supervoice. They stopped at the boxes of CDs, and the boy said he didn't use his computer for playing games. 'Not even Minesweeper, Sam?' the man joked. The boy tried to hide his disappointment when the man said he was going to England to take up a new job the following week. It was hard to find a friend and lose him so quickly. 'Tell you what,' the man said, 'I remembered you saying you'd be here today. Just in case, I brought some things you might like. *Cinemania* on movies, *Compton's Encyclopaedia* and a dictionary and some wildlife stuff. I didn't know you don't play, so I've put in *Wild 9* and *Conspiracy*. I've enough stuff to take with me, and if you'd enjoy them, it's better than throwing them out.'

This time he'd brought his car.

It really wasn't difficult.

BOOK FIVE

The Naylor Boys

CHAPTER TWENTY-FIVE

The day started badly before it started. In the small hours Meldrum had wakened and lain sweating in the dark. He had The Fear. It had come over him at intervals most of his life, the sense that there was an abyss into which you could fall – into prison, or on to the streets, the slide into poverty, to sleeping rough. Shameful and not to be acknowledged by his daytime self, it had been with him for as long as he could remember; perhaps from his father, a man who failed slowly in a small business; or from his mother's fear, for him on a bike, in the water, in the whole dangerous place that was the world.

He couldn't get back to sleep and as the window lightened he thought about David Slater, who had wanted to be a policeman called Meldrum. Searching for Richard Nicolson, they had gone through the routine as before, airports, hotels, boarding houses, everywhere there might be a chance of intercepting the giant of a man who had signed into the Viewforth boarding house. As before, he'd vanished, seemingly effortlessly, off the face of the earth. Chief Constable Baird wasn't a happy man. It was a mess. Hard to see how it could get worse.

He was out of bed, sitting at the table in the kitchen, when the phone rang. It was half seven and he was unshaven and late, drinking coffee and trying to persuade himself he wanted to eat a yesterday's roll spread with a triangle of processed cheese.

'Good morning.'

That was all it took for him to recognise the voice.

'Heuk? How the hell did you get this number?'

'You're in the telephone book. I mean, I just looked you up. I was surprised you weren't ex-directory. Given your job, I'd thought you would be.'

Meldrum chewed a corner off the roll and drank coffee.

'Hello?' Heuk's voice asked. 'Are you still there?'

'Not for long. I'm going for a shower.'

'I'm sorry to call you so early.'

'I don't like being called at home.'

Meldrum had got it into his head that Heuk was phoning about their unexpected meeting at Brennan's dinner party.

'I apologise for that. Thing is, I have to go to work. I didn't think you'd mind being phoned at home, if it was important.'

Absurdly, irrationally, Meldrum imagined being asked whether he'd slept with Harriet.

'Important?'

'You asked me before about the man who caused the trouble at Iain Bower's funeral. And I said I knew nothing about him. That was a lie. I told myself it was a long time ago, and I couldn't be sure. In my heart, of course, I knew there couldn't be two people that size and with the same name. But even if it was him, I felt why should I get him into trouble for something as pathetic as peeing into a grave? That was a bad mistake. This description you've put out in connection with the Slater murder, it's the same man, isn't it? The one at Iain's funeral?'

'Absolutely no doubt.'

'I don't know anything about Slater, or why he was murdered. But there's a very good reason why Richard Nicolson might have killed Iain Bower. I haven't been able to sleep all night for thinking about it.'

'What reason would that be?'

'A boy in the Naylor Home was called Richard Nicolson.'

CHAPTER TWENTY-SIX

'It's not mine,' Heuk said. The office, he meant. 'I wish it was. I have to share.'

Rather than using the small conference table, however, he had gone straight for the seat behind the desk. Meldrum wondered if he thought that might give him a psychological advantage.

'You told me on the phone you can identify Richard Nicolson. I take it that's his real name?'

'Oh, yes. He was at the Naylor, when I was there.'

'Before we start, are you willing to talk about the Naylor Home in front of my sergeant?'

'Yes.'

'A full statement?'

'As full as you like.'

'I'll remind you that on a previous occasion you told me you would deny everything you'd told me about the conditions there.'

'Did I say that?'

'I think you know you did.'

'Hmm.' Heuk made a little humming sound of agreement, nodding and smiling. The effect was disconcertingly childlike.

'But you've changed your mind? Can I ask why?'

Meldrum expected him to say David Slater's murder made him realise he had to tell the truth.

Insead Heuk said, 'Sometimes I decide. Then I think, what does it matter, what does it matter?' The same pantomime of nod and smile. 'I change my mind.'

'If you're making a statement,' Shields said, 'the best plan is to tell the truth.'

'Then I hope you have your notebook, or one of those little recorder things.' He swung the chair half from them so that he was looking out of the window as he spoke. 'The Naylor Home was a place for boys. The youngest when I was there was seven, some of the oldest were sixteen. The numbers varied, boys came and went. Thinking about it later, I worked out there might have been somewhere between sixty and eighty of us and maybe ten staff, something like that. There was a Headmaster — Doward, his name was — if you saw him in the morning, he'd be a bastard, if you got him later he'd be nice more often than not. He'd a drink problem, but he could afford it, he skimmed the budget. The Naylor was cold during the winter, especially at night, and the food was bad all the year round. Probably Doward wasn't the only one making a profit, butcher and baker and candlestick-maker, eh? Anyway, it's possible being a crook was what made him afraid of Frank Bower, or maybe what Frank gave him was a quiet life. No trouble with Frank in charge.' He glanced at them, moving only his eyes. 'No trouble at all.'

Meldrum could sense Shields's impatience with this speculation. Shields liked facts and dates, and the names spelled out in full. Get it all correctly transcribed and you were half-way to covering your backside: good police procedure.

'No trouble,' Meldrum repeated. 'Would you like to explain what you mean by that, sir?'

'Second winter I was there a boy went missing. I can't remember his name. Tommy, no, Jimmy, sure that was it, doesn't matter. One morning there were only two staff to supervise at breakfast — and they spent most of the time whispering to one another. Word went round like lightning, somebody had skipped out of the younger ones' dormitory during the night and the rest of the staff were searching the buildings and grounds for him. Things got back to some kind of routine by the middle of the morning, except that police appeared and started interviewing the younger boys. One of them said Jimmy hadn't been in the dormitory at all that night. The police soon established that had to be a mistake, though, for Frank Bower himself had checked at lights out and said everyone was in bed and accounted for.'

'Are you saying Bower was lying?'

Heuk smiled and went on, 'That was a long day. It was dark before they found his body. I suppose they were looking in the wrong places. You know, the path over the moor into the town or cars on the main road to Glasgow. But apparently he'd headed the other way down to the shore. He was in his pyjamas and bare feet and he'd frozen to death. All curled up in a ball with his arms folded round his head.'

He stopped talking and sat in silence for so long Meldrum asked, 'What happened then?'

'Wouldn't you think that would cause a scandal? Wouldn't you think it would be in the newspapers? And on television!' he exclaimed as if that idea had just occurred to him. 'Of course, they picked what we saw on the television. Maybe it was in the papers. I've never checked, I do research, it's part of my job, and I've never checked on that. It must have been in the papers, but even if it was we didn't see newspapers. I suppose there would be some kind of an enquiry. They have to hold those things, don't they? They *must* have done. But for us, living in the place, nothing changed. Him dying didn't make any difference at all.'

'Why are you telling us this?'

'There was a high wall round the Naylor. And the gates were locked at night. It's true there was one tree grew near the wall. You could have climbed that, but the branches looked thin near the top and they didn't touch the wall. Hard to imagine a small boy in pyjamas and bare feet reaching out, maybe even having to jump across. And then what? It would be a long drop to the ground.'

Meldrum asked, 'Is that an accusation?' Shields was taking notes again.

'Accusation?'

'Are you suggesting the boy's death wasn't an accident?'

'If I was, it would be too late to do anything about it, wouldn't it? Anyway, nobody could ever say it was *impossible* for him to climb the wall or get down the other side. If you're unhappy enough, you'll try anything.' Heuk swung round again to face them. He was smiling. 'And there would have been an enquiry, so I expect it went through all of that and found everything was just as it should have been.'

Holding his gaze, Meldrum nodded slowly. 'You've spent a lot of time going over what happened there.'

'I'd put it out of my head. But then I met Iain Bower again. It was just bad luck. I didn't know he worked for the company when I took the CIMD job.'

'Why bad luck?'

'For him, I mean. That's what I thought. Maybe he'd put the Naylor Home behind him. Me appearing out of the blue, I assume, must have turned his mind back to everything that happened that summer. Someone in Brussels said to me, Bower's such a camp little shit! I was taken aback when she said that to me. I mean, everyone always liked him so much. Maybe women have an instinct about that kind of thing. I've been blaming myself, thinking I might have started him off again.'

'Doing what?'

'As a paedophile.'

'Are you saying you're a paedophile?' Shields asked. There was no emphasis in the question, just a routine attempt at clarification. It was nicely done.

'I don't think so,' Heuk said in the same tone. Intentional or not, it had an effect of mockery. 'I'm *saying* that I don't know what Iain Bower did in the years between, and when I met him again – you can imagine it was difficult for both of us – at first it didn't even occur to me anything might be wrong. But then I began to wonder. And, *no*, he didn't confess to me. I couldn't tell you one thing he said, or anything he did that made me suspect, but I did begin to wonder. Not at once, not for a long time. Certainly, there wasn't anything I could have gone to the police with.' He turned to Meldrum, the hand patting along his moustache covering his mouth. 'That's why I was so grateful to you for drawing my attention to the news about Guichard.'

'I can't see anything to be grateful for in what Guichard did.'

'Oh, horrible! But, you see, if there was a group and Bower was part of it, he must have been doing these things before I ever met him again. In that case, there's nothing for me to feel guilty about. When he came back to Edinburgh, retiring so early, it must have been because he was afraid of a police investigation. Suppose, though, he couldn't stop. No matter how afraid he was of being caught. Suppose he was out of control. Suppose he couldn't hide what he was any more. Couldn't that have been why he was killed?'

'You're suggesting someone murdered him because he'd interfered with their child?' Meldrum asked. The Great Balewa Theory, he thought, watching Shields lean forward.

'I hadn't thought of that,' Heuk said.

'What?' Was the bastard trying to be funny?

'Oh, I see it might be a possibility! It's just that it wasn't what occurred to me. What I thought was that maybe someone felt threatened by the way he was behaving. If he was out of control, he'd get caught, probably sooner than later. Then there had to be a danger of being exposed with him. That's what I thought of when I heard he'd been killed.'

'But, when Bower was killed, you didn't know Jean-Philippe Guichard was a paedophile. Isn't that what you told us?'

'I wasn't thinking about Guichard! Not Guichard! Not any of those people in Belgium! I was talking about Iain's brother.'

'Frank Bower killed his brother Iain?' Shields asked, wanting him to spell it out for the record.

Heuk shrugged.

'That would be a serious allegation,' Meldrum said. 'Have you any proof?'

'I'm not accusing anyone.' He smiled. 'I'm just telling you what occurred to me. I can't help what went through my mind. I doubt if there's a law against thinking.'

'What makes you think,' the tiniest of pauses stressed the word, 'Frank Bower would have any need to fear exposure?'

'I told you what went on in the Naylor Home.'

A long time ago. A Home that had been closed years ago. A Home whose records had apparently disappeared.

'Are you suggesting he's involved with child abuse now?' As he spoke, Meldrum had a sudden image of the frightened child looking down at them from the stair as Frank Bower led them into the hall at Kilbracken House.

'I don't know anything about Frank Bower now,' Heuk said. 'I can only tell you about the Naylor Home.'

'Tell me about it then.'

'Richard Nicolson, you mean.'

'That's why we're here.'

'Richard Nicolson arrived in the Naylor about a month after me. I was eleven, nearly twelve, he was a year younger. All of us had a bad time in that place. But not like him. Already at ten he was as tall as Frank Bower. That made him a target.'

'Frank Bower treated him badly?'

'He made his life hell.'

'And did Iain Bower treat him badly?'

Heuk nodded. 'But since I talked to you on the phone, I've changed my mind. I don't believe the Richard Nicolson I knew was capable of harming anyone. If he killed this man Slater, it must have been by accident. He's very strong.'

'Pissing into Bower's grave,' Shields said, 'seems like he felt pretty angry with him.'

'If everyone who'd been tormented as a child took revenge, there wouldn't be enough policemen in the world,' Heuk said. 'But it doesn't happen. I know there are cases where a brutal father gets killed, say, but that's because the wife or son is still living with him. He's killed because he's a bastard to them right there and then, not because of something he did thirty years earlier. Isn't that your experience?'

'Yes,' Meldrum agreed. But he was thinking it was the first time he'd seen Heuk agitated. 'But that doesn't mean it couldn't happen.'

'I'm not saying people forget their childhood. Maybe you wake sweating in the night, and curse someone. But the years go by. You get attached to life by so many threads. Everybody can nurse a grievance, but most people aren't killers.'

'All you're saying is, it would take an uncommon man.'

'Right!' Shields said. 'And this Nicolson's a big bastard.'

Unexpectedly, Heuk laughed. 'But I'll take a bet with you he didn't kill Iain Bower.'

'Why not?'

The desk was clear apart from an executive toy, four metal balls suspended on a frame. Heuk drew back the nearest, let it go and watched attentively as the four balls knocked and swung in line.

'Giant body, dwarf heart,' he said. 'If you won't take my word for it, ask Paddy Turnbull.'

That was as far as it went. Heuk claimed to have no idea where Nicolson would be now. He hadn't seen or heard from him since they were in the Naylor Home. As for revenging childhood injuries, he grinned and reminded them he'd been in Belgium when Iain Bower was murdered. It was an alibi Meldrum had already tested and confirmed.

As he came out of the room with them, he said, 'Nice office. Up here, they all are. Only problem is that you can't open the windows. I'm told it's because, being on the fifth floor, the architects were afraid someone might jump.'

CHAPTER TWENTY-SEVEN

No trace of Richard Nicolson ever having done military service. A National Insurance number with a last payment shown in April of 1983. Contemporary with that, an address in Huddersfield which had turned out to be a lodging house, the ownership of which had changed hands. No record of his ever having applied for a passport.

On the way back from interviewing Heuk, as they discussed Nicolson's vanishing trick, a call detoured them to a garage on the outskirts of the city. It was well off any direct route between the flat where Iain Bower had been killed and Kilbracken in the Borders. For that reason, it hadn't been one of the places checked for petrol sales on the night of the murder.

'I'm glad to be able to help,' the garage owner said.

His name was George Handley, and, glad or not, with flushed face and popping eyes he didn't look happy or well. In the course of an investigation into secondhand car dealings, his VAT records had been examined. The computer had flagged up Frank Bower's name from Meldrum's earlier enquiry. At 1.08 after midnight, Bower had bought petrol to the value of £23.75 p, paid for it with a Bank of Scotland Visa card and signed his name. That put him in Edinburgh on the night and around the time his brother was murdered.

'It's not enough,' Meldrum would tell CC Baird later. 'Motive will be a problem. We'll look closer at the inheritance angle, but Frank's lifestyle doesn't suggest he needed to kill Iain for his money. On the other hand, the theory that Frank killed to protect himself would be hard to stand up. In the first place we'd have to prove that Iain was a paedophile, then

that he'd become so reckless Frank was sure he was going to be caught.
And after all that, you'd have to find – and prove – what Frank was
doing that meant he couldn't risk exposure by his brother. It wouldn't be
easy to persuade the Crown Office we could win in court. And if it did
get as far as a trial, there's no telling which way a jury would jump.' At
that point, Baird, who was nobody's fool, had said, 'No chance anyway
while a smart defence could raise the possibility of this Richard Nicolson
having killed Bower. Hard to convict Bower, unless you can get Nicolson
out of the frame.' 'All the same,' Meldrum had said, turning stubborn,
'the Visa may not be enough, but it could be a long step to being enough.
Let's see how Frank Bower reacts when we hit him with it.'

It was when he went back to the office after talking to Baird that
Shields told him the boy Sam Chaney had disappeared.

'I was in the canteen,' he said. 'Pure bloody chance, Guthrie was
behind me in the queue. Him and Tommy Black got the call yesterday.
As far as they can tell, the boy hasn't been seen since Saturday.'

'This is Monday.'

'Exactly. The boy went out on Saturday morning. Didn't come back.
And it was the middle of Sunday afternoon before his mother did
anything. Could you fucking believe it?' He dialled with a forefinger on
the air, and said in falsetto mimicry, 'Hello, 999? I just pulled my head
out my arse and I think I might have a wee problem.' He laughed, then
stopped at the look on Meldrum's face. 'This was Guthrie at my back
doing the funny stuff. He's a right clown. I asked him what he was on
about, and that's when I learned it was the Chaney kid.' He shook his
head. 'Right enough, some cunts shouldn't be allowed to have children.'

Meldrum collected his jacket from the back of the chair. 'Come on.'

'Where?'

'Where do you think?'

Shields caught up with him in the corridor. 'It's being handled,
nothing to do with us. They'll not like us sticking our noses in.'

Meldrum spared him a glance. Nothing to do with them? It was hard
to know where to begin. Naylor Home, Chaney, Heuk, Balewa, Iain
Bower, Jean-Philippe Guichard. He decided not to bother.

Too impatient to wait for the lift, he started down the stairs, taking
them two at a time.

As they stopped outside the Chaney house, a man was standing beside
a car in the drive opposite. Meldrum realised where he'd parked blocked

half the man's exit on to the narrow road, and called, 'Have I left you enough room?' The man stared and then, instead of getting into the car, turned and went into his house without a word. Up the street, a woman appeared with two children, looked and saw them at the Chaney's gate and scuttled into her house.

The door was opened, not by Val Chaney, but by a red-cheeked, unsmiling woman. 'No,' she said. She looked about seventeen, but was probably older since she was in police uniform.

'Police,' Shields said, and Meldrum showed identification, stopping her scepticism in its tracks.

'I thought you were reporters.'

'Don't worry. Protecting her's what you're here for.'

'Ask me,' she said, speaking softly in the hall, 'she wouldn't mind her picture in the paper.'

'I didn't ask you,' Meldrum said.

All the same, Val Chaney came as a surprise. For one thing, she'd brushed her hair. On the couch, an ashtray in her lap, she was sitting up and leaning forward. Eyes brighter, movements more defined, she seemed connected to the world in a way she hadn't been before.

'Have you found him?' she asked.

The dark, crowded little room, too, was somehow different. He remembered papers and magazines in piles and scattered across the floor. Now all of them had been tidied away.

'I'm sorry,' he said.

'You were here before. When you caught that man outside. Is he the one that's taken Sam? Is that why you're here again?'

'No, nothing to do with him.'

'But he was watching the house, wasn't he? Is that not why you chased him?'

Meldrum was conscious of the policewoman's attentiveness. She was doing everything but pull out her notebook.

'Whatever happened, there's no way the man outside your house could have been involved.'

'How can you be so sure?'

Because his name was David Slater, and he has an unbreakable alibi, being dead at the time.

Not wanting to go into that, he said, 'He's in prison at the moment.'

'Oh.' She sat back.

'I understand your son's been missing since Saturday?'

'But I didn't know. I've told your lot over and over again. Sam went out, like he does every Saturday morning.'

'Do you know where he goes?'

'Not exactly. Into town. He goes round the shops, I suppose. And he'd be by himself, he doesn't have any pals. I've been through all this. I went out too. You need out sometimes or you'd go crazy. Even if it's just to the pictures on your own. When I got back I thought he'd gone to bed.' She'd been looking at him, but now her gaze flickered away. 'I stood outside his door and shouted, Good night, Sam! I even thought I heard him say something, because I was expecting it, I suppose.'

Leaving aside the self-serving lie at the end, he was inclined to believe her.

'What happened next morning?'

'I got up late, made something to eat. It never occurred to me, not for a minute, he wasn't in his room. He spends his life in there with that computer Keith got him. I didn't bother him, he doesn't like to be bothered. But when I did look, he wasn't there and his bed wasn't slept in. So I called the police.'

'What time was that?' Meldrum asked.

'All right!' Val Chaney said. 'I didn't call you right away. But you don't, do you? You think there must be a mistake. You try to work it out. It takes a while.'

'While you were thinking, did you phone around his friends?'

'I told you, he doesn't have any.'

'What about your husband?'

'What about him?'

'I supposed you phoned and told him what had happened?'

'I did phone him.' Before he could ask if Chaney had told her to report the boy missing, she went on, 'Keith would like to be here. I mean, he would be if he could. But he can't get away. He has his work to do. They can't spare him.'

As they left the house, a car was pulling up behind theirs. Meldrum recognised the man frowning at the sight of them as DI Cockburn from South Division.

'Anything on the boy?' Meldrum asked.

'No, but what are you doing here?'

'Different enquiry.'

'What enquiry? Nobody's told me.'

'I'll pass on the file to you. See what you think.'

'. . . Right.'

'Get anything at the computer places?' Meldrum asked, opening the door of his car, ready to get in.

'How do you mean?'

'Christ sake!' Meldrum said. 'Boy's out on a Saturday. His only interest in life's computers. It's worth checking the stores.'

'Oh, *those* computer places. Couldn't believe you meant something so fucking obvious.'

How to make friends and influence people.

CHAPTER TWENTY-EIGHT

No mist this time on the run to Kilbracken. On a clear morning with an early touch of frost, a pale cloudless sky slipped like a card behind the hills on either side, they made good time. The gate to the pier at the near end of the village was closed.

Meldrum got out of the car, put his elbows back and stretched. He leaned on the fence, lacing his fingers between the mesh, and looked out over the loch. A small wind, blowing towards the island, darkened the surface of the water.

Through his window, Shields grumbled, 'We're too early.'

'Not that much. There's a boat coming now.'

It took about fifteen minutes to get to them. Meldrum paced back and forward, the wind fresh in his face on each turn. Shields rolled up the window and read his paper until the boat docked.

Instead of Chaney, whom Meldrum had been hoping to see, it was Don Simon, bulky and fit-looking in jeans and heavy pullover, who came up the pier key in hand and opened the gate. 'Sorry to keep you waiting,' he said, and to Meldrum's surprise offered a handshake.

The water was choppier than it had looked, and there was no chance to talk until they landed on the island. Even then they were inside the wall, making their way through the lower garden up to the house, before Simon began on what concerned him. Where the path narrowed he'd contrived to have Shields step on ahead of them.

'You're here again about the murder of Frank's brother?'

'Among other things,' Meldrum said.

'Other things?'

Meldrum looked back at him, and left it at a nod. The path underfoot, slimed with damp earth and moss, made for treacherous walking.

'We love this place,' Simon's voice said behind him. 'More than that, Rachel *needs* to be here. She'd be ill if we had to leave. The way the world is makes her ill. She can't bear it. I don't want her to break down again.'

The path widened. Looking up, Meldrum saw Shields climbing the slippery flight of broken stone steps, hands in pockets.

Beside him, Simon asked, 'Is it a fraud?'

'What?'

'Kilbracken. Buying the island.'

'I'm here only in connection with a murder investigation.'

'We sold our house and car. We put our savings and everything we had into the community. I believe everything's as it should be. But, of course, I've had my own thoughts.' Looking down at them, Shields had reached the top. Simon started up the steps. 'I'm not a fool,' he said.

There was no one in the hall. Simon led them past the library where they'd talked to Frank Bower, and towards the back of the house. The first passage was panelled in wood, the second tiled to waist-height, the third dingy with faded paint. Carpets, by this point, had given way to stone setts striking up chill under their feet. Every door they'd passed had been shut. Meldrum tried to remember how many families had put their money together to buy the island. He imagined a turn in the corridor, a sudden wave of noise, stepping into a kitchen with a roaring fire, stewpots bubbling on a stove, a well-lit bustling place with men and women round a great farm table, children playing on the floor.

By contrast, when Simon opened a door it was to show them into a room not much wider than the passage and furnished only with a battered desk and half a dozen upright wooden seats piled in a row against the wall. A tiny iron grate askew in the fireplace was filled with yellowing crumpled newspapers spotted with soot from the chimney. Cracked linoleum covered most of the floor. It was cold.

'If you wait here,' Simon said, 'Keith will be along in a minute.'

'Mainly, we're here to see Mr Bower.'

But Simon left without answering.

'I can feel my balls shrivelling,' Shields complained. 'It's freezing. What the hell does he think he's playing at putting us in here?'

'Not him, Bower. Playing silly buggers,' Meldrum said.

'Because of what you said about his brother? Stupid bastard's asking for trouble.'

'He's not doing himself any favours.'

'We shouldn't wait here. Come on and we'll go back up to that library. See if he's there.'

Before Meldrum could respond, there was a tap on the open door and Keith Chaney edged in.

'What do you want?' he asked. 'I'm working on a boiler through there. Not that I'm a heating engineer. But if I can't do it, nobody else will. They've never got their hands dirty in their life. Organic gardening? That'll be right! Cunts'll starve to death.'

He was in overalls and as he spoke kept his head down, busily wiping oil from his fingers on to a bit of rag.

'I'm sorry about your son.'

'What?'

'Sam.'

'So?'

'He's disappeared. He's been missing for three days. Are you saying you haven't been told?'

'I knew.'

'Your wife phoned you.'

'That's right.'

'And that would be on?'

'Sunday. Look, it's nothing to do with me.'

'He's your son, isn't he?' Meldrum asked, trying to keep the contempt out of his voice.

'No, he isn't. That's why my wife and I – my first wife and I – broke up. She'd been having an affair. I'm not the boy's father.'

'But you kept him?'

'She didn't want him.'

Poor little bastard, Meldrum thought. He saw the boy in the doorway, the light glowing behind him in the room with the drawn curtains. Spends half his life in there, his mother – no, the second Mrs Chaney had said.

'You know Val and me're separated?' He looked from Meldrum to Shields. 'Thought not. She won't admit it. Tells lies to everybody, pretending it hasn't happened. As if that'll change anything.'

'So Sam isn't – hasn't been since your first wife left – living with either one of his natural parents?'

'I told you, I'm not his father.'

'But you kept him after his mother left you. How long were Sam and you together before you met the present Mrs Chaney?'

He thought about it. 'Three or four years.'

'With you looking after him on your own?'

'Right! So what?'

'Were you fond of him?'

'. . . I suppose.'

'Well, you'd have to've been. To keep him. A lot of men, finding out he wasn't theirs, would have been angry with him.'

'Wasn't his fault.'

'Good for you. You looked after him, you were fond of him.' Chaney nodded agreement. 'So why, for Christ's sake, aren't you in Edinburgh? He's disappeared. Don't you care?'

'I haven't been off the island in a week. I can prove I was here on Sunday.'

Meldrum studied him in silence. 'I never said you weren't,' he told him at last. Turning to Shields, he said, 'Think he was at a dinner party on Sunday?'

'Eh, right,' Shields said; if not picking up the ball, at least juggling it in the air.

'The night Iain Bower was killed, we've been told there was a dinner for the Simons. You were at it, your boss was at it, what was the name of that other couple?'

'The Parkers,' Shields said.

'One big happy family. You'd have thought everybody on the island would have been there. Funny, that. So the day your son was abducted, were you all at another party that day?'

The red flush had drained from Chaney's cheeks, leaving him very white.

'I never said anything about a fucking party. All I meant was, working around, you see people all the time. Plenty of people saw me here on Sunday.'

'Tell you what, you go and get your boss and he can confirm that for us.'

'I'm not sure where he is.'

'Find him.'

As they waited, Shields leaned against the wall, staring moodily at his feet. It could be his way of expressing disapproval of getting into the stuff about Sam Chaney's disappearance. On the other hand, maybe he was just resenting the way they were being treated; or resenting Meldrum for not kicking up hell about it. Meldrum found himself shivering. Whatever bill of goods Simon and the others had been sold to bring them to this island, they'd found a cold paradise.

When Frank Bower put in an appearance, he stayed in the doorway, more in the corridor than in the room.

'The boat didn't leave the island on Sunday, and Chaney was here. What the hell has that got to do with my brother? I've complained to your Chief Constable. I'll complain again.'

He'd begun to turn away, when Meldrum asked, 'Would you look at this, please?'

Bower took the paper and glanced at it.

'What's this?'

'It's a Visa payment, used to buy petrol. Could I draw your attention to the date?'

'It's not one I'll forget,' Bower said grimly. 'It's the day Iain was murdered.'

'Is that your signature?'

'No, it bloody well isn't. It's no better than an adequate forgery.' He held the paper out at arm's length. Meldrum took it.

'That's not the opinion we've been given,' he said.

'You get your expert, I'll get mine,' Bower sneered. 'Not that it matters. That card was stolen. And I reported it. To the Visa people. Soon as I realised.'

'I know,' Meldrum said. 'You reported it the morning after your brother's death.'

'But it had been gone for over a week before that. I'm pretty sure I left it on a shop counter in Dumfries the previous Saturday. Between then and until I got the call about Iain, I'd never opened my wallet. We don't use plastic on the island.'

'Unfortunate coincidence.'

'That's exactly what it was.'

'It's a pity it wasn't used for other purchases. If somebody had it for a week after it was stolen, you'd think it would have been used. For a lot of stuff within the first twenty-four hours. That'd be the usual pattern.'

'I don't know anything about such things.'

The honest civilian's answer: plain and flat: hard to refute: ideal for the witness box.

'Can I come back to Mr Chaney?'

'What about him?'

'When he left his wife and came to work for you, he didn't bring his son with him. Do you think that was because he was afraid the boy might not be safe here?'

'What do you mean safe?'

'We've been building up a picture of the Naylor Home since we saw you last. Your brother worked there for a summer. Neil Heuk was in care there. Chaney, of course. He seems to be devoted to you. Patrick Turnbull, the minister who conducted your brother's funeral, you must have remembered him?'

'So what?'

'Oh, and Richard Nicolson – he was at the funeral, too.'

'Nicolson?'

'You don't remember a boy called Richard Nicolson?'

Bower kept his eyes on Meldrum, as he eased a handkerchief from his pocket and rubbed it across his upper lip. His heavy face showed no expression.

'I put a lot of boys through my hands. If you've done your homework, you'll know I worked there a long time.'

'I'm surprised you don't remember Nicolson. I'm told he was exceptional. I'm told as an eleven-year-old, he was tall enough to look even you in the eye. But I'm told that would have been a very bad idea, so maybe he didn't.'

'You don't want to believe anything Heuk tells you.'

'But you do remember Nicolson?'

'Vaguely. He didn't make much of an impression. What about him?'

'He was the one who pissed in Iain's grave.'

'Was he?'

'You were there when it happened. I would have thought you would have recognised him. Why didn't you?'

'I'd my eyes shut. I was praying.'

'That's not what you said at the time. You didn't say you hadn't seen him, you said you didn't recognise him.'

'Shock. Didn't you tell me I'd remember things better once I got over the shock?'

'Why do you think Nicolson pissed on your brother?'

'You try to help scum, that's the thanks you get.' Without any transition, he was suddenly in a rage. Face stroke-purple, jowls shaking, spittle flying from his lips. 'You think kids can't be evil? Heuk threw a chip pan in a man's face. We'd boys had raped six-year-olds. Turnbull? He turned up in a parish not ten miles from here. And he fucked a fifteen-year-old girl. Man of God? He should be in jail. We got the dregs in the Naylor. *And they don't change.*'

He stopped abruptly, as if suddenly hearing himself. It was quiet after the shouting. He looked from one face to the other. His tongue licked over his lips.

'I'm not sleeping,' he said. 'I keep dreaming about my brother.'

Emerging from the passage into the hall again, Meldrum placed the strangeness he felt. There were no boots or umbrellas or coat stands, no bikes, no children's toys; nothing to show anyone lived here. There was no sound of voices. Dust settled through a shaft of light.

Already, the house was stirring, as if with an expectation of ghosts.

CHAPTER TWENTY-NINE

They went down to the boat in silence, and the same silence carried them back across the loch. On the jetty in Kilbracken village, Meldrum stood watching as Simon pushed the boat off. It swung in a lazy half circle, the engine note rose; he watched it stretch a wake of white foam. When he turned, Shields was walking back up the slope towards the car.

He went through the gate and Shields pushed it shut.

Shields said, 'He's forgotten to lock it.'

'Maybe he was in too much of a hurry.'

'To get back to that bloody place!'

'To get away from us.'

As they settled into the car, Shields shook his head in disbelief and said, 'The way Bower was yelling, they must have heard him a mile away.' It sounded as if the idea amused him, but then he went on, 'And not a peep out of anybody in the place. Gave me the creeps.'

Meldrum was staring ahead. Half to himself, he said, 'Next time we leave there, I want to take Bower with us.'

In handcuffs.

He started the car.

'Home sweet home,' Shields said.

Meldrum, however, was turning left. 'Let's see if Macdonald's in.'

'The old guy that was in the police?'

'That's him.'

'Nice one. Get a coffee, eh? Take the chill out our bones.'

Meldrum grunted. He'd forgotten about Macdonald's coffees.

When they got to the house at the end of the village, however, though they were hospitably received, perhaps because it was before noon there was no suggestion this time of a dram of whisky in the coffee.

There was no doubt, though, that Macdonald was glad to see them. He was wound up because he'd just had a phonecall from his brother.

'There's been a right to fish for salmon on the Solway for four hundred years. Now the haaf nets are to be banned because of EC regulations. It'll put my brother-in-law, a decent hard-working ordinary man, on the dole at fifty-eight. What good'll that do anybody? I'll tell you who it'll suit. Every duke and lord with his estate and his riparian rights to the fishing on the river. They've always grudged the salmon the haaf nets take out of the Firth. Those are the gentry would charge you for the air you breathe if they could get away with it.'

'I suppose they look after the countryside,' Meldrum offered. It was the kind of bromide designed to let people, who might have been too outspoken, beat a retreat into platitudes.

'Bollocks!' Macdonald said. 'Dumfries Hunt's just a joke. Tearing up the land in their red coats – all day to catch just one fox, when they catch one at all. But my father had to kill foxes – once they got a taste for lamb, his flock would just be a larder; it's a lot easier for them than hunting. If my father lost a lamb, he'd go out with his gun and shoot half a dozen of them – because he knew the countryside, every tree on it and the run of the fields. Folk blether about conservation in Africa or wherever. And they know nothing of their own country. They don't have an idea what's going on.'

None of this talk squared at all with Meldrum's notion of country coppers, who'd always struck him as great admirers of the gentry, intent on leaving no forelock untugged. Maybe getting to retirement and the pension made the difference.

'Pity to be indoors when the sun's shining,' Macdonald said. 'I've bushes to prune. We can talk outside, if you'd like. You stay here and enjoy the warm,' he told Shields, who didn't argue.

He'd built out a wall from the side of the house. Facing south-east, the plot was out of the wind and full of bushes.

'Redcurrant, blackberry, Tay berries, blaeberry and gooseberries.' He had put on just a body warmer, and had rolled up his shirtsleeves over thick forearms. 'I get jam from it and puddings. We used to get wine too. But my wife was the winemaker. I never learned the trick of it.'

Meldrum put up the collar of his coat and plunged his hands into his pockets. He watched the secateurs slice through the branches. 'My father's people were farmers,' he said.

Macdonald nodded, separating the old wood from the new. 'Over there. Along the edge of the water's where my father's place was. When I think of my childhood, Kilbracken was time warped, lost to the world. This is where I always planned to retire, though my wife might have settled for staying in Annan. She came for my sake. But when I got here, that Kilbracken I remembered was gone – and the people with it. The fellows I knew as a boy. I tell you, we got up to some tricks. I mind one Hallowe'en we blocked the chimneys in the village. There was hell to pay about that. And another time, this lad was courting one of the farm girls. They used to go down this particular wee brae, and there was a gate they'd sit on, just to chat, like, and admire the view. It was a five-bar metal gate. And this night, some of the boys lifted it and sat it back so it was off its hinges. When young love got on it, it fell over. They broke their ankles.'

'Boys will be boys,' Meldrum said drily.

Macdonald gave a big snuffling half laugh. 'Oh, don't tell me. I know. We were barbarians. But *innocent* barbarians.'

Meldrum watched as he stacked the cut branches on one side and moved to the next bush.

'I'm surprised you're not asking me why we're back again.'

Macdonald grinned up at him. 'Because I knew you'd get round to it. You wouldn't be here unless you'd something to ask me.'

He listened as Meldrum took him through as much of the story as he cared to risk. A kind of solidity about Macdonald made you feel you could trust him; but Meldrum had been caught like that before. When it came to Patrick Turnbull, for example, he gave no indication of any connection with Iain Bower's murder, confining himself to what Bower had said about the minister featuring in some local scandal.

'That's typical of Bower,' Macdonald said. 'The man's a vicious creature. I know the story. Everyone for thirty miles round chewed it over. From all I hear of Turnbull – I only met him once – he was a good minister. If he'd a fault, it was asking too much of himself. Suddenly the rumour was going round that he'd interfered with this girl, who was only fifteen. The truth is, he was fancied by the mother and daughter both. When he'd have nothing to do with her, the mother dropped hints about the girl, made scenes. To cap it all, her husband, the local grocer, was an elder in the kirk. The better kind of people gave it no credence, but one fine morning Dr Turnbull was gone. Then people decided he must have been guilty, and some kind of face-saving deal had been struck. That fellow Bower might have been involved in persuading the kirk session, somebody told me that. Anyway, Turnbull left without putting up a fight. Maybe fighting wasn't his style.'

'But you think he was innocent?'

'Nothing surer. He was a victim. He's that kind of man is catnip to some women. They can't bear his mind on higher things.'

When they went back inside, Meldrum caught Macdonald as his glance went straight to the bottle of whisky on the sideboard. Shields, legs stretched in front of the fire, was still sipping at his coffee. The bottle was half empty. He'd no idea how full it had been before they went out, but Macdonald was allowing himself a faint grim smile. It seemed even retired policemen liked to keep their hands in for the craft of setting traps for human nature.

CHAPTER THIRTY

S unday mornings that were real Sunday mornings and not just another working day, Meldrum went out for breakfast. After Carole left him, days with nothing to do were hard; and an empty Sunday the hardest of all. Waking up on a day like that, the best way to start filling the hours had been to get out from between four walls and into the world. Over time that had eased, the way time eases everything, but the habit had stayed with him. There were places in Leith Walk or off Princes Street or over the Bridges where you could get eggs and bacon and coffee. A breath of air and buying a paper to read through over a slow breakfast wasn't the worst way to start a day. He put on his coat and went down the stairs whistling.

He was taken aback to open the door of the close and find Patrick Turnbull on the pavement studying the list of names on the entryphone.

'The answer to a prayer,' Turnbull said. 'Your name isn't here.'

'There's a reason for that,' Meldrum said.

'My apologies. I've been away. I had to get out of Edinburgh. Last night I came back to find messages you'd been trying to get hold of me. Official messages, of course. I know it isn't appropriate to come here.'

'There isn't anything that won't keep till tomorrow.'

'Not for me. I haven't been sleeping.'

Dark under the eyes, he did look underslept, the grey hair not helping, lank and almost to his shoulders. Despite the fresh breeze, he was coatless and the jacket looked to be the same one the woman drunk had vomited over.

'I was going for breakfast. If you want to walk with me, you're welcome.'

They started up the hill in the direction of Princes Street.

'How did you know where my flat was?' Meldrum was having the experience, unusual for a man of his height, of having to hurry his pace. 'I'm not in the phone book.'

'You'd spoken to me about Jim Pleat, the man on Radio Leith. You reminded me that I'd actually been on a programme of his. So I asked him, and he told me.'

'I didn't know he knew. I don't advertise where I live.'

'I'd the impression you were friends.'

'He's never set foot in the flat.'

'He knew where it was.'

'He takes a pride in knowing things.'

Bewley's didn't open until ten on a Sunday, so instead Meldrum settled for a place down a flight of steps into a basement cafe. He got his bacon and eggs and coffee, so that it was like other Sunday mornings, except he'd a companion and no paper.

Turnbull ate nothing but drank his way through two pots of tea as he talked about how it had been at the Naylor Home.

'Jesus said that to lust in your heart was damnable – and that has troubled me to the point of despair. I told myself for a long time, No, that He was simply excessive, unrealistic in saying that. Of course, there is and has to be a difference between the thought and the deed. But then later I came to see that in the deeper sense what He said is true – as everything He says is, if you find the deeper sense. If you lust in your heart, you can't ever be safe. I dread getting older – I never get drunk – the greatest danger for me is loss of control. I control myself every waking moment.'

From when he recognised Richard Nicolson at Iain Bower's funeral, he'd known that finally the bitter past would be uncovered.

It took a long time to tell, a time full of sighs and vacancies. At the Naylor Home, Turnbull as a fifteen-year-old had done his best to protect the weaker, in particular Richard Nicolson, the grotesquely outsized ten-year-old. In that mission, he had defied beatings, beatings of an unimaginable savagery, beatings so extreme that they had ended in dreams of martyrdom. 'I'd stumbled on a text in the Bible where Jesus tells his disciples it would be better for those who hurt children if a millstone were tied around their necks and they were cast into the sea. When I was older, its mixture of compassion with harshness gave me a difficulty. Jesus says some harsh things. But *then*, when I doubted Christ, when my faith wavered, *then* I was saved by that saying. I won't say it was that one text which made me a Christian, I think I'd found my faith, but it burned Christ into me.'

Whether because of that or some tough inborn integument of the spirit, it became true in the course of his suffering that he would have died rather than submit.

A waitress's hand came down in front of Meldrum and lifted his plate away.

It was like the breaking of a spell. Turnbull's words had been hard won with nothing false in them or any note of self-praise. The lantern jaw, wide gash of a mouth, intent dark eyes: it was a striking face, but one familiar enough on the streets of Glasgow or Edinburgh. Yet Meldrum had looked on it with something like awe as the story unfolded.

'All right?' the waitress said. 'You haven't eaten much.'

He stared at the plate. Spilled yolk of the half-eaten egg had been stirred about among bacon slices larded with congealed fat.

It was a relief to be back out on the street. They went down the hill and across Princes Street. Though the sky was cloudy, the weather had changed so that the air was mild as they went into the Gardens. Near the bandstand, they found a quiet bench on the grass beside the Norwegian stone: 1939–1945: in memory of a time of exile.

Turnbull's resistance had made a great difficulty for Frank Bower. Like other tyrants he ruled through fear, and like them hated and feared nothing more than an unbreakable defiance. Even single instances of it were intolerable, perhaps because of the power of example, perhaps because of the inner amazement every tyrant must feel at the ease of his tyranny. Out of his need Bower found a way. In the end, he broke and tamed Turnbull by arranging his seduction by the twelve-year-old Neil Heuk. As he spoke of it, the braced tension that was the mark of Turnbull's physical presence unwound. For him, it had been the sin against the Holy Ghost, the greatest of sins, for which he had spent his life repenting. 'It almost destroyed me.'

It was approaching the time when Turnbull's congregation would be gathering. As they walked up through the park towards the Waverley exit, Meldrum glanced at his watch. 'You'll be hard pressed to make it,' he said.

'It's never easy. If I preached this sermon, my congregation would drag me out of the pulpit. Or would, if they cared enough.' He bent and plucked a thick dark green stalk of grass from a clump at the base of a tree. Torn into two pieces, one folded across the other, he held it up as a cross. 'What should we do? Would you find me a grasshopper? If you did, would I crucify it? We're nothing, I'd tell them. How could I explain to them, heresy like that helps me to forgive? You have to find some way to forgive or the soul dies in you.'

'Forgive Bower?'

'Both of them. Both brothers. I tried to help Iain, and was sorry when he left the Doune Apartments. He did speak to me of repentance. And I'm sure that summer at the Naylor Home ruined his life.'

Meldrum thought of the Balewa family and said nothing.

As they climbed the steps to the gate, Turnbull threw away the plait of grass he'd been holding. 'I'm sorry to have inflicted that on you. As if I had any right to talk of forgiving others. I fill myself with disgust. I ruined Neil Heuk's life. And nothing I do could earn poor Richard's forgiveness, not if I began by crawling to Italy on my knees.'

'Right place for a pilgrimage,' Meldrum said as casually as he could manage.

Italy.

Nicolson was in Italy.

BOOK SIX

Under the Yoke

CHAPTER THIRTY-ONE

T hey had done everything by the book. As soon as word came that
Richard Nicolson had been found, arrangements for his extradi-
tion to face the charge of murdering David Slater were put in hand. The
opening part of the process had been the hardest, coaxing from an
unwitting Turnbull enough pieces of the jigsaw for a search to be
initiated. The key piece of information had been his manner of earning a
living. Like Meldrum himself, Nicolson had served his time to become a
journeyman joiner. Unlike Meldrum, he had gone on to become an
exceptional craftsman. In Huddersfield, his last recorded address in
England, he had worked as a cabinetmaker. It was from there, aged
twenty-five, that he had disappeared; now as it seemed, to Italy.
According to Turnbull, who had never lost touch with him, sometime
during his second year in that country a chance meeting had led
indirectly to some work in a film studio. There had been trouble with
unions, of course, and it hadn't lasted long, but it had given a place for
the hunt to start. He was a foreigner and that helped. In his own line his
remarkable skill had made him memorable. Above all, his size and
physique were so far out of the ordinary range that any description of
them made for instant recall.

When Meldrum flew in with Shields to Ciampino airport outside
Rome, it was with the expectation that taking Nicolson back would be a
formality. The forensic evidence in the Slater case was strong against
him; and the fact he'd lived for so long under an assumed name with
forged papers made him an embarrassment the Italian authorities were
happy to be rid of as quickly as possible. Looking down at bristling

aerials and balconies hung with washing on the shabby apartment buildings that lined the perimeter of the airport, it hadn't occurred to Meldrum there might be a problem.

A plump thirty-plus, Renato Fulcini was the younger but clearly more senior of the two policemen who met them. He spoke English fluently with a marked American accent. His offering the barest of greetings accompanied by a tight-lipped frown gave the disconcerting first impression that he was in a rage, which turned out to be the case. Perhaps in his turn wary of their reaction, he kept his news to himself until they were in the car and out of the public gaze.

There had been a defect in the warrant or its execution. For the moment, it didn't matter whether the fault had been at their end, as Fulcini suggested, or with the Italians. While they were in the air between Heathrow and Rome, Richard Nicolson, appealing his arrest in front of a magistrate, had promptly taken himself off. Fulcini had been at the airport awaiting their arrival when he'd been told.

'Nothing should have happened until you were here. It was not well handled. It was handled badly enough to make you wonder. Is there any reason to believe Mr Nicolson has friends in the right places?'

'Surely you'd know that better than I would?'

'I meant in England.'

'Nicolson hasn't lived in England – *or* Scotland – since 1983.' The news had put Meldrum's own temper on a short fuse.

'Of course he has. You know he must have. How else could he have killed Slater? Isn't that so?'

Killing someone, Meldrum thought, would take a hell of a lot less time than making friends in high places. Isn't that so? In the front, Shields stared ahead, the driver concentrated on his driving, both making a production of not listening.

Meldrum took a deep breath and asked quietly, 'Do we have any idea where Nicolson is now?'

'He has the key for a summer place in Anzio,' Fulcini said, matching the change of tone. 'It's possible he may not know that we know about it. It seems worth a gamble. Would you agree?'

CHAPTER THIRTY-TWO

According to Fulcini, the run down the coast was something under fifty kilometres. They'd made most of it in reasonably light traffic and, glancing at his watch as they stopped, Meldrum saw it was just before one o'clock. He couldn't remember if he'd reset the time getting off the plane; either way he was hungry.

They were parked outside a small hotel. Opposite, a gap in a wall showed a glimpse of blue sky and water. As they began to walk, however, the sea disappeared behind high wooden fencing. There was no pavement on that side and the road was narrow with a scattering of broken places like pock-marks on skin. The villas they were passing had small front gardens with palm trees and bushes that looked overgrown and somehow uncared for. There were no parked cars and all the shutters were closed. There was graffiti painted on the fence and on some of the garden walls.

'This isn't the way I pictured Anzio,' Shields said.

Fulcini said, 'We're a couple of miles from the port here. And the vacation situation isn't good. People go to Majorca or Minorca or Cuba.'

'No,' Shields said. 'The beach, I mean. I saw it in a film. The Americans landed on it during the war. John Wayne, I think it was. Or maybe Bob Mitchum.'

They came to a corner and Fulcini stopped. Another narrow street, as full of empty sunlight, climbed away to their left. A dog from the hard-edged black shadow under a wall yelped twice like a squeezed toy and lay down. 'From now on, keep behind us,' Fulcini said. 'Third house from here.'

Meldrum saw he had drawn a gun. He cradled it in his left arm, elbow bent against his chest. The driver had done the same

'Do we have to have those?'

Walking ahead, Fulcini said without looking round. 'People don't make a fool of me twice. If he resists arrest, I'll shoot him. As often as I have to.'

Directly opposite the third house, torn cartons and rolls of what might have been roofing felt were scattered round a pile of rubble stacked beside the fence.

Fulcini went through the gate followed by the driver. They were holding the guns now with both hands, pointing the way with outstretched arms. The shutters on this house, too, were closed. The driver crouched level with the front of the house. Meldrum pushed past him and followed Fulcini round to the back. There was a patio with a round wooden table and four chairs tipped over to lean against it. He had the foolish thought that it seemed a nice place to relax in the sun.

Fulcini was trying the door. He shrugged as he turned to Meldrum, then swung round again and kicked it just under the handle. It burst open under the single impact. He was a man with a lot of anger in him.

The house was empty. There was no food in the kitchen. In the big shaded room at the front, Fulcini ran his hand across the face of a carved wooden cabinet. 'The bastard has talent. New furniture. Restorations. For most of the last ten years, he's been working for private clients. Wonderful pieces, the client doesn't get charged too much, Nicolson gets cash in hand, no tax, everybody's happy. He'd been working on this place off and on for the last couple of months.'

At the front gate again, they were about to walk back to the car, when Shields pointed in the other direction and asked, 'See there? Do you think that'll be steps down to the beach? I'm not coming this far without seeing the beach at Anzio.'

Fulcini said, 'If you're thinking of John Wayne, it's the wrong beach.'

'Near enough,' Shields said. 'There were steps back where the car's parked. I'll be there as fast as you are.'

Edinburgh's finest, Meldrum thought, watching him hurry off, arse going like a metronome. Busy with their separate thoughts, they went along in silence. When they reached the car, Fulcini sat with the door open, his legs swung out, as he talked on the phone. There was no sign of life about the little hotel opposite, but the windows were unshuttered and a van of some kind was parked at the front entrance. Meldrum wondered about suggesting going in and seeing if they could get something to eat. He wasn't a fan of Italian food, but a pizza would go down well, a whole pizza, say one a foot across. Failing that, a bag of crisps. Any flavour.

Fulcini leaned out of the car and said, 'They've had a message from Nicolson. He wants to give himself up. But he's put a time limit on it. Christ's name, where's your sergeant?'

'I'll get him.'

But when he ran down the dozen rickety steps, Shields wasn't in sight. After an instant of pure disbelief, he looked in the other direction. No one. Nothing. Gone; like a conjuring trick. Where had the bloody man vanished?

For the lack of any better idea, he started to plough along through the sand the way Shields should have come.

He found him almost at once seated at the side of a small hut, perhaps some kind of beach vendor, still with its shutters up. Meldrum had almost passed when he glimpsed him from the corner of his eye and swung round. Chin on hand, Shields was looking out across the white beach at the sea.

Seeing Meldrum, he smiled with a kind of spontaneous pleasure, and said as if sharing the experience, 'It's just no' real, is it?'

'What the fuck do you think you're doing?' Meldrum yelled. 'We're waiting for you, you fucking idiot!'

Taken off his guard, Shields blundered to his feet. Purple-faced, he shouted, 'And fuck you as well! That's right out of order. Who in hell you think you're talking to?'

'Nicolson's ready to give himself up,' Meldrum said and turned on his heel.

He heard Shields puffing along trying to catch up.

'Where is he? Was he hiding?'

Meldrum kept going without answering.

Behind him, Shields said, 'It's not my fault Henderson got killed.'

Meldrum spun round. '*What?*'

'You heard me. I don't know what happened in America. Maybe it's right what they say, if you'd handled it better he wouldn't have got killed. All I know is I'm not Henderson. And that's why you've had a scunner at me from the minute I started with you. Maybe I'm not as smart as Henderson, but I'm smarter than you think I am!'

The tide had passed the turn and was moving quickly up the beach. Very faintly, Meldrum could hear the thin barking of a dog. If it was the one they'd seen earlier, it was a good distance away. Showed how quiet it was.

'They're waiting for us,' he said. 'We've wasted enough time.'

But when he got to the steps, he heard Shields at his back having the last word.

'I'll tell you another thing that pisses me off about you! You always have to do the driving. Every sodding time. I never get near the wheel of a car.'

CHAPTER THIRTY-THREE

It was raining in Perugia. This came as a surprise to Meldrum, an untravelled northerner who only once, a long time ago on his honeymoon, had come to Italy and associated it with sunshine. On the other hand, on the drive north from Rome, it had occurred to him that country this fertile and pleasant didn't happen only with fine weather, and so the surprise wasn't complete. What he hadn't expected was it falling in torrents. While Fulcini was phoning again, he'd walked along under the shelter of the covered walkway round the Palazzo looking for a lavatory. Pissing eased one discomfort, but he was still hungry. When he came out, the rain seemed heavier than ever. He walked to the corner to get a view of the valley below the town, but it was hidden in mist.

When he came back, the three of them were at the escalator entrance; the two Italians wearing matching expressions of impatience. It had been his turn to keep them waiting.

As they rode down, Fulcini said, 'Another message. He's playing games with us.'

'Why?'

'Once I get hold of him, he'll tell me,' Fulcini promised grimly.

Following instructions, they'd parked at the bottom of the hill. The idea had been that Nicolson would be waiting for them at the top of the escalators that went from the car parks up through the excavated Roman caverns to the square at the top.

Back in the car, Shields belched loudly. Like Meldrum, he must have been travel-weary and hungry. 'How far is what do you call it?' he asked.

'Castiglione del Lago,' Fulcini said. 'It's about sixteen kilometres.'

'You know how to get there?'

'I think we can manage,' Fulcini said drily. Turning to Meldrum, he said quietly, 'We used to holiday at the lake when I was a child.'

'Which lake's that?'

'Lake Trasimeno. It's really not far. Maybe the bastard will keep his word this time. What's your saying? Third time lucky?'

'Third time lucky,' Meldrum said.

After that they lapsed into silence. It wasn't far, not much more than ten miles, but it was enough to leave the rain behind and the lake when they got there spread out like an inland sea under the late afternoon sun. They came to a street and a corner so tight the houses seemed to press in on either side.

'Is this it?'

'No. This is San Feliciano. Just a fishing village.'

Afterwards it would be a place Meldrum would remember for the rest of his life. Then he hardly spared a glance as they ran through it. The road stayed close by the water. 'Over there,' Fulcini said, pointing across the lake.

Castiglione del Lago showed as white walls and towers on the ridge of a promontory, stuck out like a hitchhiker's thumb into the water.

'Is that a castle?'

'The Rock of the Lion,' Fulcini said. The sight of it had put a smile on his face; perhaps because of childhood memories.

It was a routine again of following Nicolson's instructions; and so they parked at the end of a row of cars in front of a large brown building, and from there walked up a narrow bustling street lined with shops and eating places oddly reminiscent for Meldrum of far off holiday towns from his own childhood. The street finished in a small square and they looked round until they found the place where they'd been told to sit, taking one of the outside tables.

Going to Anzio, Meldrum had asked if the police there had been contacted. The same question had cropped up about Perugia. This time, he didn't bother. He'd finally understood that for Fulcini this was a matter of pride to be settled personally. The other reason he didn't ask was because he no longer thought it mattered. When or wherever, Nicolson surrendered or got caught, Meldrum had given up on it being that day. They ordered sandwiches and glasses of wine. After the first glass, they had a second. Nobody made any objections. It occurred to Meldrum he wasn't the only one who'd given up.

Chair turned slightly so he could sprawl out his legs, Fulcini had maintained the improvement in his mood. When Shields remarked on his American accent, he explained that – 'not once but twice' – he'd had the privilege of secondments to the USA, with the FBI and with the New York Police Department.

'To be truthful, I learned more in New York. As professionals yourselves, does that surprise you? I spent ten days working with the vice cops. That was an interesting experience. This Puerto Rican sergeant introduced me to a dress designer, and he took me along to talk to his dominatrix. This was off duty, but purely for research purposes, you understand. She was half Chinese, a beautiful girl. And with a college education. She said what she did took intelligence, like being an actress. She explained that by telling us a joke. What's the difference between an SM client and a computer?' Meldrum shook his head. 'You only need to punch information into a computer once.'

The driver, who'd shown no sign of understanding English, joined in the laughter, which surprised Meldrum. Maybe he was laughing only out of politeness, much like Meldrum himself. It wasn't much of a joke.

Encouraged, Fulcini said, 'She had another one.' He thought for a moment, getting it straight before he told it. 'Yes. What's the difference between an SM client and floor tiles? You have to lay floor tiles before you can walk all over them!' He looked round. 'That one depends on a pun. You know that American word? Getting laid, yes?'

Those who hadn't laughed, laughed. The driver joined in.

Fulcini sipped his wine. Above his head there was a stone laid into the wall. When they'd sat down at first, he'd translated it for them: to the memory of the men of the Resistance executed by the Fascists.

'I asked her,' Fulcini said, 'what was the worst thing she had heard of between a dominatrix and a client. She told me of this woman who had sliced a man's scrotum, taken out his testicles and shown them to him. Then she put them back and sewed him up.' When he paused this time, only the driver laughed, which meant he didn't understand English after all or had an odd sense of humour. 'What was the charge for that? I asked her. Three hundred dollars, she told me. But she said she'd worked for as little as seventy.'

Meldrum pushed away his glass and said, 'He's not coming.' He'd had enough.

'*Il topo.*'

'What?'

'I'm told that's what the other carpenters in the studios called him. The mouse.'

'Well, the mouse isn't coming.'

'No . . . We'll go back. Decide what you want to do in the morning, eh? After you've slept on it.'

'We'll have to find somewhere to do that.'

'Let me know what your budget is. I'll find you a place.' He got up and stretched. 'A strange day.'

'Frustrating.'

But Fulcini shrugged and went on, 'If you'd told me this morning I'd be here.' He looked round and smiled. Childhood memories.

Two streets went back down the hill, the busy one they'd come up and a quieter one that ran parallel to it. As a last gesture, it was agreed they should split up and cover both. They watched the driver and Shields stroll across the square in the direction of the quiet street and set off themselves down the other one.

They were no sooner in it than they saw him. He would have been hard to miss, freakishly large, head and shoulders above the tallest. People turned round to stare after him. Going away from them, he was walking not running, and they did the same, not wanting to start some kind of panic in the busy street. For the same reason, Meldrum thought, No guns, thank God.

'What's he playing at? He told us he'd be here.'

'Maybe he's changed his mind,' Fulcini said.

They were both panting, with excitement as much as the pace.

By the bottom of the hill, they hadn't gained on him, but they hadn't lost ground either.

'He must have a car.' Fulcini put his hand inside his jacket. 'If he tries to drive off, get out of the way.'

Guns after all.

As if he'd heard them, Nicolson swerved unexpectedly away from the row of cars and instead, three at a time, took the steps in front of the brown building and went inside. Now they began to run.

There was an entrance hall with a desk under a sign, *Percorso*

Monumentale. Through an arch on the right, Meldrum could see into a long room with a painted ceiling and exhibition cases like a museum. There was no one in it, but an arch at the end suggested a room beyond and the possibility of another exit. While Fulcini wasted time at the desk, Nicolson was getting away.

But when the Italian turned from talking to the woman, he headed not for the gallery but a door at the side of the arch. Meldrum went after him across a cramped landing and up flights of stairs, the last two of uncovered stone where there would barely have been room for anyone coming down to squeeze past. They stepped out through a door into an explosion of light and space. Over a stone wall they could see down into an inner courtyard. The other way they looked out across the blue spread of Lake Trasimeno. They were on top of the castle wall.

In front of them was a covered passage, in effect a long tunnel with a circle of pale light at the far end. It was dark, but as they hurried along, sunlight fell in slants from slots cut for archery or musket fire. As they passed one, Fulcini turned and shook his gun to indicate that he had drawn it again. His forehead shone with sweat, but his lips were drawn back in a grimace that showed his teeth. It was like a grin, mirthless, though, and full of excitement. Fulcini was a man hunter. Meldrum wanted to call out, Nicolson's no good to me dead.

In another moment, bursting out into the open, they ran across light and space and plunged into the second passage.

There was no light at the end of it.

It was blocked.

The light was blocked.

Fulcini was shouting in Italian.

Nicolson filled the whole tunnel, blocking the light, and Meldrum was running even as he understood.

Fulcini shouted in English now, 'Halt or I'll fire! Halt or—'

The gun was a thunder clap in the closed space. It was like being punched in the face. Meldrum opened his eyes to see Fulcini plucked from the tunnel. Held by the shoulder, he must have been thrown a dozen feet. He sat against the wall at the entry to the next passage. Blood was coming from his mouth and both legs were folded under him like a broken doll.

Nicolson stood by the wall, one fist on top of it.

In a voice startlingly thin and high, he cried, 'Don't come near me. If you do, I'll jump.' He was so tall it seemed he might as easily step over. His whole body was shuddering. He swayed as his legs shook under him.

'It's all right.' Meldrum could smell the animal sweat of panic. 'Don't be frightened. I'm not going to hurt you.'

'Is he dead?'

Meldrum went over and crouched beside Fulcini. As he felt for a pulse in the neck, the body settled under his hand. 'He's all right.' He probed and probed again, and in reward for the certainty of his words felt it, thready, almost imperceptible, but there.

'He's breathing,' he said, but when he looked up, Nicolson was gone.

He eased Fulcini down, supporting his head, and turned him on his side. That way he wouldn't choke on his blood; no way of knowing what damage moving him had caused.

As he finished, he heard voices, a man's voice and then a girl's laughter. In the passage, he walked past them without a word. They couldn't miss Fulcini; his job was to find the driver so that he could report what had happened.

As he hurried through the entrance hall, the woman behind the desk called after him. He came out of the entrance, expecting to see Shields and the driver. He cursed them, thinking they'd been stupid enough to go searching back up the other street, then realised they would be waiting in the car. He ran down the steps, and along to it. They weren't there. As he turned from peering in, a horn sounded and the door of a van at the end of the line swung open. As he stared at it, the horn sounded again.

Nicolson was folded down into the driving seat.

'I didn't mean to hurt him,' he said. 'But they won't believe me. I can't face what they'll do to me.'

Meldrum climbed in and sat beside him. Nicolson reached across and drew the door shut.

'If we went to the airport, couldn't you just take me back?'

'I'd do my best.'

'I couldn't bear to be beaten.'

He started the engine. As the van began to move, instinctively Meldrum reached for the handle.

'The door's locked,' Nicolson said.

CHAPTER THIRTY-FOUR

S an Feliciano was a fishing village. From where he sat opposite
Nicolson, through the big window Meldrum could see two con-
centric circles of stakes about half a mile from the shore. The fish must
be driven into it and somehow netted between the stakes. He remembered Macdonald, the retired policeman at Kilbracken, talking about his
brother and haaf net fishing on the Solway. What had he said? They'd
done it that way going on for four hundred years? For how long, then,
had they been sinking stakes into the water of the lake out there? San
Feliciano. The Happy Place, Nicolson had said as they drove into it. It
wouldn't be difficult to imagine being happy here: sun on the water, fruit
from the trees; and the fishing, of course. Certainly more sun than ever
you'd see on the Solway. On the other hand, nothing they caught here
could compare with a sweet-fleshed homecoming salmon, fattened to
fight the river, the king of fish. The truth was you could be happy
anywhere.

Given the chance.

On the wall above a cabinet, there was a big black and white photograph
in a silver frame. It showed a group of a dozen or so men, formally dressed,
standing in a half circle outside a building presumably newly opened. They
were all smiling except for the one in the centre, a pigeon-chested, plump-
jowled Mussolini look-alike, glaring at the camera. The carpenter in
Meldrum remarked on how fine the cabinet was. It reminded him of the
one in Anzio; another fine piece done for a client by the same master
craftsman. Nicolson, though, had given no explanation, just unlocked the
door of the villa and waved him inside.

They had been sitting here for hours. In the beginning he'd tried to argue and cajole, now the plan was simpler: to let the giant purge his fear, talk himself out, till he saw there was nothing for it but to give himself up. The plan had to be simple, since there was no other choice.

Nicolson insisted Meldrum drink with him and kept refilling his glass no matter how slowly it was sipped. He himself was drinking steadily, topping up regularly from a bottle of whisky on the floor by his chair. There was no food in the house, but the drinks cabinet was full. No problem with the drinks.

Despite himself, as Nicolson's voice went on and on, going over the same ground endlessly, Meldrum's mind wandered. Waves of weariness washed over him.

'Because I haven't had any education, because I work with my hands, doesn't make me a stupid man. I read all the time. I know about cowardice. In the First World War, soldiers in the trenches knew they'd been sent to France as machine-gun fodder and every natural instinct told them to run away. But they stayed. Amazingly, thousands of them found it easier to go mad than run away. I tell you, cowards could save the world.'

It had turned out Carole and he weren't the only honeymoon couple on their package tour to Italy. The boy of the other couple had been about twenty, thin-faced, energetic, self-absorbed, with something foxy and unreliable about him that didn't in the long run promise too much for the girl. It had seemed to Meldrum then that his own marriage would last for ever. In Rome, they'd seen the Pope on his throne outside the Vatican, a tiny white figure, diminished across the vast square. That had pleased Carole enormously. Later they'd stood looking up at the Colosseum, built by Jewish slave labour, where the Christians were eaten by lions. The walls were all pitted with holes where the metal rods that held the stones together had been pulled out to be used over the centuries in other buildings. It was a wonder the place was still standing.

'You think that policeman will be all right? It was the shock of the noise. What did he want to shoot at me for? Why would he do that? I picked him up and threw him when he ran out of the tunnel with the gun. I didn't know what I was doing. I woke up and David Slater was standing over me stark naked. I didn't mean to hurt him, I didn't mean to hurt either of them.'

The guide who said: I always think of Garibaldi as the muscle and

King Victor Emmanuel as the brain of our revolution. That was under the statue on the hill above Rome. Funny, he'd forgotten whether the statue was of the King or the other fellow, but remembered what the guide had said. Maybe because he'd written it down that night in the hotel, and decided he'd read up all the history stuff when he got home and surprise Carole. That was part of being young and on honeymoon, proving yourself, improving yourself. When they got home, of course, he hadn't got round to it. He'd been too busy when he got back to work.

'You're one of the brave ones. I can tell. You could agree with me that a war was stupid, but it wouldn't make any difference. When the crunch came, you'd find you couldn't run away. Do you know the bravest person I ever knew? Paddy Turnbull. His heroism destroyed me, I can't live up to it.'

Carole's grandfather had been in the First World War, in the trenches in France, when he was sixteen. When his son was called up in 1943, he'd told him, never volunteer, the ones who ask for a regiment go first. The son had teased him, but he hadn't volunteered for anything and (to his disgust and his father's delight) he'd finished up in the Pay Corps at Redford Barracks in Edinburgh.

Meldrum's head went up with a jerk that hurt his neck. If he'd slept it could only have been for a second, but Nicolson wasn't in the room. He blundered to his feet, knocking over a small table. At the window, he saw the van was still parked outside. There had been a phone on the table he'd knocked over. He realised he'd no idea what the code here would be for emergency services. Would he get someone who could speak English? He was so tired he could hardly think. While he was listening to the dialling tone, Nicolson came into the room. 'I heard you,' he said. 'That's why I had to come back.' He tore the cord out of the phone and threw the handset into the corner. When they'd sat down, he had to get up again because the whisky was finished. He rummaged in the cabinet, clumsily to the sound of breaking glass, and found a bottle of brandy. Ignoring Meldrum's refusal, he refilled both their glasses.

'You know the bravest thing I ever did? Pissing in that grave. If I'd just been able to do that and not care, I'd have thought better of myself. Even as late as this. But when I'd pissed out the last drop – and I didn't hurry and it flowed, God, how it flowed – I looked up and saw Frank Bower, watching me like a promise of punishment to come. He knew who I was. He knew who I was all right. I turned and ran. And when I got into the taxi, I'd pissed myself. So you see there was still some left – not to the last drop at all, I couldn't even do that right.'

On a morning, they'd gone to Pisa, to what they called the square of the miracle, though the miracle when you got close depended on great blocks as counterweights stacked against the base of the leaning tower. When you'd done with miracles, you went out through the gate and along by the wall of the town past lines of stalls with Sengalese selling postcards and leather belts and Man United football strips.

'When soldiers came out of the trenches not able to talk or jigging about like puppets or walking like syphilitics, they got sent to hospitals like Maghull in Lancashire. The army was so desperate to get them back into the fighting they even let Freudian psychologists have a go at them. And they searched them like purses for a trauma in their childhood. Never mind the guns, they told the poor devils, Mummy fucking Daddy did the damage.'

A big ball-faced farmer type grinning and trudging up the steps to stand under the statue of David on the hill above Florence. I want to see which of you's the better man, his wife had shouted.

'Slater shouldn't have come at me in the night. I ran away when I saw Frank Bower, because I wasn't different, hadn't changed, was still the coward they'd made me. From the window, you could almost see where Hannibal beat the Romans. He was always beating them, of course, not that it did him any good in the end. This time he made the prisoners walk under the yoke to show they gave in for good and wouldn't fight him any more. I expect all the brave ones had been killed. The first time I met Frank Bower, it wasn't my fault I was taller than him. He looked up at me and said, I'll break you. They'd come in the night for me. *I was ten years old.* And no one but Paddy had pity on me. Look at me, I should never have been afraid, I wasn't made to be afraid. I crawled and howled and they taught me fear.'

An inverted man, legs spread, was cut with a saw down the middle from the anus; he didn't die till the cut reached the navel – blood to the head kept him conscious. That was in San Gimignano. Their party had trailed into its torture museum after a busload of other tourists. The Etruscans built their houses on the hills, the guide said, the Romans in the valleys. There was water in the valleys. Take your pick. San Gimignano sat on top of a hill. It had towers built so that when its families were tired of fighting everyone else they could fight one another.

Music, bands, the crowd cheering, with Carole looking down from the tower at the piazza full of cyclists lined up in ranks waiting for the signal to start the race; afterwards, high above the purple landscape on the terrace behind the little convent, *antico convento del 1200*, they drank wine. They had a good time, that morning in San Gimignano.

'I have a commission to make a whole room, everything in it, every piece, for a man in Siena. A little fat man, who raises money for making films, steals most of it and uses what's left to make porn. They say, even if you know what he is, there's a magic in the way he describes each new project. It's worth listening to him, because he believes the dream he sells. If only, they say, he had the courage not to steal. And because I wanted that to be true, I would have made something wonderful for him. It won't happen now.'

Thinking back, he regretted the nature that made him waste energy on worrying over how to order a meal in a foreign language or get hung up on stupid disappointments like the Sistine Chapel not having a dome for a roof just a barrel vault for God to lean over to reach out his finger to Moses. And the way it rained today, they were in Perugia, lashing down, mist and all, like an October afternoon at home. Had he complained about that? No wonder Carole had wearied of him at last.

He heard a voice, real or in a dream, telling him, 'Neil Heuk was worse than Frank Bower.'

And another, real or in a dream, telling how the Emperor Tiberius with his finger could poke a hole in a sound apple or the skull of a boy.

It was the cold that wakened him.

How does a man afraid of pain kill himself? He found Nicolson on a bed. His arms were spread out, he was on his back. He was so tall that his legs stretched off the end of the bed and his feet were on the floor, which would have been funny if it hadn't been for the foam on his lips and the tablet bottles scattered round him.

It was dark when he ran outside. All the way to the next house, the still air was heavy with the sweetness of flowers. He beat on the door until a light came on, and even then couldn't stop himself from knocking. The man who answered, fiftyish, grey hair standing on end, opened the door no more than half-way, ready to slam it shut again. He'd pulled on a pair of trousers, but was naked to the waist and his feet were bare. Despite being apprehensive and startled out of sleep, he looked intelligent and competent. The only difficulty was that he didn't speak English.

Meldrum explained and pointed. *Non capisco*, the man said. In your neighbour's house, someone is dying. *Non capisco. Non capisco.*

'Jesus fucking Christ, you cunt!' Meldrum cried.

The door was pulled a little further open. A woman in a dressing gown had arrived behind the man.

'Is something wrong?' she asked.

CHAPTER THIRTY-FIVE

He was in a room in another town. He didn't even know which one; they'd been brought here by ambulance. An Italian policeman was sitting on a chair by the door outside in the corridor. In a room on the floor below, Fulcini was being cared for. His injuries were serious, which made the authorities unhappy and assertive. Whoever was picked as being at fault, it wouldn't be Fulcini. Meldrum had been questioned, and would be questioned again. All the same, tomorrow at the latest, he'd join Shields at the airport in Rome.

'Put it this way, we can keep him alive,' the doctor said.

'Can he hear us?'

'I wouldn't like to think so. But I'm not one of those who would be dogmatic. There is brain activity. See, his eyelids are flickering. Put it this way, if he has dreams, let them be pleasant.'

'There's no question of him being able to travel?' Meldrum asked.

'You could try, at the danger of his life,' the doctor said, 'but what would be the point? I thought you understood. He didn't get here in time.'

Meldrum watched the steady pulsing that matched the beat of Nicolson's heart.

'I needed it spelled out,' he said. 'For my own people.'

'He knew what he wanted. He must have been saving up painkillers, maybe for a long time. Certainly, what he took was enough to kill three men.' The doctor sighed. 'Sometimes to be strong isn't an advantage.'

BOOK SEVEN

Dancing Mahoun

CHAPTER THIRTY-SIX

When Meldrum, off the plane, heard that his daughter Betty had been forced off the road, his first thought was that Neil Heuk had been responsible. His second, because Baby Sandy had also been in the car, was to make a blinding connection to Carole's story of how their grandchild had disappeared while she was shopping at the Gyle. At the time, he'd hardly paid attention to her account of the man who'd given her a row for carelessness and then walked away in the wrong direction. But if he tried to tell anyone that now he believed the man might have been Neil Heuk, he'd be marked as having lost the place. Told he was too exhausted to think straight. Obsessed with the Naylor Home. And it was true he was deadly tired; couldn't stop hearing Nicolson's voice. Near the end of his tether, his thoughts were full of a murderous rage.

Baby Sandy had been an accident. There was every sensible reason why he shouldn't have been born. Sandy and she had made their plans. She would take her degree and Sandy would take up his scholarship. They would go to Italy where the award would let Sandy paint for a year and she would find work of some kind. Then they would come home and she would find a job as a teacher and support them both until Sandy made his name as an artist.

Meantime they'd had a quiet wedding and lived together because they were in love. One month her period didn't come. Now she looked after the baby and Sandy worked as an art teacher. Her mother had been wonderful. Her father had behaved as if it was the end of the world.

Betty rubbed the baby's cheek with the backs of her fingers, smiling as she listened to him chuckle. He should be in the back seat, but she couldn't resist having him near so she could reach out and touch him as she drove. For Sandy and her, their baby wasn't the end of the world but the beginning, worth all the sacrifices and the changes of plan. Her father didn't understand. When little Sandy was old enough, she'd get a job. You didn't need a degree to get a job. Or she'd finish her degree, why not? And Sandy could give up teaching and not be tired any more and start painting seriously again.

'Soon see Daddy, darling,' she said aloud.

She glanced at her watch. She'd just under forty minutes to pick up Sandy from school; from there to Sainsbury's at Cameron Toll to shop for the weekend. The car was small, a Peugeot Trio, and ten years old; but it had made an enormous difference to their lives. Her mother had helped them to buy it. Nice euphemistic way of saying had given them the money, she thought.

She couldn't have got from Edinburgh out here to Pencaitland on the bus, not with Baby Sandy and all his paraphernalia of nappies and bottles and blankets and woolly toys. It had been good to see Tracey. They'd been friends since second year at university. Tracey had finished her degree, a 2.2 in Honours English, and was back home in Pencaitland while she wrote off for jobs. Her parents being away on holiday, as they often were since her father's retirement, she got bored and depressed. The visit had cheered her up: there was the benefit of the car again.

At the crossroads by the war memorial, Betty hesitated, trying to decide. Straight ahead would take her to the motorway, left into the village to the road through Dalkeith. She had time to go the scenic route, she told herself. The truth was, the lighter the traffic, the fewer people to rush past as you dawdled along at forty. She turned left, along by the paper shop, and down to the traffic lights at the narrow bridge. She was held up by a red light, then ran up out of the village past the whisky distillery and on to the open road.

The road wound back and forward and then there was a long straight stretch. She was half-way along it when the car appeared behind her.

Tracey had been so pleased to see her, and so nice with Baby Sandy. She glanced aside. He'd fallen asleep, head over to one side. It didn't look comfortable, but he was sleeping serenely.

The car had closed the gap. It loomed large in the rear mirror. Too fast, it was coming too fast.

She pulled in tight to the side of the road. An image of a man leaning forward over the wheel. Behind her, a horn yapped once, twice, then in a single unbroken blare that didn't stop. The noise filled the car. Baby Sandy was awake and crying. She couldn't get in any closer to the side. Why didn't he pass? The car juddered and bounced. She'd hit something on the verge. As she fought to straighten it, suddenly her mind was working, quickly and clearly, because she had to save her baby. Stupid to speed up – that's what he must want – this car was too slow, even if she tried – the faster she went, the more danger for Baby Sandy. She tapped the brake and the wheel wrenched and she fought it. She tapped again. Was he too close to see the warning lights? Again. There was a sickening bump. He'd hit the rear of the car. The horn blare started again. He fell back. And then he was moving out of the mirror. He was overtaking. Braking, she had the sudden awful thought that perhaps he was going to pull in front of her and force her to stop. The road ahead was empty. He was level with her. She braked hard – she would lock the doors, someone would come – the wheel juddered in her hands. He'd edged ahead and he was turning. Turning across her. Turning too soon.

The blow slapped her off the road.

The old sergeant at Dalkeith was suspicious of Meldrum.

'I can understand how you feel,' he said. 'Being a father myself.'

'I just want a look at him.'

'Your daughter and the baby are all right, though?'

'They got a shake. They're keeping them in overnight for observation.'

'But everything's okay?'

'Betty might have a bit of whiplash. That's my daughter. And she's got a broken wrist. Partly she got hurt protecting the baby. And he's fine! It's like a miracle.'

'She did well.'

'Not bad.'

'Aye.' A drawn-out double note, between a grunt and a sigh.

A constable leaned in at the open door, and said, 'There's a man at the desk, says we have an anorak belonging to his wife. She was in a crash. Car was a write-off and the anorak was in the boot. Blue, he says.'

'Second shelf, back of the cupboard. It's in a Safeway shopping bag.'

'Right.'

With a curious look at Meldrum, the constable took himself off.

'That happened about a fortnight ago. On the way into the town on the Jedburgh road. She had whiplash.'

'So can I see him?'

'He's nothing much to look at.'

'That's all I want. Just a look.'

'Do you mind if I say, I can't see why?'

Meldrum stared at him without answering.

'He's only here till the morning. He'll be moved in the morning.' The sergeant spoke slowly, not stressing his point, but making it. 'There's not a mark on him.'

'Oh.' A little ominous noise.

The sergeant plodded on. 'While he's here, I'm responsible for him.'

'You don't know me,' Meldrum said. 'That kind of stuff isn't my style.'

'My mistake.' The sergeant got to his feet. 'It's just that, being a father myself, and with the bairn being in the car, I could understand you being angry.'

Meldrum grunted and left it at that.

There were a couple of holding cells at the end of a corridor.

'I don't want to talk to him,' Meldrum said. 'No need to open the door.'

The boy sitting on the edge of the cot was no more than seventeen. He'd stolen a car in Sighthill and gone for a jaunt. After his collision with Betty, he'd roared his way through Dalkeith and Eskbank, and finally been caught jumping the lights at the cross in Loanhead. He didn't seem worried about being in jail, but cheerful and alert, as if the adrenaline was still coursing through him. He had other convictions, he'd told the sergeant; he loved driving fast, it was something he wouldn't ever be able to resist. As he stared up at the door, his expression was jaunty. If he was telling the truth, his future held other expressions for him, defiant maybe, or forlorn, suicidal if things went badly enough.

'Okay.'

'That's it?'

'That's it.'

The sergeant slid the observation panel shut.

Meldrum had taken his look.

There was no way of explaining that he had needed to see with his own eyes. Despite everything he'd been told, until the moment he looked into the cell, he couldn't be sure he wouldn't see Neil Heuk.

CHAPTER THIRTY-SEVEN

'Ten little niggers,' Heuk said. 'That's not politically correct, is it? Indians? Ten little Irishmen. That would be all right, wouldn't it? Ten little Welshmen, pissing in the milk.'

'I don't know what you're talking about.'

'I'm upset,' Heuk said. 'The people I knew when I was young are dying.'

'Nicolson's not dead.'

'Worse than, by the sound of it.'

There wasn't any arguing with that.

'Can I sit down?' Meldrum asked.

Heuk thought about it. 'I don't feel comfortable about you being here.'

That, at least, was unfeigned. When he'd opened the door and seen Meldrum, his jaw had dropped.

Meldrum sat down on the couch. Instead of the easy chair, the only other comfortable piece of furniture, Heuk pulled out one of the upright wooden chairs round the small table, and sat leaning slightly forward with his hands between his knees. The room with its kitchen clutter of sink, fridge and work surfaces against the back wall, felt cramped and impersonal. Nothing there seemed to belong to the present occupant, no pictures or photographs, not even a book lying around. It was very tidy, swept, dust-free. Meldrum remembered, however, there was once-a-week maid service at the Doune Apartments. If today had been the maid's day, even the tidiness gave no clue to Heuk. The receptionist at the desk downstairs had told him about the maid the first time he had visited this building. That had been to talk to the Balewas. There was no law against Neil Heuk taking a rental at the Doune Apartments. But it felt strange to be sitting in a room identical to the ones occupied by Iain Bower and the Balewas.

'Usually people don't come to see us,' Meldrum said. 'We've to go looking for them. But not you, you're different. You come and tell me I've saved your life. You come and tell me about the Naylor Home. You tell me what a monster Frank Bower is. It seems you can't keep away from me. I felt it was time I returned the compliment.'

'I'm more upset than I would have believed possible. Poor Nicolson.'

'From what he told me, he hated your guts.'

'I don't think so,' Heuk said. 'When did he tell you that?'

'I've told you, I was there the night he took the pills.'

'The night he tried to kill himself.'

'Yes, but he knew what he was saying.'

A little crazy, but rational.

'How could you accept anything he said that night?'

'I was there.'

'But just you,' Heuk said, sounding almost sympathetic. 'If someone else had been there as a witness, that might be different. Of course, if there had been two of you, he might not have had the chance to overdose.'

I can live with that, Meldrum thought, who didn't have any other option.

'All I can tell you is he put you on a par with Frank Bower.'

'In what way?' Heuk wondered.

'For cruelty. I took it that's what he meant.'

'I was only a child myself then. You're talking about a child. You can't compare a child to a grown man.'

'Children can't be cruel?'

'In their innocence, they can be. Like young animals, slapping out with their claws, testing their strength. But for anything more, they have to be taught to be cruel.' Meldrum remembered Macdonald, the retired policeman at Kilbracken. What was it he'd said about his childhood? *Innocent barbarians.* 'I'm certain Paddy Turnbull doesn't blame Neil Heuk. Ask Paddy. Neil Heuk was only eleven years old.'

Had Heuk ever been an innocent?

'I might just do that.'

'Yes, it's true, poor Nicolson was tormented by Frank Bower. And Paddy Turnbull tried to protect him. He was incredibly brave. If things had been left to go on like that, Paddy might have been a Christian martyr. I'm not trying to be funny. Even then he believed in Jesus, maybe more than he does now. And that made him absolutely fearless. A Christian martyr in the making. Because Frank couldn't give in, not in front of the whole school. If that's what it took, he would have had to kill Paddy, because he'd no choice. But he didn't want it to happen, that's why he came to me. Frank told me I could save both of them, and he taught me how.'

'Tell me about it,' Meldrum said. 'Your good deed.'

'Oh, many a true word spoken in jest.' Hands between his knees, Heuk rocked gently back and forward with a kind of smile. 'Turnbull had always been good to me. Kindness was rare in that place, he was kind to all of us. But Frank made me understand that it wasn't so simple, it never is. He wants you, he told me. That's what it's about, he told me, he wants you. Well, it didn't happen at once. The first time I touched Paddy, he was shocked. And the time after that and all the other times, shocked or angry. He must have wanted to run away, but there wasn't anywhere to run to. Frank saw that we'd be together, jobs we were given that meant we'd be alone. Every step of the way, he resisted me. Until one night, he'd been terribly beaten and I put my arms round him. He began to cry, he never cried. And that night he buggered me, and the light went on and Frank was there. No more God for Paddy.' Heuk rubbed his hands down his face and yawned. 'And after all he didn't die. So it was a kind of good deed.'

Meldrum got up and went to the window. He stared at the building opposite.

Behind him, Heuk's voice asked, 'Do I disgust you?'

This flat was on the second floor, and so all you could see was the building on the other side of the street. You had to imagine the Forth behind it, the dark rolling waters and Fife on the further shore.

Without looking round, he said, 'You like to play games. It would be stupid to play them with me.'

'In case you get angry? What would you do to me?'

He turned his head and looked down at Heuk. 'Now you disgust me.'

Heuk nodded, not showing any particular emotion, just acknowledging it.

Meldrum sat down again. 'What about the other boy?'

'What other boy?' Heuk blinked and stared, disconcerted.

'You want me to believe Frank Bower was afraid he might kill Turnbull. But what about the boy who was found dead on the beach outside the Naylor Home? The story was he'd run away, but you accused Bower of killing him. According to you, Bower could get away with anything then. So what did he have to be afraid of? If he could kill one child, why not another?'

Heuk leaned back with a sigh. 'Why not? Like you say, people play games. Maybe it was a game he was playing with us.'

'That's it?'

'We were children. You play games with children.'

'So it's all down to Frank?'

'You said it yourself, if once why not twice? God knows, what Frank's done in his life. I'm sure he killed his brother.'

'You told us that before. We've been through all that.'

'Are you going to arrest Frank?'

Meldrum studied him thoughtfully. 'Not a chance. I'll tell you something I shouldn't tell you. This morning the Chief Constable used those exact words. Not a chance of arresting Frank Bower. There might be a motive, but it would take a lot of proving. We have something about him buying petrol the night of the murder, but I think Frank's covered himself with that. But the worst thing is Nicolson. He had the motive, and we can't prove he wasn't in Edinburgh the night Iain was murdered. Any defence lawyer of Frank's would love him. And we can't do anything about Nicolson, not one thing. He can't give us an alibi. He can't confess. He's a vegetable, but he'll save Frank's skin.'

Without a moment's hesitation, Heuk asked, 'What about Keith Chaney's boy, then? Have you questioned Frank about Keith Chaney's boy?'

'Why would I do that?'

'The boy's missing, isn't he?'

'There's not the slightest reason to believe that could be down to Bower.'

'Down to him. We're all down to him. Why shouldn't Sam Chaney be down to him?'

Meldrum thought about explaining that Frank Bower had been at Kilbracken the day Sam went missing, as had Keith Chaney. There wasn't any doubt about that – DI Cockburn's detectives had taken witness statements from everyone on the island.

Instead, he shook his head and got up. Time to get out. Just for today he'd lost his stomach for the games Heuk wanted to play.

CHAPTER THIRTY-EIGHT

B etty sat with the baby on her knee, while Sandy fussed around their kitchen making tea.

'If only I'd been there,' he said again.

'You'll learn,' Meldrum said. 'Golden rule, husbands are never there when they're needed.'

'Like policemen,' Sandy said.

Meldrum just about managed a smile. In fact, unreasonably he felt Sandy should have been there and, totally unreasonably, angry with him for not being.

'Are you sure you're both all right?' he asked Betty.

'I've told you, Dad. I have a headache, that's all. And Baby Sandy doesn't seem to be up or down. They checked everything. They were very thorough.'

It was the third time he'd asked the same question.

'And very nice,' Sandy said. 'Like the police. Apart from the first one.'

Betty frowned at him.

'What?' Meldrum felt a surge of protective anger.

'He didn't mean any harm,' Betty said. 'He was wondering about road rage. So he asked me if I'd done anything to annoy the other driver.'

' 'Bloody fool,' Sandy said.

'How long will you have to wear the collar?' Meldrum asked. Second time for that question.

She eased her head slightly back and forward. The collar went over her shoulders and up to her chin. A Philadelphia collar, apparently they called it.

'Six weeks. And no, I've not to take it off at night.'

'Did I ask you that already?'

'Hmm-mm.'

Sandy said, 'They showed me what to do. When she's lying down, you unfasten it and sort of slip it out from under her. Give it a wipe. Put powder on. It's to avoid getting a heat rash. It'll be worth it to make sure there's no after-effects.'

'The baby's all right, that's the main thing,' Betty said. Her eyes filled with tears.

Sandy sat on the arm of the chair and hugged her round the shoulders. 'And you. You're *both* the main thing. And you're both all right.' To Meldrum he said, 'It's the shock.'

Betty flapped a hand at him. 'Don't bloody well talk about me as if I wasn't here!'

Over her head he made a see-what-I-mean? face. Meldrum ignored him.

'You could say she was amazingly lucky,' Sandy said, getting up and starting to pour the tea, 'apart from the bad luck of it happening at all. Once I was sure Betty and Sandy were all right, I phoned to see if they'd caught the maniac who forced her off the road. The sergeant told me the fence was badly maintained, so when the car hit it the posts tore out. The wires were already hanging nearly to the ground. Sheep had been out on the road, so the farmer had been warned to do something about it. The sergeant said, tell your wife she should try the lottery, the fence was due to be fixed the next morning.'

'Do we have to talk about it?' Betty asked.

'I'm sorry, love. That was bloody stupid of me. I'm so relieved, I'm just babbling on.' He gave her a cup and then handed one to Meldrum. 'She got an arm over to hold Sandy in his chair – and she thought of switching off the engine *and* somehow or other she managed to do that as well.' He grinned at her. 'How many arms have you got?' To Meldrum he said, 'She was terrific. I couldn't have done it.'

'Yes, you could,' she said. 'If Baby Sandy was in the car.'

'And you,' he said fondly.

Love's young dream. Meldrum was feeling just a touch superfluous. 'Are you not having a cup?' he asked Sandy.

'No. I'm going to take the chance while you're here to get some shopping in. Betty's mum's going to look after her tomorrow while I'm at school.'

'She's staying off school?' Meldrum exclaimed. It was unheard of for Carole to take a day off.

'I told them there wasn't any need!' Betty said.

'I didn't mean that the way it sounded,' Meldrum said. 'It's just – you know your mum. A workaholic.'

'Takes one to know one,' Betty said, but she was smiling.

'I'm glad she'll be with you tomorrow. Rest as much as you can. You either do it now, or pay for it later.'

'That's me told,' she said to Sandy.

Pulling on his coat, he left in a welter of promises about being as quick as he could.

No sooner was he out of the door than Betty put down her cup and pulled a face.

'Pour me another cup, would you, Dad? I can't stop him putting sugar in it – he's got this theory it's good for shock. Maybe one cup at the time, I keep telling him, not the day after. But you know Sandy, he's so stubborn once he gets an idea into his head. I'll finish up the fittest diabetic in Edinburgh, if he goes on like this. Anyway, I *hate* sugar.'

He emptied the tea down the sink and ran the tap. On impulse, he went over and hugged her.

'Thank God you're all right.' He ran a hand over the baby's hair and down over the eyes to cover them. When he took his hand away, his grandson laughed up at him. 'Both of you.'

'Thank who? I thought you were an atheist.'

'Agnostic.'

'Same difference.'

'Only to the priest-ridden.' He'd meant that as a joke, but she didn't smile.

As he poured her tea, he said, 'I'm just back from Italy. Official business, don't ask. It was funny being back there.'

'When were you ever in Italy? You never go anywhere.'

'Your mum and I went there on honeymoon. Don't tell me you didn't know that? You must remember the photograph we had framed? Sitting on a wall with the whole of Rome spread out behind us. A young chap that was on his honeymoon, too, took it for us, and I took one of them.' He smiled at the memory.

'Hmm-mm.' Sipping her tea, Betty bent her head over the baby.

'This visit I didn't see any of the places Carole and I went to together. Drove round the edge of Rome, that was about the nearest. It brought a lot back, though. It's wonderful how much you remember. Not everything, of course. You can see why people keep diaries. Bother is, when there's anything worth writing down you're probably too busy to write it down. We saw the Pope. He was about that size.' He measured a little gap between finger and thumb. 'Which Pope would that be? I knew at the time.'

'Don't ask me,' Betty said.

'And the Sistine Chapel, we saw it. Carole said to me, You must be the only person in the whole world who was disappointed in the Sistine Chapel.' He laughed to himself. 'But, honestly, that's how I felt. It was the crush of people and all the schoolkids and the noise. The place was going like a fairground. Maybe if you could have sat quietly on your own. The church I went to as a kid was a little wooden church. It didn't hold all that many people, and it was never even half full. But it was quiet. We both loved Florence, though. And Siena and—'

'Let it go, Dad.'

'What?'

'You should let it go.'

'I don't know what you mean.'

'I'm saying it was a long time ago.'

Comfortable and affectionate, he'd been drifting along. Now he spread his hands, trying to understand. 'That's what makes it worth—'

'You and Mum aren't married any more. Not for years.'

'That doesn't stop me remembering. Your life is all the bits that happened in it. You can't pick and choose. Of course I remember things. Even if I wanted to, I couldn't let them go.'

'I don't mean then. I mean now.'

'What things?'

'When you go to see her.' She made a face of distress mixed with exasperation. 'God! I don't mean you shouldn't go to see her. Of course you should see her. But it's as if you can't get it into your head you're not still married. You won't make her happy, don't make her unhappy. Don't make her unhappy. She's confused. You're not going to get back together – and if you did, wouldn't it be the same? – wouldn't you make her unhappy again?'

'Did Carole say this to you?'

'Not in so many words. You know she wouldn't.'

He thought of one thing after another to say, and didn't say any of them. By temperament and training, he was a man who thought before he reacted. There were times when it was best to say nothing.

'Now you're hurt,' she said.

'No, no, no. Just a bit taken aback. Let me think about it.'

'I shouldn't have said anything.'

'Don't feel like that. I hope you can always tell me what you think.'

They began to talk again about the accident. It was the safest topic.

'The car kept rolling forward and I couldn't find the brake. When it stopped, it was so quiet I thought I heard crickets in the grass. And then Baby Sandy started crying. It's the sweetest sound I've ever heard.'

After a time, Sandy arrived back with three full plastic bags from Safeway clutched in each fist and Meldrum helped him unpack them and put the loaves and packets and cans away. When they were finished, he agreed, yes, a coffee would be great – or a beer – yes, a beer would be fine, too. The three of them sat talking and he looked at Betty and wondered, How close was I to her, even when I took our closeness as being natural as breathing? Didn't I spend my time on those long walks with her talking about myself, *my* ideas, *my* thoughts – one-way traffic, me to her. Maybe that's the difference between fathers and mothers, with mothers maybe it's two-way traffic. He felt a parent's anger. Why couldn't you stay young and be my child for ever? And the other side of that coin, Why am I getting old?

Before he made his escape, all of that confusion was settling down. Even at its worst, he knew perfectly well what mattered was that Betty and Baby Sandy hadn't been hurt.

The after-effect, though, was to make him see his relationship with Carole in a different light. He'd taken it for granted, and got it wrong, it seemed, that her feelings and his were pretty much alike.

Anger and envy of the old for the young.

And self-pity.

Don't forget self-pity.

CHAPTER THIRTY-NINE

C hief Constable Baird was of the opinion the time had come to let the Iain Bower enquiry run down. Of course, murder was the most serious of crimes, and the Bower file wouldn't ever be closed. On the other hand, theft, burglary, fraud, grievous bodily harm and all the rest kept rolling along the conveyor belt; and inevitably homicides, too, culpable and otherwise. Crime was an industry that rode out recessions and fed off prosperity. Police resources were limited and his job was to see they were used to best effect.

'Anyway, it seems this Nicolson probably killed him.'

'I don't think so,' Meldrum said.

'I know you don't. The difference from the last time we had this conversation is that Nicolson's confessed to murdering Slater.'

'But not to killing Bower.'

'Well, if there had been a chance to question him properly, he might have.'

Meldrum didn't even try to argue with that. It was hard to see what he could have done differently. If there was a fault, most of it lay with Fulcini and his pride and his damned gun, which had frightened Nicolson out of surrendering. All the same, there weren't any medals on offer for keeping a man company until he was ready to try to kill himself. You couldn't call it a good career move.

'What do we do about Frank Bower?' he asked.

Baird kept a tidy desk. He folded his hands on its swept expanse and began to tap along his knuckles, right then left, in a gesture of controlled irritation. 'We've been through that too, have we not? As far as his brother's death goes, there's no case against him. And no prospect of making one that could justify keeping after him. Look at the options. Iain Bower could have been killed by Nicolson – and probably was. Or by a homosexual pick-up. Or – least likely – he messed about with a kid and got killed because of that. We've spent a lot of man hours checking those possibilities. Not a single lead to suggest using up more would be justified. And that takes us back to where we started. Time to put this one on the back burner.'

It was true, Meldrum thought, that the newspapers hadn't made as much of the murder of Iain Bower as he'd feared and then wished they would. No pressure from editorials, articles, readers' letters, to find the murderer. There was a chemistry in these things, and Bower had come into the city as a stranger.

'What about the Naylor Home?' he asked.

'You've other things to do. Crimes that happened this month, not forty years ago.'

'Thirty years ago.'

'Thirty years ago,' Baird said, fastidiously separating each word as if to examine it for relevance. The knuckle-tapping had speeded up.

Meldrum took a slow breath. 'I know Nicolson has only himself to blame for the awful state he's in. He did it to himself, but I haven't been able to get him out of my head.' It was the nearest he could manage to an apology. 'Frank Bower's ruined a lot of lives. I mean, this is children we're talking about.'

'I don't need to be reminded of that.'

The edge of feeling in Baird's voice surprised Meldrum. Then he remembered that John Brennan, the man who knew everything and everybody, had told him Baird's nephew had died of cancer. He's a cold fish, Brennan had said, but he was upset at the funeral; of course, he's always been very close to his younger brother.

'No matter how long ago it was, Bower shouldn't be allowed to get away with it,' Meldrum said stubbornly.

'If what you've been told is true. We're talking about allegations. One of your witnesses, Nicolson, won't be making any more statements. And the more I hear of this fellow Heuk, the less I'd be inclined to take his word.' Baird held up a hand, silencing Meldrum. 'But, of course, the Naylor Home thing has got to be looked into. There wasn't ever any question that it wouldn't be. Not by you, though. Even if you didn't have more urgent things on your plate, I've a feeling you're too involved. I'll put somebody on to it.'

Right. Some young constable, or old hand going through the motions.

'Neil Heuk would be the place to start. The records of the Home have vanished, but if we could get a list of names out of him it would be something to work on.'

'I'll mention that.'

That was it. Finished. Double line. Nowhere to go. Don't get too involved. It happened. Join the professionals.

Having made his point, Baird slipped into man manager mode, getting up from behind the desk and walking him to the door. Being patronised was all Meldrum needed to send him back to his office in a black rage. As he went in, Shields was putting down the phone.

Since his outburst on the beach at Anzio, the sergeant had been visibly conscientious and busy. His spectacular loss of temper would have led with any other boss either to the air being cleared between them or to a fast reassignment. With Meldrum, it had been ignored as if it had never happened. Bobbie Shields, a sociable man, was showing signs of increasing discomfort.

'Somebody at reception wanted to see you. Turned up about an hour ago, claiming he'd information about the Bower murder. I could check and see if he's still there.'

'Why didn't you deal with whoever it is?'

'I tried, but he won't talk to anybody but the man in charge. I asked him who he was, what it was about. All I could get out of him was his name. Name, rank and number stuff, like in the war. Boer War by the look of him.'

'So what was his name?'

He waited impatiently while Shields searched for his scratchpad.

'James Arthur Curdie.'

A tree around, Meldrum would have chopped it down; a garden, he'd have dug it. His only way out of a black mood was physical. He ran down the stairs with Shields rolling in his wake.

At a glance, he knew Curdie was going to be a waste of time. Shields, to be fair to him, had pretty much said the same thing. Years in the job gave you an instinct. Curdie looked somewhere in his mid seventies, a lean old man with an eyepatch, who had to be reassured twice that, yes, Meldrum was the man in charge of the Bower investigation.

'Can we go somewhere to talk?' he asked. 'Somewhere *private*, I mean.'

'Exactly what I was going to suggest, sir.' Looking over the old man's head, Meldrum had a view of the front entrance. 'Eh, sergeant, could you take Mr Curdie along? I'll join you in a moment, sir.'

He intercepted Balewa, before he reached the reception desk.

'Detective Inspector, good morning! What a surprise! It was you I was hoping to see. If you could give me a moment, I would be grateful.'

'Is this in connection with the murder of Iain Bower?'

'No.' Balewa shook a finger in denial. 'Not directly, no. Could you speak to me now?'

'I have someone to see. I'm sorry.'

'The thing is, I didn't want to talk to someone who would misunderstand. I know you will see why I am concerned.'

Meldrum hesitated. 'It would have to be quick.'

In the interview room, Balewa eyed the tape deck warily. 'Do you have to put that on?'

'Not if you just want to take a moment to tell me something.'

'Could it be off, please? Thank you. I'll be honest with you, I don't want to be accused of slandering someone. This could be quite innocent. I'm sure it is, in fact. It was my wife who insisted you should be told. I'd like you to treat what I say on that basis.'

Meldrum made no secret of looking at his watch. 'If you've something to tell, I'm listening.'

'There's a man who's come to the Apartments. I met him in the lift and we had a conversation. The weather and what had been in the newspaper, you know, quite casual and ordinary. But when I mentioned it to my wife, she became upset. I told her not to be foolish, of course. But it's true he seems to be going out of his way to speak to me. And he has asked about my family. And yesterday he invited my wife and me and 'your charming little boy', that's what he said, 'your charming little boy', to afternoon tea on Sunday. Telling it like this, I feel foolish. If it wasn't for – for what happened before, we wouldn't be giving it a single thought. We'd be pleased in fact – the way we were before. It isn't anything but a horrible coincidence. I'm sure it's quite innocent. But my wife wouldn't rest until I agreed to come to see you.'

'Did this new neighbour tell you his name?'

'Mr Heuk.' Balewa held out his curved forefinger. 'Heuk, like for a jacket, to hold up a jacket, you know. We made a joke of it. Is anything wrong?'

'No,' Meldrum said. 'You did the right thing. I'll talk to this man, make sure everything's above board. In the meantime, I agree with your wife. It doesn't do any harm to take precautions.' He forced a smile. 'If he invites you, I wouldn't have tea with him on a Sunday.'

He went back up to his office lost in thought. At his desk, he took a blank sheet of paper and covered it with random lines as he went over the implications of what Balewa had told him. After a quarter of an hour, the phone rang.

'He's still here,' Shields announced without preamble.

'What?' That was when he remembered James Arthur Curdie, who by that time had been kept waiting for almost two hours. 'Oh, Christ!'

He went down faster than he'd come up, but the old man was remarkably cheerful.

'I must apologise,' Meldrum said. 'It's been a very busy morning.'

'Not for me,' Curdie said.

'I'm sorry. You could have spoken to someone else, of course.'

'Have you got a Charter?'

'How do you mean?'

'Like the hospitals. They have a Charter. Promise they'll deal with you within ten minutes. That means you see the nurse at the desk straight away, then wait an hour to see the doctor. Or, in your case, two.'

'At least I see the sergeant's got you a cup of tea.'

'I've had more tea than I can handle at my age. I've had to go to the lavatory twice. Can we start? You'd better put that thing on.'

Meldrum nodded to Shields, who switched on the tape. They went through the preliminaries. Curdie gave his address.

'But that's the same building! You live in the building where Iain Bower was murdered?'

'Floor below. My flat was right underneath him. Still is. He's the one that's gone, poor fellow.'

'But you must have been interviewed.' Glancing at Shields, Meldrum could see Curdie's name didn't ring a bell for him either. 'Everybody in the building was interviewed.'

'They'd have had a bother with me. I was in South Africa visiting my son. A very violent place, Johannesburg. My son couldn't believe me when I told him I'd come back to a murder in Edinburgh. I just missed it, I told him.'

Iain Bower's body had been found at ten o'clock on the Friday morning, when a neighbour who'd first noticed his door lying open at just after eight finally decided to investigate. By then, however, Curdie had been gone. Up at half five, he had left in a taxi to catch the seven o'clock shuttle from Edinburgh Airport, and by the time the body was found was in a lounge at Heathrow patiently waiting for his flight to South Africa.

'It must have been about eleven o'clock. This was the night before I left, the Thursday night. I couldn't give you the exact time, but it was quite late. It was late enough that I almost didn't go up. I didn't want to disturb Mr Bower, if it was too late. The thing was, I didn't want to go away without trying to make sure the repair would be done. Did I say about the repair? There was something wrong with the roof gutter so that water was coming down on his balcony *and* on mine, which was underneath his. There was a storm of rain that night, and that's when I noticed it. So I made up my mind and went up to see him. He told me he had reported it. But when I got home from Johannesburg, the gutter still wasn't repaired. I'm afraid he didn't tell me the truth. No doubt he *intended* to report it the next day. But he didn't get the chance, poor man.'

'I'm grateful to you, Mr Curdie,' Meldrum said. 'It's helpful to us in establishing the time of death.' This was politic, but not strictly true. 'I wonder, apart from discussing the gutter repair, did you and Mr Bower chat at all? He didn't say anything to you about expecting a visitor?'

'Of course not. I barely knew the man.'

'Well, it was good of you to come and see us.' Meldrum started to ease his chair back.

'I'd been introduced to him, of course. At an owners' meeting about parking spaces. Can't say I took to him. I'd have paid more attention to him if I'd known he was going to be murdered. I've lived a long time, but I've never met anyone who's been murdered before. My son thought I was joking when I phoned him. I missed the murder, I told him, but I'm pretty sure I saw the murderer.'

'I beg your pardon?'

'I finished talking to Bower. Didn't take long. My impression, he wasn't really interested. I'd walked up and I was going to walk down – worst thing you can do with age is give in to it – but to get to the stairs I had to pass the lift. As I came to it, the doors opened and this man stepped out. I wouldn't have paid him any attention, if he hadn't seemed upset at seeing me. By that time, I was desperate to get to my bed.'

'Can you describe him?'

'I can do better than that. It was Iain Bower's brother.'

'Frank Bower?' Shields asked. 'How did you know?'

'I asked.'

'Could you explain that?' Meldrum asked.

'When I was introduced to Iain Bower at the owners' meeting, I said to him, Bower? That's an unusual name. Any relation to Frank Bower? And he said, yes, he was his brother.'

'But how did you know Frank Bower?'

'He was the leading light in the Rotary Club I belonged to years ago. Very popular figure. But I said to my late wife, I wouldn't like to get on the wrong side of him. Some people go into teaching for the wrong reasons, I told her. I was in education, you see. Physics, chemistry, taught maths when there was a shortage, head teacher before I retired. She liked him, though. And, give him his due, he was an excellent speaker. Could hold people in the palm of his hand. I'm not sure how good an influence he was. Something about him never sat right with me.'

'You're sure it was Frank Bower you saw?'

'Nothing wrong with my eyesight.'

'That corridor isn't brightly lit. How good a look did you get? Did you speak to him?'

'I did not. He didn't recognise me. And I didn't care for the expression on his face. I pretended I'd hardly noticed him. Played at being an old buffer lost in his thoughts, you know. I tell you, I was glad to lock my own door behind me.'

'When did you last see him? I mean, when you knew him before?'

'Oh, I know what you're implying. Over twenty years ago. But I'll pick his photograph out of a hundred, if you like. Or I'll pick *him* out of one of your line-ups, if you like. Frank Bower isn't a man you forget.' He looked from one to the other and smiled. 'Are you glad I waited?'

'We certainly are.'

'I thought you might be.'

CHAPTER FORTY

T he local policeman was a stolid forty-year-old called Leitch, whom
Meldrum had got in touch with about fixing up a boat to take
them to the island. With a constable, he was there to meet them when
they drove up the track on the eastern side of the loch. Waiting his turn
to get into the farmer's boat, Meldrum drew the sharp clean air deep into
his lungs. As the boat left the pier, he watched a pair of mallard rise and
fall in the choppy water of its wake.

The first indication of things going wrong came when Leitch told
them he'd gone out to the island the day before.

'What took you out there?' Meldrum leaned forward so abruptly, he
had the illusion for an instant of the boat dipping under him.

'Just a coincidence. Your man was there. I spoke to him. Lightning
striking twice in the same place, I said, when I got your call today.'

'That's what's bothering me.' To check Bower was on the island,
Shields had phoned Kilbracken House after they'd got the warrant, on
the pretext they needed more information on his stolen Visa card. He
hadn't spoken to Bower, who was apparently shooting at the far end of
the island, but no doubt when he got back Bower would have been told
of the call. Meldrum had an uneasy feeling that Shields plus Leitch might
have added up, from Bower's point of view, to a suspicious amount of
police interest.

'I had a good reason for being there,' Leitch said, sounding defensive.

'What was that?'

'There was a bit of a dispute at the weekend. One of the women on
the island was accused of shoplifting in Dumfries. I spoke to this Mrs

Parker, but Bower himself came in while I was talking to her. He was playing the laird, very much the man in charge. I'll tell you, he wasn't very civil. He'll be singing a different tune today.'

'It's a pity you were there yesterday of all days. I don't suppose you're at the island that often?'

'That's the first time I ever had occasion to be there. I was interested to get a look at it. There's always rumours fly about when folk keep themselves too much to themselves.'

'I don't suppose it matters. But whatever else he is, Bower isn't stupid.'

'I can't imagine there'll be any problem.'

'Let's hope not,' Meldrum said grimly.

They left the farmer with the boat and set off towards the House. As they came on to the terrace in front of it, Chaney came out of the front entrance with a pale, tall, beak-nosed man, who frowned at Leitch and said, 'I hope you're not here to bother my wife again.'

Ignoring him, Meldrum said to Chaney, 'We want to see Mr Bower. Tell him we're here.'

Seeing a little twitch of the lips, almost a smile, Meldrum knew suddenly what he was going to hear, even before Chaney said it. Frank Bower had left the island the previous night. Asked where he'd gone, Chaney said, 'He didn't tell me.'

'Last night?' Shields repeated. 'I phoned about three hours ago. I was told he was out shooting. Some woman that didn't sound all that sober. What the hell's going on here?'

Parker, the shoplifter's husband, stared at him in alarm. 'I do hope that wasn't my wife. Oh, dear, she hasn't been well. She's been under sedation.'

He, too, claimed to have no idea where Frank might have gone.

'In that case,' Meldrum said, 'let's ask Mrs Bower.'

'Oh, I don't know about that,' Parker said. He glanced to Chaney for support. 'May Bower doesn't keep at all well.'

Paradise seemed to have more than its share of invalids.

Chaney, however, knew when it was time to bow to the inevitable.

They waited in the library, the room they'd been shown into the first time they came to the island. This time, however, there was no fire. When May Bower appeared, she was wearing an outdoor coat with a fur collar. She didn't, however, comment on the eccentricity of this or the coldness in the room. Instead, she held out a hand and shook Meldrum's very graciously as he introduced himself.

'Frank will be sorry that he's not here to see you,' she said. 'He's very busy, of course, but he always makes time if he's really needed. You can count on him to lend a hand in getting things done. He's always been like that. He has a strong sense of civic responsibility. I think that comes from being in public service for so many years.' In a childish gesture, which might have been charming in a very young woman, she put a hand across her mouth. 'Oh dear, if Frank heard me, he wouldn't be pleased. He'd tell you plenty of businessmen show a responsibility to the community they live in. The right sort of businessmen, you know. The sort you meet in the Rotary Club.'

Feeling slightly stunned, Meldrum tried for firm ground.

'Can you tell us how we could get in touch with your husband?'

'They told me he'd gone when I woke up this morning,' she said vaguely. 'I didn't know he'd been called away. He's a businessman now, you see.'

'So he has to go away often?'

'Oh, yes. Well. Sometimes.'

'Do you know where he goes? I suppose he'll phone or send you a letter or a card when he's away?'

Her eyes slid away from him. She stared up intently, as if studying the far corner of the ceiling. The effect was disconcerting.

'I think I was happiest,' she said, 'when my husband worked in the Naylor Home. He was so well thought of by everyone.'

'Councillor Nolan,' Meldrum suggested.

'Yes!' The brightness of her smile shamed him. 'And Michael Forbes. He was our local MP. Oh, all kinds of people. Everybody knew Frank. We had Lord Crombie once to dinner. Those were such happy years. Not that I'm unhappy now.'

Once started, she proved difficult to stop. As if stimulated by each attempt to get her to leave, she would go over in more or less the same terms how good their life had been when they lived in a house in the grounds of the Naylor Home. Just as Meldrum was beginning to wonder if they'd have to carry her out or leave themselves, she dozed off for an instant, and when she jerked awake shook hands with all of them and left.

Chaney had been told to wait outside, and as she left he came in.

Frank Bower had knocked at the door of his room after dinner. He was carrying a case, not an overnight bag, a proper suitcase. Yes, he'd thought it was odd, but, no, he hadn't asked. You didn't question Frank. You just didn't. Because of the case, they'd taken the four by four down to the pier, and then he'd taken him over in the boat. They'd walked up to the car and put the case in the boot – yes, he'd been carrying the case for Frank, of course he had, why? The last he'd seen of Frank was him getting into the car. Volvo, he couldn't remember the licence number. Volvo S80, Meldrum told him; don't worry, we have the number.

When told Richard Nicolson was in a coma, Chaney showed no surprise, but had an odd reaction. He went over to the hearth and pointed.

'See that?'

Meldrum went close.

'What?'

'The face.'

Set into the massive stone overmantel was a face in relief. It was easy to miss, lost among an exuberant detailing of fronds and grape bunches. Once focussed on, though, it was extraordinary. It took a moment to realise how strongly it reminded him of another face. A face which he had never forgotten though he'd seen it only once and many years before.

Coming out of the Sistine Chapel, he'd noticed a door in the corner because they'd been told of an exit leading to a short cut into St Peter's Square. Beside it, he'd seen a man talking to one of the Vatican guides. A tall, bulky man with an air of authority, a man with hanging shoulders, fleshy nose, wide down-turned mouth. It was the look on his face that was unforgettable, though it might only have been an accident of the moment; and one lent a deception of meaning because of the disagreement with Carole about the Chapel, already casting its shadow. His look was one that might have been scorn or perhaps disillusionment or simply infinite weariness. Standing near the heart of one of the world's great places of pilgrimage, involved in its business, his look said that in this crowded temple God was absent.

He had glanced at Meldrum and, without words, had seemed to ask him, And so if He is not here, then where?

'See under it?' Chaney said.

Under the stone face a verse was carved:

Mahoun gart cry ane dance
For idle herts
An hauns
An aa by time's mischance.

'I didn't make out who it was at first,' Chaney said. 'But as soon as one of the smart arses here told me Mahoun was the Devil, I saw right away it was Frank.'

On the way to the boat, he walked at Meldrum's side, talking softly all the way.

'Heuk was about the worst thing that happened to Nicolson. He would slap his face, and the rest of us would laugh, you couldn't help laughing. Nicolson could have picked him up with one hand. But if he crossed Heuk, Frank beat the shit out of him. It was funny when I was in Brussels, I could see right through Heuk – he hated everybody liking Iain so much. And the thing was nobody there knew Heuk or what he'd done, not the way I did. But nobody had any time for him. You know how there's a kind of man dogs will bark at in the street. People were like that with Heuk, they . . . sniffed him out. If I told you the things Heuk made Nicolson do. He'd squeeze him by the balls and make him sing "She Loves You", funniest thing you ever heard. And then he'd run off and tell Frank some lie or other and Frank would tell him to fetch Nicolson, and the two of them would take him into a room and shut the door. It didn't matter that Frank knew he was making it up half the time. Frank was grooming Heuk for stardom.'

At least the air blowing across the loch, cold on cheeks and lips, still felt clean.

'Lord Crombie, eh?' Shields said, looking round at Meldrum from his seat in the middle of the boat.

More or less in the dark about what had been going on, Leitch had been keeping a low profile. Now he asked, 'Mrs Bower, you mean? Did you notice that as well? Going on about what a big man her husband was. And all these friends he's supposed to have had. Apart from anything else, I wondered if she was a wee bit mental, like not the full shilling. Take all this rich friends stuff with a pinch of salt, I thought. I've come across it, more than once, folk claiming to be on great terms with Lord Home or the Duke of Buccleuch – and them the kind you know fine wouldn't get over the doorstep. *Lord* Crombie!'

'Do you know who you're talking about?' Shields asked, grinning.

'How do you mean?'

'Crombie's a Law Lord. A judge in the High Court.'

'All the same,' Leitch said, 'it doesn't mean Bower knew him. Do you think he knew him?'

Lord Crombie was just over the five-foot mark, a dandy, always impeccably dressed. After the reductive fashion of police humour, he was known irreverently as Little Lord Fondletheboy, which had to be a calumny. What else could it be?

'I wouldn't be surprised,' Meldrum said.

CHAPTER FORTY-ONE

B etty watched fascinated as the tray tilted and its contents started to slide towards her. She didn't even try to take evasive action. The Philadelphia collar held her by the neck as if to say, don't look away; and she watched it happening in slow motion. She knew she was going to be soaked at best, burned at worst, and then the man dipped and tipped the tray so deftly the other way everything slid back into its place – and stopped.

It really was very well done.

'I'm so sorry,' he said. 'I slipped on something.'

There was nothing to be seen on the floor, but perhaps it had been kicked under the table.

'I don't know how you managed to save yourself,' she said. 'I was sure everything was coming off.'

'Coming right at you, too. Oh, how awful,' he said, 'and the baby – I've just seen him!' Baby Sandy, in his pushchair, tucked close to the table at her side, was fast asleep. 'He's missed all the excitement.'

'So he has!'

Laughing, the adrenalin still flowing, it seemed natural that he should sit opposite her.

'If it's not anyone's seat?'

'No. That's all right.'

Once they got talking, she explained that she was waiting to meet her mother, but that she wasn't expecting her for another half hour at least.

'She'll be off doing some shopping,' he assumed.

'No,' Betty said. 'She'll be coming from the school she works in.'

'She's a teacher?'

'Head teacher, actually.'

'I can see you're proud of her.'

'She's going to help me pick a present for my husband's birthday – then she'll come back with me for dinner. John Lewis is a good place to meet – it's handy for the car park. If we can get an hour of shopping, that's about as much as the baby will put up with.'

Looking out through the angled wall of glass, she saw Eduardo Paolozzi's 'Left Foot' outside the Cathedral and a foreshortened panorama ending in a frieze of buildings on the Forth's edge. Beyond that looked less like water than a valley filled with mist. I'm chattering on, she thought, that's not like me. Her nerves must be more upset than she'd realised. After the car crash, the last thing she needed was any more excitement. The thought amused her: a spilled tray (in fact a tray that had been prevented from spilling) didn't qualify as much of an accident.

As if he'd read her mind, the man said, 'You'll be glad to get that thing off,' pointing at the collar.

'You get used to it. It's worth it not to have any after-effects.'

As they talked on, she wished she hadn't agreed to him sitting down. She had time to kill while she waited for Carole, and normally she enjoyed company. She just found she wasn't enjoying talking to him. It would have been hard to say exactly why. Maybe it was that he'd bought two pastries instead of one, big cream-laden confections that he sucked off the spoon. He was perfectly pleasant and courteous, though.

'I first heard them when I was at school. One of the masters had singles and he'd let me hear them sometimes. Kind of a special treat, you might say. And he'd one of their albums, too, Revolver, and later on he got Abbey Road. Not Sergeant Pepper, though. I don't know why. It was years later, before I heard it. The Beatles can't mean so much to someone younger like you. But I don't think they go out of fashion, do you?'

Nothing wrong with any of that. Maybe it was his eyes. They stuck out a little and were an unattractive shade of green. And she didn't like men with moustaches. Despite her best efforts not to be rude, she couldn't help her answers becoming monosyllabic. Fortunately, he seemed not to notice. He's lonely, she thought; either that or the sound of his own voice is enough for him.

'They talk about men being gossips,' he was saying. 'I'm sure women are worse. One time I was talking to this woman and I mentioned a colleague. This was when I worked abroad. I can't remember what I said, something about he'd be taking his family back to England for Christmas. Oh, haven't you heard? she said. That marriage has broken up. I was amazed. Well, I hadn't heard a thing. Nobody had told me. I'll bet there wasn't a woman in the building didn't know. Don't you think so?'

'Hmm.'

'I'll bet. Come on, wouldn't you bet they did?'

'Probably.'

'I told her I'd always felt sorry for him, because his wife was a bit of an invalid. How did you know? she said. I suppose he told you. Then she said, he was always fortunate in having the sympathy of lots of sensitive, intelligent women. But in the end he preferred to fuck this shopgirl, who's only twenty-five. He'll have her, she said, but he's lost his children.'

Betty didn't like the four-letter word. She didn't have to listen to it from her husband or her father, and she was damned if she wanted to hear it from a stranger. It was a relief to see Carole, who had just come in and was hovering at the entrance looking around for her.

The man stood up, blocking her view.

As she gave him an automatic smile, he leaned over and said, 'Speaking of losing a child, I always feel the rule should be prevention is better than curettage.'

'*What?*'

'It's a joke.'

When Carole arrived, she sat down at once without even a peep at Baby Sandy, which was very unusual. Frowning, she asked, 'Who was that odd-looking man, who was sitting with you?'

'A complete stranger. And he didn't just look odd, he was odd. Bloody odd.'

Fucking odd.

'I don't know,' Carole said. 'For a minute as he passed me, I thought I recognised him. It'll come to me. I'm sure I've seen him somewhere before.'

CHAPTER FORTY-TWO

They got back empty-handed to Edinburgh just before two in the afternoon. It was after three when they arrived outside the flat in Morningside which Frank Bower had inherited from his brother. By then the machinery of the hunt had been set in motion.

Meldrum went over to check with the police car which had been keeping a watch on the building since his morning phone call from Kilbracken.

As he walked back to join Shields and the locksmith, a lean old man with an eyepatch emerged from the front door of the building, shopping bag in hand.

'Good morning, Mr Curdie.'

It took a moment for the old man to focus on him. 'Isn't that strange?' he said. 'I was thinking about that poor man who was killed, and here you are! It's almost as though I hadn't missed his murder at all. Have you arrested his brother?'

'Not yet.'

Curdie turned and stared up at the balcony of the murder flat. 'Is he there? I heard it was his now, but I didn't think he was staying in it. I don't like the idea of him being there.'

'I doubt it,' Meldrum said. 'He has a house in the country.'

'So why are you here?'

Meldrum smiled, but didn't say anything.

'I'll let you get on with it,' Curdie said. He held up the empty shopping bag and gave it a shake. 'I like to buy things fresh. There's all kinds of shops in Morningside Road. The exercise is good for me, and hearing a voice apart from my own keeps me cheerful. Good morning again, then.'

Looking after him, Shields said, 'I get to that stage, they can shoot me.'

'He'll not have a family,' the locksmith said. 'I've got six brothers.'

The front door opened at a push.

'Folk can't be bothered using their key,' the locksmith said. 'So much for security.'

As they went up in the lift, Shields said to him, 'I've just got the one. A wee boy. A great wee fellow. I wouldn't mind more, but the wife had a hard time. So that'll likely be it.'

'When you've only the one, you can do more for him. Give him a good start.'

'Right enough.'

They were silent as they went along the corridor. It didn't matter whether you were expecting anything to happen or not, this was the moment when there was always an edge of tension.

Meldrum knocked the door. Waiting, it wasn't hard to read into the silence the sound of footsteps padding around inside.

'Let's do it.'

Opening it took the locksmith no time at all.

Once inside, they went along the hall quickly, checking the bathroom, the small second bedroom, the kitchen. Through the living room, then, to the main bedroom. Coming out of the en suite bathroom, Meldrum was surprised to see the headboard of the bed still had splash marks where the blood had been. He'd have thought Bower's first task, once he had occupation of the flat, would have been to get the stains removed.

It made a particular impression on him, since the bed – which had been left by the police with just the bare mattress – had been made up with pillows and sheets; and the blankets were thrown back as if someone had just got up. The idea of Frank sleeping under that uncleaned headboard was macabre.

In the living room, Shields was turning from the patio doors. 'He's not on the balcony. Unless he's hiding behind a flower pot.'

Through the glass, Meldrum saw the ski track drawn like a double scar down the rump of the distant hill.

'What size is he then?' the locksmith asked, taking a look out on to the balcony. Presumably, he was joking.

'What now?'

'Well, Bower's been here. At least, somebody's slept in the bedroom, presumably him. So we go over the drawers, the desk, the lot. Anywhere he might have left a letter or . . .' He lost the thread of what he was saying.

'What is it?' Shields asked.

Meldrum shook his head, trying to place what was bothering him.

'Need me for anything else?' the locksmith asked.

'Check the desk isn't locked – inside as well, of course. Cupboards in the hall. All the sideboards. Dressing table and stuff in the bedrooms. There's a drawer in the table beside the bed . . .'

Table beside the bed.

He walked over and looked into the main bedroom. Even from the doorway, he could make out the details of the photograph on the table.

Side by side in shirtsleeves, two men in a garden. Frank, the taller of the two brothers, was smiling. Iain, though, was scowling as if oppressed by the weight of the arm thrown round his shoulders. It might only have been because the sun was in his eyes.

As he went into the room, Shields followed him and asked again, 'What's wrong?'

Meldrum pointed.

'What? Am I missing something?'

'The photograph. I knew something was wrong in here. It went missing after the flat was broken into. Remember?'

'It can't be the same one.'

'Looks like it.'

Shields picked up the photograph for a closer look. As he did so, Meldrum bent over the headboard and scraped at one of the stains with his thumbnail. He studied the result for a moment, then he put his knee on the bed and leaned forward on his hands so that he could look over it.

The body was on its back, squeezed between the bed and the wall. Though the front of the skull had been crushed in, enough of the face was left to make it recognisable as Frank Bower. One untouched, very light blue eye was open.

CHAPTER FORTY-THREE

Cowan laid the two photographs side by side. One was the picture of the Bower brothers taken in a garden. The other showed Iain with two boys of about eleven or twelve, one on either side of him. The background displayed not simply a garden but the same garden, with so identical an arrangement of flowers and bushes behind the figures it suggested the two photographs had been taken from almost the same spot. Iain Bower frowned even more intensely in the second photograph than he had done in the one with his brother. The boys with him, dressed in shorts and blue shirts which gave the effect of a uniform, were caught for ever as they smiled intensely into the camera, teeth showing in a kind of grimace.

'When I dismantled the frame, I found this photograph behind the other one,' Cowan said. 'Do you have any idea why it would be hidden?'

'Start with who hid it in the first place,' Meldrum said. 'It belonged to Iain Bower. My guess would be that it was a photograph he was ashamed of, but he couldn't bear to get rid of it. So he hid it behind the one of him and his brother.'

'Ashamed of?'

'I think both those photographs were taken in the garden of a kind of reformatory called the Naylor Home.' He laid a finger on the boy on Iain Bower's left. 'You've heard me talk about Neil Heuk.'

'Not only you,' Cowan said. 'Henry Stanley is fascinated by him. You wouldn't mind if I tell him about this?'

'Can't see why not.' Meldrum smiled. 'Knife's practically on the strength.'

Cowan studied the boy in the photograph. 'So this is Heuk? Are you sure?'

'Beyond a doubt. It's the eyes. They're unusual.'

'What about the other boy?'

'I thought it might be a guy called Keith Chaney. More I look at it, though, the less certain I am. Probably not.'

'You should show it to Heuk.'

'That's an idea,' Meldrum said. 'You ever think of taking up police work?'

'Sarky bastard. But it would be worth finding out. He could be a suspect, couldn't he?'

How many boys had suffered in the Naylor Home? No shortage of suspects. Except that the records of the Home had conveniently gone missing.

And suspects for what? Cowan and everyone else seemed to be assuming, because both bodies had been found in the flat, both beaten to death, that whoever killed Iain Bower had also killed Frank. In fact, despite the efforts of Cowan and his team, there was no forensic evidence to support that.

'It doesn't help that the murder weapon is missing this time,' Cowan had said. 'Hard, self-evidently. Round-edged. Didn't splinter or leave any traces in the wounds. We've concentrated on finding fingerprints new from last time and occurring in more than one location. That gave us three sets — all of them found in the bedroom, bathroom, kitchen and living room. As you'd expect, one set belongs to Bower himself. It might be a fair guess that one of the others belongs to your murderer.'

Meldrum had been turning over in his mind that it must have been Frank Bower who'd taken the photograph from the flat in the first place. Since it had belonged to Iain, it seemed possible that Frank hadn't even known about the second photograph hidden behind the first. All the same, he had taken the risk of a clumsily faked burglary in order to remove it. That suggested an irrationally strong fear, a desperation, in case any police investigation uncovered a connection to the Naylor Home. To avoid that, it had been worth the risk of removing even so tenuous a connection to the past from the murder scene.

Leitch, the local policeman who'd gone with them to the island, had described Bower as behaving like the lord and master of Kilbracken. That had been Meldrum's impression, too. Bower on Kilbracken had been a very different man from Bower in Edinburgh. But suppose what he had set up on the island was being put at risk by his younger brother's return from Belgium. Would Frank Bower have killed to protect it?

Every instinct Meldrum had said, yes. Everything he knew about Frank Bower, down even to the standing of the photograph again beside the murder bed, confirmed an image of evil. Though he could see no way of ever proving it, he had no doubt Frank Bower had killed his brother.

Which left the question, who had killed Frank?

The only sure thing was that it hadn't been Nicolson. He had to be innocent. None more so.

CHAPTER FORTY-FOUR

'S he's in her room too drunk to come out. But then that's her normal condition.'

To Meldrum's eye, it looked as if Don Simon had sunk a few himself that morning. It was one way of dealing with the cold. The stones of Kilbracken House, having spent two hundred years soaking up north winds and mist, were releasing them in a distillation of raw air.

'If so, she has a reason now.'

Simon scrubbed a hand over his face. 'I know, the grieving widow. Aren't I nasty? If you want to talk to her, I'll take you up. All I'm telling you is it'll be a waste of time.'

From the hall, they could hear the noise of Shields and the others moving around in the library.

'It can wait,' Meldrum decided. 'Once we're finished down here, we'll do the private apartments upstairs. The ones occupied by the Bowers.'

This time he'd come armed with a search warrant.

'Do the lot, if you want. Nobody to stop you.'

Meldrum had already been told that Chaney was gone. Simon had caught him packing a bag the previous evening, his air ticket booked from Newcastle to London.

'Is there anywhere warmer than this where we could talk?'

The chill was creeping into his bones.

'Nowhere down here,' Simon said. Apart from cheeks that were redder than ever, he showed no sign of feeling the cold. In addition to being acclimatised, he had the advantages of alcohol and an extra layer of fat. 'They've let the kitchen fire go out.'

He led the way up the stairs. There was an upper hall with an elaborately elegant cornice, pictures and a statue in a niche. The pictures were very large, but done in muddy colours; they looked uninteresting, but the frames might have been worth something. The carpet in the long corridor was threadbare.

'Bower's only been dead a day. Are you trying to tell me everyone's gone?'

'You know what they say about sinking ships and rats? They've been leaving for days now. The Parkers hung on till this morning. Chaney was supposed to take them across, but he was up early and took the boat and went off by himself. The Parkers had to get somebody from the village to take them across. Last time I'll clap eyes on them in this life with any luck.'

He opened a door into a room which took Meldrum by surprise. It was a comfortable drawing room with large windows looking over the loch and a big fire of logs blazing in the hearth, the first worthwhile fire Meldrum had seen in that house. There were deep chairs, two couches, tables with china ornaments, a long sideboard with a tray holding a decanter and six glasses.

'Bedroom through there,' Simon said. 'Rachel's lying down at present, having a rest. I'd appreciate it if she wasn't disturbed.'

Meldrum nodded. 'Of course. This is a pleasant room.' He made no attempt to hide how unexpected that was.

'The furniture's ours. It cost a fortune to bring it over here. Now somehow or other it'll have to go back. Where to, God knows. I suppose we'll do what the others have done. Stay in a hotel till we find a place and get things organised. It'll be like starting over again, no, not *like*, we are starting over again, an adventure. Except that we're a bit old and a bit short of cash for adventures. I suspect most of our money's gone. Do you want a whisky? I suppose not. On duty and all that, eh?'

'A small one.'

Call it medicinal.

The bottle was set handily on a table beside the armchair nearest the fire. Simon poured half a tumbler and handed it to Meldrum, who was about to protest until he saw how much went into the other one.

Tumbler in hand, Simon wandered over to the window.

'Even now,' he said, 'I love this place. It's all been a swindle, you know. I got that out of Chaney last night. I should have known sooner.

The signs were there. Getting plainer all the time since his brother died. But there's none so blind as those who're desperate not to see. We were true believers, we really were.' He ran a hand through his hair, and gave a series of dry barking coughs, mimicking laughter. 'The Parkers phoned the village this morning, and a man called Macdonald arrives in his boat to fetch them over. Very obliging – and eaten up with curiosity, of course. He's been running a campaign of sorts against us. I don't know what he imagined – that we were some sort of Devil worshippers. You know the type – too much inbreeding and an overactive imagination. And there he is, has the bloody nerve to turn up this morning to fetch the Parkers over. I kept out of the way and let them get on with it.' The generous light from the window shone pink on his scalp where the mane of white hair was thinning. 'Anyway, before they left Parker came in here to tell me that, according to Macdonald, the MOD had taken over the island during the war. For experiments in chemical warfare, rumour has it among the peasantry. I thought I'd better tell you, Parker said, I know how much you two worry about your health. Want another one?'

Meldrum shook his head. Simon's tumbler was empty. He refilled it and dropped into the chair by the fire. Meldrum stayed standing. The whisky had warmed him and he was ready to go. There was one thing left, not that it mattered any more.

'Frank Bower's alibi for the night his brother was killed. There wasn't any party, was there?'

'Of course not. He persuaded us to go along with it. He'd a story why we should and it made a kind of sense at the time. Rachel believed everything he told her, and I believed it for her sake.'

'If Frank Bower had lived, you'd both be facing a perjury charge.'

'I know that. I can't blame you for thinking I'm a fool. Everybody else will, and that hurts. All *right*, we were a ship of fools. That doesn't make us different from the rest of you. Put it this way, we're all in the same boat.' He gave the same dry laugh, then made a gesture of disgust. 'You don't understand a word of what I'm talking about, do you?'

'Since he is dead, you don't have to worry about perjury.' Just anthrax or mustard gas, he thought, or whatever else they were clowning around with to defend civilisation.

Don Simon, however, had wound down. Slumped in his chair, he stared into the flames, empty glass in hand.

'Once you go away, I'll knock at her door again. Maybe this time I can persuade her to let me in. She sleeps with a chair jammed under the handle. She has bad dreams, you see. The world's too much for her.'

CHAPTER FORTY-FIVE

'You know, your Kilbracken menagerie reminds me of a funny story,' Knife Stanley said. 'Did you ever hear about the man in New York who couldn't stop thinking about all the street violence and the corruption and the fact that the world seemed to be heading for Armageddon? He got obsessed, his wife got worried. Instead of cancelling the papers and giving up television, they decided to find the safest place on the planet. After an enormous amount of research – this was before the Internet, but he was a librarian – they found it. He sold up everything he had and moved his family to these little islands off Argentina. And the next year the Falklands War broke out.'

'Very funny,' Meldrum said. 'But it doesn't describe even part of the truth about Kilbracken House.'

'Dear fellow, you can't describe part of the truth. That's like handing a skin to a Martian and telling him, imagine a banana.'

Meldrum suspected that of not making much sense but, hearing it delivered by the little man in a deep cultivated voice with so much confidence, it was hard to be sure. Instead of arguing, he went up to the bar. Everybody needed someone to confide in, and Knife Stanley suited Meldrum. His ego meant he was infinitely more intrigued by himself than whoever he happened to be with, and Meldrum found that relaxing. When he came back with the drinks, he told him about how after coming back from Kilbracken he and Shields had gone to the Doune Apartments.

The receptionist there had said, 'Mr Heuk? I haven't seen him today. Are you sure he isn't in his apartment?'

'If he is, he isn't answering the door.'

'Would you like me to phone him?'

'Why not? But if he isn't in we'll need a key.'

Heuk's place was like the *Marie Celeste*, only tidier. All the cups were washed, the pans were clean, there wasn't anything lying on the chairs. The bed was made, with the top sheet pulled taut enough to bounce a coin.

'Either he left so early reception wasn't open, or he didn't sleep here.'

It didn't seem, though, that he'd vacated the apartment. There was a coat and a couple of suits in the little cupboard fitted as a wardrobe, shirts folded on a shelf, drawers of underwear and sweaters. A briefcase under the bed held a litter of papers, among them four letters carrying the same male signature but written in what Meldrum, because of the Belgian connection, took to be Flemish. There were Bank of Scotland monthly statements, the most recent showing a carry-over of £1100, and notice of a new postal account with Dunfermline Direct which had been opened with a lump sum payment of £11,600.

'He's not broke,' Shields said.

'No. But if that's his lot, he hasn't accumulated much. Most professional people of his age, apart from savings, would own their own place.'

As they came out of the flat and Meldrum was locking the door, the lift stopped along the corridor. Balewa leaned out, saw them and stepped back. They heard the lift doors closing. Meldrum and Shields looked at one another. 'Let's have a word.'

The wife opened the door at the first knock, as if the Balewas had been expecting them. She didn't say anything. She didn't invite them in.

'We were in the building anyway, so I thought I'd see how you're getting along,' Meldrum said. 'Nothing to worry about.'

She sighed and glanced behind her. 'I know.'

Balewa was on the couch holding the boy on his knee. Seeing them come in, he tried for a smile.

'Did you see me looking out of the lift? I was startled when I saw you. That's why I didn't stop to say hello.'

'Hello, now,' Meldrum said with a smile. 'What made you look out?'

'I heard voices. I wondered who was there.'

'But why stop at that floor at all?'

He expected him to say he'd pressed the wrong button. He might or might not believe him, but it wasn't something you could disprove.

The wife, however, said sharply, 'Tell the truth. You did nothing wrong, not so?'

Balewa gave her a hard stare, his face expressionless. It was the look a man gave his wife when she was being naive. Meldrum could almost hear him thinking, We're foreigners, they're the police. What has right or wrong got to do with it?

'Your wife's right, sir.'

Balewa said, 'We had an altercation.'

'You and Heuk?'

'I've done my best to avoid him, but he was in the lift. That was not yesterday. The day before. Did he tell you?'

'No.'

Balewa looked more cheerful. 'Perhaps he is ashamed.'

'He wasn't there.'

'But you were coming out of his flat! Has he run away?'

'Why should he? What happened when you met him?'

'We chatted. It was normal. He was polite. Then he said, You have a beautiful son. That came out of the blue. It had nothing to do with what we'd been talking about. And after that,' frowning and nodding down at the child, 'he said something I can't repeat. I hit him. If he's gone, it's because he's frightened to face me.'

'I don't think so!' the wife said. 'Tell them what you told me.'

Balewa hesitated, overcoming his reluctance. 'He had blood coming from his mouth and he laughed at me.'

'I want you to protect us,' the wife said, 'from that man.'

When Meldrum finished his story, Knife Stanley had him go over it again. He offered his opinion that Balewa's wife had got it exactly right in being afraid. If it was true that Iain Bower had been out of control, how could you describe Heuk's behaviour? The same only more so. He must know that by following in Iain Bower's footsteps, if he did anything wrong he ran ten times the risk of being caught.

'He wants to be caught,' Meldrum said.

'Hmm-mm.' Knife nodded thoughtfully, then picked up their empty glasses and took them with him to the bar.

On his return, he resumed where they'd left off, beginning to speak as he sat down. 'At a guess, he's weary of his primal fantasy, the one which set the direction of his sexuality. The difficulty for him is that if he contemplates giving it up, then he's afraid his sexual drive will stop with it. That would mean impotence and, worse, impotence towards life, as if the only meaningful next event were death itself. The horrible implication of that is that he may commit his crimes not because he's driven to them by the strength of his sexual appetite but because of its weakness, worn down by repetition in his fantasy to being a ritual without energy. So that for him paedophilia is a kind of vampirism. You got it right. He does want to be caught. But he'd be better pleased if we still had the death sentence.' He drained half his glass as if in a silent toast to his ingenuity. 'I think there's an affinity between you two. That's why he chose you.'

'No,' Meldrum said. 'He didn't choose me because we're alike. It was just my bad luck.'

'I like you, Jim. You're not clever, but you're a good listener.'

That amused Meldrum.

Knife frowned at his smile. 'Or is that what you want people to think? I suppose I'll have to commit a murder to find out.'

Like many clever men, Knife Stanley didn't hold his drink well. Among other things, it encouraged him towards the telling of jokes.

'There were these two psychiatrists who met for lunch every fortnight, a regular date neither of them would break – old friends going back to university days,' he explained. 'They'd discuss cases together, and help too with advice and sharing about their own lives. One day one says to the other, "Strangest thing at breakfast this morning. I started to say something to my wife, and it came out quite differently." As you can imagine, the friend pricks up his ears. "That's interesting. What happened?" "No, after all, it was nothing. Not worth talking about." "Come *on*," his friend says. "You and I know these slips of the tongue can be subtly revealing. They are like clues. We should pay attention. On you go." "Well," the first one says, "I looked across at my wife, and I meant to say to her, 'Pass the butter, darling.' And instead, I said, 'You've ruined my life, you bitch!'" '

'I heard it as, You've ruined my life, you bastard – wife to her husband.'

'Well, actually, the way I heard it the husband said, You *fucking* bitch!'

He put a comic venom into the adjective.

Not long after that, Meldrum decided he'd had enough. The sociable

Stanley upbraided him for desertion, then spotted a group of university colleagues and was homing in on them as he left.

A sharp wind spun papers along the gutters as he came out into the High Street. He was surprised when a glance at his watch told him it was only eight o'clock. He'd been in the pub about an hour and a half. The idea had been to have a quick pint before he went home to eat, but then he'd been ambushed by Stanley.

He started to walk up the Lawnmarket in the direction of the Castle. As he went, he was tempted by the idea of going into the Ensign Ewart, then decided he didn't feel like drinking on his own. All the same, having found the car where he'd parked it, as he drove down Johnston Terrace he saw a woman standing at the top of the steps that led down to Victoria Terrace and suddenly it felt altogether too early to go home.

He cruised the radio channels. A gospel singer accompanied by a choir was singing *Operator, operator, get me Jesus on the line*. If you have a star button, press now. For night prayers, press one. For yield not to temptation, press two. For forgiveness of sins, press three. The line is busy, you're in the queue, please hold, please hold. *Operator, I've been waiting quarter of an hour – and this music is driving me crazy.*

Every year it seemed to get harder to get a good fish supper. Only Italians made a good fish supper. The decline had started when they stopped cooking chips in lard.

As he worked this out, something he'd done before and would probably do again, he was winding his way up to Tollcross, where there was a good fish supper shop. There would have been, in all honesty, ones as good if he'd turned towards home, but he'd already been through that. He got to opposite the Cameo and slowed to park, but there weren't any spaces, so it was farewell to the good fish supper.

He was into Craiglockhart before he realised where he was going. Earlier in the day, he'd thought about Chaney's wife and that she'd have to be seen at some point to find out if Chaney had been in contact with her. Now, as he unwove the tangle of narrow streets, he checked the time and made up his mind it was too late to pay a visit. He should head for his own place, and call it a day. All the same, her child was missing. He hoped Cockburn had found a more sympathetic policewoman to look after her. Whether she was the mother or not, you couldn't live with a child without caring for him.

He came in at the wrong end of the street and, unsure in the dark, parked three or four houses away. When he switched off the engine, he could hear the silence. It wasn't twenty past eight yet. Was it too late?

While he sat trying to decide, he noticed three or four children playing with a ball. A light, on at the side, illuminated the drive and open paved area in front of a bungalow. They were muffled up in coats and scarves, and had different kinds of bats, one like a baseball bat carried by a boy of about eight, a slightly older girl swinging a hockey stick. As he watched, one of them, a boy older than the others, came to the car and peered in at him. He lowered the window. 'Sorry, I think our ball's rolled under your car.' He started the car, took it down past two of the houses and stopped, running two wheels on to the pavement because of the mean narrowness of the street. As he got out of the car, he saw the heads of the children peeping round the hedge of their drive at him. It made an unpleasant impression. He turned from them and walked down to the Chaneys' gate. The house crouched under trees that had been left to grow for too many years. There were no lights showing, but the curtains were drawn. As he studied the house, he was startled by a heavy banging. It came from the bungalow up the street, bats and sticks being thumped on the path or against a tree. *Bang. Bang. Bang.* After a moment, two of the children came out, dithering ready to run back in, and shouted towards him, 'Stranger! Stranger!'

Bang. Bang. Bang.

'Stranger! Stranger!'

The street stayed quiet. Nobody seemed to pay any attention. Everybody was minding his own business. Neighbourhood Watch wasn't working. It was that kind of street. He knocked the door and waited. After a time, a light came on in the hall.

Val Chaney, if anything, looked better than the last time he'd seen her. Her hair ruffled up looked fuller and the yawn took away the discontent around her mouth. She was in a dressing gown and her legs and feet were bare. He wondered if she'd been sleeping. That was one way of coping. Maybe she looked better because she'd been sleeping.

'Sorry if I've disturbed you,' he said. 'DI Meldrum. I was here before.'

'I know who you are.'

'Your husband's left Kilbracken.'

She didn't show any surprise. After a pause, she said, 'You'd better come in.'

The sitting room smelled like an overnight ashtray. He sat down on the couch, and was surprised when she took a seat beside him. Maybe she did that because it was easier than clearing a chair.

'Have you had any more news about Sam?' he asked. He wanted to get that out of the way, in case she thought he might have brought some and was afraid to ask.

'What's that got to do with you?'

He blinked. 'Sorry?'

'That's the other fellow.'

'Detective Inspector Cockburn, you mean?'

'He's a sour-faced bugger. You'd think he blamed me for letting the boy go to the shops. How could I stop him going to the town on a Saturday? They do what they want at that age. I told him, Wait till you've got kids.'

Sam was ten, Meldrum remembered. As for Cockburn, to the best of his recollection, the DI had three children. On the other hand, Val Chaney seemed to be cured of her apathy and back in touch with the world again. Excitement was obviously good for her.

'No word of the boy then,' he said.

'He could have run away.'

'Why would he do that?'

'They don't need a reason.' She smiled and let it turn into another wide-mouthed yawn. 'Like you lot. You know what you want.'

'Your husband's left Kilbracken. He won't be going back there.'

'You told me that.'

He studied her for moment. She smiled again and stuck a hand into the gown to scratch her shoulder. He saw enough to tell him she was naked under it.

'Has he contacted you?'

'He's not much of a one for writing.'

'You've got a phone in the hall. Is it working?'

'I pay my bills.'

'If he does get in touch, phone me. I'll give you the number. Or if he turns up here, of course.'

She made a face. 'No chance.' She smiled again. 'You've nothing to worry about there.'

He'd been looking at it without seeing it. A black leather jacket draped round an upright chair at the side of the table. She followed his gaze. Seeing what he was looking at, she giggled, an odd sobbing noise, half apprehension, half swagger.

He recognised the jacket.

He went up the stairs three at a time, and shoved the first door on the landing with the heel of his hand. As it shuddered back, he saw a naked rump and a face upside down beside it, as its owner felt around under the bed.

Shields straightened up, holding the shoe he'd been searching for. 'What the fuck are you doing here?' he demanded.

ALMOST THERE

I 'd only been in Brussels a month, new job, same old life. It was a Sunday morning and the phone rang. I let it go on for a bit. It wasn't a convenient moment. I had all the gear spread out ready on the bed. When it didn't stop, I picked up the phone.

'Is that you, Neil? Are you there?'

I couldn't believe it.

'Yes?' I said.

'It's me. It's Dad.'

The last time I'd heard his voice, I'd been seventeen. But I knew who it was all right; I'd known right away.

'Dad who?'

'Frank Lees!' He sounded indignant. 'I've had some bother finding you.'

'I was going to ask how you'd done that.'

'Your Aunt Mary.'

In a moment of weakness, I'd sent her a postcard. She was my father's sister and she'd been kind to me, particularly after my father died.

'What do you want?'

'Your mother's dead. We were having our breakfast, and she reached for the loaf and passed away. It was that quick. I don't think she even knew it was happening. God felt it was time for her to go home, son. She didn't have any pain.'

'Right you are.'

'Did you hear what I just told you?'

'You've always had a loud voice,' I said and held the phone away from my ear. He was very loud for a while, though with the handset against my crotch I couldn't make out the words. When he'd quietened, I put the phone back to my ear.

' – the crematorium, we went to a hotel in Busby for a meal. About a dozen of us, friends of your mother, your Aunt Mary, my brother and his wife. Fuck, I don't know why I'm bothering. Only reason, I thought your mother would want you to know.'

'What were you doing in Busby? That's a long way from Lambhill.'

As a matter of fact, it was right on the other side of Glasgow.

'What're you talking about?'

'My father's buried in Lambhill.'

'So?'

'It'll not be easy for them to find one another.'

'When, for God's sake!'

'At the Great Day of Judgement.'

'Jesus Christ!'

'Exactly,' I said and put the phone down.

I stood in front of the mirror and put the elastic bands round my head. They made the skin on my face stick out in lumps. I lay on the bed and began. After a while, I stopped and put on the nipple clamps. I began again. She *left* me she *left* me she *left* me she *left* mesheleftmesheleftmeshe-leftmesheleftmesheleftmesheleftmesheleftsheleftshesheshesheshesheleftleftleftleftleftleftle

My heart exploded. I know what an orgasm is. This was different, it was my heart. For my life, I rolled off the bed. I lay face up on the floor. As the pain eased, a dull suffocation filled my chest and pressed down on my shoulders and my neck. I lay for a long time before one hand crept up and took off the clamps. Clamps were cancer, breast cancer. Pain was my heart and when it stopped I'd be dead.

She left me when she married that bastard.

she left me me me me

BOOK EIGHT

Night Prayers

CHAPTER FORTY-SIX

H ead bowed, shoe dangling between his spread thighs, Shields had
sat on the edge of the bed, naked and muttering, 'Wasn't me did
the chasing, she was gagging for it. Mind the day you ran out of here
after Slater? She was after me, soon as you were out the room. Was I ever
round this way on my own? Be sure not to pass the door without coming
in. Don't worry about the time, she wasn't an early bedder.'

Thinking about that on the way home, Meldrum was turning into
Leith Walk, when he took the radio call. Sick of brooding over the
encounter with Shields, not able to face going back to his empty flat, he
did a U-turn and headed for Joppa.

Half a dozen marked and plain cars were parked on both sides of the
narrow entry. He flashed his card at the constable keeping guard. As he
walked down the lane, he could sense as much as see the great space of
open water ahead. The high wall of wet stone on his right was striped by
a bar of vivid light. As he came out of the lane, he saw floodlamps
dazzling down from the walkway and from the shore below.

A figure detached itself from the group and came towards him.

'Meldrum? What are you doing here?' DI Cockburn asked.

'I'm on the computer for Keith Chaney.'

'It's a mix-up then. This is a kid.'

'Sam Chaney?'

'That's what we're assuming. Want to take a look?'

'I might recognise him.'

For some reason, this made Cockburn grin.

'Come on then. Here, you! Give us some light.'

The constable looked about eighteen, Meldrum thought. The light from his torch swung in an erratic arc as they walked back towards the lane. This would be his first experience of a murder victim. You got accustomed, but not even old hands like Cockburn and himself forgot the first one.

'There's steps at this end,' Cockburn said. 'For what they're worth. Watch you don't go on your arse.'

The walkway was squeezed between a ten-foot wall with ladders at intervals up to garden gates and on the other side great black blocks of stone, square-cut, man-made, ugly remnants of coastal defence from a war that had been over for two generations.

They picked their way down the broken steps. Pebbles ground under their feet. Down here the water shone like oil. The constable's torch paled and vanished as they came into the pool of light. Two stones with another resting on them made a narrow space into which the body had been folded. Drawn out, it lay now on its side, surrounded by a litter of plastic and cardboard that had been thrust into the hole to conceal it.

'Identifying him might not be so easy,' Cockburn said. 'The rats have chewed off most of his face.'

Meldrum had seen worse than vacant eye sockets and grinning bone. The trouble came when he saw a glint of light in the cavity of the chest and, bending down, recognised the glittering disc of silver and blue as a cd-rom for a computer.

Straightening up, he said, 'This is Sam Chaney.'

He'd seen the title on the disc and remembered the boy's scorn when he'd asked him if he played games on his computer. This disc was for a game. Of course, it was. Sam Chaney had only been a child.

Cockburn glanced away to the young constable, who was coping manfully. When he turned back, the look he gave Meldrum was an odd mixture of indignation with him and embarrassment.

Old hands don't cry.

CHAPTER FORTY-SEVEN

Please, God, look after Mummy and Daddy. Please, God, look after all my friends and relations. Those had been the night prayers when he was a child.

Meldrum was almost asleep.

Gentle Jesus, meek and mild, look upon this little child. If I should die before I wake, I pray Thee, Lord, my soul to take (a little child he'd lain some mornings in bed by the open window listening to the murmur of his mother's voice talking below in the kitchen) God bless and look after Carole (the robin had flown in and beaten itself against the glass of the window and he'd caught it only when it was exhausted and he had thought it must die feeling its heart beat so fast and taken it outside and sat on the bench and it had rested in the nest of his opened hands before unfolding its wings) God bless and look after my daughter Betty, and make her happy and keep her safe, God bless and look after her husband Sandy (autumns he'd look out from his bedroom at the three tall trees opposite the house and the tops of them would be full of rooks) God bless and look after Baby Sandy and let him be happy and do something with his life (blunt-tailed black-wedge bodies on the high branches cruel attentive heads turning this way and that) look after Baby Sandy, keep all the horrors away from my grandson, please, God, look after him (and they would rise and circle take little flights from one branch to the next and then be at rest for a time hung like black fruit in the high leafless tops of the three trees) God bless all the people I work with. God have mercy on Sam Chaney. For Jesus' sake, amen. God, help me to be a better man. Amen.

He slept.

It was dark and he was standing in the hall. He had no idea how he'd got there or why. Then the buzzer rang again and he fumbled for the phone; asked, 'Who is it?' and, without waiting for an answer, pressed the button to open the door downstairs.

Shivering, he wondered, Why's Shields here in the middle of the night? He had the unpleasant thought that perhaps Shields hadn't been able to sleep and had come to plead with him about Val Chaney. Of course, I can't forget it, he'd have to tell him. Call me a bastard. But it gets reported. That's it. Period.

But when he opened the door, it was the Reverend Patrick Turnbull.

'Are you looking for Neil Heuk?' he asked. 'I have to know. It's very important.'

'Is it about Sam Chaney?'

Turnbull stared. Clearly, the question meant nothing to him.

'Never mind,' Meldrum said. 'Have a seat through there. The light switch is just inside the door. I'll be with you in a minute.'

In the bedroom, he put on a sweatshirt and pulled jeans over the underpants he'd slept in.

When he went through, Turnbull was leaning forward, elbows of the vomit-stained jacket on knees, running the fingers of both hands through his shoulder-length grey hair. As he looked up, the hands as if without his knowledge kept repeating the same action. The taut body had gone slack. The face he turned to Meldrum was that of an old man.

'I've listened to a damned soul,' he said. 'All my life, I've blamed myself for what happened to Richard Nicolson. Only blamed myself, and to such an extent no blame was left to share with anybody else. But it wasn't just me, Neil Heuk *did* play his part in all of it. He was more than a victim. Did you know that?'

'Yes.'

'Was I the only one who didn't?'

'Does it matter?'

'When I looked up from my suffering in that place, I was blind to everything but the face of Jesus and how He pitied me. Tonight Heuk made me see the Naylor Home through his eyes. *And he has never left it.* Like a devil in hell, he's spent his life inflicting pain. I don't know what gave him the right to tell me such things. Things no one should hear, on and on and on, I couldn't make him stop. I asked him, Do you want me to kill you? He laughed at that. Please, he said.'

'Whatever you did then, you don't have to tell me! I don't want to know.'

'Oh, I didn't kill him. Do you know what prevented me?'

'Maybe you realised, he's not afraid to kill himself. If he tried to make you do it instead, it's because he wanted you to have the guilt of it.'

'Yes, yes. I understood that, of course. I'd seen the world through his eyes.' Impatiently, Turnbull dismissed the obvious. 'But his mistake was that he couldn't share the seeing without sharing what was felt. Those who most suffer the pains of Hell are its demons. Emptiness and the despair of salvation. I pitied him.'

He laid his head back. His eyes closed, flickered open, closed again. Meldrum started to speak, then watched instead the muscles of the grey face slowly unclench.

After a while, he got up quietly and went into the bathroom. He ran the cold tap, poured double handfuls of water over his head, smashed them up against his eyes. Gasping, he contemplated the face in the mirror. Its lips wrenched back seemed like a parody of a smile.

What had Jimmy Pleat said about Turnbull after he'd had him on his radio show? *Not a man who went in for knock knock jokes.*

Meldrum, restored to himself, no saint, went back to take up the struggle.

Watching the door, Turnbull was awake.

'I won't tell you where he is,' he said, 'but I'll take you there.'

Being driven down Leith Walk, Meldrum assumed they were going to Turnbull's church. He had an image of the room in the vestry and Heuk alone by the electric fire studying its illusion of dancing flames. Before they reached the bottom of the Walk, however, Turnbull turned left into a side street. Not long afterwards, Meldrum recognised one shop then another and realised they were approaching the corner on which Turnbull and he had stood talking the night they met.

'Heuk came to your home?'

'To the manse, yes.'

'You think he'll still be there?'

'It's you he wants to see.'

They came into a street of substantial houses. Turnbull slowed the car.

'Don't turn in,' Meldrum said.

Turnbull stopped across a drive; the gate lay open.

'What is it?'

'I'll give you my keys. Go back to my flat, and wait for me.'

'Why can't I go in with you? I should be there.'

'Because it's me he wants to see.'

He stood and watched the car swing across the road, bump two wheels on the pavement, and roar off the way they'd come. Too fast to be safe, he thought; why do so many ministers drive too fast?

As he approached the house, he could see into a room where the lights were on. It seemed to be empty. The front door was open.

The hall was brightly lit, and listening to the silence he made his way slowly down a long corridor towards the back of the house. All the lights were on in the kitchen, too. Half a loaf sat in the middle of the table surrounded by crumbs. A knife with a black handle lay beside it and a pot of jam with the top off. He picked up the knife and touched its edge. A line of blood sprang out on his fingers. As he looked at it, he heard music and a singer, slurring across the notes like Sinatra, and then a man's voice joining in with an exuberant in-the-bath kind of harmonising.

He found Heuk in the front room. Wearing an overcoat, bread and jam on a plate in his lap, he was sprawled in a deep armchair which had concealed him from the window. He nodded and smiled at Meldrum, then joined again in the song, beating time to the music with a clenched fist on the arm of his chair.

For a damned soul, Heuk looked to be in good spirits.

In the hearth in front of an empty grate, a small cheap radio was supplying the music. Meldrum went over and pulled the plug.

'Three in the morning,' Heuk said, 'and you can still get music. There really isn't any excuse to be lonely.'

'All the same, it's a bad time,' Meldrum said. He took the opposite chair. 'Ask any doctor. If you're sick enough, it's the time of night when you slip away.'

Heuk poked the slice of bread with his finger. 'I felt hungry, but the notion's gone off me.' He laughed. 'Typical Paddy. There's practically nothing to eat in the house, but he's got a dozen pots of strawberry jam. From a lady in the congregation, I suppose. Made with love and sugar. All the ladies love Paddy. Pity he's not interested in them. He isn't, you know. Do you think he might have killed Iain Bower?'

'Not a chance.'

'What about Frank then? He could have killed Frank.'

'You don't expect me to believe that.'

'No . . .' He lost interest in the idea. 'Frank killed Iain. He as good as admitted it to me. And I killed Frank, of course. He phoned me, and I went to meet him at Iain's flat. He buggered me. For old times' sake, he said, though I was too old for his taste. Afterwards I dreamed I was in the Naylor again, and when I woke up Frank was standing over me naked. I chased him into the kitchen – no, not again, never again, I was saying – I hit him and he fell over. Only when I woke up, there he was snoring beside me in the bed. I lay there for a while, and then I thought, Why not? and I got up and beat his head in.'

'It's a good story,' Meldrum said.

Heuk stared at him. 'It's a confession,' he said.

'If you say so.'

'Good enough – if the law hadn't changed – listen, you could come and see me hung.'

'Chaney's as much a suspect as you. Probably a better one, since he's run off to London.'

Heuk chopped at the air in frustration. Then, unexpectedly, he smiled. 'Fine, chalk Frank's killing up to Keith then. Why not? And Paddy can absolve him, give him a cuddle, down on their knees together, say the Lord's Prayer, sing a hymn. Don't you find there's something disgusting about forgiveness? If you convict Keith, do me a favour. Tell him Neil hoped they'd shut him in Barlinnie and throw away the key.'

'Like hanging,' Meldrum said, 'that doesn't happen any more. He'd be out in eight years.'

'What is it you want?' He licked his lips. 'Are you trying to find out what happened to Sam Chaney?'

It was cold in the room. Meldrum watched the grey breath come from the other man's mouth in little panting breaths like gasps at the moment of orgasm. 'I was thinking about Brussels,' he said. 'When we met by accident in the street.'

'Brussels?' Heuk looked puzzled, then his frown cleared. 'We're in the wrong house for that,' he said. 'You don't break your neck jumping out of a first-floor window, you break your ankles.' He looked for a response. Meldrum said nothing. 'Or maybe you think I should join a monastery instead.' A little smile curled the corners of his mouth. 'How about a teaching order?'

'Or how about, you miserable bastard,' Meldrum said, 'you doing us all a favour and cutting your throat?'

Heuk sighed. He picked up the slice of bread and took a great, mouth-cramming bite out of it. Chewing luxuriously, he stood up. He seemed to have got his appetite back. He turned at the door. Still chewing, a red smear of jam at the corner of his mouth, he said, 'You didn't need me to tell you where Sam Chaney is, did you?'

When Meldrum didn't answer, he shrugged.

'What does it matter?'

Meldrum watched the clock, waiting for it to reach the hour. Once, a car went past. Once, he imagined a shout from the street. Later, he found himself on his feet without any memory of standing up.

Five minutes had gone by.

Some time after he sat down again, he began shivering. The shuddering went down through his arms and his jaws shook. It was cold and the front door was lying open. Anyone could walk in.

His long dead grandfather, latest in a line of tenant farmers, had worked his sons like bonded slaves. When the eldest rebelled, it had been to run off to town, get married, have a child. Left with the burden, his brothers to the day of his death didn't forgive him; and, growing up, it had been unclear to Meldrum how far his father had forgiven himself. They'd never talked about it, as they'd never talked about anything that mattered. Like the day his father had decided to have the family dog, old and turned vicious, put to sleep. Meldrum had wept and yelled that he hated him, but his father had only stared and gathered the dog up and gone out without a word. The poor creature's being done a kindness, his mother told him, but he'd been too young to understand.

The clock chimed the hour.

He didn't have to go and look to know that it was over.

He went into the hall and had started to dial for help, when he remembered he didn't know where to tell them to come. He went outside and checked the street name and the number on the gate. Standing again by the phone, he saw a patch of light thrown across the end of the corridor that led to the back of the house. A loaf of bread set in a scatter of crumbs. A knife on a table. A knife with a black handle. The light must come from the open door of the kitchen. He stared at it as he gave the address to the constable who'd taken the call.. He explained how he'd been asked to come to the house.

'What time would that be?'

What would Turnbull say when he was questioned? That he'd left him at the manse hours ago? Maybe, maybe not; no way of telling. Some passerby might have glanced in and seen him with Heuk. The room had been brightly lit. But perhaps you couldn't see in from the street? He hadn't checked.

'Are you there?' the voice asked.

What did it matter?

As he opened his fist, the slash across his fingers leaked bright drops of blood.

'I got here about ten minutes ago,' he said. 'Unfortunately, I was too late.'

CHAPTER FORTY-EIGHT

After the questioning about Heuk's suicide, instead of going home, Meldrum drove out past Fairmilehead. As the sun was rising, he pulled in by a farm gate and got out of the car.

He jumped over a fence and walked up the hill. Grazing cattle watched him from big moist eyes. In this isolation, they seemed like a herd of wild creatures. He was following an old sheep track to the brow of the hill, when he came on a rabbit crouched at the side of the path. Ears back, it didn't move a muscle as he passed within a couple of feet. When he turned and went back, it stayed motionless apart from a faint quivering of its long laid-back ears. Then he noticed the eyes, shut and swollen.

What happened to a helpless creature, out in the open like this, but tearing and pulling, stabbing and slashing, being dragged and tugged apart and burrowed into. He had no stick with him, no boulder to drop on it. No stomach for killing. Anyway, how could he be sure it was sick? The swelling might be only an impression. The eyes didn't leak pus. Suffering asked hard questions.

It wasn't enough just wanting to help.

Instead of going back into Edinburgh through Fairmilehead, he turned down on to the City Bypass and headed south. Even this early, there was a lot of traffic; but when now was it ever quiet?

Though he'd never been there, of course, he knew where Shields lived.

He came off the motorway and through a roundabout and past an estate wall down into the port. He didn't stop until he came to the river, where he parked and sat for a while trying to summon the energy to get out. What was it he'd said to Turnbull during the night? 'Heuk's not afraid to die, but he wants you to have the guilt of it.'

When Shields opened the door, his jaw dropped. You read about that happening, but you didn't often see it, Meldrum thought.

'What's wrong?'

'Eh . . .' It wasn't easy to explain.

'It's – Christ, it's not seven o'clock.' Shields was in slippers and he'd pulled an old jersey on over his pyjama jacket. Reluctantly, he said, 'I suppose you'd better come in.'

As he stepped inside, Meldrum caught a flicker of movement at the top of the stairs. It was a child's face peering round the corner. Instantly, conscious of being seen, the child vanished. Unaware, Shields was tramping down the hall. Meldrum followed him into a small sitting room. Through patio doors he could see a lawn, flower borders, a slatted wooden fence.

'Want a coffee?' Shields was asking. 'Don't mind me saying, but you look terrible. You have a rough night?'

Drinking, he meant. Meldrum wasn't a heavy drinker; but no shame if he had been. Teetotal wasn't part of the job description.

'Kind of. A lot going on.'

'Is that why you're here?'

A wave of tiredness went over Meldrum. 'I wouldn't mind a coffee.'

When Shields came back with it, he said, as if it was something that should be explained, 'Normally the wife would be up. But Alec was sick a couple of times during the night.'

'Right.' Alec. If he'd ever been told the name of Shields's son, he'd forgotten it.

'Gets everything that's going. He's just started nursery school.'

He sipped his coffee. There was sugar in it. How the fuck could Shields work with somebody day in day out and not know if they took sugar? 'Right,' he said again. Didn't seem to be anything else to say. Grass in the garden was well cut. Grass had to be cut often. After Carole left him, the garden had got to be a wilderness.

'So?' Shields stirred restlessly. 'Something happen?'

Meldrum laughed at that, then stopped. 'It was a busy night.' By the time it finished being busy, it was too late for bed and too early for work. So why not turn up here? He should tell Shields so he could see, put like that, it made sense. Instead he said, 'That stuff about you and Val

Chaney last night. I won't report it. I thought I'd tell you, in case you were worried.'

'I wasn't worried.'

Of course not, Meldrum thought, hard man like you. Then he saw what a mistake he'd just made. He'd shown weakness. In this job, showing weakness wasn't a good idea. Everybody had to find his own way of getting through the days. His had been to keep people at a distance. Let them get too close, and who knew what might happen. You could splinter into pieces.

'I'm off,' he said. 'Keep away from the Chaney woman, and we can both forget her.'

Shields chewed his lip, staring up at him, then got to his feet.

'Appreciate it,' he said and held out his hand.

Meldrum ignored it. He wasn't displeased to see the look of dislike that came and went at once. He could live with that. There was after all, as the man had said, something disgusting about forgiveness.

As they went down the hall, a small singing noise made him turn and look up.

The boy on the landing above was three, maybe turning four. He was clutching a child-size beanbag, arms stretched half round it to get a grip. Swaying on the edge at the top of the stairs, he sang to himself, calculating, gathering his resolve. Before they could move or make a sound, he launched himself into space. The bag slid and swung and it seemed for an absurd moment he might make it, and then it had shaken him loose. His head came sickeningly close to the wall, his shoulder hit a step. He was at the bottom, sprawled across the bag.

Shields gathered him up and sat on the bottom step. He made odd grumbling, crooning noises as he hugged him. The boy held up an arm, dangling at the elbow. Meldrum crouched down beside them, and checked the back of the child's head, his eyes, made him grip a finger.

'Bobbie, Bobbie,' he said, 'he's all right.'

Shields's face was the colour of putty. 'It's my fault,' he said. He put his head down and rocked back and forward, holding his son as if he would never let him go. When the mother came down, Meldrum left them together.

The night was over. As he walked back to the car, he had to screw up his eyes against the brightness of the sun. In the middle of the river, a swan was paddling hard against the current. Two others, on the far side,

knowing the river, moved fast where the water was slack. There was a
crying of gulls overhead. He took a deep breath that turned into a yawn.
On his lips, the air tasted of salt. He had cramp at the back of one leg, his
head ached, he was stiff all over. It was going to be another long day.
    But the boy was all right.

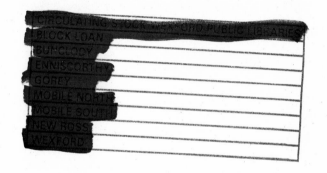

CIRCULATING STOCK WEXFORD PUBLIC LIBRARIES

BLOCK LOAN	
BUNCLODY	
ENNISCORTHY	
GOREY	
MOBILE NORTH	
MOBILE SOUTH	
NEW ROSS	
WEXFORD	

Mob Sth 8/08   w/d 8/09